HIDING UNDER THE LEAVES

THE SLAB

First edition, published in the UK November 2025 by The Slab Press
The Slab 004 (softback) 10 9 8 7 6 5 4 3 2 1
Introduction copyright © 2025 by Donna Scott
This compilation copyright © 2025 by Donna Scott
All Stories copyright ©2025 by the respective authors.

ISBN: 978-1-7384268-6-7 (softback)
978-1-7384268-7-4 (e-book)

Cover design by Kev Rooney
https://cultofnyx.substack.com/
Typesetting by Donna Scott

https://theslab.press

HIDING UNDER THE LEAVES

THE SLAB

Table of Contents

Introduction
Donna Scott

What is folk horror? Trying to pin a particular definition on what might constitute this 'subgenre' can sometimes feel like comparing hazelnuts with cobnuts.

Hazelnuts are the sort of horror that everyone knows. Chopped up in chocolate or blitzed with cocoa and palm oil to make a commercial spread, they can be sweet horror, kid-friendly horror; perhaps the body horror of rotting teeth, the monstrous corporation that has you in its power; screaming creatures running from fiery destruction.

Nobody puts cobnuts in factory-made chocolate. They are uncommon, foraged-for things. They are found in hedgerows and they don't look like the little brown nuts in shells that we know, not at first glance. Our prehistoric ancestors ate them, treasuring the sight of catkins and flowers in the spring and marking the places they saw them to return for the sticky green pods in early autumn. The cobbe, the cobylle, the cobble, and the filbert: all of these are old names, too. Filbert is the 14th century name for the nut, as it ripened around the 7th Century Frankish abbot St Philbert's feast day on 22nd August. In essence, when we get down to the nut of the matter, the very kernel, we may find there is no difference between all these names, only a sensation, a certain ambiance or tone, a desired distinction. Hence, British Michelin-starred chefs now discovering raw cobs for their menus. It uses language to evoke a sense of "terroir": the flavours and character of the geographical landscape in which the food is served. The same may be true of folk horror.

The term "folk horror" doesn't seem to have been used to denote a subgenre of horror before 1970, when reviewer Rod Cooper used it to describe *The Devil's Touch*, later renamed *Blood on Satan's Claw*. The next use was by the film's director Piers Haggard in 2004, and then that film was also referenced along with the term by Mark Gatiss in a 2010 documentary, *A History of Horror*. Gatiss went further in referencing other films that he felt fitted this subgenre: *Witchfinder General* (1968) and *The Wicker Man* (1973) along with some archetypal tropes: "the countryside as symbols or as imagery"; "people subject to superstitions"; "living in the woods". It's a term that seems much older than it is, though it is in fact a fairly recent one that collects together a number of horror elements that have been around for some time: the supernatural; folklore; death traditions and rituals; the afterlife; the nature of evil, and the demonic. It is more people-centred than the Gothic, but there is considerable overlap.

Gatiss is, of course, one of *The League of Gentlemen* – a sketch comedy team that have been creating various horror-tinged and distinctly British comedies for the BBC since 1999. As the catalyst for the surge in creators seeking to fit

8

their work to this term over the past 15 years, the work of Gatiss, along with Steve Pemberton, Reece Shearsmith, and Jeremy Dyson, arguably helps to add to people's ideas of what the subgenre actually is. Gatiss didn't coin the phrase, but he popularised it and helped to define its flavour and character.

With folk-horror finding a firm footing in popular culture and offering interesting variations on the cumulated tropes to reflect the cultures of its creators around the world, we have almost come back to consider folk horror in terms of 'terroir' rather than terror. Every continent has its version of folk horror, and there are so many interesting books and films to discover.

I may be particularly partial to British folk horror, with its woodland tales, and creepy fairy stories, but I have also always loved the stories of Angela Carter, who drew on folk stories from all over the world, producing some of the most lyrical and unsettling fiction. I've been delighted to expand my reading recently to all manner of folkish horror, from Shirley Jackson to Andrew Michael Hurley to Stephen Graham Jones.

Consider this anthology then as a taster of some of the amazing folk horror that is out there. Many of these writers have made a name in the genre already, and some are rising stars. I drew this list of treasures from hundreds of submissions of original fiction. I have no doubt they will speak to you in some way, whispering of old, forgotten things; will give you a glimpse of something ancient, powerful, unspeakable…

Carry a bookmark with you into these woods. I would hate for you to lose your place. Take care as you read, for you are shortly about to discover what is hiding under the leaves.

Donna Scott
August, 2025

Rumours Overheard in the School Playground Relating to Miss Angeline Holst

Tim Major

She's a wonder, isn't she? A real miracle worker. The school's lucky to have her.

Aw, look at her dabbing away at that boy's knee. Did you even see him fall? I don't think anyone did. All I saw was Miss Holst dashing out of the school reception like there's no tomorrow. She must have a sixth sense. I suppose you have to, to do her job.

What *is* her actual title? Receptionist? School office

manager? I don't know. How about school angel? That would sum up Miss Holst, wouldn't it? She's just adorable. My Sammy adores her; I can tell you that. I wouldn't be surprised if they all just pretend to fall over and graze their knees, just to have Miss Holst rush over and tend to them. I swear that boy over there hasn't taken his eyes from hers the entire time. And he stopped crying the moment she appeared.

Do you think she dyes her hair? Veronica says she's older than you'd think. And it's so curly, isn't it? Must take a lot of work, if it's not natural. How old would you guess? Thirty-five? Gone forty?

We should invite her out for drinks some time, maybe. She might be fun when you get to know her.

No. No. It wouldn't be quite right, would it? We wouldn't think of socialising with one of our kids' teachers, would we? Inappropriate. An invisible line in the sand. And anyway, Miss Holst isn't a parent. She wouldn't want to hear us banging on about Sammy and Olivia and all the other kids. A busman's holiday, it'd be. Besides, there's something about her, isn't there? When it's directed at the kids her smile's like a ray of sunshine. When it's directed anywhere else... Well, you've seen it too. It's cold, isn't it? Beautiful but cold, like Elsa in *Frozen*. I suppose she just prefers children, and fair play to her.

It seems like that boy was crying wolf after all. Look at him! Not a scratch on him. And look, do you see what Miss Holst's holding in her hand? That's not Savlon or any over-the-counter ointment, I can tell you that. I wouldn't be surprised if she makes her own. She looks the type—all organic and self-grown.

I don't like the way that boy's looking at Miss Holst. And why's she still out here in the playground, staring at him? She should be back behind her desk. It's making everyone nervous. She's acting like she's that boy's mother. I've a good mind to go and tell her to—

Oh, look, Sammy's class is coming out. There's Sammy now. Cheerio, Neil! Same time tomorrow.

Rahul says she lives alone. Big house, too. Huntsman's Crescent. D'you know it? The cul-de-sac just off Finnemore Road. I *know*! We viewed a house there once, way back. Desperately wanted it, but it was hard fought and came to nothing. Offers went in the very day it was put on the market, *way* over the asking price. God knows how much Miss Holst paid for it.

I mean, how would you even begin to fill a house like that, on your own? Those are family houses. You'd only buy one if you were at least *expecting* to start a family. But apparently there's no man on the scene—and no woman either, let's be politically correct. And yet here she is, every day, looking… what would you call it? Salon fresh. She smells like the perfume counter at Fenwick's, too. Just gorgeous. But it makes you wonder, doesn't it, if it's not *for* anyone? Makes you wonder if she's trying to snare somebody. You ought to watch out, Neil!

Apparently on Hallowe'en her house was the only one in the cul-de-sac that wasn't all done up. They have a great tradition on Huntsman's Crescent of welcoming trick-or-treaters. Rubber skeletons, spiderwebs, even these projectors that project ghosts onto the clouds. The whole works. Sammy's always loved the place, insists on making a beeline for Huntsman's Crescent every year. Fills his plastic bucket all the way to the brim, and then he'll be chomping sweeties for weeks to come, inevitably ending up at the dentist for a stern word. But that's what Hallowe'en's all about, isn't it? Not for Miss Angeline Holst, though. Rahul doesn't know if she took a trip away to avoid the whole thing. But he's minded to think she was in the house, watching from darkened rooms and not taking part. Or else maybe she was out on the streets herself, childless, guzzling sweets. What a thought!

Speaking of guzzling, did you know she doesn't eat in the canteen? Or at her desk either. Apparently, some of the children have seen her sneaking off to the gazebo. I mean that shelter over there—I know, I know, 'gazebo' is a generous word for it. Miss Holst sits in there each lunchtime, all hunched over. No lunchbox. No sandwich and packet of crisps. Sammy didn't want to tell me at first, until I pressed him about it. He said he didn't want to tell tales and that the kids he'd heard talking about it were just being mean. And that's probably true, but sometimes there's no smoke without fire, don't you think? Because what other explanation can there be? What other behaviour could be mistaken for somebody hunched over in a gazebo, reaching down to the wooden floorboards and picking out the grubs and those little flies that are always in there because of the damp? And pulling them up wriggling and pushing them into her mouth? I can just see her doing it. And my Sammy's no liar.

Speak of the devil—there he is now.

How've you been? Sorry I didn't end up seeing you on Friday, or yesterday. Did Becky enjoy forest school on Friday afternoon? Sammy was sad to have missed it. Still. I don't know if you heard, but we actually did one better. There was a last-minute cancellation at Center Parcs in Penrith for the long weekend. I know! Lucky us! So we decided to beg off work and school on Friday, spent the morning packing and then off we went. Then we were wiped out yesterday, of course. And sure, I know it's wrong, keeping Sammy off school for a couple of days. But school's not everything, is it? And there's loads of educational things going on at

Center Parcs, probably more than there is here at school, ha! Navigating using maps, treasure hunts. Physical dexterity on the climbing walls. Mainly we spent our time on the water slides and in the jacuzzi, but the point stands.

Oh Christ. Miss Holst's caught my eye. Is she beckoning to me?

Hold onto Sammy's bike, would you, Neil? And wish me luck.

All right. It's all right. No, I'm okay. Really, I am.

Look! I just shivered. Properly shivered, even though it's warmer than it's been for days. That's what happens when Miss Holst gets her claws into you, isn't it?

I'll tell it like it is: I don't like her. I don't like the way she makes me feel.

She's so *judgy*. You can tell she's never been directly responsible for children herself. She's one of those non-parents who think they know everything about parenting, even though it's all from books and TV instead of lived bloody experience. She doesn't know what it's like. She can't imagine what a *nightmare* Sammy can be, and how much I've given up over the years. She just sees the presentable version of Sammy that trots in to school, beaming up at her and telling her she has a beautiful smile. And she doesn't even have to teach the monsters! When they all head into their classes, she sits there at her desk, filing her nails, waiting for parents to email or call and then she can turn her supercilious attitude on them, full force.

Here's what happened. She asked me to clarify the reason for Sammy's absence. And I told her straight. I told her Sammy was feeling very poorly and I also told her we had to go and visit Sammy's grandad, which is true, because he *was* there at Center Parcs with us, and it's true that it was sort of a last chance, because who knows how many more Center Parcs trips he's got in him?

And Miss Holst's just watching me while I'm saying all that. With this sort of glint in her eye. And here's the awful bit, Neil. I go completely cold, while I'm speaking. Icy. She's staring at me and I'm shuddering with cold. Have you ever noticed how dark her eyes are? It's like there's no pupils, or that they're *all* pupils. I felt like I was falling into them.

There's something not right about her, anyway.

She didn't actually call me a liar—not that I was lying, but you know what I mean. She didn't actually tell me she knew Sammy wasn't ill. But she said he seemed bright and alert this morning, and he'd seemed chirpy on Thursday too.

So I said, well, it must have come on quick, then.

And she said there's been a bug going around.

So I said, that must be it. Sammy must have caught the bug.

And Miss Holst reacted in a really weird way. She looked out of the window, staring out here, at the playground. For a while she watched all the young ones running around, the ones who've come with parents to collect their older brothers and sisters.

And you know what she said? She said in this really quiet voice: that wasn't my intention.

Did you hear me, Neil? She said: *that wasn't my intention.*

I mean…

How would you interpret that?

I know it's mad. I know she couldn't actually be responsible for making the children ill.

But that's what she said, wasn't it? She said that wasn't my intention.

Was that a confession? Was she saying it wasn't her intention to have Sammy catch the bug that's going around? Or maybe she meant she hadn't meant for so many children to get ill—but she's still confessing that she somehow caused the illness, isn't she? Am I going crazy, Neil? Because that's what I take from what she said.

Somebody should look into those little pots of ointment she brings into school. There are rules for a reason.

I tell you what, Neil. That woman makes me feel unsafe bringing Sammy here. She's a menace.

The more I hear about her, the more nervous I get.

Did you realise she knew all about Mrs Fitch, the head of Year 3, and Mr Donnelly the Year 1 class assistant? You heard all about what they were getting up to, didn't you? Mrs Fitch being married with three kids, and her and Mr Donnelly having all those dirty weekends in Leeds and then the whole thing eventually coming tumbling down? Miss Holst knew about all that way before anyone else did. Eddie Piper reckons she was trying to extort them, which is the main reason why Mrs Fitch ended up taking such a long leave of absence. And then Mr Donnelly had that awful accident, falling off his bike at the underpass. Terrible. I'm not saying Miss Holst was responsible somehow, but it makes you think.

I swear Miss Holst knows everything that goes on in this school. Apparently, she knew about Vic wanting to transition before her parents did. I mean *his* parents. That's not right, is it? Miss Holst's worming her way into everyone's lives. And speaking of worms, when I last saw her in the office, she was wiping her lips with a napkin and I swear I saw one of those grubs she likes to eat, right there in the corner of her mouth before she slurped it down.

I'm not going to stand for it.

I've already been in touch with the headteacher about her. He said she'd been nothing but a credit to the school. That's all very well from his perspective. All he cares about is an efficiently run school office, and newsletters sent out and absences logged, all that sort of thing. He can't see the nightmare she's become, the havoc she's… what's the word? Wreaking. And when I pushed harder the headteacher finally said she wasn't his hire anyway, that she'd been sent by the multi-academy trust, and that I should take it up with them.

And I will, Neil. I'm on the warpath. These are our children we're talking about, our precious children.

Speaking of which, here come the Year 4s! Over here, Sammy! What's that he's carrying? Some sort of art project. Another clay Viking settlement or something. No, don't rush, Sammy, you'll trip—

Oh look, he went and tripped. Bloody stupid idiot.

Hold my bag, would you? Just need to— Just need to get my breath.

It's been a day. I've been on a quest.

Nearly there. Five more deep breaths. There.

You know I told you Miss Holst was a central hire by the multi-academy trust? Well, I'm not one to be put off by a glib answer. I called the MAT this morning. Called and called and called. No answer for ages, and then when there *was* an answer it was pretty bloody unsatisfactory. So I went over there, didn't I? I took the Land Rover and went on over there.

They did *not* appreciate me barging into their offices. They tried everything they could to get rid of me. I've been there for *hours*, Neil.

But I got my answer. My answer about Miss Angeline Holst.

And you'll never guess what.

The multi-academy trust has no record of her. None whatsoever. They had no idea who I was talking about.

At first, that is. Eventually they said they'd found her

record, and that she was highly qualified and had a string of school appointments before this one, and that they were lucky to have her on their books.

But the woman who told me this, she looked properly frightened. I don't know whether she was scared of being unveiled as incompetent, or whether she was afraid of Miss Holst, which seems more likely. And I went and called Miss Holst a witch, joking but not really joking, you know? And this woman's reaction turned even stranger.

Your *face*, Neil! I can tell that you see what this means.

It means somebody deeply unsafe is preying on our children.

Think about it: she treats the children so kindly, but with parents she's cold to the point of being insulting. She knows everything about the kids, but also everything about us parents—all our family goings-on, all our secrets. And she lives alone and she eats worms and she stalks the streets on Hallowe'en night, watching from the shadows. And her hair curls so nicely because it's been crisped in the fires of hell— that's what Lianne thinks, anyway.

It's all coming to a head, Neil. We've all been talking about it, me and the other parents. And we need to know that we can count on you, when the time comes. Because it's clear that official measures aren't going to work. The headteacher and the MAT are under her spell. We'll never get rid of her that way.

You realise you can't afford not to act, right? Because if she knows about Mrs Fitch and Mr Donnelly, you can be sure she knows about us too, Neil. You can tell yourself all you like that it was a one-time thing. Everyone's going to know about it soon enough, if we let Miss Angeline Holst have her way. She won't stop until she's destroyed us.

So here's the deal: we pick up the kids as usual, take them

home, cook and serve up their chicken drummers and potato smiles. Then we come back, after dusk. No, not with the kids, Neil. They're old enough to look after themselves these days, at least for an hour. You need to stop mollycoddling.

You see, all the staff are staying late tonight. Some sort of planning meeting. The teachers will all be in the hall, doing a workshop. And Miss Holst will be in the office. Alone.

We're not suggesting violence! No pitchforks at dawn or anything like that. But it might be dangerous all the same. It might get messy. So it'd be in your interests if you're able to defend yourself, Neil. Use your imagination.

Tumulus

Frazer Lee

The drive to the long barrow passed by in a blur of wheat fields and queues of tourist traffic at roundabouts and service stations. At first, due to the elevation, it seemed as though the minibus was floating above the ancient landscape. Then the road began to snake ever downwards between rolling hills, hunkering down into the secrets of the landscape. When at last Barry pulled into the lay-by, Tomas saw only one other car parked there. It was a welcome sign that it wouldn't be crowded. Barry turned off the engine and then hopped out to open the sliding passenger door.

"Thanks for bringing me at such short notice," Tomas said.

"No probs, dude," Barry replied with a flick of his thinning dreadlocks. "Kris told us you'd be back someday. Said we were to take care of you. Follow his instructions."

"I'm sure he did."

Barry slid the minibus door shut and Tomas breathed in

the fresh Wiltshire air, welcome relief after the stale smoke inside the van. It was getting easier to talk about Kris without bursting into tears most days. And it made him smile to think of his control freak boyfriend leaving instructions with Barry and his group of weirdo new agers. How typically Kris.

He reached inside the van and under his seat to retrieve the plastic carrier bag. As he did so, Barry placed a firm but gentle hand on Tomas's arm. Before Tomas could react, he wiped something across Tomas's forehead using his thumb. Tomas recoiled and dabbed at his skin. A slick of oil coated his fingers. He sniffed it and winced at the overpowering scent of patchouli.

"A blessing for you," Barry explained. "Kris's instructions."

"Right…" Tomas said. *More hippy bullshit.*

"There won't be many up there at this time of day, if any at all," Barry said, staring into the distance. "If there are, just wait it out. Better to do what you have to do on your own."

"Got it," Tomas replied, eager to be on his way.

"Oh, one more thing. Just before you do the, erm, deed. Drink this."

Barry handed Tomas a small, pewter hipflask. It had a strange symbol like a knot engraved on it. The flask felt warm and heavy in his hand, and Tomas remembered how alive Kris had felt when they nuzzled together inside the long barrow. Before the confession. Before Kris had passed.

"Kris's—"

"Instructions. Got it," Tomas said. Pocketing the hipflask, he started walking.

"We'll come for you when you're done," Barry called out after him. "Take you to the bonfire for a final goodbye."

"Righto," Tomas said over his shoulder as he walked up the path holding onto his carrier bag.

He didn't glance back until he'd reached the first gate.

Barry and his battered old tour bus were gone, as was the lone car he had seen on arrival. A cool breeze rustled the dying leaves of a gnarled tree, its branches grasping at the wilderness beyond the metal fence. Kris had dubbed it the 'wee-wee tree' on their first visit, a year ago. Tomas smiled, remembering how they had spied a guy taking a pee against the tree from the window of Barry's minibus.

"Eww," Kris had said, "Putting me off my picnic, that." He had put his untouched sandwich back in its Tupperware. "Not that hungry anyway."

Kris rarely was, back then. The meds either made him sick, or sleepy, or both. Tomas had wondered how long it might be until he was spoon-feeding soup into his lover's mouth, wiping away drool with a napkin. The thought had made him shudder. He hated himself for it, but he knew he was dreading what was yet to come. He'd considered his options more than once, but the guilt won out every time.

"You don't have to stay with me out of duty," Kris had said, after the doctor delivered the prognosis they were both dreading.

Tomas had found Kris's candour increasingly difficult to deal with. Too often, Tomas just muttered something about needing to pop out for supplies. Then he'd hit their favourite bar on Old Compton Street, followed by a succession of seedy dives. Kris had once stirred from his post-treatment slumber when Tomas had staggered, blind-drunk, back to their flat.

"You stink Tomas, and you're getting fat," Kris said before falling asleep again, vomit bowl on the floor next to him yellow with bile that matched the pallor of his skin.

As the tumour worsened, Kris's personality had changed with it. The doctors had warned of sudden mood swings, but

Tomas wasn't ready for what came next. The treatment made Kris sick and he could no longer stomach their favourite dishes. They stopped eating out, and in a matter of days, Kris had gone full vegan. Tomas worried all the time about Kris getting enough nutrients, watching his lover's once tight body begin to waste away. Then, along with raw food deliveries, the online orders had started arriving from esoteric bookshops and crystal healing websites. Kris joined an online group called 'Megalifers', which had a logo of a stone circle with a big, yellow smiley face at its centre. *Megaloafers*, Tomas called them, to Kris's annoyance.

Soon after, Kris started burning incense sticks and weird oils in a burner heated by tea light candles. Their flat had started to smell like a Camden head shop, the pungent scents barely cloaking the taint of Kris's illness that seemed to cling to every surface of the soft furnishings in their room. When the night sweats became torrents, Tomas took to sleeping on the sofa next to an open window. Even the carbon emissions from the nearby high street were preferable to the stench of their flat. In lucid moments, Kris asked Tomas if he thought the spiritual healers he had been reading about on *Megaloafers* could help cure his tumour. Give him—give them—a few more months, or even years. Tomas had gotten angry then. The doctors had told them it was incurable, that their priority should be making Kris as comfortable as possible. What use would some crackpot healer be in the face of an unstoppable cancer? Furious, Tomas had smashed the oil burner against the wall. Screamed at him to 'get real'. Kris did so, saying that the oil had left a stain and lamenting how Tomas would never get their landlord deposit back. And wasn't that a shame because he'd surely want to move after Kris died? Tomas had broken down, then.

Unable to bear the rift between them, Tomas took it upon

himself to scroll through the threads on *Megaloafers* in search of a peace stone. It turned out that the stone was rather a large collection of them. He'd found Kris's bookmarked thread about guided tours of ancient sites in Wiltshire. His browser history contained several blog pages about West Kennet burial mound. Morbid, of course, but typically Kris to fixate on something so esoteric and ancient to distract him from the problem of his here-and-now. The prospect of spending time in a minibus with a bunch of smelly hippies (who probably had not a pay check between them) was anathema to Tomas. But he told himself to man-up and booked two places on the next tour. He thought about not telling Kris about it, in case he became too ill to go, but then changed tack. If Kris had something to look forward to, it might lift his spirits a bit. His gamble worked. Kris even ate a little lunch and had asked for some watered-down wine to go with it by way of a celebration. The drink had made him puke his guts up, but Kris said it was worth it.

The look on Kris's face that day, when he helped him out of Barry's tour bus and into the Wiltshire drizzle was priceless. *At last I've done something right*, Tomas thought.

"Wow," Kris whispered at the sight of Silbury Hill dominating the landscape on the other side of the A-road. "I'll race you to the top—after we've seen the long barrow." Kris's legs wobbled a bit and he leaned against Tomas for support.

"Can't climb it I'm afraid, the guide said it's open to grazing animals only," Tomas said.

"Then we'll have a munch on some grass together," Kris joked, but Tomas could hear the strain in his voice.

What should have been a ten-minute walk turned into three of them. Kris was so knackered by the time that they had reached the first gate Tomas had to insist they stop for a while. They rested by the 'wee-wee tree' with Tomas gently suggesting they could come back another day. Determined, Kris wouldn't have any of it. He seemed energised by the landscape and described how thousands upon thousands of feet had walked this path over the centuries for rituals and feasts, and now—selfies.

Tomas half-carried him the last of the way to the long barrow, Kris's arm slung over his shoulder. Kris joked all the while and breathlessly quoted from movies he loved.

"I can't carry it… But I can carry you!"

Tomas laughed along until they reached their destination. The long barrow was a narrow, low hill, overgrown with grass and wild flowers. It was capped at one end by a huge upright stone that looked, to Tomas, like a monstrous tongue protruding from a mouth of wonky teeth. Kris murmured about how beautiful it all was, but to Tomas it just seemed desolate. The worsening rain was driving the last of the tourists back to their cars, leaving Tomas propping Kris up at the mouth of the barrow.

"Help me inside," Kris said.

"We can avoid getting drenched for a bit, at least," Tomas replied, casting an envious glance at the tourists beating a retreat in their polyester rain macs and destined for warm pubs and tea rooms.

The pounding rain felt less intense in the shelter of the capstone. Tomas stopped still on the gravel threshold, holding onto Kris. The interior of the barrow was pitch dark, reminding him of a disused railway tunnel he used to play in as a boy.

"Let me get my phone light on," Tomas said.

"Don't be silly," Kris said, "your eyes will adjust in no time."

"That's as maybe, but I don't want you falling over in there. Too far from the road for me to get help without leaving you up here on your own." Tomas wiped a slick of rain from his phone screen and thumbed the flashlight app.

"Spoilsport," Kris groaned.

Inside, a section of modern, reinforced concrete ceiling bordered overhanging rocks and stones, wedged together at chaotic angles. Tomas felt as though he was entering the crawlspace beneath a landslide rather than something that had been fashioned by human hands. To his left and right, he saw tiny chambers set back from the pathway that led deeper inside the barrow.

"That's where they found the remains of over forty of our ancestors," Kris said, sounding awed.

Tomas bristled at the thought of all those old bones. "Yours maybe," he retorted, "I'm from Norwegian blood, remember."

"Who's to say your ancestors didn't come here too, on their Viking ships?"

"Always with the Vikings," Tomas said.

"Is it true they wore helmets with horns on?"

"Don't go there."

"So easy to tease," Kris said. He chuckled, but his mirth soon gave way to a hacking cough. He doubled over and Tomas just grabbed hold of his waist in time to stop Kris from toppling headfirst against the rocks.

"Jesus, Kris. It's the damp air. Should never have brought you."

"Don't… be… silly. Just… need to… sit down," Kris wheezed.

"Okay, but where?" the thought of sitting in a darkened tomb gave Tomas the creeps.

"In there… look, there's a stone bench to sit on."

Tomas grimaced at Kris's suggestion, but giving his lover a breather took precedent. The entrance to the burial chamber was narrow, formed of two upright stones either side with a mosaic of little ones filling in the gaps.

"Jenga of the ancients," Tomas muttered.

"You always find a way to urbanise everything," Kris said, when he got his breath back.

"Only natural when you're on a day out in some old duffer's grave."

He set Kris down on the stone, which was high enough to make a suitable seat, and just wide enough for two. Holding onto Kris's shoulder to keep him steady, and to avoid knocking into him, Tomas pivoted on his heels and slid in beside him.

"Turn that bloody light off," Kris said, "you're spoiling the atmos."

Tomas killed the light and, thankful he was nearest the chamber opening, could just see a slash of muddy light from the mouth of the barrow. As his eyes adjusted, he began to see minute details in the rock above and around them. One stone glimmered with mineral deposits, and another was pockmarked with boreholes the width of an adult's index finger. The space where two of the larger stones met had created a little alcove with a ledge beneath them, and someone had placed a corn dolly there atop multi-coloured blobs of melted candlewax. The dolly's stumpy arms and legs looked comical, but Tomas looked away when his eyes found the featureless face in the semi-darkness.

"It's so peaceful here," Kris said with a sigh. His breathing had steadied, and he sounded less wheezy.

Tomas felt Kris's cold, wet cheek nuzzling into his neck and tried not to shiver. To him, this place was anything *but* peaceful. He felt as though the cold walls were closing in on him and clamped his eyes shut against an imagined image of each stone bearing Kris's name. Tomas realised he was panting.

"Hey, what's wrong?" Kris whispered.

"This place. You, me, us. All of this. It's just… wrong," Tomas said, and the tears followed. He sobbed, but he couldn't hold them back any longer.

"It's just the cycle of life, babe," Kris said.

"Yeah, but it's not fair," Tomas retorted, his tears beginning to burn hot with anger. "We had years ahead of us. *Years*. But now we can't… Because of that *thing* in your head."

"My tumour is as much a part of me as you are," Kris said. "An extension of my cells, of who I am. Trust me, I wanted a full life too, but if this is all I've had, I'm grateful. A couple of years with you has given me a lifetime of happiness—"

Tomas sniffled.

"—and I mean that. Really mean it. For once I'm not snarking. I'm grateful for what we've had."

Despair coiled in the pit of Tomas's stomach. His feelings were overwhelming. A rush of fear, guilt, rage, sorrow, all at once. Mostly guilt. The words left him before he could stop himself.

"Kris. I haven't been honest with you."

Kris sighed again, heavier this time. Tomas expected him to move away, to recoil, but he remained nuzzled into his neck.

"Oh. I wondered when we were going to have *this* conversation."

Tomas was dumbstruck.

"You great lummox. Booze and fast food don't hide the smell of other guys. How many? And don't say *Five Guys* or I might actually scream."

The fact that Kris was joking made Tomas feel ten times worse. "I'm so sorry…"

"Sorry *now*, maybe. Fun at the time though, wasn't it? Bastard."

"I didn't want to hurt you…"

"But you did it anyway. Really quite the fan of 'popping down the shops'. Can't tell you how many times I woke up alone, in agony, calling your name. But you weren't there were you? I know. I *knew*. You were out partying."

Cold wind sent a smattering of rain into the entrance to the barrow. Tomas felt his tears, icy on his face.

"If I could go back and change things, be a better person, I would," Tomas started, "but I can't. God, Kris, I didn't want to tell you like this!"

Kris smiled at that; Tomas could feel it against his neck. "You've never been a good liar, babe. I know I wasn't your only good time guy in Ibiza, so I never really expected to be the one for you in London either. Look. If our roles were reversed, maybe I'd do the same."

"Really?"

Tomas leaned into Kris and then felt him recoil slightly.

"No, actually. You don't get off that easily."

Tomas fell silent. Kris pulled away from his shoulder and sat bolt upright. His silhouette looked like the old Kris somehow. Stronger. The guy Tomas had fallen for.

"You only told me so you could feel better, I get that. But now I have to carry it with me in what little time I might have left? Quite selfish of you, really. I've been dreaming of coming here and, when we sat down, I felt more at peace than I have ever felt in my life. I felt ready for whatever shit this fucking cancer might throw at me next. But now, all I feel is…"

"What?" Tomas asked, hearing the fear in his own voice.

"I want to get out of here. And I know you've been itching to ever since we arrived. But I want you to promise me something first."

"Anything."

"After I'm dead, I want you to bring me back here. I want to be at peace, with the ancestors. In this beautiful, ancient landscape where no one judges, or points and prods, or takes endless blood samples."

"I don't think we could get permission to bury you up here," Tomas said, "it's all protected, like the hill."

"Not a burial. Just scatter my ashes, you idiot," Kris said with a chuckle, but there was also vitriol in his voice. Hearing that resolve reminded Tomas of their first months together, when they had the whole world at their feet. He realised now that he loved Kris more than ever.

"I don't want to let you go. I love you Kris, please believe me. I just wanted us to stay together, for you to get well again."

"I know," Kris said. Then he sighed. "What if I told you there was a way we could be together forever?"

"And what's that?"

"When you pop your clogs, have your ashes scattered here too."

Tomas smiled through the pain. "That'd be quite romantic. Weird, but romantic."

"Hold that thought," Kris said before pecking Tomas on the cheek. "Now. You can take me for a nice pub lunch. So long as you eat most of it. And you can drink a glass of wine on my behalf, too."

Tomas felt his skin flush. "Really?"

"Really. Let's just focus on the time we have left, yes?"

The funeral had been a miserable affair. Everyone wanted to tell Tomas how sorry they were for his loss, what a fantastic friend Kris had been, and how they 'wished they could have visited more often, but'.

After the cremation, Tomas had gone to sign for the ashes. The clerk at the undertakers handed them over, boxed up and in a carrier bag with Kris's name stapled to it on a little ticket. They were so heavy. Tomas placed the bag inside the wardrobe when he got home and shut the door. And there the ashes had remained. Until now.

The biting wind picked up as he neared the long barrow's looming capstone, a monolithic marker on the brow of the hill. Nobody was around and the only sound was the bleating of sheep from a distant field. Tomas tried to summon some comfort at being back on Kris's hallowed ground, but he found none. All he felt was tired and woozy from lack of sleep and food. The morsel of bitter-tasting cake that Barry had given him earlier simmered in the acid of his stomach. He swallowed against the dryness in his throat and approached the entrance.

Dying petals from long-since forgotten flowers littered the gravel at his feet, which crunched beneath his walking boots. The sounds echoed off the wall formed by the capstone and its neighbours, incongruous in the stillness. He passed beneath the modern cement lintel and then drew a steadying breath before walking a short distance into the darkness.

Tomas halted when he was adjacent with the entrance to the burial chamber. He could just make out the shape of the stone seat in the gloom where he had confessed to Kris. Reaching into the carrier bag, Tomas located the tea light candle and lighter Barry had given him. After a couple of tries, the candle flickered into life, casting undulating shadows across the rocks. He sidled into the chamber and placed the tea light on the little alcove beside the stone bench.

Thankfully, the disturbing little corn dolly with its featureless face had long since gone. Tomas turned and slid down onto the stone, but not before bumping his head inside the cramped space. Cursing, he wondered how both of them had managed to sit together at all, then he remembered Kris's frailty from those last days.

Tomas freed the heavy box of ashes from the plastic bag and set it on the stone seat beside him. Wiping away his tears, Tomas remembered the hipflask and pulled it from his pocket. He unscrewed the cap and smelled the tang of spiced rum. Of course—the first drink they had enjoyed together on Ibiza. Raising it to the flickering candlelight on the craggy wall, Tomas made a toast through his sobs. He downed the contents in one, enjoying the sharp burn at the back of his throat.

Tomas removed the tape seal from the lid of the box and flipped it open. Inside, was another, thicker plastic bag, loosely knotted closed. He untied the plastic and gazed down, for the first time, at Kris's mortal remains. They looked mundane, somehow, like the remnants of a fire pit. He found himself wishing Kris's last wish had been to have his ashes made into a firework. That would have been more befitting for a trailblazer like him.

He placed the box between his feet and a tear slid from his cheek onto the grey powder, making a little exclamation mark there. Tomas's head began to ache, and his near-empty stomach churned from the alcohol. A ringing started in his ears and his hands felt hot, then freezing cold. He pushed the ashes over and onto the gravel floor then lifted the upturned box, shaking it to release the final, mortal remains of Kris. His Kris. Tomas leaned back and watched a swirl of ashes rising as though borne on an invisible last breath. They shimmered bright in the light of the candle, and then they were gone.

Tomas jolted at the sound of a sharp whisper. He must have zoned out for a while because the tea light had burned out. It was so dark. He listened intently. Just the wind outside the barrow.

Fumbling in the dark for his phone, Tomas's stomach sank. He must have left it on Barry's minibus. No matter. The entrance wasn't far away. He lurched into a half-standing position and fumbled his way around to the entrance of the chamber. Or where he thought the entrance should be, because his shaking hands found only a solid wall of stone. He had gotten himself all disorientated in the dark. Turning to his right, he searched the blackness with his fingertips. More rocks piled up the ceiling above him. He began to probe the gaps and crevices with his fingers, trying to find something, anything that might lead him out.

Panic gripped him, along with another overpowering sensation. His throat felt like it was on fire. He clutched at his Adam's apple and gagged at a plume of rising bile that lapped at the back of his tongue. He doubled over in agony as a sharp spike of pain barrelled through his stomach and deep into his guts. His intestines squirmed hot inside of him and he tried to scream, but only a raw scraping sound would come from his impoverished vocal cords. Another jab of molten hot pain and he struck his head on a protruding rock. Warm blood trickled across his nose, its salt tang mingling with the scented oil that Barry had dabbed onto his forehead.

Kris's instructions.

Tomas fell to his knees, his skin a slick of cold gooseflesh.

We'll come for you when you're done.

He coughed up bloody bile. Tasted rum and ruin on his tongue.

Take you to the bonfire for a final goodbye.

34

Poison closed his throat. He couldn't breathe. His lungs burned. Dying organs cremated in the burial chamber of his ravaged body.

Said we were to take care of you. Follow his instructions.

Tomas clawed at the wall and felt the nails rip away from his fingers. He felt the weight of aeons bearing down on him, crushing him in the void behind the impenetrable capstone.

What if I told you there was a way we could be together forever?

No One Knows The Old Ways Anymore And It Will Be The End of Everything

LJ McMenemy

You've noticed the birds get more rowdy at this time of day, as if the setting sun triggers them to warn of approaching darkness. Even on this, your third night, it's still unsettling, this sudden cacophony in the midst of the utter stillness of the woods. And it's still a surprise to hear birds at this time, especially when it's later than it looks—but twilight comes so much closer to the witching hour at the summer solstice.

You get to work stoking the campfire and pray the solar lighting lasts longer this night than the last few. Without it, you're thrust into the dim, illuminated only by the speckles of moonlight that manage to creep through the thick canopy of trees stretching so high it hurts your neck to seek its top.

In the old tin shepherd's hut—more well-worn and "well-loved" than the listing's photo would have you think—you hurriedly use the last vestiges of your phone battery to search for extra candles, but it's extra matches that are AWOL. You make a note for a shopping trip tomorrow; tonight, you might finally just have to deal with the dark.

At least out here it doesn't feel like the walls are closing in. It doesn't feel like the air is suffocating, like the ground itself is trying to crush you into dust…

No one would've thought you could last this long in the wilderness. Too much of a city girl. You've never even camped at a music festival, preferring to find a local B&B within commuting distance. Back then, you didn't listen to the talk of "missing the full experience"; you'd rather have a real shower to warm you up at the end of those long days. You can't deal with mud caked on your skin, not even for a beauty treatment. It's too much sensory overload.

Yet here you are: no shower since you left civilisation, crouching on your haunches and stoking a campfire, alone in the middle of an ancient woodland and covered in dust. Senses both dulled and heightened. You tell yourself it was your only choice, really. You needed space. You needed time to think. Life is too, too noisy. How are you meant to figure out who you are and what you're meant to do if you're surrounded by the noise of London all the damn time? You told yourself that a week in the woods would clear your mind, help you figure out what a woman should be at this age, past 40 yet without the expected trappings and baggage. When there's no man, no kids, no career… Nothing but a whole big pile of steaming nothing.

Sure, in your haste to leave the city you didn't realise it was the summer solstice this week, but why would you? And anyway, does it matter when it means you got this hut cheap? Everyone else who's called to this sort of thing, to commune with nature at the solstice, has headed for Stonehenge so this "boutique glamping opportunity" was lying empty. You're doing the owners a favour. Besides, heading out here is not running away. It's not. It's running *to*—towards your future.

Stoke the fire again to stop it dying. You need to get the flame to take in a much sturdier way. You've only had brief glimpses of phone signal out here—at least, that's all you've noticed between reading in the dappled sunlight and walking through the woods and pouring your heart into your journal—and you've seized those moments to search for campfire tips. You need twigs, they said. Sticks. Kindling. The big logs available for purchase at the landowner's homestead at a "bargain price" will only get you so far if you don't have kindling. If only you were surrounded by the discarded waste of trees, right?

As daylight starts to wane, you head off to wander the beaten path, picking up sticks of varying sizes, wincing each time. You try not to think about what's pissed on these sticks, try not to focus on their rough texture, the patches of lichen, the tiny things that are probably crawling all over them. They are a means to an end.

A means to an end. That's all. Like this trip.

Solstice time
Praise the light
Demand what's right
The land has might

Back on that first night in the woods, fresh from the city, you could've sworn you heard movement around the campsite while you were lying in bed. That's why you lit all the available candles and, fire hazards be damned, slept surrounded by tea lights. The next morning you inspected every inch of the area outside, getting to know all the bushes, the birds that hide in the trees, the cheeky ones that swoop in to steal your food supplies from the little outdoor kitchen.

It wasn't until late that afternoon—no, it must have been the evening, given the light was fading so quickly—that you noticed the little grey squirrel watching you. It sat just on the edge of the clearing where you stood, the clearing that contained the hut and the campfire and the outdoor kitchen and the table and chairs, the clearing at the end of a messy overgrown walking trail that led back towards the owner's homestead where your car sat, waiting to take you back to civilisation once you'd figured your shit out (or the end of the week, whichever came quicker). The squirrel gave a little flick of its tail, once, then twice, and your body buzzed with the thrill of nature in proximity. You always were a sucker for a cute animal reel, but this one was right in front of you, right in touching distance. You felt it calling to you, almost magnetic was the pull, and as you took your first step to reach out to say hello, it disappeared into the brush with another flick of its tail. You thought it wanted you to follow, but it was getting dark, and cold, and you needed to get the fire going and to eat and… well, you were just a bit wary of walking unaided into the woods with no guidance and no light. You were sure the squirrel would understand. You thought you might see it again the next day, maybe, and make friends.

But again that night, the sounds of movement around the campsite kept you awake, searching for more tea lights to stave off the darkness within. And when you awoke, it was not squirrel prints or bird feathers that awaited you; it looked like footprints that went right up to the hut before disappearing seemingly into the fire pit. Or were you imagining that, bereft of sleep and a wild imagination stirred by the setting?

Either way, that was this morning. The beginning of day three in the woods. The third night draws nearer, and you still need to find better kindling for the fire. And you'll need to keep it going long enough to light some candles, because the solar lights really aren't lasting, and it'll take your last matches to get the fire in good shape.

> *Solstice time*
> *We have our needs*
> *Our spirit feeds*
> *Or yours recedes.*

By now, deeper along the trail in your search for twigs and kindling, you're no longer paying attention to the rustling in the bushes—it's noises higher up in the canopy that draw your eye further, tracing the long and winding trunk of the yew tree spreading at a fork in the path. You don't know how you know it's a yew given your knowledge of nature is pretty non-existent, but the name pops into your mind as you approach it and the fork. You don't remember a fork. Could've sworn there was just one straight trail which would eventually take you back to civilisation. But this new path—if in fact it is new—feels like it's pulling you. Like a wall had been put up, an energetic field telling you the other way was now forbidden to you, that you needed to follow the rustling, follow the feeling—no, follow the little grey squirrel that's now returned, appearing at your feet, tugging your shoelace, beckoning you onward.

Still wielding your stick haul, you take a few tentative steps along this new path—spotting silver birch, meadow foxtail, deadly nightshade, and a darting pine marten—and then freeze. The squirrel turns back to see what's holding you up, but you're blinded by sudden light, a radiating golden glow somewhere up ahead, like the sun has set right here in the ancient woodland and is now making the bracken its bed for the night. Still you are drawn onward, an echo calling you, pulling you towards the centre of the woods, and you take it step by step by feel and vibe instead of sight. You come to a clumsy stop as that blinding light recedes, and as the floating orbs stop dancing in your eyes and your vision returns you find yourself standing in front of a giant oak. Clearly ancient, its size dwarfs all around it: as wide as a Routemaster is long, bark chipping off at all angles, branches twisted and turning and covered in moss, holes of decay yawning in its ancient trunk. Standing before it makes you feel insignificant, like a tiny ant that knows it will be stood on at any moment, squished into oblivion, overcome by the might of the more powerful being.

You stand in awe of the wise old oak, knowing the squirrel stays by your side from its gentle nibble at your leg. And then it's not beside you anymore; it's a streak in your peripheral vision and then it's running up the oak's trunk, settling in the lowest branch, watching you carefully, waiting for what's to come.

It's then that the deepest roots rise from the earth and grab your feet, holding you still, pulling you down to your knees. And threads of pendulous sedge crawl up your thighs and your torso and split; two forks going around your arms to bind them to your side, and a third spinning around your neck, around your head, weaving your lips closed. You try but you can't move, trapped by the land, forced to genuflect in front of the ancient oak. The tears escaping your eyes drop from your chin onto a newly-sprouted patch of red campion; if you'd properly listened to those folklore podcasts, you'd know you should start looking for fairies hidden no longer.

Instead, you're glued to the spot, staring at the world in front of you.

Now the birds are flying in for the show, branches filling with jays and treecreepers and wood warblers and chaffinches and nuthatches and nightjars and little red robins—how do you know all these names?!—while woodcocks and red kites and tawny owls gather on the ground around you. In the shaft of moonlight now bright above (when did it get dark— how long were you enthralled?!) dance spores of death cap and fly agaric, slowly waltzing towards your nasal passages. The entirety of creation sits and waits for what's to come.

Through its roots, through its branches, through its spores hitting your neural networks, the land shows you the past, the present, and the future. You're shown the very thing you came here for, to understand your place in the world, and nature shows you its suggested course is the only way forward. You must relent. You must give in. You were fated to be here, right here, right now. And so you believe it's the only way it can be and you nod and you relent, you welcome them in, the oldest spirits of the woods. You understand they need you, need you to do their bidding, to bring them sustenance because it's been so long, oh so long since anyone came to visit. They're glad you came. They were beginning to worry, to wonder, to fear they'd been forgotten but not now, not now you are here to save them, to restore them, to bring them back to glory if only you'd give the sign that you know what to do, that you were sent here for the ritual, that you know your place and your reason for being and your purpose in life. Just give a little sign, a flicker of recognition, and the spirits will free you to start proceedings.

The spirits poke at your brain, looking under forgotten rocks and in every nook and cranny of your being and you feel their sadness as they realise you do not know the ritual, that you have not been sent as their tribute. And you feel the shift as their sadness turns to anger, and you are a disappointment, you are a traitor, you are just like all the others and they shall have their revenge.

And you're rooted to the ground, the pendulous sage joined by roots of the oak and roots of the yew and roots of the silver birch, all stalking up your legs, your arms. You stiffen and your eyes are wild as you slowly and then very quickly indeed turn to wood. And you are now a tree in this ancient woodland, and your roots touch the roots and mycelium network of the forest and you are alone no more. You are among the many who came before you and did not have the knowledge necessary to free the spirits and set them loose on this world in need. No one knows the old ways anymore, and it will be the end of everything.

Before, humans knew they needed to make offerings. The spirits of tree and land demanded a sacrifice each solstice as payment to live here, but humanity moved to the city and abandoned the woods and their spirits. And now the spirits are angry from years of neglect. They will take what they can when they can.

Stay safe out there. Make sure you don't venture into their path accidentally. Don't follow stray animals further into the woods in search of a selfie. Don't look into strange and sudden light. Wrong time, wrong place could be fatal. After all, plenty go missing in the wilderness…

And they may still be there, hidden in plain sight, consumed by the land, now part of the ecosystem and unable to scream.

Mister Persimmon
Rachel Henderson

Are you ready to meet Mister Persimmon?

Of course you are. Since the leaves turned brown and the winter rains began, you've thought of nothing else. You're focused. You're committed. You're prepared.

Have you pictured his face? Maybe it belongs to your neighbour across the road—the one with three underfed kids and four overdue bank loans—his wrinkled forehead, his drinker's nose. Or the bastard who hangs around the truck stop, all crusty lips and bleeding gums, shrieking for bus fare and spitting when you reject him. Friends, enemies, family, strangers: so many prospects.

Possibly he has no face at all. Could be you close your eyes and see a smooth drum of flesh, featureless as an egg. You can no more imagine the details of his face than you can imagine your fields in July, green and flourishing, because right this minute it's January and right this minute your fields are dead. Imagination can't tell the future. You trust what you see with your eyes—soggy farmland outside the kitchen window, stack of bills on the dining room table, *jump-jump-jumping* jaw muscle in the bathroom mirror—and your eyes have never steered you wrong.

So—have you pictured Mister Persimmon with your own face?

It's okay to say you haven't—a lie, most likely, but as far as lies go, there are worse to tell. If you're not lying—if you truly haven't pictured it—maybe you're overly confident. Or overly stupid. Blind to the risks, in either case, which is a dangerous way to exist. There's no shame in being a little afraid.

Anyway, you're picturing it right now. Mister Persimmon, with your own face.

What a terrifying thought.

Lucky for you, you're focused—committed—prepared. You grew up with the stories, cautionary tales wrapped in gold leaf: your father's beer-soured whispers, your mother's husk-dry sobs. Years ago, farmers in the feed store shut up when you approached—now that you're older, they let you join their circle. The first time one invited you orchard wassailing—invited you to meet Mister Persimmon—you turned him down flat. There was nothing enticing about that man's oversized smile, or his shuffling feet, or the way his hands shook when he showed you the covenant, breathlessly waiting for a signature you refused to give.

Isn't it incredible, how a small taste of life has changed you? How your family's debts became your own, how bad choices compound your misery, how good choices do nothing to help? Once the hunger begins, there's no beating it back. Hunger lives as long as you do.

That's why you joined up this time, finally, after years of watching others—braver, dumber, more desperate—leave for the orchard to meet Mister Persimmon. You took the papers and signed on the line, just like you always promised your mother you wouldn't. Farmers in the feed store clapped you on the back and offered titbits of advice. Some of the advice they gave, you'd already heard: expand your stomach. Cook a Christmas dinner big enough to feed a church hall and spend the next eleven days feasting alone, always feasting, feasting at breakfast and lunch and suppertime and all the moments in between. Other advice they gave was entirely new: harden your palate. Leave leftovers on the counter to spoil—not spoil to poison, only a touch—and hold the rotten pieces in your mouth until you can't stand it. Hold them until your bile is rising and your nausea crests. Then, hold them even longer.

They reminded you not to start before Christmastide.

They suggested you practice crawling around on your hands and knees.

They encouraged you to go to bed at dawn and sleep until dusk on Twelfth Night. To collect your thoughts. To fast before the wassail begins.

All these things you have done. Eleven days feasting on dry turkey, sour cranberries, shrivelled beans, doughy pie. Eleven days of mouldy morsels, held under your tongue, as your insides kicked and your throat constricted. Your knees are bruised from inching back-and-forth across the linoleum floor—your palms are scraped raw. Today, while the sun is out, you lie in bed with your eyes squeezed shut, breathing deeply, hoping stillness is as good as sleep, knowing full well it is not. You think about your stomach, stretched thin and hanging loose, a deflated balloon inside your abdomen, ready for tonight's contest. You think about the farmers, all full of advice and swagger—how they asked what you'll do with your riches if you conquer the orchard, if you come out big-man-on-top after the wassailing's finished, and how they laughed when you said you'd leave this place forever and make a better life somewhere else. They laughed because it's the same answer they gave, once upon a time. It's the same answer everyone gives. Everyone hopes they'll be the next champion.

You lie in bed all day and wonder how it will feel to meet Mister Persimmon.

The smiling, shuffling farmer who first offered you the covenant described the relief of it all: seeing Mister Persimmon, in the flesh, after a hard night's wassail. Meeting Mister Persimmon in the orchard means you have nothing to be scared of, not anymore—he's right there beside you, and he has someone else's face. That farmer claimed he's met Mister Persimmon every year since coming of age, more years than you've been alive. Never conquered the orchard in all those years—others have wassailed better, eaten more fruit, more quickly—but he's still walked out of the orchard, every time. Something to be said for that.

You, though—you'll only meet Mister Persimmon once. Because you're going to conquer the orchard. Only one man wins a golden future on wassail night, one man out of all the dozens who try, and that man must be you. You know all the stories. Your father used to mutter about the winners, those Wassailers Triumphant, getting top dollar for acres not worth a nickel, oil rights and water rights and mineral rights for patches of grow-nothing dirt, men who ditch their single-wides and drive away in factory-fresh trucks, leaving behind a cloud of diesel exhaust and envy. Fortune always kisses the man who conquers the orchard. And this year, that man is you.

You know this, because you're focused.

Committed.

Prepared.

Good thing you are, since it's finally wassail night, it's finally sunset, and it's finally time to head to the orchard and meet Mister Persimmon. You take your place among the others—friends, enemies, family, strangers—in the dirt, on your hands and knees. Perhaps you overdid it the past eleven days, practicing on your kitchen floor—your joints are creaking-stiff and the wet leaves sting your shredded palms. The trees feel too tall overhead. Even though it's wintertime they're deader than you expected, skeletal and grey, and you wonder what kind of trees they are, because between all the whispers and advice and stories and warnings, nobody mentioned the trees.

You look down at all the rotten fruit.

Persimmon is the wrong name. Close, but wrong. The fruits' outsides are orange and puckered, their stems are flat and leafy, but bits of pulp bulge from tears in the skin, and those bits are nightmare-black, darker than anything you've ever seen. They smell like rancid ham soaked in warm vinegar. Beetles skitter away to make a meal elsewhere. Nobody has a name for this fruit.

Nobody knows where that sound comes from, either—the low, sickening horn blast pulsing through the orchard—but everyone knows what it means.

The wassailing has begun.

Time to eat.

You shove your face into the nearest fruit. Chewing isn't necessary—the decayed pulp is so soft it simply oozes into your throat, one long clod of fruit flesh—and when it enters your oesophagus you cough, come right to the brink of retching, clench your fists and fight to banish the putrid taste that clings to your lips and teeth and tongue. It slides back, back, back—you swallow—take a breath—and it's finished. The first fruit is safe.

But this isn't enough to become the champion.

You need to eat faster. You need to eat more.

Above all—you need to keep it down.

The next fruit isn't any easier. Gamy juice dribbles over your lips and chin. The urge to spit is overwhelming until you glance at your fellow wassailers, munching their way across the orchard floor like it's covered in ripe strawberries, so you swallow again. And again. And again.

The skin, the pulp, the juice, the seeds.

How to tell bad fruit from worse fruit? They're all decomposing—all dusted with white mould—all have the potential to raise Mister Persimmon, to end the wassailing in an instant. Nobody gave you the trick to choosing the right fruit because there is no trick. You must eat, eat, eat—eat and keep it down. Eat all you can handle and then eat more. Pray the next bite isn't so foul, so viscous, it gags you the moment it hits your tonsils. Pray that even if you don't eat the most fruit, even if you can't conquer the orchard, you can still gulp back the bubble of puke threatening to crown. Pray you can walk out of here, just like that smiling, shuffling farmer— walk out, and try again next year.

After some time in the orchard, with the trees stretching taller and the shadows growing colder, you stop praying. It's pointless. Exhausting. Besides, you need your energy to eat.

And eat.

And eat.

Your stomach twists around itself after the tenth or twentieth or thirtieth fruit. When you crawl forward, searching the ground for more, pain stabs at your guts. Even with all the sounds around you—the squelch of damp earth, the smack of other mouths—you hear your digestive system struggling to keep up, fierce pops and molten gurgles. You can also hear your heartbeat, although you try not to—its quickening rhythm accelerates your nausea. Each *thump-thump-thump* drives you further inside yourself, pushing you into the soup of hot, rank fruit and gastric acid, holding you under until you're certain you'll drown if you don't take a breath, absolutely certain, no matter what that breath might cost you.

You take a deep, luxurious breath, and vomit onto the orchard floor.

At last, you're going to meet Mister Persimmon.

And as it turns out, he has your own face.

What a shame.

Because you've never come to wassail night before, you might be surprised how quickly the change happens. Sick is still dripping from your nose when your limbs soften and curl inward. You collapse into the sticky puddle of your failure—bright orange flecks punctuating the silky blackness—and try to call for help before realizing your tongue has dissolved to sludge and slipped back into your throat. Feeble, boneless, you roll onto your side. At first, you think the sensation of bursting skin and seeping mush comes from the fruit beneath you, crushed by your weight, but then the others scoop you up. They scoop you up and you see your stomach—the slough, the split, the pulp—and you'd vomit again, if you had muscles left to do it.

How does it feel, now that you're Mister Persimmon?

Unjust, of course. You were focused, committed, and prepared. You followed the advice from the farmers; ignored the warnings from your mother. You were as worthy as the others—worthier, maybe. Bad fortune can only follow a person for so long before they get a break.

And you were so sure that person would be you.

No telling yet who the champion is tonight—you surely can't, with your liquefied eyes and dangle-down ears—but it's probably one of the men hauling you over to the nearest tree. A bootstrapping bastard, someone with a stronger stomach or dumber luck. He pours your fruit flesh out of its skin and onto the tree roots, already thinking about his factory-fresh truck, his golden future, his shiny new life, while your life soaks the dirt for next year's wassail champion.

If it's any consolation, any at all—you make a fine Mister Persimmon.

The Forgiveness Tree
Paul Crosby

As the Harwich branch line breaks out of the post-industrialism of Colchester's east end, and pulls clear of the brownfield that buttresses it, the ambiguous majesty of the estuary begins to reveal itself, at least to those of its passengers who are able to tear themselves away from their phones. This is a low country, as low as it gets without joining the other remnants of Doggerland beneath the North Sea silt and salt. It is in constant negotiation with the sea; in winter it is prone to waterlogging, trees standing hunched against the wind with their ankles in water. And it is winter, as Jules peers out of the grimy window, habitually scanning the landscape, the way he always used to, looking for one tree in particular that he's never quite managed to spot. His friend Rob claimed to have seen it, but Rob was prone to claim all sorts of things.

He hasn't been this way in years, not since his dad moved into the home: there's nothing left in Harwich for him now, other than discarded chip wrappers and raw memories. Today he's only got a ticket as far as Wrabness, with its woodland burial ground. Jules's dad would probably have scorned the whole idea of a "green burial", although he had never expressed any particular opinion on funeral matters. But Annie had insisted, and Jules had agreed to it to keep the peace, since his sister was his only remaining family now. Not that the peace had been kept for very long. So Dad was planted in the ground, with a stubby oak sapling rooted over the top of him. They had gone for the cheaper wooden plaque option to identify it, and this is why Jules has a small tin of varnish and a brush in his bag, the banality of which he finds hilarious, although he's not entirely sure why. Is it a peace offering? A libation? An expiation?

Jules is on the train en route to visit his dad's tree, but that isn't the one he's looking for now. He's a couple of stops short of Wrabness, at the point on the line when he is reminded of the story of the Forgiveness Tree. It's supposed to be somewhere here, in the woods outside Ostley, the oldest tree in the area, an oak that has clung fast to the mud for more than eight hundred years. He's shaky on the exact details of the story, but it's something to do with forgiveness or absolution as its name suggests. How appropriate for today, he thinks. But he still can't see it, despite Rob's claim to have seen it from the train. He's picturing an ancient, gnarled oak, knots and whorls resembling the faces of humanity's ancestors, but now that he considers it, it's probably just a degraded memory of something from a film. He doesn't think he's ever seen a photo.

As the train begins to slow for the station, it occurs to him that he's never tried using modern technology to find it, and out of bored curiosity, he puts the name into a mapping app. There it is: a pin labelled "Forgiveness Tree", just outside Ostley. It can't be more than a short walk from the station. A few moments later, he's on the platform, without having made a conscious decision. He checks the timetable. The next train is an hour away, so there should be plenty of time to get there and back, but it's the last one, so he'd better not miss it. The wind is disordered, gusting, and the rain comes in waves.

Led by his phone, Jules follows the high street back west, looking for the footpath. He reaches what is obviously the edge of the small town centre very quickly, but he can't spot the beginning of the path. He notices he is standing outside the church, so he goes in, immediately relieved to be out of the weather. Inside, the lights are off, and before his eyes can adjust, he is startled by a small man in dusty jacket and jeans, with a lined but smiling face.

"Welcome to St. Mary's," he says. "There's no service today, but please feel free to look round."

"Er, thanks," says Jules. "Actually, I was wondering if you could give me directions. I'm looking for a tree." Too late, it strikes Jules how odd this sounds out loud. "The Forgiveness Tree?"

He is reassured by the recognition on the man's face. "Ah! Yes. Our local legend. Hold on a moment."

He turns to a rack of tourist brochures to one side of the door and flips through them. "You're in luck, there's one left." He pushes a dog-eared pamphlet into Jules' hand. "It's a wonderfully creepy story. They say one of Matthew Hopkins' accomplices fled here, after murdering a man in a local pub during a drunken fight. In his haste to escape justice, he ran into the forest. He..."

"Yes," says Jules. "I know the story. So the tree is real?"

The man smiles again, and nods.

"Can you tell me how to find it?"

The man points, indicating a southerly direction, beyond the church. "Through the churchyard and keep going. Take the path across the field, up toward the woods. In fact it's likely to be the same route taken by the murderer: he supposedly did the deed in the courtyard of the Rose, just up the High Street. I think we might have some more literature..."

"I'm in a bit of a hurry, sorry," says Jules.

The man is visibly disappointed to be cut off, and Jules adds awkwardly: "I've got to get back for the last train. Thanks for all your help."

On his way out, a thought strikes him: if forgiveness is really what he's after today, a church is probably the best opportunity he'll get, and he's just missed it.

Now that he looks again, a disintegrating wooden fingerpost points down a walled alleyway next to the church. As Jules enters, it funnels the wind at him, and he angles his hood against the squalls of rain aimed his way. He sees he's still holding the pamphlet, and stuffs it into his pocket to preserve it. The weather relents a little when he reaches the churchyard, around which the crumbling red brick walls continue. Between the puddles and the gravestones, the snowdrops are already coming out; on a kinder day, this would be a pleasant place to stop for a while, but Jules is keen to keep moving, already regretting his decision to get off the train.

Each of the walls, in the cardinal directions, has an opening, all but the one through which he entered with its own low wooden door. The one to the east appears to be a short-cut back to the station that isn't shown on the map. To the west, a footpath in the direction of Manningtree, and eventually Colchester and home. (If that's still home?) In front of him, the blue line on his phone map cuts across the railway tracks, and beyond that, the woods where his destination apparently lies. He pauses briefly, before choosing the latter.

He was wondering how he would cross the train line, but after making his way down a muddy bramble-lined path from the churchyard, his unspoken question is answered by a short foot tunnel, bored through the grimy brickwork shoring up the embankment. A gush of rainwater gets a direct hit down his collar when he enters, and he wriggles uncomfortably as he splashes through the surprising darkness of the tunnel. Emerging at the other end, he is startled by a leering face that someone has painted in considerable detail to one side of the entrance. It looks knowing, somehow, and Jules suppresses an urge to protest his innocence, rehearse all of his justifications to it.

Looking down from the tracks, he finds that they form an abrupt boundary: he was expecting Ostley to extend further to the south, but now he can see that before him is the woodland that he was looking at from the train. The path continues downward from the railway line, but between him and the woods there is a field, grazed by a few scattered sheep, their coats glistening wet as they tear at the meagre winter growth. He stands above the lowest point of the field, which is occupied by a stretch of standing water. The wind rises again as he descends toward it, and he hunches into his coat. Essex cold, Essex mud.

He turns right to make his way around the oversized puddle, wishing he'd picked better shoes; the cemetery in Wrabness won't be any better. This reminds him about the train. He'd better keep an eye on the time. He glances at his watch: OK for now.

It takes a few false starts to find ground that is unsodden enough for Jules to pick his way up to the field boundary.

Checking his phone again, he remembers that the map app only gives a rough location, and it might be slightly or even totally wrong. There aren't any crowdsourced photos of the tree either, as if previous visitors are part of an informal conspiracy to ensure that no one can take the lazy option. He will have to do the hard work of finding and identifying it himself, picking it out of the line-up.

He walks around the perimeter of the field and tries to recall exactly what Rob had said about the tree. It looked like a clenched fist, he'd said, clutching something white that he couldn't quite see. Blossom, or remnant snow, Jules had vaguely assumed, but now that he focuses on the remaining scraps of this memory, he's fairly sure Rob had said it was late summer. Then again, Rob had tried to freak him out with all sorts of embellished folklore on the nightshift that they shared a few years ago.

Jules doesn't have Rob's number to follow it up: he lost track of him after they both moved on to other things, and it turned out that the job was the only connective tissue in their friendship. Not just that, but it had been a bad year. It was around then that they moved his dad to the home, after he'd got confused and come a cropper one too many times, alone in his house, and started getting aggressive with the home help. Annie had insisted on the place in Colchester so that he was near to her, but it always seemed like it was Jules that had to get the early train up from Stratford to see him.

Jules swears as a straggling root nearly sends him sprawling in the mud. The uncertain path has stuck to the field boundary so far, but now it strikes out across the field toward the woods, as if it has suddenly made up its mind.

At the top of an incline, the path passes through a kissing gate, and splits, one branch continuing straight toward the bulk of the woods, the other bearing left and downhill again, toward what looks like bramble and low willows, with taller trees beyond that. The route on the phone map doesn't closely correspond to either, and Jules is still frowning at it when he becomes aware that a pair of dog walkers are waiting for him to step away from the gate and let them through.

Jules mumbles an apology, then says: "Um, I'm looking for a tree. I don't know if you've heard of it. It's called the Forgiveness Tree." The name makes him self-conscious again. "Or something like that."

"Is that the magic tree they talk about? Isn't that just a story?" The woman holding her restless labrador's lead looks over toward the woods. "I'm not sure."

"No, it's real, definitely," says the rotund man accompanying her. "Well. There's a big oak, an old one. Over that way, I think." He points to the lower woods. "I haven't been down there in years though."

The woman looks sceptical. "That one? Didn't some kids set fire to it, and burn it down?"

The man shakes his head. "That was a different one."

"It was in the papers," she insists.

"No, it's still there. I think. If that's the one you're after."

The woman looks at Jules' increasingly sodden state. "What you doing this for, anyway? It's a horrible day."

"You should go to the pub. It's what I'm doing!" The man beams, as if proud of an elegant solution to a previously intractable problem.

"I've got to catch a train." Jules fails to resist the urge to look at his watch.

"But the station's that way." The woman frowns and waggles the end of the dog's lead toward the town.

"Thanks," says Jules. "So the tree's over there?"

"Yes," says the man.

"No," says the woman. "Yes."

"OK, thanks again," says Jules, already walking toward the trees in the bottom corner of the field. The wind gusts again, now behind him like a hand in the small of his back, hurrying him on.

As he feared, the slope takes him back down to the water level, murky standing water criss-crossed with sinewy old bramble growth and fallen branches. He tests the going with a pointed foot, but the ground has the consistency of a bloated sponge. Eventually he finds the trunk of a fallen tree and edges his way along it, his city clothes feeling increasingly ridiculous to him. But he reaches the far side with a sense of triumph; then his cockiness gets the better of him, and he immediately gets a shoelace caught on the spiny tangles underfoot, slips while trying to unhook it, and sprawls in the muck.

Jules picks himself up and carries out a quick inspection: more wet than muddy, but he's torn his coat. He has a sudden flash of perspective, of how ridiculous this situation is, when he was supposed to be miles away by now tending his father's grave. If Annie saw him in this state, she would not be forgiving. Not that forgiveness has ever been a strength of hers, even before what happened happened. Even in her absence, he can't help mentally adding her into the scene, the disapproving older sister standing over him in judgement. This last year, after he lost the Stratford flat and had to move in with her and Richard in Colchester while he looked for work, had hardly improved their relationship. If anything, it's just exaggerated the worst aspects of it, the younger brother constantly messing up, his big sister resentfully clearing up afterwards. He flinches again at the raw memory of their last conversation, the day she threw him out: *It's not about the money, Jules. It would take the rest of your life to repay us for a betrayal like this.* But he was fully aware that his shame wasn't about the money he'd taken from them; that wasn't the half of it. Still, he would rather Annie thought of him as merely a thief, rather than what he really was.

Forgiveness: isn't that what this tree is supposed to do for you? Jules told the volunteer in the church that he knows the story, but he can't recall the details all that well. As he picks his way through the brambles to drier ground, he remembers the leaflet, and fishes it out of his pocket. But his fall in the bog has completely ruined it. It's illegible now. What was supposed to happen when you climb the tree? Some grandiose word like absolution, or restitution. He hopes it isn't much further into the woods, because it's not too long before he'll have to turn back if he wants to get the train. As he pushes through the tangles, he judges that the path is taking him back in the direction of the tracks, although he can't see them through the thick growth. But he supposes that would make sense, if Rob really did see the tree from the train.

The thought of his old colleague shakes another memory loose: Rob had called the tree by another name. *Old Boney.* Had he given Jules an explanation for it? Too long ago now.

The undergrowth seems to relent slightly as the ground dries out, and Jules realises that he is climbing, and steeply at that. He worries that he has got turned around, because he didn't see a hill in this direction earlier. It's hard going, his feet getting little purchase on dark mud left slick by the season's rains. He wonders why he followed the dog walkers' directions, despite their obvious uncertainty; he knows he should turn back, but he's invested too much in this now. He also knows that this is faulty reasoning, but a stubborn part of him is intent on seeing it through. He is halfway through an imagined rehearsal of telling Dad about his quest for the Forgiveness Tree, before he remembers that his destination isn't the assisted living flat in Harwich, but a plot under a tree in Wrabness. And if he's going to say something there, he knows what it ought to be. *Not yet.*

At this thought, the foliage opens out, and he is in a clearing, thickly carpeted by the mulch and papery skeletons of uncounted autumns past; he can't see any footprints. Before him, the buttressed trunk of a huge oak squats at the centre of a web of thick, tortured roots, which rear up from the soil as if someone has tried to wrench the tree bodily from the earth. Spindly branches shoot from the stubby remnants of older, much thicker boughs, but a smattering of last season's leaves still cling to them, proving that this colossal methuselah isn't dead yet. What is left of its crown is open, inviting, with a flattened area in the middle, a crow's nest large enough to accommodate an adult human. It's obviously the Forgiveness Tree; it can't really be anything else.

Jules takes a step forward, then another. Each one is a struggle, thanks to the yielding depth of humous, and the wind and rain pick up again, as if they have been waiting for their moment, but he wades his way to the base of the trunk and looks up. He's never climbed a tree before. What did the story say? You climb the tree, and you're forgiven for whatever it is? He imagines the Witchfinder General's accomplice, scared and exhausted, perhaps drenched and muddied by a day like this one. Did he climb the tree in the story? Jules has a feeling he did. Was the witchfinder forgiven? He must have done much worse things. Worse than... anyway, surely Dad would have understood?

It doesn't look too hard, he decides, and digging his fingers into the grimy bark of the stump of a broken branch, he puts one foot into a crevice and pushes off the ground. But his toehold is less firm than he hopes, and he skids back down, bashing his shin on the way. Everything is wet and lubricated by moss.

62

Glancing at his watch, Jules realises that he's out of time; he has to go now. One more attempt, though. He tries the same route again, with the same result. In frustration, he takes off his belt and throws the buckle over a higher branch to give himself a bit of extra reach. He swings, scrambles, lands on his backside in the loam again. Brushing the worst of it off, he gets to his feet, fully intending to retrace his steps, sprint the last hundred metres or so up the high street, and catch the train. But instead, he turns back to the tree. He's going to do this. He was never going to catch that train to Wrabness anyway.

And with this admission, the tree accepts him. Reaching up, he finds the true way, the correct branch to catch hold of; the right crevice over here that will fit the toe of his boot. Hand over hand, he progresses upward, as if he is gliding up toward the canopy. The tree shows him the way, guiding him from foothold to handhold.

When he reaches the top, the Forgiveness Tree's secrets are revealed to him; he sees how it works now. The hollow at the top is bigger than he expected, and there is plenty of room to lie down. Old Boney makes a surprisingly comfortable bed, and he nestles into the remains of his predecessors.

He has made it to the heart of the Forgiveness Tree, and he is ready to receive its benediction. Or was it absolution? Jules still can't quite grasp the word from the story. But he feels at peace now, and the things that he has been keeping out of his mind's eye can come into focus. He is able to confront the memory of standing over his father's bed holding a pillow, having convinced himself that what was left of Dad would never know, wasn't really him anymore. Jules needed the inheritance sooner rather than later; thanks to Richard's investments, Annie never would.

The branches cradle him, almost caressing him as they

close about him. In a half-sleeping state, Jules is in touching distance of the word, the name of the Forgiveness Tree's gift. Was it retribution? He's so tired. He doesn't want to think about it anymore, and he closes his eyes, ready to sleep long and deep, as the seasons turn.

Up above the low wood, the trains will continue to pass. If a passenger happens to stare into its heart at the right moment, they might see an old, old oak, its crown clenched like a closed fist. And if they are particularly sharp-sighted, they may catch a glimpse of something held within its branches, something white. Something that might be the leftovers of last night's snow, or early blossom, but isn't.

Teas at the House
Sam Hicks

Blue twine hung loose around the rabbit's neck. It lay on its side, straining black eyes, stiff legs, ears without a twitch. Its pelt, the colour of a river bed, quivered madly. Above, sycamores and nettles danced and stilled, danced and stilled.

Irene bent down, fascinated and a little moved, and so heard the last sound that issued from its mouth. Nearly, faintly, the beginning of a word:

"Muh—"

The eyes lost life. The frantic heartbeat stopped.

It was as though it had been waiting for her to walk across the field towards the corner stile on that exact day, at that exact time, so she might bear witness. But where would you be if you believed every creature—why not every plant?—could foresee, and fear, their death? How would you be able to eat, to drink, to touch anything that ever lived? Irene squinted up, just as the sun was hidden by cloud. She'd better get moving. Despite the heat, rain might be on the way. Adjusting her rucksack more to the middle, she climbed over the stile.

It was a time, the 1950s, when it was rare to see a lone woman hiking. But Irene—a doer, an organiser, a natural pick for the team—responded to the jeers of the gallants outside the village pubs with firm, indulgent smiles, and waved cheerily at those who called out from cars on the narrow country roads. She wasn't one to be cowed. She enjoyed maintaining her own brisk pace and not having to stop for someone else to catch their breath. She liked not having to carry a conversation, and the fudgy squish of mud beneath her boots, and the burn in her legs as she tackled the hills, and the sense of solitary wonder she found when, on reaching a high place, she saw the landscape surrounding her as though she were the centre of a vast green circle.

It was the first chance in months she'd had to wrest a Saturday for herself. How good it felt, catching the train from London Bridge, seeing the suburbs give way to fields and trees and bright little streams, and alighting at the tiny station where an early fall of sycamore seeds littered the deserted platform and roses grew around the ticket office door. The day was still opening, still had its waking newness, as she walked through the quiet village and up towards the hills. She'd seen no one since the churchyard where a woman knelt by a new grave, arranging cornflowers in a vase. It was too hot, perhaps, for anyone but mourners, and her, to venture far from their shaded houses, their riversides, their gardens.

She checked her map; this stile led to a path between fields, and if she remembered her planned route rightly, there'd soon be another footpath, heading up through farmland to woods. The path was shaded by field maple and elder, their leaves turned flaccid in the heat, and below them brambles, casting their slashed shadows. Now and then, through a small gap, she'd catch sight of a field's rough-grazed grass, but it was only by luck she spotted the footpath sign; a smudge of yellow caught her eye, and going closer, there was the pointer, deep within a bank of ivy by the side of a metal gate. She consulted her compass. The direction matched a faint line in the grass.

A cruciform shadow moved over her, halfway across, and looking up, she saw a bird, a hawk of some kind, scarlet for a moment in the sunlight, lazily circling as though observing her, then tacking swiftly off. The humidity was building—could there be a thunderstorm coming?—and sweat glued her shirt to her back as she took the field's incline. Clenched lumps of dung dotted the cropped grass; the sheep she found as she neared the field's edge, laid out in the shade of leaning oaks beside a lurid green pond.

The stile was half-buried by hedge. Using her bag as a shield, she clambered carefully. The ground rose in a sun-greyed wave across a field so wide it was hard to tell if it was bushes she saw at the distant borders or stranded lumps of rock. Irene shielded her eyes. A man was up on the crest of the hill, plodding along, back bent, shoulders stooped. She had the impression of old age, a flat cap over lank grey hair, a sagging jacket that would be a second skin no matter what the season. She sensed a world of manure and mud and hard-baked resentment. He stopped, facing downhill. Irene didn't move. He raised a hand. He waved, very slowly, more of a signal than a greeting, and not knowing entirely why, Irene gripped the Swiss Army knife she always kept in her shorts pocket. He was waiting for her to return the gesture, and she wasn't going to do any such thing, not without knowing how it might be taken. She, the indomitable Irene, found she was edging back towards the stile. The old man removed his cap. He circled it back and forth in his hands as if ruminating on something before sending it back to his head with a decisive flip and turning away. His heavy trudge along the ridge resumed, and he became smaller, became less, until, at the field's far limit, he dipped out of sight.

Irene slipped off her rucksack, took out her water bottle. He was passing through to another field, checking on the sheep. Just going about his day. No reason to get the jitters. An old man like that. As if she couldn't cope with the likes of him. Once, on one of her hikes, a hulking farm lad had followed her across four fields. Finally tiring of it, she'd stopped, and as he closed in, when she could see the warring confusion and compulsion in his eyes, she'd taken out her Swiss Army knife and, with the tip of its largest blade, had begun to clean her fingernails with the greatest care and precision. The overgrown boy watched impassively at one safe remove, before mumbling, "Excuse me, Miss. Didn't mean no bother," and lumbering away. She had an instinct for these situations. The first rule was: always do the unexpected.

She took a long swig of water, disappointingly warm and unrefreshing, while she read the map. The woods weren't far, and then, shortly after, she'd meet the main river where she could follow an easy, meandering path back to the village. She'd stop in the woods to eat her sandwiches. In fact, she was so hungry, with six miles already under her belt, that she was tempted to have one now. She rifled through her bag, grabbed the white package. But it wasn't her neat, waxed paper-wrapped lunch. It was that buffoon Daniel Seal's last book, *Manchester Orpheus.* She swore.

She'd taken the call from her assistant, Eddie, that morning, just as she was about to leave—that was it—book and sandwiches, both of them white rectangles, side by side on the kitchen table. When she'd taken ownership of the publishing house after her dear father's death, Eddie had been one of the many staff who'd treated her with a suspicion that bordered on contempt, but who nowadays found it impossible to decide the simplest thing themselves. They vied for her attention. They squabbled, invented problems. She blamed herself; she'd made herself too useful, proved her worth a bit too much. She'd become, to them, what she'd never had any desire to be. A mother.

"Danny won't accept the edits for the last chapters of the new one." Eddie's whine always set her teeth on edge. "Says we can go whistle. Says it doesn't matter if he lifted whole paragraphs from *Manchester Orpheus*. It's a symbolic excavation of his own text, he says. What should we do about him?"

Why did he even ask? He already knew. "Oh, Eddie. Book the usual table for two, you know how it goes by now. Monday lunch at *Bertolet*. He'll come round in the end. Doesn't he always?"

It amazed her, how Danny Seal ever managed to write anything near passable, let alone outstanding, when he had all the emotional sophistication of a dog. A good Bordeaux, a rare steak, flattery, a promise of an interview in *The Journal*, and he'd be a happy boy again. You only had to throw him a couple of bones. Oh the idiot. Now he'd stolen the food from her mouth, more or less.

She stomped up the hill, seething, almost wanting the old man from the ridge to come back, so she could punch him in the face, just like she did to Jerry Dunstable that time he tried to take advantage. But you had to be boiling with rage for that, and she hadn't been gripped by rage when she saw the man. It had been doubt, if anything: the feeling that she might have gone the wrong way, even though she knew hadn't. Something in the way he'd waved, perhaps. The way it had been more a signal than a greeting.

Was it just the length of the grass, pale and feathery and dry, that made it seem as though the ground were sinking the higher up she went, and that gave her, when she reached the top, the oddest feeling of having grown shorter; of being in some way out of proportion? She took another gulp of water. The trees bordering the fields somehow contrived, even from that relative height, to hide any view further than a mile; their overlap erased the fields and created the illusion that the farmland was now forest. She headed towards the field gate, thinking of her missed lunch, of how long she'd have to wait before she found anything to eat, and anxious she might start to flag, with five miles yet to go. Nowhere on her route looked remotely like a settlement big enough to keep a shop.

Beyond the gate the trail was the downhill margin of a maize field. The plants, intimidatingly tall, amplified the breeze, so it seemed as if it were chasing her, and she was glad to be free of its clap and chatter and rush when, at the lower corner, a few yards of rutted track appeared, and then a slab of steel and concrete crossing a rust-coloured stream; the bridge into the woods.

She moved through a hover of tiny flies, more implied than seen, and entered peaty woodland light, passing, at the head of the path, a leafless dying oak, and finding herself among conifers and papery birch, quiet now that the breeze had dropped, and below them, fallen moss-furred branches, and, where the light was dappled, the delicate arcing plumes of ferns and the last green leaves of wild garlic. As she walked, she almost held her breath in reverence at the silence. Only the water bottle sloshing in her rucksack broke the stillness with its tinny voice.

After a while, the trees, those skinny rivals for the sun, gave way to a looser space of ash and hazel, and beeches whose smooth, exploratory roots tried, and failed, to trip her. At the first bend, beside a lengthy run of holly wilder and taller than she'd ever seen before, she made another map stop. Yes, the woods definitely ran for less than a mile, with a single, clear way through. She'd begun to think they must be bigger, but then maybe they held, as some wooded areas seemed to do, a memory of greater, ancient forests and the awe they'd once awoken within the human soul. She saw the two stately gateposts behind her only when she readied to move off. A handmade sign hung from the open gate, with the likeness of a pointing hand, and in neatly painted script, *"Teas at the House"*.

"Thank you!" she said. Starvation might be averted after all.

Her watch showed just after half past two. But how did it get so late when she'd maintained such a steady pace? And would it be too early for teas? This was, she'd heard, the kind of thing the gentry were resorting to as their houses became more difficult to keep, and as their wealth, ever a source of mystery, began to dwindle. But—how lovely. Scones and jam, perhaps, and sandwiches. It couldn't have come at a better time. Presumably as an inducement, posies of sweet violets had been tied to the bars of the gates. She put her nose to one but immediately pulled away. Clearly not as fresh as they looked; there was a putrid stink about them, like flowers that had been left in the vase too long and filled the water with rot.

The driveway through the gardens, more properly described as parkland, wasn't as long as she'd feared; you'd often walk for a mile or so through thoroughly exhausting landscaping before coming in sight of the main event. But the wide track, glinting a sandy gold in the re-emergent sun, led directly to the old carriage turning circle fronting the house, no more than two hundred yards away. It was imposing, all right. One of those white Georgian confections, whose architect, drunk on dreams of Grecian temples, had installed, around the central entrance, soaring Corinthian columns, rising at roof level to a triangular pediment. She gazed hopefully about. Definitely too early. The lofty double doors were not thrown open in welcome, Perhaps the teas began at three, or four.

It was unusual, eccentric really, when she looked at it, the layout of this place. The grounds of these houses usually went in for a gracious open sweep, but here the trees weren't organised to improve on nature's lack of plan, but chaotically, so they blocked the eye and stole any sense of fuller grandeur. Low-spreading cedars, crooked mulberries, horse chestnuts, white willow, copper beech. You'd think the whole arrangement had been cobbled together in a day, not over centuries; a rushed and unsophisticated job. Had she seen the house on the map, but overlooked it? Somewhere like this would usually earn a mention. But it was easy enough to skip a word and a dot. There'd been no nameplate at the gates, had there? She glanced back to the house.

Irene had stopped only a short way from the entrance, yet it was, she supposed, likely enough that the little girl had been hiding behind one of the columns all the while. Even so, on seeing her, she gave a start.

Maybe about ten years old—Irene wasn't good with children's ages—and all done up in a funny white dress that reached to her ankles. It reminded her, the dress, of the outfits they'd been forced into for school plays; a shapeless thing, run up by an inexpert seamstress, with blue velvet ribbons tacked to the sleeves for opulence and cheap gold braid around the neck. She had the look of an antique peg doll; her cheeks too pink, her eyes too big, her neck surprisingly thick where it rose from the crust of braid. Her head, wisped about with fly-away fair hair, was noticeably too large for her slight frame. For one moment, perhaps because of the strangely knowing stillness of her gaze, Irene wondered if this was not a child, but a very small old woman. But no; her skin was unlined and her hair, what little there was of it, was golden.

"Hello," Irene said in the light, amused tone she'd heard others adopt with children. "Do you live here? Is it open for teas yet, do you know?"

The girl stared on, and Irene began to doubt whether she'd actually seen the sign by the gates, if she'd mistaken it somehow, and was now trespassing where she'd no right to go. What was wrong with the girl? Her eyes widened, unblinking, like a cat disturbed in its night time prowl. She nodded robotically and pointed at a sign by the doors, which, like her, seemed to have fallen from the sky. Had she put it there? Before Irene could ask, the girl was picking up her skirts and scampering off, clearing the house, leaping the shallow terraced steps and away into the trees. A child unaccustomed to people, evidently.

The new sign said teas would be served from three. Was it worth waiting? It would add time to the walk. But she was so hungry, just the thought of egg and cress sandwiches and Victoria sponge made her stomach growl, and at least she was the first there, so she'd be at the front of the queue, if one ever decided to form. Her wrist watch read a quarter to three. Yes, it was worth it. She'd only to kick her heels for a few minutes more.

It had to be a deliberate plan, how the trees were offset. Wandering away from the driveway, she found that after passing between any two the longer vista was hidden in the same way that, earlier, the trees had hidden the fields from the summit of the hill. Why would they want to make everything seem closer, rather than lengthening the view? Wasn't this way of life all about display? But it was obviously cherished, for all its oddness. The grass was well-watered and lush; cared for, no doubt, by a fleet of gardeners with generational ties to the house. The flower beds, scattered whimsically, were crammed with perfect blooms; the blousier kind of dahlias, chrysanthemums, lilies. But how long would this family's way of life survive, now they'd been forced to admit the hoi polloi, like any small-town tearoom? A shadow coasted over. A large bird, a hawk very like the one she'd already seen, was losing height, floating down in easy, swinging increments, sinking below the dark levels of a cedar. Was it the same one? What an unnerving idea, that it might have followed her. Arms suddenly goose-fleshed, she turned and walked back to the house. The sign by the doors had vanished, but those doors were now, thank heavens, open.

She'd already formed an idea of the interior; an entrance hall with the kind of glorious balustraded staircase made for the descents of beautifully dressed ladies, and, of course, lined with priceless portraits. There'd be a statue or two, huge Chinese vases, and a high-ceilinged reception room, emptied of anything thievable, set out for the teas. But, of course, this place would have to be *eccentric*. The staircase, towards the rear of a considerable but largely vacant space, curved around the walls of an internal tower, with the flights between the landings hanging like the precarious paths of a sheer white precipice. The dome of frosted glass at the very top was effectively concealed, it seemed, by the house's gracious façade. Another hand-written sign was propped at the foot of the stairs; an upwards arrow and the words; *Please admire The View.*

So would the teas be served here at the front, or at the back somewhere? The first door on the right had glass panels, and—oh yes—there was a room behind that seemed to be expecting guests. Tables for four draped in white linen, China cups and saucers set out in readiness. She tried the door handle, but it rattled resistantly. What should she do, then? Should she go in search of the begrudging ladies of the house? It was surely three by now. She checked. Five minutes to go. *The View* it was then. It would be rather embarrassing, anyway, to be found waiting outside the door.

The stone steps deadened her footfall as well as any fine carpet would, and it was, perhaps, the presence of the domed void above her head, the feeling of spiralling upwards as she followed the curve of the banister, that left her a little dizzy. A lengthy corridor led from the first landing and leaning against the open door of the facing room, yet another arrowed sign. She imagined the genteel lady of the house seated at her writing desk with a pile of card, gently sobbing as she painting arrow after arrow with her best watercolour brush.

Just as she'd conjectured; this house must be seeing out its last days. The furniture had fled the long, high-ceilinged room—auctioned off, probably—apart from two freestanding marble pillars balanced on avian claws Thick white candles, showing signs of recent burn, had been planted among the carved fruits spilling from their tops. Well, why not? Cheaper than electricity, and you could tell yourself candlelight was romantic. *Enfilade* was the word she remembered, as she crossed the mosaic parquet floor; that was the term for this interior arrangement. Through the wide golden frame of the central door she could see all the other rooms, and the diminishing perspective gave, as it was intended to, a sense of endlessness.

The elaborate ceiling must once have been the height of

fashion; concentric circles on white plaster, borders crammed with creatures from the zodiac and various hybrids of more obscure mythologies, all finely modelled and finished in gleaming gilt. Unsullied by fixtures, or the damage caused by their removal; nothing to indicate where they'd suspended the obligatory chandeliers. Inset into the mantelpiece of the great, garlanded fireplace was a blank heraldic shield; one that had proved to be in the end, it seemed, an appropriate coat of arms. It was rather poignant, but not altogether unsatisfying, that the scions of this house, this once unimaginable wealth, had been reduced to catering to the appetites of the common herd.

The windows measured twelve feet high, she estimated. She imagined a team of servants, unhooking the yards of silk brocade that once hung there, before selling it to be cut up and changed to everyday dimensions. Was this, then *The View?* But the grounds, even from above, did not give up their secrets lightly. She'd anticipated seeing along the driveway, all the way up to the gates, and the arrangement of the grounds on either side making, from on high, more thematic sense, but the windows were more to the side than she'd supposed, and she could only see the turning circle and the initial section of the approach. The trees were in the way, appearing, from there, to be even closer together than at ground level. Nor could she tell which trees belonged to the woods outside or to the land of the house. There must be a subtle slope running down from the estate's borders, so that, being higher, the trees inside concealed their untamed cousins.

She was aware of the passage of time as she crossed the room to the central doorway, and she wondered if, by some spatial artistry, an illusion of unusual distance had been built into the design. But when she reached the other side, looking back, she knew it could only have taken seconds to cross, not the minutes it had felt like.

The rays of a stylised sun spread across the ceiling of the second room; a room that was smaller, but still impressive in scale, and, like the first, lacking any furnishings to detract from its profligate share of space. Irene went to the windows. It didn't matter, though, if she stood at the nearest or the furthest; at any chosen point, she saw exactly the same first section of the driveway, which now, beneath a blue and cloudless sky, had a transparent glitter about it, as though it had turned to glass. Did *The View* earn its name because of this quality; the way what was outside followed you, like the moonlight on water? Was that why it was signposted so specifically, with capitals for emphasis? To let you know it was something special? There was movement down there; someone must have just come from the house.

It was like seeing a living version of one of those nineteenth century journals that reported, with lurid illustrations, the juiciest crimes *du jour*. A woman, dressed in what looked like a Victorian riding habit, running as though hotly pursued, stumbling and clumsy and panicked, movements hopelessly hindered by the bulk of her full skirts. But as far as Irene could tell, there was no swarthy assailant or top-hatted assassin giving chase. She moved to the far end of the room, but it was no use; there was no chance of seeing the woman now she must be further along the driveway. She was already hidden by the trees. What on earth had she been doing? Was she playing a game? If only Irene had managed a clearer look at her face. She'd probably see more of the driveway from the next room. She'd probably see the woman laughing with the strange little girl, feigning delight and disbelief at being caught.

It was a dramatically smaller space, the next room; roughly

half the size of the one preceding. Empty again, and with a ceiling not worked in gold relief, but with deeply cut wooden leaves. Irene paused at each of the three windows. The rest of the driveway, and the gates, still weren't visible, and how could they be when the trees appeared to have moved much closer to the house, so that, after the turning circle, everything sank into crowding woods? The gardens had become impenetrable. Naturally, it was impossible. But didn't they say that the simplest explanation was usually right? And didn't the creators of this house, the devotees of *enfilade*, love optical illusion? That's what *The View* was. An optical illusion. Just this floor, and everything normal everywhere else. An entertainment. She wouldn't be surprised if it had been famous once, if all the minor aristocrats had come from miles around, lining up their carriages in their eagerness to see the wonders worked by the architect, how he'd angled the house, or the windows, to transform what lay outside. But her mind struggled. It was such an unsettling kind of optical illusion. One that filled you not with wonder, but a feeling of being trapped. And why did all the trees grow like that? Was that part of the spectacle? From all their crowns, dual branches twisted, imitating horns.

She passed through the last doorway. The final room had seemed to glow from afar, but close up it was poky, brown and musty-aired, the low ceiling unembellished, the furniture a pair of thin iron beds and their filthy blankets pushed against two walls. Why leave this room open at all? Who'd want to see this? As miserable as the dens tramps made for themselves in the bombsites of the East End. Why on earth didn't they keep this one locked? Why expose themselves in this way? Next to one bed, what looked like a child's drawings, black pencil or charcoal, had been tacked to the wall.

There were a dozen or so. Whoever's work they were—a

girl's she imagined, from the subject matter—must have been copying from a history book. The female figures, mouths and eyes at crazy angles, hands with identical length fingers, necks non-existent, were dressed in costume that ranged from the Victorian to the medieval; bustles, regency classical, ballooning skirts you could balance a tray on, hanging sleeves, wimples. The one at the very top wore an outfit which a Victorian lady might chose for riding; a tight bodice, a skirt gathered to the side, a version of high laced boots. In thick capitals was written, as it was on all the others, beneath the round or square or pointed toes, the word 'MAMA'.

Was this the work of the girl she'd seen in the gardens? Did she sleep in here? Or was it a room she was sent to as punishment? And was the woman in Victorian fancy dress her mother? Irene's thoughts grew clearer. She understood all she needed to. It didn't matter to her, none of it. It was a place she was passing through; the dying days of a country dynasty turned strange by the loss of the status that had once protected them from themselves. Children out of control. Parents going out of their heads and running around in peculiar clothes. All that was left to them was this folly of a house, the pittance they made from afternoon teas, and *The View*.

She felt more herself, fully prepared for the optical absurdity she was bound to find as she went to the only window. The trees were a few feet from the house. The turning circle had gone. She looked up. The sky had sunk, and one cumulus cloud hung, as white and flat and unshadowed as an amateurishly painted prop.

"Stop it, please!" she said.

It was only the *View*. The architect's trick. Yes: a trick

"Stop it!" She slapped her face.

But there were fibres trailing from the cloud, the broken

threads of a torn canvas. And from the sky fell flakes of blue, dropping onto the trees like tainted snow .

She took the stairs in lurches, hand sliding down the banister but gripping it tightly to keep contact with something hard and real. She'd flung herself from the end room, through a blur of gold and darkness, finding the landing deserted, knocking over the sign with the pointing arrow in her rush, and already she was dreaming ahead to the moment that, when it was all over, she'd remember and wonder at, and dismiss, what had happened to her. She was in reaching distance of the world she'd left. Outside, the unreality of *The View* would be proved. It would all snap back into place. She'd soon be on the path through the woods, and onto the meandering river route. Tea in the village, train, home. Danny Seal on Monday.

She slipped on the very last step, twisting her ankle. She hopped a short way, assessing the damage. It wasn't too bad. She could move forwards. It was only when she tried turning it to the left that she felt a blunt ache. The door to the tea room was open, the tables pushed together to form one long, white-draped line. Laid out inside was a banquet dreamt up by a child's mind; porcelain tiers of little sponge cakes, iced in pink and yellow and studded with glacé cherries, silver stands heaving with chocolate cakes and strawberry tarts, custard slices and cream éclairs and buns. The sight of it made her gag. The girl stood at the far end of the table. Her too-large blue eyes shone with infantile triumph.

Irene forgot how to speak. She intended to say, "I'm sorry, I won't be staying for the tea after all," but nothing came, only a kind of moan. The front doors were open, but the space was filled with a static mass of leaves. It was, she knew, the same with all the windows; those she'd run past upstairs, those down here.

The girl was coming closer, unhurriedly walking the length

of the table. Her hands, Irene noticed with a shudder, were coated with downy hairs. She stopped by a plate of pink meringues; smiling, conniving.

"Mama?" she said. "Is it you? Have you come to me again?"

The Tiddy Mun

Kev Rooney

Boston, Lincolnshire.
1641

They rode north, out of Boston, with the death of the day. The sky was ablaze, a sunset unlike any Ambrose Shiveley could recall. Overhead, pastel shades of violet and pink bled and mingled westward into smouldering red, and deep, crisp orange. Yellow-white burned the horizon, painfully bright; he thought of the sky above Landshut. The glorious light lit among reeds and gorse and made stark silhouettes of the winter-bare trees that grew rare and stunted out across the fens. To the east, to his right, the first stars of night glittered above and below, bright flames reflected back to heaven in the glassy waters of mere and marsh.

Grey clouds, thin as wood smoke, scudded across the

luminous brilliance, chasing a flock of lapwings as they swirled home to roost. Bitter winds carried the evensong of redwing and plover and the distant, mournful cry of an owl; carried, too, the bitter tang of damp and rot. His father's engineers called this lowland, lower than the sea was high, like the Dutch lands to the east. The tides seeped in like a canker, forming pools and stale bogs, drowning plant life, decaying it to rich peat below the turgid waters. It was a land at war with itself.

At his back rode Garrett, Migs and Oliver. Ostensibly men of his employ, in truth his brothers; no, closer than brothers. Confederates. Bound by acts of valour and glory.

And guilt.

The creaking of their saddles and the rustling of their cloaks; the musical clink of bridle and buckle; the wet thump of their horse's hooves upon the road; they were each as loud as musket fire, as clashing steel, against the desolation of the fenland around them, yet they gave no echo back to his ears. The marsh swallowed the sounds and coddled them to silence.

The sky was ablaze, but winter in the fens was unwelcoming as the grave.

"God's teats, 'tis cold," muttered Migsett breathing on his hands, as though mere breath had any chance of warming them through his heavy leather gauntlets.

"Watch yer tongue," Oliver snapped, single eye chillier than the marsh water at the road side, " 'for the Lord will not hold him guiltless that taketh his name in vain'."

Ambrose smirked as Migsett murmured reproachfully and sought to beat some life into his fingers instead. Oliver was eldest and godliest of them, and while it seemed a fool's errand to reprimand an Englishman for swearing, there was no arguing with a well quoted verse.

"You're not wrong though, Migs," Ambrose mused back over his shoulder, "a sky like damnation's inferno, yet the air is sharp as hoar frost."

"'Tis said the devil himself resides in a frozen wasteland," offered Garrett, and Oliver baulked and spat beside the road at mention of that accursed creature, "or at least, so Dante would have it."

"Trust only a catholic to be so contrary," Oliver growled and the others laughed, though when Ambrose glanced backward to him, he realised Oliver wasn't even smiling at all. He simply rolled with the saddle, baleful eye peering from behind his lank hair at the road ahead. Mockery of the papists was a serious business to him.

"Even the trenches at Breda were warmer than this," Migsett complained again, vigorously rubbing his hands together.

"'Twas hot enough in the press of the breach," Ambrose said quietly, "let that memory warm you a while."

They rode on in silence for a spell then, each man looking back, across time and across the sea, to a Dutch city held by Spanish papists. To a siege, and the roar of flintlock and cannon and undermined walls collapsing, and a chaotic charge into the breach. To the crush of the living at their side, and the faces of the dead by their hands. To a blur of exhilarating horror, where every second survived was an exultant victory. To the thrill of it, the unreality of it. The nightmare of it. To everything before and since.

The sunset was fading from the sky and more stars had appeared, cold and sharp as ice shards in the dark. The land spread away in every direction, flat to the horizon where it blurred with the night sky. The faintest shimmer of mist was rising like spider silk in the east. The sole landmark still visible was the tower of St Botolph's to the south, impossibly tall, crowned with a ring of pinnacles, and burning like a sconce where it caught the day's last light.

"There's a new life below the mire," Ambrose said into the dark, "land more fertile than any in this kingdom. Once the drains are complete 'tis ours for the taking."

"Your father's for the taking," Migs said with a smirk.

Ambrose rankled a touch then. His lip still smarted where his father had struck him that evening, in their rooms in Boston. Him, a cavalry officer with near a decade's service in the continental wars, and he'd stood and taken the blow, timid as a child. Honour thy mother and thy father, he'd been taught. Ambrose's father, whose warlike portrait hung in their hall in Sussex, resplendent in half plate, yet who Ambrose had only ever seen raise arms against his own wife. Honour thy mother…

For daring to suggest they leave this pursuit until morning, he'd taken a fist to the mouth. Taken it wordlessly. For honour… and with an eye to the future.

"The King grants the land to my father, he gifts it to me and I let it to you," said Ambrose with only a trace of irritation, "and we all sit back and grow fat on the bounty. No more trenches. No more breaches."

"Once the drains are complete," Migs said.

"Aye."

The thud of their horse's hooves and the splash of a strand of Oliver's spit on the roadside was the only sound for a moment. The companions thought on. They each knew why they were there.

"'Tis said there is no reward without work," Migs sighed.

"'Whatsoever ye do, do it heartily,'" quoted Garrett with only the slightest trace of irony.

"'For God shall bring every work into judgment, with every secret thing, whether it be good, or whether it be evil.'"

86

replied Oliver and Ambrose turned in his saddle to look hard upon the old sergeant.

Ambrose was not so pious as Oliver. Few men were, outside of a pulpit. Ambrose had seen the war on the continent as an adventure, where Oliver had seen a crusade. He was the eldest of the four, and the longest serving, but not a gentleman. Still, he had ridden in the cavalry of His Majesty Gustavus Adolphus and had been there at Lutzen in '32 when the Swedish king was slain. He'd received a pike to the flank at Landshut, and a broken leg at Nordlingen. He had suffered much and seen more.

Right now, all he appeared to see was the road.

"And which is it with our work this night?" Ambrose asked.

Oliver's left eye was fixed straight ahead. He'd lost the right one when the Swedes lost a king.

"Well," he mused in a voice like shifting gravel, "the sluice gates o' your father stand blackened by arson. His embankments tumbled. The hard labour of good Christian men, wasted. His Lordship, yer father, wasting good money in pursuit o' the King's commands; commands now opposed."

"And 'the powers that be are ordained of God'," offered Garrett, "so the vandals oppose the Lord's work."

Oliver nodded sagely.

"Aye. An' the drain-tumblin' dwellers o' th' fen are godless folk, 'tis said, little more than idle beasts, leeches on the rump o' civilisation. Savage as the aborigine o' the colonies..."

"So, savage beasts are vandalising my father's drains, opposing the progress ordered by the divine right of the King himself, and all to preserve their godless, wretched way of life out here in the bogs," Ambrose said. "Do you then, Oliver, judge our task to be one of good, or of evil?"

The elder man said nothing for a moment, then simply shrugged.

"I only follow orders, Master Shiveley. Judgement is the Lord's domain."

Garrett chuckled lightly and Ambrose scowled somewhat but supposed he could ask nothing more than that.

"So be it," Ambrose said, facing ahead once more, "we ride these bastards down and the Lord can judge us at his—and our—leisure."

"Would have been preferable to ride them down in the morning," Migsett muttered, pushing one of his gauntleted hands up into the warm pit of his arm.

Ambrose sighed, breath fogging the air about his head, and repeated his father's words.

"The sluice gate smoulders still," he said, "and the arsonists fled north. By morning they'll have vanished. But they won't outrun our horses this night..."

Each man gazed into the darkness there about. The sunset was an ember in the west and the black night yawned naked and shameless above them. To the east, a grotesquely swollen moon, ghastly in its redness, was rising through the mist. All was silent. The fenland seemed to be holding its breath.

Nothing moved. Nothing sang. Of men or bastards, arsonists or no, there was no sign.

They rode on.

They saw the lantern sometime later, as the moon rose higher and the mist grew thicker. Ahead and to their right, it danced slowly north across the flat landscape, here disappearing behind a reed bank, there passing behind a gnarled blackthorn. The fen was lit a weak and waxy amber by the bulbous moon and the light moved alone, suspended in shadow. Presently it vanished.

The horsemen sat silent and waited, for some footfall, or watery splash, or whispered word to betray their quarry, out across the mire, but the night remained unnaturally still. Ambrose bade them ride on.

There was little conversation among the men now as they strained eyes and ears into the distance, ever watchful for some hint of their quarry. The road snaked ahead, beyond the limits of sight. Distance and time became difficult to judge. They rode through a thick bank of freezing fog that swept in from nowhere and enveloped them in soft, almost tangible gloom. It soaked deep into their garments, nipped at nose and ear, and tasted bitter in the throat. Migsett muttered sour complaints to himself as he huddled into his cloak.

Then they were through and the light hung above the road ahead. Lights, indeed. Ambrose asked for Oliver's spyglass and tried to look closer. The thick lenses blurred the light and the slightest twitch of his hands danced the image about, but he gained an impression of windows, lit from within.

"Appears to be a village…" he said eventually.

"That may be where our vandals were headed," Garrett said.

"There may be an inn," Migs said quietly, "there may be a fire."

"Someone'll know somethin'" Oliver growled, "jus' gotta ask the right questions…"

It was further out than he thought. Distance became abstract in the darkness and the village seemed to draw no closer. Ambrose was just able to discern the silhouettes of clustered buildings ahead when the lantern returned, ahead of them and to the right, moving like a fallen, drifting star.

Ambrose had Oliver's spyglass, still. He peered through the lens, failing to find his mark at first and having to check twice where the light had moved to. Then he found it.

For a moment he could make no sense of what he saw. It was a blur of light and shade and motion, motion that seemed uncanny despite his lack of recognition. Then his awareness adjusted and the image seemed to resolve before his eyes.

A yawning pit opened in Ambrose's guts. Dark vertigo crowded at his mind. His chest froze. His spine froze. Winter pierced him through.

Lit starkly from below, and by sinister moonlight above, he was watching… something… some beast, stalking through the bog. Hunched, curved and ragged was its back, long and crooked were its limbs; they lanced into the fen water, rising and jabbing in a skittering dance across the bog. A round head lolled below the bulk of its shoulders and below that was the light, a swaying brilliance that pricked at his eyes. The beast's scuttling brought to mind harvestmen and crabs, and awful things that crawled in the dark.

Then its head snapped round and stared straight at him, and Ambrose dropped the spyglass.

He heard commotion around him, questions, exclamations, the crisp tinkle of a shattering lens. His mount stirred beneath him. The light was gone, and so the creature was gone, and he did not know where. Bile rose in his throat; his spine crawled with an icy flame and every instinct in his body screamed to flee.

His mind flitted back to Breda, to a moment he often recalled. When a mine below the defensive wall had misfired, a concussive blow to the senses that blinded and deafened him and threw him from his horse. Earth and rock, and the bodies of Scottish and Dutch soldiers who had only been a little closer than Ambrose, rained from the sky, pattered and thumped to the ground around him.

He had not then felt this afraid.

He was afraid to stay; the thought of explaining his return to his father made him terrified to leave. Deaf, once again, to the words of his men, Ambrose spurred his horse blindly into the village.

It wasn't much of a village. The track simply widened to a sizeable flat of high ground and the locals had filled the space as best they could. Rough, single storey cottages lined either side of the road, leading to a surprisingly handsome looking inn at village end.

He galloped along the street. The smell of peat smoke was in the air, and pig shit from a sty away to the left. Golden eyes blinked, startled, in the darkness ahead and a cat shaped phantom bolted across the open ground before him, disappearing silently behind a wood shack.

Lights burned in the ground floor windows of the inn, and from the lanterns hanging either side of its door. It stood tall above the surrounding cottages, with peaked roof, curved half beams and herringbone brickwork between. There was a distant, muted sound of conversation from within, but both windows and doors were closed fast against the bitter cold. Ambrose spied a tiny stable yard at the rear but drew his horse to a clattering halt by the front door. He dismounted unsteadily, adjusted his sword belt and transferred his flintlocks to his waistband, all the while searching the misty horizon beyond the circle of lantern light. Nothing moved in the darkness there.

Hooves thundered to a halt and his men reined in beside him. They practically shouted their questions at him. Ambrose ignored them and entered the inn.

Smoky heat engulfed him, shrouded him, invaded him. It coated his face and his eyes and his lungs. He thought of cannon fire and the press of the breach. His left hand clung tight to the pommel of his sabre. What conversation there was had mainly stilled at the sound of hooves. Eyes gazed from shaded nooks at the newcomer. Someone was tuning a fiddle. A peat fire blazed at the back of the room.

He gazed about the low, dark room like a lunatic, like an idiot, until gradually the conversation died altogether. The only sound was the pop and crackle of the fire grate.

"Shut that bloody door," someone called gruffly from his right.

"Something in the fen," Ambrose said quietly, pointing behind him, "there's something out there."

"Well tell it to come in and stop letting all the bloody heat out!" the gruff voice quipped and there was general laughter.

Ambrose was wearing a heavy, caped coat against the night and so they hadn't seen his flintlocks. He showed them now.

Benches scraped and figures stumbled over one another in their haste to move away from him, as he waved the pistol about the place in a trembling hand that could barely hold the weight. He was vaguely aware of his men at his back. He thought he heard the whisper of steel on leather as a blade was unsheathed. Everything but one had become a little unclear.

"There's something out there!" he roared again, and his voice sounded like madness in his own ears. "What is out there?!"

"M' lords," a large man said, sidling across the room, hands empty and raised, apron flapping round his knees. Ambrose reckoned him the keeper. "Good sirs, please. Please. There's no call for this, sir. Please lower yer arms."

Ambrose trained the flintlock on the man, as though to focus him to the question. The inn-keep froze.

"There is something in the fen," Ambrose said, almost levelly. "Some demon. Some… thing. What. Is. It?"

The inn keeper's mouth moved in silence, as though trying on answers as a child tries on adult clothes, only to find that none of them fit. Ambrose took a step towards him.

92

"'Tis the Tiddy Mun," whispered a voice from beside the fire. Ambrose turned there and blinked his eyes against the blaze in the hearth, bright as sunset. He made out a small figure, bundled in clothes and shawls, perched on a milking stool. A face like sun-withered fruit held his gaze from within deep black sockets.

"Tha's enough, mother!" the inn keeper snapped at her over his shoulder, but she only laughed like a dusting of snow across cobbles.

"I'll nae be silenced in m' own inn, y' lummock. T'out of way, so I may speak t' this... *gentleman*."

Ambrose heard the venom in that last word, yet he lowered the flintlock and stepped closer to her, bending below the great central beam of the taproom as he did. The temperature rose, and he felt flushed, like the devil ascending circles of hell. Sweat gathered beneath his hat, in the pits of his arms and the small of his back. He loomed over the tiny woman, yet she gazed up at him with gleeful malice.

"You've seen th' Tiddy Mun," she whispered.

At his back, the inn keeper tried to interrupt again but Ambrose waved him quiet with the flintlock, without turning.

"What is it?" he asked the woman.

"A wraith," she said, voice in danger of being lost in the crackle of the fire, "an angel tha' watches o'er the wild folk, an' guides they t' good huntin' an' fishin'."

"'Tis a creature of the devil," Ambrose spat. "The good Lord would never create such madness as I saw."

"Peh," she spat in return, "'tis a child o' neither."

"What then?"

She gestured to the door, and the night and the fens beyond.

"'Tis born o' th' land, an' the sea. Here they're one, an' neither. The water creeps e'er in, 'pon the world o' men.

'Twere forest here, once, all th' way t' th' east an' th' lands yonder."

"*Pappekak*," growled Oliver, behind him, "only thing t' th' east is cold sea 'fore the Dutch coast."

"Forest says I," she hissed at him, "'til th' seas rose up an' drowned land an' stone an' grove, an' hid 'em from t' light. An' rose up still, an' made all 'ereabouts mire. An' all th' ancient things that dwelled in the deep can walk th' land now, cause t'ain't one nor t'other. 'Tis twixt."

Ambrose gazed down at the small woman and watched as the dancing flames made shadows writhe in the deep trenches of her face. Ten minutes prior he would have called her mad. Ten minutes prior, he hadn't seen what he'd seen.

"Y' saw its light?" she whispered playfully.

Ambrose nodded stiffly.

"Tha's 'ow it leads yer," she smiled, "leads those who live wild round th' hidden paths o' th' fen…"

The smile grew wide, like a fissure in a rotten gourd.

"An' it leads theivin', greedy, southern shits like you to drown in th' cold an' th' mud, down where it meks its 'ome…"

She laughed then, a sound like dried rushes blown through abandoned places, and Ambrose angrily raised the flintlock. She only laughed the harder, wheezing with the joy of it.

"We're looking for the men who attacked the Boston drains this afternoon," said Garrett behind him, and his clear, steady voice 'midst the heat and the smoke and the lunacy was like a lighthouse to a mind cast adrift. Ambrose slowly lowered the pistol with an unsteady hand and turned away, feeling the small, black eyes of the old woman on his neck as he did so.

"They've broken the law, and we're to see to it they face justice," Garrett went on. "The king has ordered the fenland drained for agriculture. The *king*. This thing *will* happen. It cannot be stopped. Name the arsonists and the vandals and you'll be rewarded."

"Shelter 'em…" Oliver growled, "Well. It ain't so long since the bodies o' vandals were used as ballast in the very drains they'd tumbled. You wan' t' share their fate?"

Ambrose felt his mind settle, somewhat. He looked about him, properly, for the first time. The patrons numbered just over a dozen, men and women of every age. They were well cowed, slunk back in the shadows and against the walls, holding still for fear of drawing attention. Oliver, Migs and Garrett stood in the centre of the room, under a low ceiling of beams and rolling plaster, weapons naked in their hands. For a moment, no one spoke.

"T' hell wit' king," the old woman whispered by the fire, "foolish, craven creature. T'ain't his land, t'ain't -"

"To hell?" said Ambrose, turning back. "Treason."

And he discharged the flintlock into her face.

The roar was like cannon-fire in the closeness of the room and for a moment Ambrose was deafened by a pressure in his ears, as the old woman tumbled from her stool sideways into the fire, crimson coif trailing loose from her ravaged skull. Then his hearing returned and resolved into a dozen screeches, from all around. The inn patrons were panicked and charging the door, now blocked by Migs and Garrett, while Oliver laid about himself with his sabre. Blood sprayed where the blade met flesh, and people fell, twitching and screaming upon the flags.

The inn keeper was shrieking too, staring at his dead mother where she blazed in the grate. A big man, Ambrose reflected, but no stomach for war. He felled the keeper with the butt of his discharged flintlock and pulled the second from his waistband, aiming for the inn keeper's left eye. A pistol roared elsewhere in the taproom, and another, and was answered by ragged screams. For a moment Ambrose thought the stench of the pigsty had found its way into the taproom before he realised he was smelling something else entirely.

Blood bubbled from the innkeeper's split lips and he shielded his face with his hands as Ambrose loomed above him.

"Th' Slodgers!" he slurred with his swollen mouth, "Th' Slodgers attacked yer drains! Not th' bloody Tiddy Mun! They live on th' fens, travel on stilts cause there ain't no paths! Sling lanterns round their necks in the dark! Th' bloody Slodgers!"

Ambrose frowned, confused for a moment. Realisation dawned, and with it anger. At himself and at these people; at these feral, stupid, foul smelling, godless people.

"You know the fens?" he asked the inn keeper, balled up at his feet. The big man shook his head; his whole body shook generally.

"Who knows the fens?"

"Elias! Elias Punt!"

"He here?"

Again the head shook.

"Where?"

"Down th' road! Out o' th' village! Twenty yards!"

Ambrose shot the inn keeper dead and started for the door. The floor was more blood than stone, and his boots slipped twice as he stepped across and around the patron's bodies. Thick black smoke was starting to roll across the ceiling. The inn keeper's mother, her milking stool and a nearby table were blazing merrily and the smell reminded Ambrose that he hadn't eaten that evening.

He retrieved shot and powder from the bandolier on his horse then ordered Oliver to move the mounts away from the inn. Bright, flickering light was streaming through the windows.

Glass panes were popping and tinkling to the ground. Soon the lead cames would bubble and flow.

His sergeant gathered the reins in arms that were slick to the shoulder. His single eye glittered hard in the firelight.

Ambrose marched up the road, reloading as he went. He blinked rapidly to try and regain his night vision, though the light from the burning inn was growing steadily brighter. Ahead, a short way up the road where it began to narrow again, he saw a shack beside the water, almost hidden by bushes. A small jetty projected out from the back of the building on its far side. Ambrose saw a man there, a panicked man, moving rapidly.

"Elias Punt!" he roared. "Cease and be still, by order of the King! Or I'll shoot you dead!"

He watched the man hesitate, saw him weigh his chances. Saw the man stand straight, clasp his hands and drop to his knees on the jetty. The swollen planks creaked loudly beneath Ambrose's boots.

"Lord of light, dear sweet Lord, deliver me, please deliver your child," the man sobbed. He looked to be older than Methuselah, with tangled white whiskers and crinkled brown skin. He wore patchwork clothes of animal hide, topped by an ancient felt bonnet with a forlorn, threadbare feather hanging limp from the brim. His feet were bare.

"You know the Slodgers?" Ambrose asked him from behind the muzzle of a flintlock.

"Aye, m'lord," Punt mumbled wetly.

"Take us to them now, and deliver us back safe, and no harm shall befall you. Understood?"

Punt nodded weakly.

"Aye m'lord."

At the end of the jetty was tied a long flat-bottomed vessel of what appeared, by moonlight, to be good repair. Ambrose waved his men across and watched each of them onto the boat, as Punt stood by with the mooring rope ready to loose and a long, thick pole at his side. Oliver, Migs and Garrett were blood caked, drenched in the stuff. They moved in silence and did not meet his eye.

Ambrose climbed last onto the boat and crowded in beside Migs. He signalled for Punt to cast off. The old man stood at the stern and propelled them out across the water with long thrusts of his pole. Light from the burning inn danced gaily across them and glittered in the mirror surface of the mire, breaking into a shimmering mosaic of oranges and yellows as the boat passed through.

Punt steered them deftly through the fen, the flat bottom of his craft drifting across reed beds as though they weren't there. A mist bank drifted ghostly ahead of them. They slipped within. Phantasmal, pale tendrils masked the stars in the sky and clung chill to their skin and clothes.

"How far to the Slodgers, Punt?" Ambrose asked over his shoulder.

"Just over yonder, m'lord," the old man said. The mists made his voice sound oddly flat and detached.

"Slodgers," muttered Migs, fidgeting with his gloves. The tan leather was soaked black. "Odd word that. Slodgers."

"Jus' th' name for the fen folk m'lord. Jus' a name."

Migs didn't seem to be listening. He dragged one gauntlet off his hand, then the other. The skin within was wet and pink.

"Soaked right through," he said to himself, "ruined 'em."

He stuffed the gauntlets in his waistband and began to breath on his fingers, as though kindling a fire.

"What did she say?" Oliver said suddenly, and Ambrose asked what he meant.

"The ol' woman. Jus' afore you shot her."

Something about hearing it phrased like that made Ambrose's guts crawl with ice but he tamped it down. They weren't done tonight.

"Treason," he choked, then said it again, clearer. "She wished the king dead."

T' hell with th' king…

They were looking at him, all, in silence. Not a one spoke. He could see it in their eyes, knew what they were thinking. He opened his mouth to tell them they were wrong, but they were not, and so he said nothing.

Ambrose knew why he'd killed her, and it had nothing to do with the king. Even among his father's associates there was little love for Charles, whose arrogance and follies had cast a pall across the kingdom as heavy as the mist that swirled about them now. Ambrose wasn't about to kill for that pampered knave's honour. The king was a fool. To hell with the king.

He'd killed her because the fear was on him, and there was only one way to kill the fear. He'd killed -

"I killed a woman," Garrett said across his thoughts, so soft and quiet that Ambrose wasn't sure he'd heard it at all. Garrett was staring down at the stains on his own boots.

"Killed her. Killed a few, but this woman…" he looked back at Ambrose with a regretful smile, "young and handsome, she was. Trying to get past, out the door. I slashed at her, to make her back up… I…"

He stared down at the stains on his boots.

The boat slipped on, rustling between thickets of water weed, slipping across the flat, black surface. The pole sucked and sighed as it rose and sank and pushed them forward. Beyond the boat, Ambrose could see a few yards and no more. The drifting mists crowded them, swaddled them, hid the stars above and made a sickly smear of the moon. They were alone in the world. Alone with their fears.

"Listen to me now," Ambrose growled, and they turned to him. He was a soldier, an officer, and he knew how to kill fear, as he'd known it tonight. He knew its mortal foes—hatred, rage, and greed. Once again, he found himself speaking his father's words.

"This is not the first blood you've spilled. Not by far. The Lord made soldiers of us and a battlefield of the world, to root out weak from strong. And we are the strong. They were the weak," and he gestured back, past Punt, to where he imagined the blazing inn to be.

"Theirs was not the first blood we've spilled, nor will it be the last. But the next—the next battle may be. We settle these Slodgers, these vandals, and make a show of them so fierce that none will rise against the drains again. Then we take our land and rest our bones and let others till the soil as we grow fat and old. One more fight…"

Doubt still, in the eyes of Garrett and Migs. Only so much a man could endure, he knew, but he needed them this night.

"It isn't men we hunt now!" he said, as earnest as could be, "These wild folk are little more than savages… nothing more than beasts! What does the Lord tell us of beasts, sergeant?"

Oliver's eye was a shard of glass in the shadows of his face.

"'And God said, Let us make man in our image, after our likeness: and let them have dominion over the fish of the sea, and over the fowl of the air, and over the cattle, and over all the earth, and over every creeping thing that creepeth upon the earth.'"

"Dominion over every creeping thing upon the earth," Ambrose repeated. "No better description for these vermin. They are ours to punish by law, by the king's word and by God's own decree. Find your steel boys. One more time."

He saw them nod. Experienced; professional; killers. With

no room for guilt or regret.

Or fear.

"How far?" he asked Punt.

"Over yonder, m'lord."

"You said that last time!" Ambrose snapped. "How far are these bloody Slodgers?!"

"Not goin' t' the Slodgers," Punt said, "takin' ye to him…"

"You… dirty… treacherous…!" Ambrose snarled as he dragged his flintlock loose of his waistband.

Then the whole boat listed astern, bow raising a foot out of the water, as Elias Punt launched himself into the air. Icy marsh water poured into the flat bottom of the vessel and swirled about Ambrose's arse and legs as he fell backwards. Garrett tumbled into his lap.

In his confusion he thought he saw the tiny old man land nimbly on a raised earth bank three yards away. Thought he saw Punt's naked feet extended and distorted and grossly long, the skin stretched to translucency, shiny and smooth. Thought he saw the old man glance back at him, face puffy and shining below his bonnet, skin mottled, eyes two hard, black discs bulging from the skin. Then the mists moved and Ambrose saw him no more.

The bow of the boat slapped down, but still the vessel listed and water was pouring in from portside.

"Up!" Ambrose shouted, slapping at the water in a pitiful effort to steer or propel the boat, "Get to high ground! Over there!"

They scrambled, shoved and pushed to their feet, the long, flat boat twisting violently this way and that beneath their boots. Garrett leapt first from the bow towards a jut of black and green that rose from the murk to their right. He landed with one leg in the water to the knee and swore most obscenely as he scrambled up onto the track. Oliver followed, then Ambrose. Migs was last and the boat, now unburdened of any counter-weight, listed under his feet and pitched him into the frigid water. He screamed and choked and splashed to the bank, and Oliver and Garrett dragged him out. Migs lay gasping on the thin spur of high ground, coughing water, wracked with shivers, teeth clattering like hooves in a cavalry charge.

Smoothly, the long boat slipped beneath the waters, and away.

Ambrose cast about him and saw nothing but mist and water and rough, stunted brush. The world was colourless, a patchwork of greys. Overhead, heaven was gone. No stars, no moon, no sky. Rage took him, boiled through his chest and limbs and shook him like a seizure. He wrenched his sabre from its sheath and swung it viscously through the air.

"Curse him! Curse him!" he screamed. "I'll have his head! I'll take his cods for a coin purse! Bastard! Bastard!!"

"Ambrose!" Oliver shouted, and the sergeant's bellow punched through Ambrose's fury and gave him pause. He moved on shaking legs back to his men.

Garrett and Oliver crouched beside Migs, who was sopping wet from crown to toe. He lay on his side, legs and arms drawn in like a sleeping babe, and trembled without control.

"God...!" he gasped, over and again.

"The chill is in him," rasped Oliver, "if we don't get 'im movin' he'll die."

"Lift him then," Ambrose said, and looked around again. He was fairly certain he knew from which direction they'd come, though looking backwards very little seemed familiar. "We can warm him in one of the village cottages. Here, strip his shirt."

Ambrose removed his overcoat and draped it across Migs' naked shoulders. Immediately the damp chill of the air began to press through Ambrose's doublet and shirt, tracing shivers across his flesh.

"We should move," he said and led them back along the thin track.

The high ground was no more than two feet in width, and often less. The trail loomed out of the mist ahead, as though created by their approach, twisting this way and that, and sometimes seeming to loop back on itself. Still, dark pools lay to either side, surfaces blank like mirrors that no longer cast reflections. Thick brambles and thorn bushes crowded in from the shallow banks, to tear at breeches and the skin beneath. Often the trail would branch, sometimes in multiple directions and Ambrose would have to lead them by instinct alone. It swiftly became apparent that they were lost. They walked on. There was little choice.

Garrett and Oliver were supporting Migs as Ambrose picked the way forward. He glanced up to get a bearing on the route ahead and what he took for solid ground beneath his boot turned out to be no more than a thick tangle of scrub. His boot went through and down into water, and Ambrose nearly pitched from the trail. With a curse he pulled backwards as freezing, heavy mud engulfed his foot below the waterline and held his boot fast. His leg slithered clear of the leather and the whole thing sank away with barely a ripple.

From that point on he walked with eyes downcast and tested the ground ahead with his blade. Which is why he was last to see the light.

"A lantern!" cried Garrett, pointing away to their left.

A light shone there in the mist, a yard off the ground perhaps, though it was difficult to judge. The trail branched in that direction and wound off into the mists some way ahead of the light. Ambrose recalled the lantern around the stilt walker's neck and drew his pistol. Migs could barely walk and Ambrose wasn't about to waste time bartering with some dirty Slodger to guide them out of this hell. Oliver saw the flintlock in his hand and frowned towards the light.

"Ho friend!" Oliver called into the gloom, "Who goes there?"

Garrett shot him a puzzled look.

"Do you not hear her?" he said and turned back to the light as Ambrose caught Oliver's eye. All about was silent as death.

"I hear noth—" Ambrose began.

"Oh bless you! Milady, bless you!" Garrett cried, and turned to them, cheeks wet with tears. "She is not dead! She did not die! She forgives me! She will lead us home!"

Garrett lurched along the branching trail, too far back for Ambrose to reach. Oliver made a grab for him but was weighed down by Migs and his hand fell short.

"Bless you!" Garrett cried as he stumbled into the darkness, into the mists.

They called after him, cried after him, screamed his name, but Garrett was deaf to their voices. The mist enclosed him, swirled about him, swallowed him whole.

"Oh yes, yes of course!" they heard from somewhere close by, "Yes, I shall! Oh ble—"

The light snuffed out. Mist drifted, slow and silent. Ambrose could smell salt.

"Garrett!" he called again.

Nothing.

"Come on," Ambrose told Oliver, who grunted as he took Migs' full weight across his shoulders and followed Ambrose along the branch that Garrett had taken.

Ambrose held the flintlock ready and stabbed at the ground ahead of him as he went, picking his way carefully. There was no hurry. Migs was practically dragging his feet, chattering cold and muttering, and Oliver grunted with the effort of supporting him.

The trail ended abruptly and Ambrose halted. Still, dark waters stretched away into the haze in every direction. The water was so smooth it might have been frozen. Ambrose bent forward to look into the depths. He saw a silhouette, a shadow, staring back at him from below. It moved as he did. There was nothing more.

Wordlessly he pushed the flintlock into his waistband, returned along the trail and took Migs' trembling weight upon his shoulder. Oliver nodded silently and the three of them retraced their steps.

His back and calves burned. The cold wet air had soaked through his clothing from without and his sweat, born of the effort of carrying Migs along trails almost too narrow for one man to pass, soaked him from within. He was desperately thirsty and had started to cough. He felt the chill air was coating his very lungs. Migs was limp, chin resting on his chest, mumbling fevered nonsense. Oliver muttered something that sounded like the litany. The mist and the stillness and the silence were constant. Ambrose felt that the world had gone away from them, somehow. Like they had stepped out of creation.

The trail widened to a small hillock, a little more than a yard across and three yards long. The mound squelched underfoot, though its flank bristled with tall, heavy grasses that rustled as they moved among them.

"We should rest 'ere," Oliver grunted and went to lay Migs down among the drier grass stalks.

"He hasn't long," Ambrose said, then coughed roughly for a moment. His throat felt sore and swollen. "We must keep moving."

"Can't carry you both, Master Shiveley," Oliver said, fixing him with that glass-hard eye, "Rest a moment. Gather yer strength."

Ambrose knew it to be sound advice. They laid Migs down upon his side. Relief washed through Ambrose's muscles to be free of the dead weight and he stretched up tall, then squatted down, close to the ground. He coughed again and worked at peeling his shirt from his back where it clung with a maddening chill. Oliver sat by Migs' head and gazed stolidly out into the mist.

"We should wait 'ere, fer daylight," he said.

"Migs will be dead, long before dawn," Ambrose said.

He looked down at his friend, shuddering uncontrollably in the grass, and felt nothing but fatigue. Nearly a decade he'd served on the continent with Oliver, Migs and Garrett. They'd saved his life, and he theirs, over and again. They'd marched and rode, sang and drank and killed together. Coming home was to be a new start.

But now Garrett was gone. He wasn't the first of course. There had been others down the years; companions, brothers, confederates, long since dead. War was indiscriminate. Was survival merely chance, or did his father have it right? The world, a battlefield to sort the weak from the strong…

Migs looked rather weak right then. What if they just left him there, to the mercy of the Lord? They would move faster. Ambrose could have his coat back…

"Some o' this fer kindlin'," Oliver was droning, "Flint and powder to get it started. Should keep him warm, till sun-up. Marchin' him in this state'll kill him quicker…"

"Fine," Ambrose snapped, wiping a distracted hand across his forehead. It came away dripping.

Oliver nodded and began to tear up small handfuls of

grass stalks, which he piled in the middle of the hillock. As he placed another on the mound, Ambrose noticed something on the underside of Oliver's hand, black against the white.

"You've a stow-away," he pointed out, and Oliver grunted as he turned his hand to look.

A flash of disgust crossed the sergeant's face as saw the thing, a small, curved, slug-like creature clinging to his skin. He pinched it between the thumb and forefinger of his other hand, squeezed and pulled.

"Must've been in th' grass…" he grunted as he pulled harder, face contorting with concern and then pain. It tore away from his hand with a soft pop, taking a tiny gobbet of flesh with it, and spraying a small shower of blood down over Migs. A crimson droplet welled in the hole and dribbled down Oliver's arm as he flung the thing out into the water.

"God Almighty, tha' stings!" he cursed, shaking his hand from the pain and Ambrose caught a glimpse up his sleeve.

"Oliver…" he breathed, pointed again and, standing quickly, began to check his own exposed skin. Oliver looked at Ambrose, then at his arm, then rolled back his cuff.

The short, fat worms were writhing round his forearm, half a dozen or more glistening black bodies, lashing their blunt tails as they burrowed themselves into Oliver's skin.

"God's blood!" he screamed and leapt to his feet. One flailing foot cracked loudly from the crown of Migs' head. Panicked, Oliver clumsily stepped away from his ailing friend. There was no ground behind him.

Ambrose cried out and grabbed at Oliver's hand, pulling up short as he caught sight of the worms again. Oliver, dismayed, fell backwards into the black water. It swallowed him to the chest.

"Jesus—God—shit!" he bellowed, face twisted with the shock of the cold. The waters frothed and churned about him as he fought for purchase among the grasses of the hillock.

He began to haul himself ashore, then stopped, suddenly. The waters churned, still. His single eye bulged wide. Ambrose was rooted where he stood. He watched as Oliver, making a high keening noise unlike anything Ambrose had ever heard from him, clung to the grass with one hand while the other tore at bodkin and shirt, ripping them open and hauling them up, and revealing the writhing mass of glistening black that spilled from the waistband of his breeches and up and across his belly.

Ambrose's guts twisted with horror, yet he did not move. The worms on Oliver's belly were legion. Thick as labourer's fingers, dangling like a pelt, they squirmed grotesquely as they tore at Oliver's skin and feasted on the scarlet below.

"Help—"Oliver breathed, eye wide as the hideous moon and fixed on Ambrose's own. Ambrose stared straight back and still he couldn't move.

Oliver suddenly spasmed backwards, spine arched, tendons protruding from his throat. The waters foamed white as he kicked and screamed.

"God's—balls—damn—swivin'—fuuuggghhhh!"

His rough cries choked to noxious liquid, and dark foam flecked his teeth and lips. The grasses slipped between his grasping fingers as he slid down into the water. His single eye, round as a musket-ball and conveying an eternity of horror and madness, bored into Ambrose as a cascade of writhing black worms vomited from Oliver's mouth, over his tongue and lips and chin, to spatter softly back into the mire, like spring rain. Twitching, twisting, he sank below the surface; his hand, still clutching loosely at the grass stalks, remained above, pallid and still.

Ambrose stood and screamed at the hand for perhaps a

minute or two.

When his throat was a furnace of pain and no more sound would issue forth, save a choked gurgling, he returned somewhat to his senses. The hand still protruded from the water. The silent mists still drifted by. There appeared to be no worms upon his own body. Ambrose looked down at Migs.

He lay where they had placed him, on his side among the grasses. He was perfectly still. Tentatively, using his booted foot, Ambrose rolled Migs on his back.

It was like turning a rock. The skin that had been resting on the earth was alive with motion, a patch of wriggling madness against Migs' pallid flesh. Worms, thick and black, long and fleshy, thin and scarlet, twisted and spiralled in and over one another, falling away into the folds of the coat as it fell open. Shiny, hard-shelled beetles glittered among them; long, segmented things with teeming rows of legs disappeared beneath them, and spiders on limbs like jagged hairs skittered and crawled over everything. They squirmed upon Migs' face, darting in and out of his nostrils and slackly hanging mouth. They were a glistening shell, a writhing second skin clinging to his own.

Ambrose tried to scream again but a rasp was all that would come.

Migs' lips were blue, his eye socket sunken and dark. His chest neither rose nor fell. His skin was so pale as to be almost luminous in the half-light. It looked reddened, puckered and withered where the matt of creatures were crawling upon him, biting, and supping and gnawing. Then Migs' eye opened, the eye Ambrose could see, and it found him.

"Cold…" he breathed, like winter mist over marsh water.

Ambrose ran.

He gave no thought of where he was running to. He wasn't

running *to* anything. He ran away. From the fear that rode upon his back, and in his heart, and streamed silver down his cheeks. He ran as far and as fast as he could, down random, winding trails, through bramble and thorn and thick, black mud, and fog banks that chilled his throat and stung his eyes. He ran from horror and from death.

So much death.

And that's how he found them. On a patch of raised earth, an island in a sea of mist, with three shacks stood tall on stilts, a man's height above the sodden ground. There were unlit lanterns and nets and fishing spears secured to eaves, and a jetty, and a flat-bottomed boat. There were labourer's tools, such as a man might use to collapse a drain bank. The faint smell of peat smoke, as from a fire recently burned down, haunted the air. A rangy shape, curved and tottering, rose on four long, thin legs from the shadows beneath the nearest shack and skittered towards him, an unholy snarl emitting from its maw.

Ambrose—breathless, strengthless, wheezing, panic burning in his veins—grasped at his flintlock and found it tangled in his waistband. The thing was on him then, mouth first, a sudden crushing pressure that closed on his forearm, hot and sharp. The pressure grew, then burst, an erupting powder-keg of agony; he heard bones snap like pike shafts under the charge and felt the snarling creature try to drag him to the ground.

Sobbing, trying to scream, Ambrose speared the thing through with his sword, over and again. Doors were flung wide in the shacks, and wild figures poured forth, bellowing from puckered mouths in matted faces. Pallid harpies loomed in the shadows, clutching fat, writhing larvae to their breasts, and Ambrose dragged his blade clear as the creature slumped from his ruined arm.

He lashed the sabre about him, gasping insensibilities at the teeming shadows to keep them at bay. His broken arm screamed pain with every movement, his throat felt lined with glass shards, his legs were numb and leaden. The wild things danced from his sword tip, like smoke, or fog, or fen mist, crowding to his left, then his right. He saw tools and spears in their hands. The water was at his back. He couldn't retreat.

"Ambrose."

It came from behind him, a voice gentle and sweet. Shocked, he turned.

In the darkness, across the water, a lantern, perhaps a yard or so off the ground.

"Ambrose, all is well. We forgive you."

The voice came from behind the light. A woman's voice. It sounded like he remembered his mother. Like the girl from Landshut. Like the old woman in the inn.

"Come Ambrose. Let us take you home."

Something moved behind his head, then, and the world exploded.

Salt-crusted hemp rubbed sore and bloody across his face. He was being dragged cross-country, through freezing water, across bramble and thorn. They hadn't bound his limbs, simply shattered them with a mattock, and Ambrose now floated, half sensile in a red sea of agony. There was an excruciating pressure in his skull. His dog-mauled arm throbbed with infectious fire. Every jolt wracked his body with unaccountable pain that squeezed bile up from his stomach and rough screams from his soul, and the way was not smooth.

Incurious faces watched him as they went. Ragged men, with long hair and full beards to mask the scars of disease upon their skin; women in thick white powder to mask the same. Young children ran beside him, excited to be out after dark. Sometimes they would poke at him, through the net. Sometimes they would wave. Some of them had flat, black eyes.

The lantern followed on, at a distance.

He wanted to beg them to stop, to let him go, but his lips, his voice, no longer seemed to work. He couldn't think, could barely breath. He was beyond struggling, beyond fighting. He no longer had the strength.

Suddenly, they stopped. He heard waves crashing close-by and the air was thick with salt. For a moment, Ambrose thought he smelled beech and larch and hazel. Then they rolled him from the net. Agony swelled to a sharp, dark crescendo as he tumbled, until a sudden, freezing shock mercilessly brought him back round. He was laid face up in a pool of frigid water. It plugged his ears and burned at his wounds. His broken limbs were twisted and cramped around him. They'd dropped him in a hole.

Overhead, the mists had cleared and the moon shone silver and clean. It glowed upon the high wall of earth that loomed, mountainous above him. A sea bank. Two Slodgers, shovels in hand, stepped into view. The earth was cold and wet where it struck him.

Ambrose sobbed and blubbed and pleaded for them to stop. He didn't know if they heard. He didn't know if he spoke. The children laughed and clapped their hands as they watched. Small creatures in the soil tickled against his skin and made his open wounds itch. The hole was so very, very cold.

He'd heard the devil himself resided in a frozen wasteland. Tears streamed from Ambrose's eyes.

Through a salt-water veil he saw the lantern loom behind

the Slodgers. By moonlight he saw the thing that bore it; huge, monstrous, somewhere between a horse and a spider, it squatted and watched. He saw the pulsing veins that lined the brilliant, glowing sac at the creature's throat, like the arse of a firefly. He saw the rough skin that hung from its ungodly form, folded and rippled like melted wax, and the random spray of hard black eyes that dotted its skeletal, nightmare face. He saw teeth.

"All is well," said the Tiddy Mun.

And Ambrose Shiveley saw no more.

Things that Look like Ribbons, Things that Sound Like Bells

Or: Mayday

Emma Levin

Which of the following statements are true?

❑ The lab has high ceilings and a low hum.

❑ The lab was built on top of a mains water pipe, and the whole thing growls and judders each time something contracts deep underground.

❑ When you arrive, the lab manager's face is bisected by a grin. It reminds you of the first time you went fishing, and you had to gut what you caught. You held a thrashing trout and inserted sharpened steel, and all of a sudden there was an arc of red, and something slimy and surprisingly warm started forcing itself out with the sudden release of pressure. It feels like your arrival has cut the lab manager's face open, and something unexpectedly warm is forcing itself out with the sudden release of pressure. He says you can call him Skipton.

❑　　　Like the Crystal Maze, the lab is divided into four themed zones.
❑　　　Unlike the Crystal Maze, all the rooms are broadly themed around Environmental Monitoring. These are: The Wet Lab, The Dry Lab, The Microscope Room, and The Cold Stores.
❑　　　When you arrive, you spend your first break hiding from Skipton and your new colleagues in the Cold Stores.
The other scientists resent your arrival. And they resent that they resent your arrival, projecting their annoyance both outwards and inwards. It seems easiest to avoid their irritation by pretending to familiarise yourself with the layout of the stores. The Cold Stores are, mechanically, the same as a restaurant's walk-in fridge and freezer. If a restaurant happened to serve only mud, ice, and water (maybe a step too far, even for Shoreditch?). In the fridges bottles of cloudy pondwater, thick with life, sit beside crystal-clear bottles of pro-glacial melt. Neat bags full of dark earth give the sensorially confusing impression of being in a forest, the smell of leaves slowly turning into loam. The freezer is filled with ice cores — glossy cylinders stolen from the hearts of frozen lakes. They fester in their restraints. They are things that should not see the light, their presence here is unnatural, and great efforts are required to stop them from melting

116

away, to trap them in this foreign realm. At irregular intervals, scientists slice segments off with a saw, to prod and poke and analyse, to confirm or deny our fears. Ice core science is not so different from the ancient art of divination. Of haruspicy and extispicy, reading the guts of a sacrifice. Carve off a sliver and inspect. Tell us, oh mighty ice core, will it be 1.5? 2? 2.5?

❏   You are the lab's newest recruit. Skipton tells you that this won't be for long. "You city lot," he says, pulling a greasy hand through his greasy hair, like a rake through topsoil, "you never seem to stay for long. It's like something out here disagrees with you."

❏   There are three types of aquatic organism. There's the plankton, who drift with the current; the nekton, who can move freely, independent of currents; and the benthic organisms, who live their entire lives on, under, and within the sea or river floor. They sulk at the bottom of the body of water, adapted to the darkness and the pressure. They can't leave the benthos—their adaptations mean that any attempt to bring them to the surface will result in them bursting, blinded by the light.

❏   Your move to this lab is not voluntary. You are unsure if this move is planktonic—you merely drifted in this direction—or benthic—you have fallen, and this is where you will stay.

❏   The move was instituted by your boss. Who was also now your ex.

❏   The two of you had worked together at a semi-covert government facility, analysing the City of London's wastewater. The sewers of the metropolis acted like one great communal vein. You could tell from the chemical readouts what day of the week it was — the peaks of coke and ketamine and weed and SSRIs as regular as a pulse, plotting out the hours in a series of sigmoid curves.

❑ The lab was semi-covert not because it was obscured, but because no one wanted to think about it.

❑ Many people compared your ex to a shark. She was motivated. Keen. Muscular. It was strangely compelling to watch her eviscerate something smaller.

❑ The true comparison was that she was unable to stop moving. Her success was a by-product of her neuroses. Pathological.

❑ She did not enjoy this being pointed out.

❑ Aquatic ecosystems are home to a wide variety of biological relationships which are relatively rare in terrestrial ecosystems. These include mutualistic partnerships, where two species appear to benefit from co-existence. The most charismatic example of this, and the one that people always think of after watching Finding Nemo, is the clownfish and the anemone. The poisonous anemone protects the clownfish from predators; the excretions of the clownfish provide nutrients for the anemone.

❑ The second standard example is the shark and the remora. The remora eats parasites off the surface of the shark. In return, it hitches a ride.

❑ Just as people thought of your ex as a shark, people thought of you as a remora. Something lesser, along for the ride, and benefitting from the exceptionalism of the shark.

❑ Aquatic ecosystems are also, compared to terrestrial ecosystems, home to a large number of parasites.

❑ Perhaps the worst example of this is the accurately-named 'Tongue-Eating Louse'. It's an isopod that crawls into a fish's mouth, eats its tongue, and takes its place.

❑   There is a fine line between symbiosis, mutualism, and parasitism. Between co-operation and being co-opted. And just because something is mutually beneficial doesn't mean it's not upsetting.

❑   Your ex called you a parasite. You didn't disagree.
❑   You worry that you crawled into her life and ate her conscience. The conscience-eating louse.
❑   It was probably for the best that she sent you here.

Which of the following statements are false?

❑   This new lab is more rural than you have ever lived before. At night, when the sun sets, the sky is studded with stars. You don't hear sirens, but instead an eerie stillness, which is punctured at dawn by the cacophony of birdsong and the raucous cries of diesel-powered agricultural equipment.
❑   Your new team theoretically studies the effects of industrial and agricultural pollution on freshwater ecology. You are supposed to be looking at the effects of intermittent sewage discharges, and incessant runoffs of pesticides and fertiliser.
❑   In reality, you suspect that the lab might be studying the effects of isolation on imported freshwater scientists.

❑   When you accepted the job, you had to find accommodation.
❑   The village is tiny. So you agreed to take the only available room. A lodging situation, with an ageing, crumbling landlord of an ageing, crumbling farmhouse.
❑   You arrive in the dark. Your landlord wears a head

torch. You are reminded of the anglerfish — that you are supposed to look at the light so you don't see the teeth. You wonder what your landlord's head torch is supposed to distract you from.

❑   The work at the new lab is simple. You receive samples of river water from Skipton. You prepare slides and place them under the microscope. You conduct a microscopic underwater safari, noting the species that are present and absent, their relative frequencies, and their health.

❑   Most river water is a rich soup of life. A horrifying minestrone of fish, crustaceans, and parasitic worms.

❑   Unhealthy river water may be dominated by just a few strains of toxic algae, and the atrophied remains of what came before.

❑   To a terrestrial mammal, many of the body plans of aquatic creatures appear conceptually horrifying.

❑   For example: The starfish must turn itself inside-out to eat. It extrudes its stomach out through the thin, circular opening that we would anthropomorphise as its mouth.

❑   Personally, you consider 'The Siphonophore' to be the worst underwater abomination. A deep-sea lifeform up to 40 metres long, it looks like one creature, but is in fact modular, made up of many clones of grotesque, tiny, specialised bodies. Some kill. Some eat. Some spend their entire lives as tentacles, transporting the tiny corpses from the creatures that act like poisoned barbs, to the creatures who act like mouths. But that's a creature of the deep sea. Like sharks. You're not in the realm of the shark anymore. You're in a rockpool. No, a stream. No, a stagnant puddle. Internalise this. Accept it.

❑   Your new landlord wants to be your friendlord.

❑   Your new friendlord seems to want you to turn yourself inside out. Exposing the soft parts of yourself at dinner. "So," he asks, over a bowl of tepid mashed potatoes involuted like a coral, "which of your parents do you most resent, and why?"

❑   After a few days of quiet work, your new colleagues invite you to the pub. You jump on the invitation as an opportunity to skip dinner with your friendlord.

❑   The pub is the sort you've only seen on television shows from the seventies.

❑   Everything is furnished in a sepia haze, with a couple of load-bearing regulars propping up the bar, and a dog that may or may not have been taxidermied sprawled across the floor like a rug.

❑   Water is full of things that pretend to be other things. It's called adaptive mimicry. There are things that look like rocks, and things that look like kelp. Things that want you to believe that they're helpless, and things that want you to believe that they're poisonous. Things that look like beautiful lanterns that are in fact appendages of things that will eat you whole.

❑   Your colleagues take a seat on a cracked leather chesterfield, the same colour and texture as sunburnt skin. You sit on an armchair opposite.

❑   Your colleagues drink until they can't stand.

❑   They drink until you can't stand them.

❑   You are about to make a quiet exit, when you hear the sound of bells.

❑   Hundreds of tiny bells.

❑	Approaching.

❑	The pub's door swings open, and a stream of figures process in, solemnly.

❑	They wear dark ghillie suits, twisted strips of black cloth flailing as they move, like silken ribbons, or the tentacles of a jellyfish. The suits lengthen their limbs and broaden their backs, giving the impression that they are not quite human-shaped but something bipedal, with greater heft.

❑	They wear circles of bells tethered round their ankles and shins.

❑	Each figure wears a hat with dead things crudely taped to it.

❑	Some have slender feathers angled to look like impossibly extended fox ears. Some wear antlers. One wears a cow's dismembered horns, flaps of skin around the base hinting that the horns did not come easily.

❑	Below the hats they wear Joker-esque corpse paint, which gives the impression that there are dark cavities where their eyes should be, and a yawning hole where you'd expect to find their mouth.

❑	Though you can't see a violinist, you can hear a lilting violin.

❑	You feel a drumbeat reverberate like a pulse in your chest.

❑	You can't look away.

❑	The figures communicate through roars and barks and strangled yelps.

❑	From somewhere within their costumes, they remove short, pale sticks. They crack them together viciously in interlaced, changing formations. The way they move reminds you of a bait ball, of a thousand mackerel turning in compelling unison.

❑ You can't say how long their visit lasted. Only that by the time they left, your colleagues had left without you. One of the regulars gives you a lift back to the farmhouse.

❑ The next day, in the lab, you tell Skipton about the visitors. "Morris Men," he says. "You must have seen Morris before?"

❑ You have not. Not in the flesh. Not like that.

❑ You had once seen a video of what you thought were Morris Men. They'd been dressed in white, wearing what appeared to be floral-themed bondage gear over what appeared to be shrunken cricket kits. They'd held hankies aloft in each hand, snapping them back and forth as if guiding tiny, imaginary aircraft to land. They'd been accompanied by someone mistreating an accordion, grasping each end with white knuckles, and strenuously forcing their arms apart, as if trying to tear the wailing beast in two. The accordionist had worn an expression of grim resignation, as if he was guilty about the accordion's pained howling and viewed the whole bloody enterprise as distasteful.

That was nothing like what you witnessed at the pub.

❑ Skipton gives you the samples for the day, and retreats to his office.

❑ You try to avoid treating your work like it's a mundane routine.

❑ Looking at freshwater can be surprisingly dangerous. The threats aren't huge, like sharks or rays or krakens. They're microscopic, the type that creep silently into open cuts. You need to fear the things that live in rats, and the things that live in snails. And especially the things that live in the things that live in snails.

❑   The samples that Skipton gives you seem perfectly healthy. A good blend of zooplankton and phytoplankton. Normal for the expected pH, salinity, and flow rate.

❑   At lunchtime, you search for the colleagues who had invited you to the pub. You want a repeat invitation. But you can't find your colleagues.

❑   You ask Skipton if they've called in sick. "More like called in resigned," Skipton says. "Congratulations, you're no longer the newest. Our freshest recruits should be here at two."

❑   The lab is located slightly underground. It is unclear if this is a defensive move — that it is concealing itself from the locals, hoping that they wouldn't spot it and would leave it in peace — or if this is a prelude to aggression, if, like a ray, it has buried itself such that at any moment it might spring forth, ambushing and devouring any other buildings that move too close.

❑   The village is fringed by woods on three sides — in aerial photos, it appears that it is at the centre of a great mouth closing, about to swallow it whole.

❑   When the newest recruit arrives, she hides from you in the cold stores. You think she can sense your annoyance that you would have to start making friends from scratch again.

❑   Normally, when you're looking at river water, what you really care about are invasive species. Things that supplant and displace the things that were already there. Either replacing them or devouring them.

124

❑   In the Thames, this rogue's gallery is topped by the zebra mussel and the signal crayfish.

❑   You wonder if the villagers view the scientists as a form of invasive species.

❑   That night, you return to the pub. Alone.

❑   As the fire burns low, you hear the jingle of distant bells.

❑   The procession follows the same pattern as the night before.

❑   This time, you pay attention to the dancers' faces.

❑   You observe unsettling symmetries of skin and bone, motionless despite their wildly flailing arms.

❑   Again, the dancers have painted faces. Crudely daubed shadows implying cavities which do not align with the topology of their anatomy. This, combined with the brutal angularity, gives the impression that they might have been carved from soapstone by someone who wasn't particularly skilled in the art of carving, and who wasn't particularly invested in the quality of the final product.

❑   Again, you are transfixed by the trailing ribbons and chiming bells. You can't look away. You don't want to.

❑   Time crawls past like a snail. Or something that lives in a snail.

❑   You come to at closing time, with images of ribbons flowing across your vision like headlights smeared across long-exposure photographs of motorways. Like kinaesthetic con-trails. Muscular echoes.

❑   You can't drive. You don't have a car, and don't know how.

❑	In London this wasn't a problem.
❑	In your new home, it really is.

❑	Without a kindly regular offering to give you a lift, you must walk back to your lodgings.
❑	Without streetlights, the road is treacherously dark.
❑	At some point, the pavement merges with the hedgerows, and you find yourself inching along the tarmac believing that the next car or lorry to round a bend will leave you as flat as kelp.

❑	Wishing to remain three-dimensional, you squeeze yourself through a gap in the hedgerow to walk along the field. Branches trail through your hair like grasping fingers.
❑	You know the rough direction of the farmhouse. You can cut across the fields and make it home within the hour.
❑	You force your way through the next hedge and find yourself standing in front of the river.

❑	Each day at work, Skipton gives you samples of healthy water.
❑	The river in front of you doesn't match up to the samples you have been looking at.
❑	The river in front of you is diseased. By moonlight, you watch thick chunks of foamy scum eddy across the turbid, opaque waters. It smells of death. Of decaying plant matter and rotting fish. You hear scuffling from nearby. Not wanting to anger a farmer if this is their land, or get in the way of lovers, if it's a couple seeking a bit of privacy, you panic and conceal yourself in a bush.

❑	From inside the bush, you hear bells.
❑	Hundreds of tiny bells.

❏   Approaching.

❏   You watch in confusion, as the Morris Man troupe appears, bells jingling faintly, then louder as they approach the bank.

❏   You watch in confusion as the Morris Men process straight into the scummy water, disappearing into the gloom.

❏   You watch as the ripples of their entry fade and die.

❏   You stumble home, assuming that you've drunk too much or slept too little.

❏   In bed, you cannot fall asleep.

❏   Each time you close your eyes, you keep replaying the image of the procession disappearing below the water's surface.

Which of the following statements are plausible?

❏   The next day, on your way into work, you divert via the river.

❏   It's still diseased. If anything, it looks worse in the daylight, the eddying scum having a kind of metallic petrol sheen as it swirls, like some kind of vast and lethal lava lamp.

❏   You decide to collect a small sample of water. You empty your water bottle of coffee and immerse it in the fetid stream.

❏   At work, there are new colleagues again.

❏   You eavesdrop on Skipton's induction for the newest recruit.

❏   He definitely says that the samples are from the local river. That's why you're based here, as a monitoring station.

❑   Surreptitiously, when all of your colleagues are at lunch, you prepare slides from your own river sample.

❑   Under the microscope, you can see dead copepods, listless rotifers, and strange, ribbon-like creatures you've never seen before.

❑   A quick search through the textbooks suggests they are ribbon-like creatures that *no one* has seen before.

❑   That afternoon, you invite one of your new colleagues, one who can drive, to the pub.

❑   You say that you'll meet them there.

❑   You intend to return to the river, to the spot where you saw the Morris Men submerge.

❑   You retrace your steps, concealing yourself in the same bush.

❑   You wait as late afternoon turns into dusk, and dusk melts into darkness.

❑   You wait until the moon reflects in the scummy water.

❑   It is around ten when the first Morris Man breaks the surface.

❑   The rest process out afterwards. As they travel up the bank, the jingling of the bells recedes.

❑   You watch as the last Morris Man emerges from the river, followed by a figure you haven't seen before. It looks like a horse's skull, with a mane made from plaited wheat and ribbons, and beneath it a diaphanous sheet.

❑   You wait until you can no longer hear the bells, to emerge from the bush.

❑   Your foot hits the ground with a crunch.

❑   You have stepped on a small pile of bones. Possibly deer? Or cow? Whatever it is, it had a scapula the size of your foot.

❑ You walk shakily to the pub, pushing your way through hedgerows and snaking over the road.

❑ When you enter the pub, you hear the chime of bells and crash of sticks. The Morris Men occupy the centre of the room.

❑ The horse-skull-headed-creature stands between you and the Morris Men. The diaphanous sheet is now misshapen. Distended like a stomach. It looks like it has swallowed something — or someone. You want to look away, but you can't. Like the belly of a snake, something writhes inside. It's a hand. A human hand pressing towards you from the inside. Scrabbling. Panicked. You are instantly filled with the conviction that this is not a human pretending to be a monster. It's a monster, pretending to be a human pretending to be a monster.

❑ Horrified, you lurch backwards.

❑ Whatever the creature is, it hasn't seen you. You don't think it has eyes. Perhaps it follows the bells?

❑ You shuffle ever so quietly round the side of the bar. You glance over, to see if the creature is following. Your eyes are transfixed by the Morris Men. The flailing ribbons. The cracking sticks.

❑ When you come to, it's closing time, and your new colleague is gone.

❑ You try to add up what you have seen.

❑ You write your hypothesis down on the corner of a serviette. "Whatever the Morris Man is, it's not human. It just looks like a human. Unconvincingly. The creatures seem to be in a mutualistic partnership with the creature that looks like a sheet draped below a horse's skull. Like the lantern of an anglerfish, the Morris Man is a distraction. It is deliberately ostentatious, and holds the prey rapt, while the thing that looks like a sheet hanging under a horse's skull hunts. They seem to live in freshwater during the day and emerge on land to hunt at night."

❑   The next day, at the lab, you resolve to test your hypothesis.

❑   At lunch, you revisit your clandestine slides. The ribbon-like worms have multiplied and clustered together.

❑   Some of the cells have differentiated. You can see a primitive stomach. A primitive photosensitive mass— not as sophisticated as an eye, but functionally equivalent. In textbooks, you have seen a creature like this before. The class of gelatinous animals. The siphonophore. Perhaps the Morris Man is not one creature, but thousands? Each ribbon, each bell, each angular, cartilaginous chunk of face. A small, damp lifeform, co-operating with others.

❑   You vomit into the wastepaper bin. Skipton walks in on you.

❑   Skipton asks if you are okay. He notices your microscope.

❑   He asks if he can see what you are looking at.

❑   Skipton looks down your microscope.
❑   Skipton frowns.
❑   Skipton would like a word.

Which of the following statements are regrettable?

❑   On the short walk to Skipton's office, you try to work out what angle you should take.

❑   It seems a bad idea to blurt out what you now believe. That the Morris Man and the Horse-Skull-Headed-Creature are amphibious predators.

❑   It seems a bad omen that Skipton kept giving you fake water samples. You decide to arm yourself. A letter opener. It isn't much. But you're able to slide it up your sleeve on the walk to his office without him noticing.

❑   Skipton invites you to sit and leans back in his chair until his lab coat stretches taut across his shoulders like a sail.

❑   "What's upset you?" he asks.

❑   "I think I've identified a water quality issue," you reply. He nods, as if this answer is acceptable.

❑   "What kind of issue?" he asks.

❑   Broadly speaking, aquatic organisms adopt one of two locomotive strategies. They can be sessile—staying in one place, and taking what they're given, like a barnacle—or motile, actively choosing a path of action.

❑   You have decided that you will actively take a path of action.

With or without a shark to back you up.

❑   "I believe," you say, gripping the letter-opener, "that there may be an incursion of an invasive species."

❑   "Right," he says.

❑   "A predatory invasive species." you add.

❑   "Like this one?" Skipton asks, sweeping piles of papers off his desk to reveal that it was, in fact, an enormous fish tank. Inside, one of the horse-skull-headed creatures floats in torpor. Empty. Asleep.

❑ Skipton appears to enjoy your shock. "They were here before us, I reckon," Skipton says. "Mimicking deer maybe. Or wolves. Or boars."

❑ "And if you really think about it," he continues, "it's the humans that are the invasive species. Multiplying and causing damage. This thing—this predator—is a cleansing force. Like a wolf keeping down deer numbers. Stopping them from nibbling their way into catastrophic, cascading ecosystem collapse."

❑ "You admire them?" you ask.

❑ "Who wouldn't?" he replies.

❑ "Look at it," Skipton says, stepping aside to let you see the tank. "Really look at it,"

You note that the creature's wheat and ribbon head-dress waves gently, as if each strand were a prehensile tentacle.

❑ Too late, you feel Skipton's hands on your shoulders, forcing you into the tank.

❑ You feel the rubbery membrane folding outwards, enveloping you like the stomach of a starfish.

❑ You wonder whether you'll drown before it digests you, or it'll digest you before you drown.

❑ From inside the creature, you watch Skipton's blurred silhouette leave the room.

❑ Frenetically, you stab at the beast's rubbery membrane with the letter-opener, sawing your way out.

❑ You emerge in a damp heap. The beast, perforated and motionless, floats in the tank like a waterlogged dress.

❑ Part of you wants to run. To leave this all behind.

132

❑   The part of you that admires the shark wants to go after Skipton.

❑   In some ways he's right. It's probably your lot that's caused all this. The cities. With millions of mouths, demanding pesticides and fertilisers to keep our stomachs full, and millions of pipes for when they empty. Choking the life out of streams, one trophic level at a time. Until the predators have nothing left to hunt in the water, so learn to stumble onto land.

❑   But your new colleagues don't deserve to die tonight.

❑   So you stagger to the village.

❑   You believe that the horse-skull-headed-creature is sightless. That it navigates by sound. Following the things that sound like bells.

❑   You stamp into the pub. You steal the last orders bell. You stamp back out again.

❑   You jog to the river. You are in time to see the procession of Morris Men emerge for the night's hunting.

❑   When the last Morris Man emerges, and the horse-skull-headed-creature begins to ascend from the gloomy waters, you ring your own bell.

❑   The creature appears confused at first.

❑   You ring your bell louder. Harder.

❑   The creature turns so that the skull faces you. You continue ringing the bell, and it follows you along the stream. And through the hedgerow. And into the road. And you keep ringing the bell, and ringing the bell, until you see the headlights of a lorry approaching, and you silence the bell and duck into a hedgerow, and the lorry rounds the bend and smashes into the creature, leaving it flat as kelp.

❑ Years later, the commission will determine that it was this lorry which carried fragments of the species up the M4.

❑ The commission will determine that when the lorry stopped at the M4's Eastbound Welcome Break, it transferred fragments of the species to the wheels, arches, and axles of an entire fleet of delivery lorries.

❑ The commission will determine that it was heavy rains the next day that washed these fragments into rivers across the country.

❑ The commission will determine that the spread of the species was someone's fault. But they will not know that it was you.

The Crow Who Burned
Ivor K. Hill

Trouble. I tell you, pet, I'm up to my arse in it. And it's all my fault.

Aye, it was my own folk who built up this here bonfire, and it was them who dragged me to the stake. But I may as well have bound my sorry self to it.

I'll give you my tale-end momentarily—here comes aul Conor with his stick o'fire. He slides it betwixt the boldest of the kindling, coy-like, then gives it a half-hearted rattling, and don't the sparks twinkle in his averted eyes? Don't they just.

My pyre catches.

I blow Conor a wee kiss. He sees it, and his mouth, still pretty after all these years, tightens like your bunger. I pray to Fionn—even though it was me who invented our town god—that the thought of my burning keeps aul Conor up the rest of his nights. He backs off to take his place in the gathering, there beside glary-Mary, his woman of the nasty eyes.

Conor's act of stepping forward, his firing of the wood, his scuttling retreat.

Three acts.

All of life is three acts, pet. And within them three? Triplets within triangles within three-sided squares. And that brings us neat-like to the crux of this here tale, because three acts is all you need to birth a god, and that's the learning I'm urged to impart.

We'd all been wee and less sure of ourselves back then, myself, I daresay, more than Conor and Kyle and Mary. We'd been on the stone beach, where the wrinkly wise of Imithe yet feared to tread. Away from their strictures, we could conduct some serious kiddy business or other. And it happened that one eve the first action (in making gods) would find us there.

If we'd been able to see it, I'd bet my best stockings it had been hoary and longer in the tooth than even the wisest aul wrinkler you ever did meet. I reckon the first action always comes from somewhere ancient. Or mayhap large or just far off. It doesn't matter which, as long as thinking 'bout it makes you feel small as a fairy's pecker.

Eve was gloaming its way to star-pricked black, the surf lapping against the rocks with a susurration of a thousand pretty crows, the spray drifting skyward like feathers. But the real eerie thing about the stone beach is how the stones are all six-sided pillars, some as tall as trees but most huddled beneath your feet, each perfectly sized for perching your rear, even if a wee puddle was like to greet your cheeks.

But we're talking 'bout the first action in making gods, you and me, not beaches (sorry pet, but this bastard fire's reached my bare feet and it's hard to keep my mind of it—I'm not even fond of sand between my toes).

Well, we were sat on our funny rocks with soggy arses, staring across stones and sea, and not making a peep, when the first action found us. It lashed out, mayhap at me as I remember a feeling like knuckles cracking the inside of my skull.

And so, I spilled some words: "Why are these rocks so bloody bizarre?"

The first god-making act, you see, is the question for which none have the answer. Others include 'why are we here?' 'Why does shagging feel so good?' And 'Why won't these arseholes just let me be me?'

The great tragedy in all of this—not that I've yet decided this is a tragedy, mayhap I would be more afeared of this fire after all and isn't that queer?—is that the first action is all too often followed by the second. 'Cause some sod that's too proud to admit that they don't know the answer, makes something up.

Now, aul Conor, who was young yet but already showing the signs that he'd be a right beautiful bastard in a few summers, he piped up. And indeed, he talked pure shite.

"It was giants," he said, with the chin-jutting confidence of a boyo declaring the sky to be green, "a crossway they made to reach the Picts, 'cause no boats were big enough to carry them."

Pure shite. But it would take years for that particularly monumental turd to become truly consequential.

Ah, bollocks. Some precocious spark's floated from my shins and caught the hair 'round my crotch. Did I mention they stripped me as they marched me to the stake? None mentioned why, but the rumours of my nethers died today. When they first took me, they put me in a nice warm shack for days and gave me bread and water and quiet while they hunted for the courage to appease Fionn. Sacrifice me, that is. My time in the shack was enough for the hairs I normally razor off to grow back into a thick, greying mat, but not yet curly. Doesn't need to be curly to burn though, and it makes a right pong. Let me focus on that for a moment pet, let me breathe in my own rank self as I transform into something different, something that the wind can catch and ferry away, to near and far.

Conor's watching, his face gone so pale it's painted with the lovely pink of my pyre.

Aye. The second action in making a god is the humanly daft answer to an inhumane question. And the third action? Well, in this case, it came down to me. And in time, that's what put my arse in this fire.

Seasons passed, and for the shame he claimed I brought to his door, my Da (long dead now) turfed me out of his and Ma's (longer dead), and I fled to the cold, leaky shack down the road from Imithe. It was abandoned since Lugh died (longest dead). The story goes that they'd found him stiff in his chair, so alike alive that they'd concluded he couldn't be all dead. But they still keeled the stiff-o into a hole anyway, then covered him in mud. He was still on his side, they say, in his seated posture—funny like. And so, Lugh's aul shack became my new shack. The path was overgrown, sure, but it didn't take long to fix that, not once Fergus and Dáire and even good aul Kyle began their clandestine visitations. Conor, though, he shacked with Mary.

By then, folk were less afeared of the stone beach, after we'd admitted that we'd spent so much time there when wee, and that not once had any of us been snatched by banshees or púci or Pictish selkies or kelpies or sharks or snakes or wolves or some foul pillock up to no good. As you might expect, now that the fear was a bit abated, there was a war of notions about what the stone beach might be.

138

The heart of Imithe was its mead den, and like any good Ulster town, the heart pumped drink. There you'd find the air thick with speculation like so much slung shite, especially 'round those male, those wise, and those sotted (and good luck to you if you happen across an embodiment of all three at once).

Back in my shack though, the air was cleaner. Dáire and Fergus, after their faces fell as fast as their pricks shrivelled, always left in a rush, one back to his cattle, the other back to his wife. The ravens and crows that were fond of the trees 'round my shack would cackle at their going, if never their coming. But Kyle stayed a while most times.

He's not in the crowd tonight, I don't see his gruff bake, or his deep-set blues. He wouldn't want to watch me die, I suppose. He'd tried to reason with the shite-slingers after they'd taken me, but when enough shite is slung, some will get in your eyes, and from there it's a short jaunt to your brain. Kyle had asked for proof that Fionn could cleanse our crops, never mind demand sacrifice to do so. Conor's surprise at the question would prompt eye-rolling indictment from you, pet. I just wept—the shattered weeping of the damned, my chest jerking like some púca's pulling my strings, but nary a peep from my tight, tired craw. Luckily for Conor though, glary-Mary had an answer for sweet Kyle. She did duly opine, with gravid, head-bobbing sincerity, that we mortals can't know the minds of gods.

Glary-Mary-shite-for-brains.

Anyway, back when Kyle used to visit, we'd talked about all kinds of things, in that soft space between fading satisfaction and thickening shame. We committed the first action in making gods together, asking questions unanswerable, over and over. But we never committed the second act.

It was Kyle's earnest thoughtfulness, and so his accidental

cruelty, that made me realise I was besotted with Mary's Conor. I'd been in love for donkey's years before the realisation slid into my chest like a hot spear tip into a greased stuck pig. When I admitted it to Kyle, he held me as I had a wee cry, and then he spent a good while making me feel gorgeous. And gorgeous I felt—big in ways that pleased my ego and small in ways that surely meant I'm a thing most precious.

But Kyle wasn't Conor.

Kyle isn't Conor.

And I'm not …

…

Did I pass out for a moment there, pet? I've been burned before, of course, everyone's snatched their talons from the flame. But that's not like this. I search for Conor in the crowd but can't see him through the chuffing fumes. Then the smoke billows back and forth as if a divinity's wings were descending on me, and in the gap, I see him. I see them all. They're surprised I'm not dead yet.

"Sorry!" I croak.

Now, way back when, even though Imithefolk were brave enough to talk about the stone beach, there was no agreement on the origin of the stones. Obviously. Some said they had fallen from the sky, others that they were the spears of giants. Some eejits even thought they were the aul bones of the land and that was why they stretched so far along the coast. And so, the wise of the town gathered on the nearest part of the stone beach one blustery sunny day—me included, now being in my third decade—and bickered about what we named 'the truth.'

I watched from the back, as far from all as I could, standing unremarked on the other side of the hole that scooped its way down through the stones into the wee coastal cave below. I remember thinking that it was fear that had brought us here, for if the stone beach was so close to us people, surely there was something we were meant to do with it? Mayhap we'd miss out if we didn't?

It didn't occur to anyone that the beach wasn't bothered by our wants.

Now, many folks struck poses and raised their voices to battle with the surf most heroically, and I've scraped more useful muck from my shoe. It wasn't until Conor stepped forward that I swallowed my salty sneer. He wondered aloud, voice booming, chest thrust out, muscles stretching his tunic near to bursting, and tufts of dark hair peeping over his shirt.

He asked if the giants hadn't built a bridge to the Picts, long, long ago.

There were some nods. There were some laughs. A voice asked which giant, and Conor gave the only reply any wanted to hear: "Fionn, the Bane o' the Picts!"

Conor was so lovely. Hair swept in the breeze; strands caught in the sun. And plain-glary-Mary-shite-for-brains clinging to his arm.

It was Aine who shot Conor down. She was the Wisest of the wise, her caw cutting the air how a gull wouldn't dare and carrying more weight than the stones themselves. She made strong arguments, it must be said. Why was the bridge broken? Why would Fionn even need a bridge to begin with? He's a bloody giant. He could just step over the black water and debate Picts whenever he so pleased. And if it was too far, maybe he could take a run-up?

Conor kept a polite mask on, but I saw how her words shamed him, and it was like nettles in my armpit. Mary was too cowed by Aine's feminine, brainy prowess to even raise her eyes.

So, when Aine declared that we would simply ask Fionn and find out, I saw my chance. I could be Fionn. I could be Fionn for Conor. You see, pet, in order to make a god, you can't believe in it yet, because no one can define what's already itself.

The fire's past my waist now. I've never felt pain like this. I heard once that you can only focus on one pain at a time, but whoever told me that was a lying gob. Probably my Da. My feet and legs are crushed and twisted and skinless and shrivelled, my arms are melting like tallow, and my throat's as dry from hollering as it is cloyed with sticky blood. I won't tell you about what's happening between my legs.

Ach, well.

Back to the beach. I slipped into the chute and under the stones without anyone noticing but soon knew the flaw in my plot. I could hardly hear Aine from down here over the thumping of the surf at the cave's mouth.

Now pet, depending on what kind of sod you happen to be, you might not be fond of how this all plays out. There's no need to be looking away now, it's just that what happens next involves a wee bit of the unknowable, a touch of the ambiguous. A shadow, you might say, that's there one blink and gone the next, even though you could have sworn it was shaping into a dread wolf or your dead gran or some thieving git after your baubles.

You see pet, I listened without hearing, straining for Aine's cawing above, but she was a pattering scrabble compared to the boom of the surf. Each phase of her beseeching was punctuated by the giant's close-held silence. It was during Aine's fourth pause that I spotted the crow. Or mayhap she was a raven. I don't know if she was there before me, crows are hard to see in the dark, ravens too, but I do know that she was a she, and she gave to me a nod quite wee. And I thought, *bollocks to it*, and cupped my hands around my mouth to better allow my best impression of a giant.

"Yeeeeeooooooooo!"

And, wouldn't you know, that was just when Aine had asked Fionn if the stones were what remained of his crossway for debating Picts.

Was it Fionn that made me call out in that moment? Had some tarry, fed up god sent their birdie envoy for sowing seeds of mischief?

Feck it, who cares, I'm burning alive, aren't I?

What matters, is that it was there, and it was then, and it was me. The third action in making a god was performed. The would-be believers were given their sign. Or something they could interpret as a sign, which I reckon could be any aul shite if they want to believe bad enough.

My third action caused quite the stir. Firstly, we had to refigure how big Fionn was. If he needed a bridge, he must be a short wee giant. Some of the lads found that particularly upsetting for some reason.

Regardless, the giant had spoken, and he became our town god, and while Conor never looked at me twice, he was put on a pedestal for his wisdom. And now, some score of years later, he's Wisest, which was a surprise given he's pretty and thick, and aul Fergus was ugly and clever. Indeed, it was Conor's idea that Fionn might cleanse the crops before we starve.

It was plain-vindictive-glary-Mary-shite-for-brains that pointed out that goats were too valuable to sacrifice.

It's her who wears the lone smile in my deathwatch. A wee tilt at the corner of her lip, like her tongue wants to poke through but knows it might be unseemly, so contents itself with the sweetness of teetering on the edge of pleasure. I never understood why she hated me, she knew nowt of my infatuations, surely. But I'm not above hating her back, being moral and all.

And so, they came for me. Kyle had trekked to my shack the day prior for the first time in a long while—his knees pain him nowadays—and told me that my own Imithefolk would kill me, as there was only one person living 'round the edge. Moreover, I knew that the only folk who were fond of me kept it a secret from the rest—Kyle didn't know about Fergus didn't know about Dáire didn't know about Kyle. And I don't know why I didn't leave. Maybe it'll come to me before the fire kills me.

Conor himself led them to my shack. The years weighed more politely on him than me; his shoulders only a tad drooped, the skin between his cheeks and nose hanging only a wee bit low. But he was still a looker, with that chin and the grey like salt on dark bread.

"Sorry, Ana," he said as he stepped inside, the heat from my hearth fire sucked out into the night to be replaced with that from my cheeks. Ah, feck, 'Ana' is my chosen name, sorry, I should've said. I almost didn't see Mary behind Conor, scowling that he'd called me such. No one else had chosen their name, after all.

How many times had I pictured Conor here? How many times had I mouthed his name into Kyle's shoulder as I spasmed, not five steps from where I stood? And there Conor was, with me standing before him mouth agape. Then the others came in, boyos from town that had never visited me.

Conor explained what they were going to do, as if giving me a choice. But the moment he stopped speaking, he motioned the others forward. He stopped the procession as it passed him, and again, he said sorry. I opened my mouth to tell him to go take a jaunt off a cliff, but the words wouldn't come out. Bastard tears came from my eyes instead. And then a cry slipped my lips, small-like, the pitch cracking as a twig between a babe's thumbs. And the boyos carted me off as I battled my sobs and lost.

I can see Conor, now. He's turning from my pyre, a sick look on his face. Mary notices and cuts me a glare as if I'm spiting her with my death, the sour eejit.

Why didn't I leave after Kyle warned me? Did I think Conor would protect me, just because I loved him once? I'd never even told him. And he would never have left his Mary for one such as me.

I'm a gentle soul, aye. And thick as mud. But it won't be me I hate for this.

Among the crowd before my pyre, comes a sudden jumble of motion and Kyle steps forth. And he is a picture, with the tendons on his neck standing out like new bones are sprouting from his skeleton, an impression emboldened by his bald, shiny pate. He's got something in his hand, he waves it at me and then at Conor, who backs up a step, arms outstretched and cautious like he's just stumbled upon a hoary boar. Then Kyle roars something to the skies above, pulls his arm back and lets fly.

It hits Conor. He topples. In the ensuing kerfuffle, Kyle is dragged back and held by three boyos, and a space opens in the mob, like a scar on a scalp. Conor lies within, Mary kneeling beside her man, her mouth slack. Shock, it might be.

Conor sits up, swaying a bit. There's something stuck to his face. He reaches up and tugs Kyle's rock free, but that's a mistake. His brains spill out.

Mary screams.

Such a sweet song.

Do there need to be gods for there to be an afterlife? Give me eternal suffering on Balor's left arse cheek as long as Conor's on the right so I can tell him to go feck himself until the sun goes out.

I laugh, blood spurting from my mouth now the hard parts are exposed. But I cease my cackle mid-breath. You see, Balor's got a big arse to be sure, but not big enough to nail me and Conor to, he's no giant. I find myself wondering about my certainty on that particular.

But then I know I'm here at last—my moment of dying.

The smoke's swallowing me up, nesting me cozy-like in black feathers. They swirl and billow and shudder as a storm come to raze all warmth. And then, the fire's gone out, and all's dark.

Dark as a crow.

I sink my talons into the smouldering stake and fix the people with one eye. I cannot say what they see—none can know the mind of another, even that of a mortal—but their fear pleases me, and I rattle my pinions.

Some few of my Fearful slip from the crowd and into the dark of night, but I have no time to give chase. The itching begins, deep in my skull. I release my caw, and some of my Fearful scream, and I spread my wings and yet more flee. My memories now join, coming together as one. Memories of a life around the edge of Imithe, and of a hundred other lives, some as ruler, most as less.

Ana knew not why she told her tale, but it was for us, for all the lives we have lived.

My Fearful stare, and Ana speaks to me.

I acquiesce.

From her tale now hatches consequence.

I caw to the folk of Imithe, and demand the unanswerable first act in shaping a god: "What made you like this?"

They quail and wail and my breast swells.

"Forgive us," one of my Fearful dares, "we are but simple folk!"

And so was the second action committed. The third is forthcoming.

Ana urges me, but she need not. For her sake, I take flight—an arrow from Lugh's bow. My talons are long and sharp and wicked as words, and I rake them across Mary's face. She begs. I bestow the kiss of my beak. She stops begging.

Many times have I have seen truth beget legend beget myth. It can take generations, or it can take the span of hours, because when mortals and gods alike reach for their truth, it is all too easy to make a leap of faith.

In time, the name of Imithe will be lost. But a skein of truth and lies shall stretch far and wide. Legend will have it that Conor and Mary wore crowns, and that Kyle wore the armour of their clan.

Legend places me in their story.

And they will name me The Morrigan.

Before I depart Imithe, Ana demands her say. Listen to how she finished her tale.

I'd be wild pleased at this scenario (me being an unkillable shape-shifting force of nature, that is) if I wasn't so fecked off.

Do you want to know what really mucks my rug? It's not that they outed me or ignored me or cuckolded each other on my flesh with nary a glimmer of warmth or sweetness for my soul. Not even that they burned me.

It's their bloody defence.

"We are but simple folk."

Regular, then? Normal? Fecking *real* mayhap?

If that were true, they'd be such a boring lot there wouldn't be a single story of theirs worth telling. So, I reckon "we are but simple folk" isn't just daft, it's a fib to boot.

Mary's done twitching. She fell over Conor's corpse. I take

my human form, easy as taking flight, and kick some mud over both of them.

Kyle's still here. Tears stand in his deep-set blues, but they aren't all sad. I blow him a wee kiss to give him something to remember me by, for he was a nice man as far as they go.

Then, ignoring the rest of the shame-obsessed, hateful, self-appointed bullies and self-disappointed wankers, I become the crow, and we feck right off.

Muddy Water
Epiphany Ferrell

"Where you been, Thelma?"

Thelma jumped. "Why are you still up? It's 3 am. I told you. I was helping Miss Marie with the Johnson baby."

She went to the refrigerator, poured a glass of tea, drank the whole thing standing by the sink. Jimmie watched the way the liquid pulsed down her throat as she swallowed, her head tipped back and her unruly dark hair brushing her shoulder blades. She'd lost weight in the past month; she seemed more angles than curves.

"You did tell me that," he said. "But I'm asking where you been."

Thelma moved around the kitchen, opening and shutting cabinets, looking for an answer. She sighed. "Don't start, Jimmie. It's been a long night."

"I'll say. Hey, Thelma. You got your shirt buttoned wrong."

Thelma picked up the empty Mason jar he'd left sitting on the table, sniffed it, glanced at Jimmie, put the jar in the sink. "I'm going to bed," she said. "I gotta work in about four hours. Don't wake me up, I'll get up myself."

She didn't cross the room to kiss him on the cheek like she always used to do.

Jimmie stayed where he'd been sitting all night, by the fireplace, holding a cast iron poker even though there was no fire on that hot July night. He hadn't shaved in three days. Thelma hadn't said a word about it.

"That's fine, Thelma," Jimmie said to the empty room. "But I sure wouldn't want the sun to go down even once without you as my girl."

"What you need a pistol for, Jimmie?" Clayton asked, putting away the guns Jimmie wasn't buying.

"Bird hunting." Jimmie put the Ruger 9 mm in the case. "Give me a couple boxes of ammo, too, Clay."

"Bird hunting with a pistol, huh. That bird wouldn't be a Thelma-bird now, Jimmie. Would it?"

Jimmie grimaced at Clayton. "Of course not, Clayton. Lord almighty, what you do think of me! It might be a Mateo-bird, though, trying to take away my girl. That's in season any old time."

"You ought not say that, Jimmie, you know I'm part-time down at the sheriff's office."

"Yeah, but you aren't there now, are you? Old friend."

"I don't think you need to worry about Mateo." Clayton sprayed Windex on the glass case, wiped it with a cloth. Without looking at Jimmie, he said, "Thelma sure spends a lot of time with that Miss Marie."

"Miss Marie," Jimmie said, putting a sneer in his voice.

"She's no Madam Nerline. Not afraid of the likes of her."

"Just leave it alone, friend," Clayton said. "You know better."

Miss Marie Landry had been to college. Jimmie wasn't alone in thinking anyone who'd gone to college and came back home to live in a shack on a swampy bend in the river had something wrong with them. Even if her aunt was Nerline Landry, whose people had been brewing potions and conjuring the Lord-only-knows out there in the swamp for at least a couple hundred years.

"Maybe I'll just go pay a visit to Madam Nerline," he told his steering wheel, his words just barely slurring. "See if she knows what her sweet, little, college-educated niece is up to."

Nerline and Jimmie's grandma had been friendly when Jimmie was a little boy. She'd brought his grandmother salves and tinctures, and his grandmother had given her flowers and herbs that needed full sun to grow. Sometimes, Miss Nerline, as he'd called her then, brought cookies.

There was a time the only way to get to the Landry place was by water. Now there was a road. Not a good one. Madame Nerline was standing on the porch when Jimmie parked his truck next to an ancient Cadillac. It wasn't a premonition, Jimmie reminded himself. Anyone could hear his truck crunching over the ruts on the gravel road from at least half a mile away.

"If it isn't little Jimmie Davis," Madame Nerline said. "I know why you're here, Jimmie. I know why you come all the way out here for the first time in your life to visit your grandmother's old friend."

Jimmie shuffled his feet. He'd sobered up some.

"Have some lemonade, I don't have any cookies," she said,

and gestured at a bent willow chair. Windchimes of unmatched silverware and others made of animal bones curtained the porch, hanging down to the railing and enclosing the space. Madam Nerline had been sewing. It looked like a little doll. A taxidermied alligator wearing a saddle took up about half the porch. Jimmie looked at it so he wouldn't stare at the doll on Madame Nerline's lap.

"Do you want to go for a ride, Jimmie?" she asked, her silky voice suggestive. "On the alligator?"

Jimmie shook his head no, gulped his lemonade. His mouth was dry.

"It don't take sixth sense to know why you're here. You been runnin' your mouth. But maybe I can help you, Jimmie Davis. First, I want you to do something for me. It's something you planned to do anyway, so it shouldn't be no problem a'tall. I want you to resolve an old quarrel for me, having to do with that road you drove here to my house. I want you to kill Mateo Harris. You must do it with witchcraft. If you shoot him, everyone will know it was you. Witchcraft is the only way."

"Aren't you the lucky man?" Madame Nerline said. "So many people wonder what goes on out here, and you get to see for yourself."

It was past midnight. Driving back out to the Landry place after dark with no stars or moon visible through the tree branches overhead had nearly been too much for Jimmie's nerves. But he didn't dare cross Madam Nerline now. He was in too far—had been since he'd stepped onto her porch.

The clammy night air clung to his bare chest. She'd given him the option of wearing his jeans, had laughed when he did. He crouched next to her fire pit, balanced on a short three-legged stool, ceaselessly pounding his fingers on a djembe, not daring to break rhythm. Madame Nerline hummed and murmured as she wove a necklace of animal bones and teeth that looked human. Jimmie stopped drumming only when she draped the necklace over his head and stepped back. His fingers felt raw.

Madame Nerline pulled a squawking black chicken from a wooden cage near the fire. Jimmie remembered how his grandmother had always set aside her white and black chickens for Nerline Landry. He forced himself not to flinch when she moved the chicken in a circle, then poised it over his head before slicing its neck. Its wild wings battered his face, its blood spattering his face and chest. Still, Madam Nerline had caught much of it in a blood-stained wooden bowl. Jimmie didn't dare wipe his face, though the running blood tickled and itched.

Madame Nerline washed a smooth, white stone in the chicken blood. She gave it to Jimmie to hold. She wiped chicken blood on his face in a cross, across his forehead and down his nose, over his lips to his chin, murmuring words Jimmie couldn't understand. "Mal pour mal," Madame Nerline said, and other things too.

"Put the stone in your shoe. You must keep it there until this is done."

Madame Nerline scraped some ash from the edge of the fire, mixed it with what was left of the chicken blood. "Drink this," she told Jimmie. Jimmie shuddered, then took the bowl and drank the blood and ash. He gagged, and Madame Nerline pursed her lips. He was ashamed.

Madame Nerline reached into another wooden cage and brought out a small black rabbit. It blinked at him in the firelight. It had a white marking on its chest that looked like a heart. She thrust it into his hands. Its heart was beating so fast against his hand, so very fast.

Jimmie followed Madame Nerline's pointing finger into the forest, the trail she described for him barely visible as the cypress thickened, their bent knees—witch's knuckles, people called them—like little trolls along the path. Just as she'd said it would, the path was visible only as he went forward. When he turned to look behind him, it was gone. If he stepped off it, he'd go straight down into the swampy water. Jimmie was convinced the bone necklace was the only thing keeping him from the alligators.

He held the black rabbit under his left arm, pressed against his side. He'd used a strip of his shirt to tie its legs to make it easier to carry. He'd lived on the edge of the forest his whole life, swimming where the river eddied and drinking with his buddies on its banks. He knew the night sounds almost as well as the day sounds. But he'd always avoided this swampy part with the dark cypress and the ghost trees. Everyone did.

As he hurried along the trail, he heard owls and the squeaking of bats, the incessant leopard frogs and piping tree frogs. He heard ripples in the water, the distant bellow and snap of alligators, a screech that might have been a bird, a scream that might have been a bobcat or even a panther. There were no visible lights, only the dimly luminescent stick Madame Nerline had given him. The stone in his shoe bruised his foot, and he was limping before he'd gone a hundred yards. When he stepped through a spiderweb across the path, he swiped it off his face without a sound but he could swear he felt the spider moving around in his hair, creeping down his neck.

The exterior lights from Mateo Harris' house shone on the water. Jimmie had never been so happy to see a house in his life. He stepped out of the woods onto the wide lawn. It was an old house; Mateo was restoring it. He didn't have an alarm system. He did have dogs—mastiffs that wore wide, studded collars. Madame Nerline had given Jimmie hunks of meat for the dogs, had laughed at his reluctance to poison them.

"It won't hurt them none," she said. "They'll sleep some and then wake up thirsty 'n mean. But they'll be a sight better off than the man you gonna kill, that's for sure."

Jimmie scanned the yard, looking for the dogs. He ran to a tree midway across the lawn. As he did, two shadows detached from near the garage. The dogs bounded across the grass toward Jimmie, barking to wake the dead, their teeth white and sharp in the floodlight. Jimmie threw a hunk of meat at the first dog. It blew right past, but the second dog stopped, sniffed, bolted it down. Jimmie hurled the rest of the meat and the first dog went back to investigate and joined the other dog chomping down the meat hunks. One of the dogs wagged its tail as Jimmie crept past. He almost laughed.

He looked up at the house. Was anyone awake in that house after all that barking? He thought he saw a figure by the window, a silhouette maybe. But already the quality of the night sky had changed. It was faintly grey in the east. He had to be back to Madame Nerline before the sun came up, she'd been adamant.

Jimmie ran to the back of the house. All he could see as he looked at the forest he'd come from was darkness and he wondered how he'd managed to stay on the path. Now he felt like he was in a spotlight.

There was an unlocked door in the second kitchen Madame Nerline had told him. Jimmie crept into the dark pantry, bumped hard into a shelf, knocked off a jar. Somehow, he caught it. Pickles. "I ought to piss in your pickles," he whispered. Catching the jar before it smashed made him feel better about himself. Braver. Deadly.

Mateo's bedroom was upstairs, toward the back of the house. Jimmie inched his way out of the pantry, through the kitchen, nearly knocking his head on a hanging display of cast-iron skillets. When the air conditioner kicked on, he jumped hard enough to rattle the bones-and-teeth necklace. The rabbit squirmed in his grip, squeaking as he gripped it harder. He pushed it against himself to smother the sounds.

Jimmie flattened himself against the wall, trying to stay in shadow, his heart pounding. He didn't have much time. His eyes adjusted to the low light in the dining room, and he saw the stairs across a wide hall, spiralling into blackness. He edged up them, one careful step at a time as if he were ascending to Hell. The third stair from the top creaked, and Jimmie froze, holding his breath until his vision swam.

He didn't have to hunt for Mateo's room; he could hear him snoring. He sidled past two empty rooms, feeling eyes on his back as he passed each door. He hoped it was true Mateo lived alone in the big house. He hoped it wasn't true the house was haunted. He wouldn't let himself turn around, but he felt like someone unseen was right behind him. Maybe Mateo's ghost would join whatever was here in this house.

The bedroom door was ajar. Though the air conditioner was running, the window was open. A gauzy curtain moved in the night air. Jimmie stepped sideways into the room, scarcely breathing. The room smelled of lilac and weed.

Mateo snorted in his sleep, gasped, and was quiet. Jimmie blinked. He hadn't even done it yet! But then the snoring resumed.

Jimmie tiptoed up to the bed and looked down at Mateo asleep. The absurdity of his situation struck him—sneaking into a powerful, rich man's bedroom with a rabbit and a faceful of chicken blood! He bared his teeth in a silent snarl. Hate had got him this far this night, hate would see him through. He held the rabbit over Mateo and began wringing its neck, his strong hands clenching on the small animal.

156

Mateo grunted, gulped for air. *It's working! I can hardly believe this but it's working!*

The rabbit struggled, fighting for its life. Its hind legs thumped against his arms as he squeezed, the sharp nails cutting his side, and it squealed, shrieking even as Jimmie squeezed harder and harder, grinding his teeth in fury and fear.

Mateo clutched at the sheet over his chest, fists clenched, his breath rattling in his throat. His eyes opened, but he didn't see Jimmie or the rabbit—his eyes were filmed with death. Mateo gagged, thrashed, and was still. The rabbit went limp in Jimmie's hands. "You filthy piece of shit," he hissed at Mateo's still form.

Mateo's eyes flashed open.

"What the fuck, man, what are you doing in my house?" Mateo roared, his voice scratchy and raw.

He sprang out of the bed straight at Jimmie, fast as a coiled snake. Mateo caught Jimmie at the waist, his strong arms holding him in a bear hug. Jimmie beat him with the dead rabbit, pummelling so hard with it for a moment he thought it, too, had come back to life.

The two men crashed to the floor. Mateo was bigger and stronger, but Jimmie was meaner. And Mateo's legs were tangled up in bed sheets. Jimmie rolled away from Mateo, got to his knees and swung the rabbit at Mateo again and again. He'd forgotten what he held in his hand, only feeling that it was a weapon. He lost his grip on the rabbit, and it smacked against the wall. Mateo reached up with his hands for Jimmie's throat. He was on his back, Jimmie with a knee on either side of him. Jimmie dropped down onto Mateo's stomach. Mateo grunted, the air driven from his lungs and his grip on Jimmie weakened.

Jimmie put his hands around Mateo's throat and squeezed,

just as he'd done to the rabbit. He pounded Mateo's head against the hardwood floor. He got up on his knees to drop down onto Mateo's stomach over and over, almost as if he was having sex with a woman. As soon as that thought entered his head, Jimmie began to laugh—mad, mirthless cackles. He kept squeezing after Mateo stopped moving, shifting so he could bring his knee down over Mateo's throat. His hands were tired.

It was done.

He made a weak attempt to lift Mateo into the bed. The scenario Madame Nerline had described was peaceful. Mateo would appear to have choked to death in his sleep. Instead, he sprawled on the floor, sheets wrapped around his ankles, livid marks on his throat.

Jimmie fled to the hallway. He was bounding down the stairs when he remembered the rabbit. His work wasn't done. He'd botched it, but he needed that rabbit. He crept back into Mateo's room, stepping gingerly around his body. *Is he breathing?* Jimmie froze. *Did his hand just twitch?* The longer he stared, the more he was sure Mateo was breathing. He kicked Mateo's head. It rocked and was still.

The sky was noticeably lighter. Where was the rabbit? Jimmie frantically threw the rest of the sheets off the bed, feeling for the little black animal. He looked around the room wildly. There was a smear of blood on the wall. The rabbit was at the bottom of the smear. Jimmie tried to rub the blood stain out with his hand. No good. He picked up the rabbit and ran down the stairs. He had less than two hours to get to Ebeneezer Holcum Cemetery.

He ran down the driveway, racing his floodlit shadow. There was no sign of Mateo's dogs.

"Go 666 steps into the cemetery," Madame Nerline had said.

"Stand still and turn slowly around and around until you see the glowing tombstone. There may be more than one, go to the first one you see glowing. Bury the rabbit. Then come back here before the sun rises."

Jimmie had played football in high school, tight end. He hadn't kept up his conditioning. Even so, Coach would have been impressed with Jimmie's time on the run to the cemetery. His lungs were on fire. He felt he was coughing blood; he could taste it at the back of his throat. His neck was sore from where Mateo had grabbed him and his left wrist was bruised. The bloody white stone in his shoe pounded his foot with every step. He held the battered rabbit by one back leg, and it bumped against him as he limp-ran.

Six hundred sixty-six steps. His panting was harsh in the silence. He had to focus to count; his brain wasn't working right. This was an old cemetery, with the bones of old families in it. Obelisks surmounted by crosses marked family plots, some of them encircled with leaning wrought-iron fences. A hill rolled away to the right, dotted with crypts and crooked tombstones. The dew rose from the grass, a light mist threading through the parts of the cemetery down the hill, and along the back by the trees. Jimmie had never liked this place, not even just to drive past it. He lost count of his steps and had to go back to the entrance and begin again. A distant police siren reminded him of what was at stake if he didn't.

At 666 steps, he stopped, turned slowly in a circle, all the way around. The air was clammy, damp, smelling of moss and rotting flowers. He felt it in his bones. He turned around once. Twice. The third time, there was a sharp ray of light, bouncing off a tombstone, then stopping behind one. It glowed.

Jimmie ran silently over the soft ground. The light

moved—headlights, from the road behind the cemetery. Was that what Madame Nerline meant by glowing? He'd pictured an ethereal light, ghost-light, blue and flickery. This light was bright and yellow-white, and now it was gone. He stopped at the tombstone that had been illuminated. *Is it the right one?* Jimmie looked around in a panic. So many of the tombstones looked the same. He didn't want to get it wrong now, not after everything that had happened that night. The morning birds were starting their pre-dawn chirping. This grave would have to do.

He knelt in front of the stone. The name was weathered with moss inside the letters. Solomon Dufresne, it looked like. "Sorry, Sol," Jimmie said, and began digging. The stale earth smelled of worms. How deep? Had Madame Nerline said? When she asked him if he had any questions, and he hadn't, she'd made a straight line with her lips and shook her head. She knew how stupid he was! How deep?!

Jimmie dug frantically, the earth disturbingly loose. Every third handful, he looked over his shoulder. He felt ghosts all around him, laughing at him, hissing at him. They called his name, taunting him, their voices like ice on his skin. Fingers stroked his cheek, something brushed his neck, leaving a frosty kiss.

"Hey Mister, come play with me!" "Give us a kiss, Jimmie. Just one." "One for each of us!" "Jimmie, over here!"

"Stay away," Jimmie shouted, startled at the madness he heard in his own voice. "Stay away from me!" Silence answered. A distant laugh—real or ghostly, he couldn't tell.

As the sky lightened, Jimmie saw he was within several feet of Katie May's grave, a girl he'd dated and dumped who'd died giving birth to a child that might have been his. It was her stroking his cheek, he was sure of it—that soft way she had of running a finger over his lips. Despite the sweat dripping off his nose, he was chilled. Shivering, even. He closed his mouth and kept it closed, afraid a spirit might enter past his lips and teeth.

He got elbow deep into the grave and he couldn't stand it any longer. The grey of early dawn cast shadows he swore were moving. He had to get out of the cemetery—the hole had to be deep enough. He thrust the rabbit in, covered it, patting the earth down as best he could.

"Oh God have mercy, the voodoo queen will have my soul!" he sobbed, and he started running. If he went by road, he'd never get there in time. He ran into the cypress forest, splashing where the water was clear, clomping where it was mucky. He lost a shoe. Sun slanted through the thick trees, and the birds sang merrily like they didn't have a care in the whole damn world. Still, Jimmie ran. He stumbled, got up, ran into a tree. He tripped over cypress knees and bruised his ribs when he fell. And he kept going.

When Jimmie crashed into the clearing at Madame Nerline's side-yard, he was covered in smelly, black mud, his dirty face streaked with blood and snot. Madame Nerline was not there.

Jimmie fell on his face next to the fire and sobbed. The sun was above the horizon.

Jimmie dreamed. He saw a small, black rabbit with a white patch on its chest like a heart hopping toward him in a ray of light that showed the delicate veins in its ears. It was such a cute little bunny, he smiled. Its nose twitched, and it hopped closer. Jimmie squinted, trying to see it better. There was something wrong. The bunny was covered in mud. One eye hung from its socket, and one front leg dangled limp and useless.

"No," Jimmie said out loud. His voice woke him. "No!" he

161

shrieked, and no echo returned his voice.

"The sun came up and where were you?" Madame Nerline said. She was sitting on the porch, rocking in her bent willow chair. "You failed. I can't keep the law from you now, Jimmie Davis."

"The rabbit didn't work," he protested. "I had to kill him with my hands."

"Mal pour mal," Madame Nerline said. "It comes back on you."

Jimmie stood, staggered toward the porch.

"Don't you come up here so filthy, Jimmie Davis," Madame Nerline said. "I don't have any cookies for you."

"Please, Madame Nerline, help me," Jimmie whispered, and looked up at Madame Nerline to see if there was mercy in her face. A small, black rabbit with a white mark on its chest and blind, dead eyes sat on her lap, nibbling lettuce.

Jimmie cried out, fell back down the steps he'd begun to climb, onto his back in the dirt.

"Go to the swamp, Jimmie," Madame Nerline said. "Drink muddy water, live in a hollow log. Like a toad. After one year and one day, come back to this clearing. Maybe I'll help you then. If you can remember what it is you wanted, if you still know your own name."

Jimmie belched, gagging, and vomited out a handful of mud, and kept retching, coughing up fat nightcrawlers, green chunks of lily pad and slimy grey-black mud. He turned to flee, but before he did, he saw Thelma, standing on the far side of the porch, her eyes wide and her hand covering her mouth, keeping herself from screaming. Marie stood next to her, her head resting on Thelma's shoulder, her arms draped loosely around Thelma's waist.

"I want my Marie to be happy, Jimmie Davis. You go on, now. Go live in the swamp, toady man. Watch out for the heron and the hognose snake. Stay hidden—hard work for a show-off like you. But talk big. Sing in the swamp. Make lots of little toads, toady man."

Jimmie ran. Or he hopped. He couldn't be sure. The forest loomed around him, the green canopy all but blocking the sun, the water likewise green with duckweed. A cottonmouth weaved a clear path through the water, and Jimmie's throat expanded as he screamed in fear.

Thelma watched Jimmie flee into the swampy forest. He wasn't a man to make empty threats. He'd always told her he'd give her a one-day head start if ever she wanted to leave him. One day, but not one night. She still wore the shadow of a bruise on her sharp cheekbone from the last time they'd quarrelled. *But he wasn't always like that. Not always.*

She put her arm around Marie, her beautiful, sweet Marie, who was smart, and kind, and gentle.

"What will happen to him, Madame Nerline?" Thelma asked, keeping her voice steady and nonchalant. "Will your craft turn him into a toad for real?"

"Wasn't craft," Madame Nerline said. "It's his own cold heart. His own hands killed Mateo. His own soul guides him deep into the swamp. It's no doing of mine. That was all make-believe and theatre last night. A stone in his shoe. The fool."

Marie squeezed Thelma's waist, and Thelma answered by pulling Marie closer. Her hair smelled like sassafras, Thelma thought, and her voice was pretty as bird song.

"Thelma," Madame Nerline said, looking down at Thelma with no hint of a smile. "You must always be true to my Marie and never hurt her heart. You understand? I could never bear to see my Marie's tears."

A heron rasped its guttural cry as it skimmed the water of

the bayou. Thelma followed it with her eyes.

"Who was that I saw you with up to Crawdad's yesterday, Thelma?" Marie asked, squeezing Thelma tight.

In the Field at Noon

Ren Graham

There was a pile of meat on the top of the hill.

Not arranged in any kind of meaningful way, though. It was just a mound of viscera barely visible in the tall, grey-gold grass. Iron slag coloured liver, a rope of intestines, a pulpy organ that might have been part of a lung. It was so bruised that it was difficult to tell.

Květa grabbed a tree branch to prod at what looked like a sheared red sheet of muscle. Gnats fluttered on its surface.

Květa glanced back towards the village.

Thatched roofs glowed in the midday sun. Summer-browned moss grew in between the cracks of the log foundations. Farmers tilled the long green stalks of buckwheat. A woman with a red headscarf hung up a dripping blouse to dry. An ox made a dry moan before lowering its head into the feeding trough. A toddler yanked on the tail of a lax barn cat.

The cat flicked its whiskers and pulled back its tail from the toddler's grasp but did not bother to get up or open its eyes. Everything was as expected.

The placement of meat in the field was odd, though. But perhaps it was a displaced kill from an animal. Maybe one of the dogs had mauled a boar and left its remains there. Animals did all sorts of strange things.

"What are you doing, way up there on the hill?"

Květa's mother called to her from the garden fence. She gestured sharply for her to come down, so Květa bowed her head and obeyed. She dropped the tree branch she had been using to prod at the meat and readjusted the pinned braid beneath her wool-lined hat. Her mother glowered at her as she approached, pointing rigidly down at the basket of soiled garments.

"These should have been washed this morning," her mother scolded. "And look at them: untouched! Now they won't have the noon sun to dry them."

She clicked her tongue and shook her head.

"I expect more from you," her mother continued. "You're not a little girl anymore."

Květa bent to lift the basket up into her arms. The dirty clothing smelled ripely of sweat and chicken manure. What could she do but bow her head and acquiesce? The laundry needed to be done. The horses' hooves needed trimming and shaping. The furnace needed coal and alloy and a sturdy set of hands on the bellows. The earth needed to be tilled, the soil fertilized, the weeds pulled. People lived, people married, people died. And still, the laundry needed to be done. Everyone had their role to play.

As she walked towards the pond on the edge of the village, a dog with a muddy muzzle fell into a trot beside her. Its eyes were watery and bulging in its skull. When Květa knelt by the

166

pond, the dog seemed to lose interest in her altogether. Its tail swayed, distracted, and it went to search a rotted log in the nearby clearing.

Květa emptied the laundry basket into the pond. She watched as the clothes darkened in the green water. A newt with a spotted belly darted away, into the pond murk, disturbed by the rippling clothes on the water's surface.

Květa retrieved each article of clothing one by one and wrung them free of pond water. She dropped them into the nearby washing basin, which was filled then with bonfire ash and smelled of stale urine. She prodded at the clothing idly with a twig, watching it swirl and discolour in the basin.

Would this be what her life was like every day after her mother had finished weaving the last towel, she intended to give with her dowry to Jaromir? Rinsing her husband-to-be's hunt-soiled clothing every morning until one day when her hands were dry and bone thin? Rinsing and rinsing until she herself dissolved into the pond water, into the stinking ammonia basin? Bone and sinew and organs, all swirling together in the linens. Perfectly clean. Perhaps this was how girls became *vodyanitsa*, one of the unquiet spirits of the river.

The dog with the bulging white eyes returned again. Tail wagging, it dropped a gummy pink filament at Květa's feet. It looked like some sort of root. Frowning, Květa knelt to get a better look.

It was not a root.

It was the connecting stalk of a human eyeball, with the white orb membrane all but chewed. The hazel iris was still partially visible.

Květa recoiled at first. But given the pile of unwholesome meat she'd seen in the field earlier, maybe it wasn't too strange. Another leftover from the mound of meat at the top of the hill.

The dog butted its head against her knee, eager for praise for bringing such a unique gift. Reluctantly, Květa gave the dog a brief scratch behind the ears. The dog gave her a slow, mouthy lick before trotting off again.

Květa had never been very fond of dogs. They barked and tracked mud over the rugs. If she spent too much time around them, she sneezed and developed hives on her forearm.

She wondered if Jaromir had dogs. She didn't know all that much about Jaromir. Not beyond the fact that he was a nobleman, and a renowned huntsman. Surely, he brought a pack of dogs with him to flush out wild boar and foxes from the brush. A pack of six or seven slavering hunting dogs, all of them smelly and nipping at her heels as they pushed and whined and demanded attention. It wasn't a very pleasing image.

There was a sudden shout from the village. Květa stood, clutching at her *oplicko* skirt. The timbre of the shout made her blood run cold in her throat. The laundry would have to wait.

As she approached the village thoroughfare, it was clear a crowd had been drawn in by the scream, too. They milled, they paced, they murmured; a hot wall of bodies. Květa had to push through to see beyond the taller field labourers grouped at the front. In the centre of the throng on a muddy embankment, a man lay flat and unmoving. His fingers were curled in a frigid rigor mortis. His eyes were wide open, the whites red like seared meat and swollen in their sockets. The man's skin was flushed with a sheen of sweat and he appeared almost red, as if he'd just drunk several tankards of beer. Spittle flecked his lips.

"*Poludnitsa*," whispered an old woman near Květa in a hoarse voice. She held a walking stick close to her chest, her hands quivering around its wooden shaft. Květa glanced back

168

at her, but the old woman would not meet anyone's eyes. She just shook her head at the ground. *"Poludnitsa, poludnitsa* has returned."

A woman collapsed at the dead man's side; her arms wrapped over his chest. She began to rock back and forth, shivering, keening. Presumably, this was his wife. Květa wondered if she would, someday, feel this way for Jaromir, too.

"Where did you find him?" The potter called above the sobs of the woman.

"He was with us in the fields," answered another of the field labourers. The man twisted his wool cap with uncertainty in his hands. "He was fine this morning."

"Call everyone in," the priest suggested, his face solemn behind his long beard. "No one should be out in the fields right now. This is an ill omen."

"The buckwheat will go to seed and make the fields fallow and weedy," another field labourer protested. "It has to be picked soon."

The priest was resolute, though. "Not today," he said. He shook his head, simultaneously directing a parishioner to place a cloth over the dead labourer's body. "If you disobey this curfew, more deaths will follow. This is the work of an unclean spirit."

"Poludnitsa!" The old woman with the cane cried suddenly.

She clutched at her heart and began to suck in great tremulous breaths. Her hysterics diverted the crowds' attention and the widow who grieved the dead labourer wailed louder. The priest pushed Květa back with a large grey palm to stand beside the frantic old woman. Květa was just another gawking body in the way. The priest set a hand on the old woman's shoulder and instructed her to repeat a hymn with him, word by word, syllable by syllable.

The crowd undulated, uncertain.

Poludnitsa. The lady of the midday sun. The wraith who stalked the fields, gleaming sickle in hand, and struck down those poor souls who toiled there. *Poludnitsa*, the bright death. The one who asked girls to dance with her until the sun set and their bodies collapsed in chthonic exhaustion.

Some in the crowd lit sticks of incense to ward off the unclean spirits, others anointed themselves with rose oil. The widow was being consoled by two sallow-faced women. A man with a dishevelled ginger beard stared between the gathering parishioners, the priest, and the tearful, hiccupping widow. Children paused their games to watch the scene unravel from a distant wooden alcove.

People waited, people whispered.

Five days passed. Five able-bodied men died.

Every day at the sun's zenith, a new body was found, in much the same condition as the field labourer before them. They weren't all field labourers, though. On the second day, the blacksmith's apprentice was found dead. On the fourth day, it was an Ottoman janissary who had only been passing through. The priest ordered two woodsmen to haul all of the dead into the field. So that they might rest under the full glare of the noon sun and be cleansed. This, he said, would appease the malevolent spirit.

Květa could feel the unease of the other villagers. They stayed out of the fields. They let the buckwheat and summer squash brown and wilt and draw gnats. If they had to be outside, people kept their heads down, shoulders hunched. No one looked anyone else in the eyes.

Jaromir visited on the sixth day, and no one died that day. He rode into town on a dark Karabair mare. The day was hot and the horse was sweating and snorting. When Jaromir removed its saddle, a lathered white foam had collected on its hide.

Květa was invited to join him by the pond for an afternoon meal. She had never been alone with him before, but her mother appeared unconcerned, and so she agreed. He likely thought the waterside location was charming, so Květa did not mention that this was the pond that all of the villagers brought their dirty laundry to on wash days. Noblemen had all the time in the world if they found ways to admire ugly grey algae and itchy pondside reeds. The wine and spicy caraway bread he brought with him were quite nice, though.

"I can't wait any longer to have you by my side," Jaromir professed. His cheeks were hot and red from the wine. Květa moved to take another slice of bread, but he gripped her wrist. Forced her to face him. "I don't care about the dowry or the ceremony of it all. I just want you up on the mountain with me."

He slid a hand on to Květa's thigh. The metal pinch of his many rings left red imprints on her skin. Květa tried to brush off his prurient grip, but he dug in his nails. It occurred to her then that it wasn't the beauty of the pond so much as its seclusion that Jaromir had desired.

"We're soon to be wed," he reminded her, his breath hot and ripe in her ear. "It won't matter what we do now."

Jaromir played with the delicate red thread hemming of her shirt collar before he leaned to lick at the base of her neck. His tongue was as moist and humid as a dog's. When Květa moved to push him back again, he only advanced. He slid a knee between her legs to part them. And then a sweaty hand.

There was a crackling sound, like a splintering log, and a heat not unlike the glowing eye of a forge.

Jaromir fell on top of her then, his mouth drooling against

her shoulder, his eyes fixed on some invisible point in space. He was nearly twice her size, his body now completely numb, and it took all of her strength to claw at the soil and pull herself out from beneath him. Her clothing was stained with the jagged wet patterns of the grass.

Jaromir's body radiated heat.

A woman in a white linen caftan stood at the edge of the pond. Her eyes and mouth were only smooth indents, as if the skin had been stretched like a drum membrane over her facial features. Her hair was bleached and fell at her shoulders in dry, wheat-like piles. She held a rusty sickle in one hand.

Poludnitsa. Poludnitsa has returned.

Wordless, the woman in the white caftan approached. It was impossible to determine her expression. Květa felt her heartbeat rise in her throat. From fear or excitement, it was impossible for her to determine.

In a gentle extension of her arm, the woman offered Květa her sickle. Květa stared down at the dull metal tool set into a crude bone handle. She took the hilt and held it in one hand. Felt the grave heft of it in her palm. What craftsman originally made this tool? It had seen the wear of many hands and many harvests.

When Květa looked up again, if only to make some kind of acknowledgement of the gift, the woman was gone.

Květa thought only briefly of the dowry she would leave behind. Surely the towels could be sold at the market. Her mother had put a decent amount of effort into the stitch work. Maybe someday the towels might serve as a dowry for another girl, wed to a nobleman or a soldier or a baker. And maybe this matchmaking would be successful. Those same towels might one day wrap the fragile body of a newborn child.

It was almost surprising how easily the sickle's curved

blade fit around Květa's inner thigh. The metal was old and rusted, but still sharp. It did not protest against the weight of her skin. It slid right through to make a perfect filet. The sickle could cut straight through tendon and bone. But it was still tiring work. Her knuckles shook, her resolve faltered. But seeing her own blood run down her ankle reinvigorated her.

The most important work was tiring.

It might even take until the sun set and rose again before each of her limbs, each digit, each organ was severed. All of this bone and fat and viscera, chaotic by its nature, collected into one neat pile.

A Walk Before Lunch

Matt Thompson

Halfway between breakfast and lunch it was suggested—by who, Nadine could never recall—that they all go out for a walk to get a breath of fresh air. Tom's parents brought the dogs along. Ever since she and Tom had arrived the animals hadn't let her get near them. Today the two shorthaired pointers, Saffron and Cynthia, bared their teeth and growled when she came within touching distance. Blix, the larger Weimaraner, sported coarse grey hair that turned to white on his belly. Once they were out of the grounds and into the adjacent meadow, he stopped dead and stared at her, holding his gaze until she turned away.

Tom didn't notice. Jayne had taken possession of him already, her arm around her son's shoulders in a gesture both protective and hostile. Lewis whistled as he walked. They strode ahead onto the public footpath leading into the low surrounding hills, leaving Nadine lagging behind.

She was glad of the solitude. At the crest of the first rise she turned back. Tom's family home looked even grander from up here, the grounds a brilliant green in the clear summer air. The few residences nearby were situated behind forbidding vehicle gates. The area had the feel of an enclave, a private community. When they arrived, she'd expressed her surprise at the size of the property. Tom had only laughed. "Don't look so nervous. You'll like them, Nadi. Dad worked his socks off to get all this. We hardly saw him when I was growing up." He gave her a brief kiss. "I wouldn't have brought you if I didn't think you were worth it. Okay? So don't worry."

But that had been two days ago, and she'd hardly seen him since then. "Family business," he'd said when she asked. She put up with the endless visits from relatives she couldn't remember the names of, and lengthy meal preparations she found herself inveigled into helping with. Jayne and Lewis were friendly enough. But it was as if her capacity for decision-making was being eroded one meal, one conversation at a time. She'd often thought that Tom had been avoiding introducing her to his family. He'd said it was because she wasn't ready for them. She assumed that meant he was, in some way, embarrassed by her. But now she was getting an inkling of what he'd meant.

Lewis hung back and fell into step beside her. He'd shucked on a tweed jacket for the excursion. They were halfway up a small rise, the dirt path flanked by shrubs and reeds. The heat from the syrupy late-summer sun had generated a bead of sweat that dangled precipitously on his overhanging upper lip. He wiped it away, leaving a white salt streak along his moustache. "So," he said. Nadine set her face into an attitude of inquisitive politeness. "You two met through work, I hear."

He picked his words out carefully, as if they had teeth.

Nadine wondered what meaning was hidden behind them. "Yes, he was a freelance contractor and I was on the sales team. We worked together on—"

Before she could finish her sentence a pair of birds erupted from a clump of bushes at the crest of the rise, screeching in alarm. Their bright red feathers were scored with deep blue streaks that looked almost painted-on.

"Oh, there they go. Horrible bloody things." Lewis picked up a flat stone and made as if to throw it. "Don't you think? Like furtive little dinosaurs. What goes on in those skulls? Nothing good, I'd wager."

The birds were too high to reach with the stone. He dropped it at his feet and scanned the sky. Nadine felt suddenly protective. "They're beautiful. I've never seen colours like that."

A volley of barks rang out from ahead. "O-ho!" Lewis grinned. One of his front teeth was a dull yellow. "Might not be a wasted walk after all."

Nadine wanted to ask what he meant. But the birds had been joined by more, seven or eight in total, their plumages like blood squibs against the deep blue sky. She hurried over the rise, almost sprinting to catch up with Tom. He was standing with his mother in a small clearing, an open space beside the path bordered by a semi-circle of thorn bushes. "What do you think, Nadi?" he said, drawing her to him. His eyes shone. The dogs strained at their leashes. "Ever seen one of these guys at work?"

"We're on a hunt?" The last thing she wanted to see was some poor item of wildlife torn into shreds by the slavering hounds.

"Don't *worry*, dear." Jayne smiled. "You can watch, for now. Ready, Tom?"

The birds skimmed low over the trees and circled around

to land. Tom unclipped the dogs' leads in unison, as if the gesture were long-practised. They scampered into the undergrowth as one, a hunting pack intent on only one thing. Nadine shivered. Tom gave her elbow a little squeeze and shot her a warning glance.

The sun beat down fiercer than ever; or maybe she was sweating anyway. Lewis clapped Tom on the shoulder. "Reckon they'll bring us something back?" he said. Jayne folded her hands and gazed at Nadine, her smile tighter than before.

"Seems they've got a scent," Tom said, to murmurs of assent from his parents.

Jayne laughed, showing too-large teeth. "They go for the weakest of the flock, did you know that?"

Nadine blinked perspiration from her eyes. "What are those birds? Parrots?"

"We're not in the tropics, love," Jayne said. "You get lots of them out here. Plenty to go around."

A warm breeze ruffled Nadine's hair. The earth emanated heat, rippling waves rising into her body and seeping along the pathways of her muscles and veins. Her head swam. "I'd like to go back," she said. "If it's okay."

"They'll be with us in a sec," Lewis said. "Seems like a good day. You don't always get a good day. Best to make the most of it."

He whacked at the ground with his hiking stick. A cloud of insects rose from the grass, enfolding Nadine in a miasma of tiny wings. She swiped them away. Tom flapped his hand until they were gone. She wondered if he'd return to the house with her right now, if she asked. That might not be a challenge she was likely to win. They'd be back to the city soon enough, where red birds didn't screech at you and dogs only hunted squirrels in the park.

She closed her eyes. Indeterminate blobs undulated across her line of sight. She smelled honeysuckle. The breeze came again, warmer this time. A low hum of conversation circled around her, stray words drifting past untethered.

She stumbled, almost falling. Opening her eyes didn't help. The blobs were all she could see. No one was talking now. At the moment her vision finally cleared a squall of noise came from the far side of the clearing. A flash of grey; and the dogs burst from the bushes, racing toward them like darting insects. Saffron held something between her teeth, something red. She dropped the bird at Lewis's feet. Blood dripped from the creature's torn throat, smeared across the dog's teeth and tongue.

"Good *girl*," Lewis said, massaging Saffron's flank. Blix and Cynthia whined and pawed the dirt, limbs trembling with excitement. "Looks like a young 'un," he said to Tom. "Fresh."

"What do you think, Nadine?" Jayne said. Her smile was a rictus now, her jaw rigid. "Beautiful, isn't it?"

"I..." Nadine swallowed. Her mouth tasted of rubber. "Are you going to bury it?"

"Bury it?" Lewis shot her a look of scorn. Tom wasn't holding her now. The sun disappeared behind a cloud. She wrapped her arms around herself, suddenly chilled.

"Don't think Saffron would be too pleased if we did that," Tom said in a soft voice. "Would she?"

"Well, who's in charge here?" Nadine replied. "The dogs or us?"

She tried to make it come out light and jocular; but her tone betrayed her, and no one was smiling. Not even Jayne, who said, "Why don't you pick it up?"

Nadine wished she could follow the trail; follow it back home where it must surely be lunchtime by now. Her stomach rumbled. Lewis narrowed his eyes, as if she had said or done something untrustworthy.

Tom laid a gentle hand onto her shoulder, increasing his pressure until she was forced to her knees in the dusty soil. Lewis grasped Saffron's leash and eased her back, away from the twitching form of the dying bird. Its feathers were an even brighter red close-up, almost scarlet. Nadine wondered what species it was. Its beak, a dulled gold, was chipped at the tip. A crack extended along the enamel almost to its face. One of its eyelids flickered a few times as it died. She supposed there was no point in refusing whatever was asked of her now. It could hardly make a difference.

She lifted it from the dirt. Saffron growled, her jaws slavering. "*Good* girl," Lewis near-whispered. "*Good* girl." Nadine raised the dead bird to eye level.

"They don't taste so bad, Nadi," Tom said. "Honest."

It was as if her life had flipped around in the space of a few minutes, reversing its steady course so that right was wrong and wrong was right. Fatigue clawed at her limbs. "You...you want me to—"

"Waste not want not, eh?" Lewis chuckled. His voice was splintering ice. "Couple of bites should do it."

Nadine's vision narrowed to a point; just she and the dead bird existed, along with the distant sound of a light aircraft and the rustle of wind in the treetops and the sound of her saliva swilling in her mouth; the feel of drool on her chin, the smell of feathers and oil and dog fur. Tom was still holding her down. She didn't suppose he'd let up until she'd done what they were asking.

She opened her mouth and bit down.

"*Good* girl," Lewis said to the dog. "Hush now." Saffron wheezed, ears flat against her skull. Feathers filled Nadine's mouth. The bird tasted like no meat she'd ever eaten. Sense impressions flooded her, flashes of coloured light and the half-memory of yawning voids, howling wind. Someone else inhabited her body now, a stranger who tugged at the flesh with their incisors, shearing the meat away in stringy chunks. Blood bubbled beneath her tongue. Her gums ached. The bird's beak poked into her cheek, sharp and cold.

Tom stood before her. She met his eyes. He stared back without expression, his hair ruffling in the breeze like leaves, like he was a gnarled, ancient tree come to hideous life, jealous of this interloper who'd stolen one of his tenants without permission, without apology.

Nadine begged off the evening gathering to take an early night. Their stuffy room, stuck like an afterthought at the top of the house, had an en-suite bathroom, for which she was eternally glad. Since morning she'd felt the bird-flesh swilling in her stomach like some alien egg-sac. She pictured enzymes breaking it down, acids dissolving its structure and spiriting its essence into her body. Her gut still hurt. Her sphincter muscles strained, sweat dampening her jeans and pooling in the small of her back.

While she was still with the family she hadn't dared complain. No one said a thing to her on the way back to the house, Tom included. The dogs followed Lewis placidly to their kennels, only Saffron giving her a sidelong glance as she was led away.

The events in the clearing flitted in and out of her memory. Had she really torn the dead bird's flesh with her own teeth? Recollections loomed like fragments of a dream, now as solid and real as the house surrounding her, now as ephemeral as a gauzy, tremulous mist. She was scared at her own passivity, her vulnerability to persuasion. It wasn't like her. Or: it wasn't like she *believed* herself to be.

She sat slumped in an overstuffed armchair for most of the afternoon, experiencing the waning heat in a half-slumbering state. Just after four o'clock she uncoiled herself to check her phone; but it wasn't upstairs where it should have been, and Tom was nowhere to be found, so she returned to her chair and dozed.

Tom nodded distractedly when she said she wouldn't be joining them for dinner. Once upstairs she pulled the curtains shut and headed for the bathroom. Everything she'd been bottling up came out as soon as she leaned over the sink; endless reams of it, the stench imbued with something almost sweet. A sharp pain wrenched at her. A feather, bedraggled with yellow mucus, lay at the crown of the mess she'd produced, its crimson hue as bright as ever.

She washed it all away, changed into her nightwear and slid into bed. The taste of bird flesh lingered on her tongue. The pillow was as soft as down, as malleable as skin. She was asleep within seconds.

The struggle back to wakefulness came in sluggish stages. No light penetrated the thick curtains. The only illumination came from the luminous clock hands on the bedside cabinet saying 3:00. Tom lay beside her, his breathing deep and even. A rattle issued from his throat; once, twice. Her brain-fuzz cleared, a little; enough for her to realise the noise was coming from outside the bedroom door, not from Tom. Something scrabbled at the wood. A low growl sounded, followed by another at a higher pitch.

Which of the dogs was it? Her stomach felt bloated again. Tom's breathing quieted. Paws padded on the hallway carpet. Again the growl, lessened now but all the more menacing for it. The paws halted their patrol. A whistling whine clawed at her ears, dying down when the stalking started back up, the animals criss-crossing the entrance in rhythmic, measured march.

She drifted back to slumber with the sound of them swelling in her consciousness, the bird-meat a glutinous lump in the pit of her gut, red feathers riffling across her line of sight as the sun beat down and Tom's parents encouraged her to take another bite.

At the breakfast table Lewis announced they'd be going for a walk again. Nadine suppressed a groan. Out on the landing dog hair had been notable by its absence. Had she imagined the events of the previous night, or even the previous day?

But her stomach still ached. The taste memory of the bird flesh lay on her tongue, unmoved by the toast and eggs and coffee. Jayne poured her another cup, despite her protestations. Dark brown grains swilled against the China. The liquid left a trail of residue as it coursed down her throat, causing her to choke. Tom glanced at her with benign concern. "Okay, Nadi?"

Nadine wondered if she'd be able to stay here if she told them she wasn't feeling well. But maybe it would seem rude; like the kind of thing Tom might hold against her. Senses dulled by her new-found passivity, she munched on soggy toast as Jayne and Lewis discussed the finer points of purebred dog breeding.

The weather was as hot, hotter even, than the previous day. They followed the same course, past the meadow and onto the footpath. Blix kept pace beside her from the moment they left. When she reached down to ruffle his coat he shied away. Had he been outside her door last night? He loped along without turning his head left or right. A thin sliver of drool hung from his jaws. She wondered what he might do if she tried to wipe it away.

There was no sign of the red birds as they approached the

rise. Tom held her hand as they walked past the spot where she had consumed the dead creature. "The path comes out by the coast," he said. "A mile or so down. Then on to Pendle. That's the next village—"

"Tom?"

"Hmm?"

She couldn't think of what to say. Who eats raw animal flesh like that? She might have caught something, some bacterial infection or worse. Lewis and Jayne were fifty yards ahead, walking arm-in-arm. Was this some initiation ritual, a humiliation meted out to those who dared challenge the authority of their family unit?

Was she the first?

The whole thing had seemed planned. Saffron padded past, an almost inaudible grumble issuing from her thick lips. They'd trapped her like the dog had trapped the bird in her sharp, sharp teeth. Unable to escape, she'd done their bidding like a servant, a slave. And Tom?

Tom had done nothing to help. Not to help *her*, anyway. It was like she'd never known him. She shook her head to try and clear away the tatter of cobwebs ensnaring her thoughts. The sun was fierce today, and she'd stupidly forgotten to bring a hat. The sound of blood hissed in her ears. From some distant place the spit of waves undulated, the two noises resonating around her skull. Blix, beside her still, stiffened. Saffron and Cynthia trotted away toward a line of trees a hundred feet from the path.

Tom leaned close, his breath warm. "Wait for it."

Nadine stopped dead. Jayne and Lewis stood motionless ahead of them. A halo of sunlight crowned their heads in gold. She strained her ears. A whisper of flight emerged from the blood-noise within her, a ruffle of oily feathers, a faraway memory of wings and air.

Nothing moved. Blix whined. Tom bent down to comfort him, his voice a low murmur.

A *crack* rang out. A bird burst from behind the treeline. Then another; red, bright, bright red, its feathers catching the light like the glistening of exposed flesh.

In a storm of colour the flock came; nine, ten, twelve, desperately lunging for the sky as Blix wrenched free and hared toward them, legs pumping across the grass in a fuzzy blur. One of the birds faltered. Low it came, too low, as if Blix were summoning it to earth and oblivion.

The dog leapt. A thump, and the bird flapped on the ground, stunned. Saffron and Cynthia pounced before it had the chance to collect itself and escape. The hounds fought for a moment, snarling and tossing their heads, a wing in each of their jaws, until Lewis called out and Cynthia retreated, still protesting.

Blix picked himself up from the dirt and trotted back to them, his head held high. The sun shone, remorseless. The family watched on, as Nadine allowed Tom to force her downward that she might receive her gift. She knew there was no purpose in resistance. The part of her that might have refused had drawn back, cowering away from the red thing that squirmed between Saffron's long teeth, viscera dribbling onto the dog's coat.

Tom and Jayne and Lewis stood in a semi-circle around her. Saffron dropped the dying bird at her knees. One of its wings was broken, circling uselessly as she lifted it as tenderly as she were able.

"*Good* girl." Saffron went to Lewis's side. Jayne petted her, not taking her eyes from Nadine for one moment. "*Good* girl. Aren't you?"

The bird's flesh was warm, almost hot. Nadine turned it over, exposing its breast. The feathers there were a darker red. Streaks of white excrement marred the smooth line of its torso. Nadine brushed the mess away and wiped her soiled fingers on the grass. Her head throbbed. Blix lay on his paws; brown eyes fixed on hers. She opened her mouth, opened it as wide as she were able, wide enough to admit the bulk of the bird's breast between her teeth, her jaw cracking as the flesh tore away and the blood squirmed beneath her tongue and into her throat.

That night she craved intimacy, but Tom turned away. She reached around to caress him. "Come on," she murmured. Wetness seeped into her nightwear. "Give me something back."

"Just go to sleep," he muttered.

"Come *on*." Downstairs, a door slammed. "No one'll hear. Who cares, anyway?"

After a brief pause, during which she hoped he was mulling her offer over, his breathing steadied into the rhythms of sleep. She rolled back over in disgust. She'd slept through most of the afternoon, assailed by dreams of crashing waves and distant, barely-seen figures. The dogs had avoided her during the evening. Blix's nose quivered when she tried to pet him. Saffron and Cynthia shied away, tense and hostile.

On the cusp of sleep the unmistakable sound of padding paws drifted in from the landing. She sat bolt upright, staring into the darkness. A scratching sounded against the door. Claws raked down the grain of the wood, accompanied by irregular wheezing. She shook Tom. He only grunted and pushed her hand away.

She waited. Another dog joined the first one, their paws patting insect-like at the door. Minutes passed by until she comprehended that the sound wasn't coming from that direction any longer. Something was outside the window,

186

scrabbling against the glass. She tiptoed silently across the carpet and risked a peep through the curtains.

A rush of colour; and a bird hurled itself into the overcast night, a cloud of bright red feathers drifting in its wake.

Nadine stifled a cry. Movement came from the courtyard. Something slipped across the concrete, a dark, elongated shape advancing too fast for her eyes to follow.

The security light snapped on. Blix stared at her, his ears pricked up. A few metres away Saffron and Cynthia sat on their haunches. The door to the kennels compound swung open. Their gazes didn't falter; wet eyes fixed on her as she stared back at them. She felt exposed, outlined there against the window. Was this how it had been for the birds they'd hunted down?

Blix barked, once, his eyes not leaving her for a moment. Saffron and Cynthia were as motionless as statues. The afterimage of their figures lingered long after the security light flipped off and she returned to bed. The padding feet on the landing returned after a while, lulling her into a deep sleep intermittently disturbed by what she thought was the cry of birds, circling above the house until dawn sent them back to their faraway nests.

She knew there would be a walk before lunch. Her phone was long gone, and she didn't bother looking for it. As the clock in the hallway struck eleven Lewis said, "Ready for another jaunt? I was thinking we could go further this time."

"Out to Pendle?" Jayne looked doubtful. "And get back how?"

"Oh, not that far, not that far. But maybe part of the way there. You won't tire, will you?"

He said this last to Nadine. Before she could reply Tom interjected: "She'll be fine. We've got the dogs, anyway."

Nadine wondered if she should ask what was meant by that. Or would it make things worse? She could have run the five miles back to the train station if necessary. But she, and they, knew she didn't have the fortitude. Not anymore.

The morning, which had been overcast, was turning to sun. A light coastal breeze wafted the cloud cover away, revealing a deep azure sky unmarred by anything other than a distant bird of prey, far, far above them. They tramped along the usual route, Jayne just in front of her and Lewis a few feet behind. So I can't go back, she mused.

So I can't get away.

Tom was ahead of her. He hadn't once turned around, just to see if she was okay. A sick dread rose inside her, catching in her throat. She would be forced to consume another bird today. Already she could see them. They passed an old oak, towering high above its neighbours. Twenty or thirty of them lined the branches, their intermittent cries echoing through the trees. Another few landed as they passed. It was as if the seasons had cycled around early, an autumnal spread of redness that almost hurt her eyes to look at it.

They tramped alongside the clearing, and then onward past the point where she had consumed yesterday's bird. The path twisted and turned, leading through tunnels of vegetation and alongside gnarled roots, moss-coated protuberances arcing from the earth in a tangle of bark. The screeching intensified. Lewis still dogged her steps, hoarse breath catching in his throat. The odour of pipe tobacco exuded from him. Jayne wore crimson breeches today, tucked into her sensible walking shoes as if she were expecting to have to protect herself against some sudden gush of fluid. Nadine had lost sight of the dogs. Maybe they wouldn't be set loose today. Maybe the birds outnumbered them so profoundly they'd win the battle on volume alone.

They climbed yet another low rise. Trees loomed close on both sides of the path. Nadine stumbled on a concealed root. Lewis caught her, his grip shockingly firm. "Steady, girl," he said. "Steady now."

The overhanging vegetation ceased with whiplash suddenness, the sun blinding her for a moment as she emerged from the gloom. They were stood at the crest of a dip in the landscape. A small dell, bounded by tightly-packed thickets, undulated into another rise a hundred metres along. Shapes, down below her, took form: Jayne, standing beside the path, Tom down on his haunches, stroking the quivering figures of the two Pointers. A red shape lay on the grass in front of them. Blix sat near enough to let them all know the prize was his to distribute, his to take back if he so desired.

Nadine approached them without speaking, her guard of honour melting away as she came closer. What would be the purpose in resisting, out here in the middle of nowhere? Blix bared his teeth when she knelt down. Saliva streamed from his mouth, pooling on the grass as he panted and grumbled.

Tom squinted up at her. "Got you a young one," he said. He caressed Cynthia's muzzle, her wet nose twitching. "Should be tender."

The bird was still alive. A single tree overlooked the clearing. Less than ten of its companions looked on from the spindly branches. She'd expected more. It was almost a disappointment, this sparse crowd for her moment of glory.

She caressed the scarlet plumage around its throat. Blank, indifferent, she raised the creature to her lips and bit into its haunches, worrying the meat loose as it thrashed and died in her sweaty grip. Cynthia moaned, sounding almost human. "*Good* girl," Lewis said, his voice tight and rough. "Good girl."

Nadine sucked the internal organs loose, letting them

slide over her tongue before she chewed them into mush. Tom looked on without expression. The sun caught his light brown hair so that it shone, wreathing his figure until he was enveloped in radiance, his parents looking on in proud approval at the blood that spilled down her shirt and soaked into her crotch, the stench of viscera clogging in her nostrils until it drowned out the surrounding honeysuckle odour and extended its tendrils deep into her throat.

They fucked that night, a violent, unprotected coupling that neither and both of them instigated. When they were done Nadine rolled over, letting his semen seep out onto the sheets.

Tom slept almost immediately. That was fine. They had nothing to say to each other now. She waited, there in the dark, for the inevitable scratching at the door. When it didn't come, she walked naked to the window and pulled back the drapes.

The sky was clear tonight, the moon bright. The dogs were sat waiting for her. Blix was at the front, his paws resting on a small, writhing object. Even from three floors up she could see the redness, the pale moonlight illuminating enough of it for her to be sure.

Saffron trotted forward, almost to the wall of the house. The security lamps snapped on all across the courtyard. Three pairs of eyes shone in the divulging gleam, unblinking lanterns beckoning her onward, the question they were asking impossible to answer by means of language.

Tom groaned and stirred. She could feel him inside her still, his issue sticky on her thighs, his breath coarse on her breasts, tongue and lips suckling at her flesh as if he wished to draw her inside him. She didn't turn around. His work was done. Her insides no longer ached. She fancied she could feel the tickle of feathers along her stomach lining, bird heart and

190

bird spleen and bird claws dissolving into pulp within the folds of her gut. A faint echo of nausea rose in her throat. She swallowed it back down, a tide of acid retreating from the exposing latitudes of her mouth.

The lamps clicked off. Saffron stirred, turning in a tight circle until the light came back on. A solitary bird skimmed the wall separating the yard from the meadow beyond. Nadine watched its wings beating like pistons, its desperate flight to freedom. When it was gone, she turned her attention back to the dogs.

Blix pawed the ground; once, twice. Nadine eased the drapes shut and went to the door, not bothering to get dressed. The landing lay in darkness. She descended the stairs without thought, her mind as blank as a blue summer sky, the carpet as soft underfoot as a grassy meadow, as a bed of feathers and fur.

When the River Flows Three Times

Gary Couzens

I take a picture of Esme asleep in her Moses basket and send it to my family and work WhatsApp groups. Esme's eyes move under closed lids. What does a three-month-old baby dream of? Everything is new, nothing routine yet. I'm scrolling through my phone when the doorbell rings.

The woman I met briefly yesterday is standing on the doorstep, a bunch of white and red roses in her hand. Her hair, almost all white, is loose to her shoulder blades; she is a little taller than me and slenderer. "Hello," she says. "I thought I'd say welcome properly as I'm your neighbour." She thrusts the roses into my hand and extends her other hand. "I'm Marilyn."

"Oh, they're lovely, Marilyn," I say. "Thank you very much.

Would you like to come in? I was just about to put the kettle on—would you like a tea or coffee?"

"That would be very nice indeed. I'd love a cup of tea. You're not too busy, are you?"

"I should carry on unpacking, shouldn't I? While Madam's asleep. But I was going to do that this afternoon. Little and often. Coffee might help me stay awake."

We go through to the kitchen. Marilyn bends over Esme's basket. "Oh she's gorgeous."

"She's had a feed and a poo, so she's sorted for now. Simples."

I make two cups of tea and cut Marilyn a slice of the gingerbread cake Matt and I bought on the way here, knowing it'll give me an excuse not to eat it all myself. "Matt's at work. His paternity leave's finished. I thought I might give birth after we moved here, but the move took so long."

"Always the way, eh? I moved here with my husband forty years ago. My daughter thinks I should move in with her and sell my house, but I don't want to. I'll be here until I get too decrepit. I like it here." Sat on a wooden chair, she sips at her hot tea. "I hope there won't be too many old people for you here. Most of the younger people in the village are those running the shops and the pub. Even the vicar's in his sixties." She looks up. "Fee...your husband called you Fee...?"

"It's Phoebe, but everyone calls me that. A lot of people can't spell Phoebe." Naila, my girlfriend for a year at university, called me Pho, hence her taking me to a local Vietnamese place for my birthday.

"Oh, I know how to spell it. It's much nicer." She raises her cup, as if toasting me. "Fee sounds like you owe somebody something. Phoebe was a titan in Greek mythology—associated with prophecy and the Moon. Did you know that?"

"I didn't. I think Mum and Dad just liked the name."

She laughs. "My parents named me after Marilyn Monroe. I never looked anything like her. I wish." She stands and gazes out of the window at the road, completely quiet at this time of day. "Just as well you've got a car. You'll need one. The bus stops at six but hardly anyone uses it. The nearest trains are three quarters of an hour's drive away. You can thank Dr Beeching for that. I guess you'll need to drive to work eventually."

"I'm on maternity leave, but I work in IT. I've been working from home since the pandemic anyway. That's what Matt and I worked out when we planned for a baby. All I need is decent broadband, but they haven't connected us yet." I yawn. "Sorry, Esme's not sleeping through the night yet. Matt was the one who wanted to live in the country as he grew up there. His dad died last year, so we sold his house and that's how we could buy this place. And the locals seem friendly."

Marilyn chuckles. "Oh, we are. We're mostly women, mostly widows actually. But we're happy to welcome a newcomer. We're always round each other's houses and Wednesday afternoons in the pub. You're very welcome to join us, you and Esme. You'll be a local before you know it."

Matt arrives home after six o'clock, an hour's drive each way for him. Unlike my bosses, his insisted on returns to the office as soon as possible after lockdown ended, rather than working from home. So the journey to and from work was the price of our relocation to this village and this house.

He kisses me. His suit jacket is over his arm and his tie loosened, his eyes tired as Esme woke us both more than once during the night. Winona, Matt's work colleague, sent us a card when Esme was born saying, *Congratulations—sleep will now be a memory*. When I turned up, heavily pregnant at Matt's work do last Christmas, one of the first things she said to me was that she didn't have a single maternal bone in her body.

"Hey, what's with the roses, Fee?"

"I've got a secret lover." He looks up, surprised. "I work fast. I was going to tell you. Actually, it's Marilyn. We met her yesterday, remember? The older lady next door. She came round with them and we had a cup of tea and a chat."

"The one with long hair?"

"Yes, that's her. She says she's making a stand for long hair in women of a certain age. She liked mine." I wear my hair short, currently dyed blue. "She said she used to wear miniskirts in the Sixties and she'd wear one now if she still had the legs for it."

Matt smiles, but I'm unconvinced by it. At that moment, there's a gurgling noise from the kitchen. Esme has just woken. I pick her up and hand her to Matt. "There you go. Greet your daughter."

"Yes, you're Daddy's little girl, aren't you, Esme? Aren't you beautiful?" As Matt lifts her up, she grins, her legs wriggling. Then he frowns. "Fee, she's done a humongous shit in her nappy. Can't you smell it?"

"Obviously her way of welcoming you home. A little gift for you."

Matt roughly hands her back to me. "Oh, for God's sake. I need a shower anyway. It's too fucking hot right now."

I take Esme away to change her, then put her back in her basket. She soon falls asleep, for which I'm glad. Weariness is a pulsing ache behind one eye. I rest my head in my hands and wait for Matt to come back downstairs. It'll be a microwaved ready meal tonight.

I park Esme's pram behind the pub and carry her inside asleep to the small room behind the bar. In the far corner by the window, sunlight putting half her face in shade, Marilyn waves. There are five others here, all women, all older than me. Marilyn introduces me to everyone, calling me Phoebe rather than Fee.

"Oh she's lovely," says the nearest, in her sixties at a guess, dabbing with her finger at the philtrum above Esme's lip.

"Now, don't get all broody, Lizzie," says Marilyn. "We're all past that sort of thing."

"Speak for yourself." Lizzie turns to me. "I had two children, two girls. The youngest was born here. I'm a grandma three times over now. I love your hair, Phoebe."

"It suits you," says Marilyn. "Mind you, I remember when the only women who ever had blue hair were old ladies with rinses. Not that I'm thinking of anyone in particular… Anyway, take a seat and I'll get you a drink. Glass of wine?"

"Diet Coke, please."

"Johnny the landlord doesn't mind us using this room as long as we buy a few things."

"Johnny's a nice but of middle-aged crumpet," says Lizzie. "I'm a widow and nearly old enough to be his mum and I would. But he's gay. Such a waste. Lovely bum."

"I'm sure his husband doesn't think so," says Marilyn as she leaves the room.

"Do your husbands come here?" I ask.

"Those of us who have them still," says Lizzie. "No, they all think all we do is chat and gossip and knit. While they're talking about the football, of course. It's nice to have some time to ourselves, isn't it? Now they'll think we're all cooing over babies. Well, we are actually."

At that, Esme stirs and begins to cry.

"Uh-oh, I think she wants feeding." I stand but Marilyn, returning from the bar, puts a hand on my shoulder. "No, you sit down. Don't worry about it. Most of us have been there."

I move Esme's head under my intentionally loose top, pushing my bra cup to one side. When I'm alone with Esme, her rhythmic sucking on my nipple relaxes me.

"It's just a normal part of life," says Marilyn. "Nothing objectionable about it. Like eating, drinking, sleeping…"

"Fucking," says Norah, the oldest here, not far off ninety, looking up from her knitting.

Marilyn laughs. "Yes, well some of us still remember that. But yes, that too."

Afterwards, Marilyn walks with me back to our houses.

"I think they liked you," says Marilyn. "Nice to have someone younger around here. Someone actually born in the twenty-first century too."

"Only just."

"Even so. When I first came here, there were people born in the nineteenth. And when they were kids there were likely people here born in the eighteenth. You look well."

"I wish I did," I say. "I'm still baby-chonked. My boobs are enormous and they're always leaking."

"You look fine. Being a little zaftig suits you. That's a lovely word—I learned it when my husband and I were in America. When I was young, being thin was all the fashion. Twiggy, for example. I was never built like a stick insect and you aren't either, Phoebe."

I sigh. "I put a dress on for the first time in ages the other day. Matt said I looked like a sack of potatoes."

Marilyn frowns. "That's not nice. He's not been the one bringing this beautiful baby girl into the world. That's something he could never do. Well, he did have something to do with it, I admit."

We walk past the small pond in the middle of the village. It is long and narrow, with muddy shores on either side, the far end of it in a gap between shrubbery.

"The Moon often rises over the end of that," says Marilyn. "It's almost if it was planned that way. I think of those ancients digging it out, however many centuries ago that was."

"I bet that's a sight. I'd like to see it."

"I'm sure you will, sooner or later."

On Saturday, Winona visits us for dinner. While she parks, Matt stands in the hallway. Through the side window, Marilyn's front room has the light on, with the curtains open as it's still light outside.

"I hope she's not spying on us," he says.

"She knows who's visiting—I told her. She's been around for tea so she knows what the inside of our house looks like."

"You're getting quite pally with her, aren't you?"

"I like her. She likes me. Anyway, it helps to get on with your neighbours, doesn't it?"

Matt opens the door to Winona. She's on her own: we invited her to bring a guest but she said she doesn't have a boyfriend at the moment. Winona is a short woman, slightly built with her hair in a pixie cut, her skirt above the knee, her feet in three-inch heels. I first met her at the Christmas do before last, a few months after Matt and I were married. Even then, standing next to her, before I was even pregnant, I was aware that I was big, broad-shouldered, taking up space. She offers her cheek to Matt and then me to kiss.

I'm cooking tonight, so I go back to the kitchen. The baby monitor sitting on the kitchen unit emits no sound, so Esme is safely asleep upstairs. I've made vegetarian this evening as Winona is one, though neither Matt nor I are.

"I saw *Love Lies Bleeding* the other night," says Winona. "It's very good. Quite strange, actually."

"Kristen Stewart's in it, isn't she?" I say.

"Yes, I'll see *Twilight* in a whole new light now. I was Team

Edward, anyway. I'm not gay but my pal Chantal thought it was really hot."

"That sounds good," says Matt. "Does she get it on with the other girl?"

"Matt…" I say. "Queer women aren't on display for you."

"Do you both get to the cinema much these days?" says Winona.

I shrug. "Not really. Well, no, not since Esme arrived. We went a lot with our Unlimited Cards before we moved, but it's quite a drive now. And there's someone else to consider."

"They do mother and baby showings sometimes. Well, father and baby too—let's not be sexist about it."

"I couldn't think of anything worse," says Matt. "Sitting there trying to watch a movie and thinking how long it'll be before one of the kids kicks off. It'll be streaming for us for the foreseeable."

"Wait until Esme gets old enough to watch things. It'll be *Peppa Pig* or *Hey Duggee* on permanent loop, or whatever the kids watch these days."

As soon as I serve the main course, Esme's cries come from the monitor. I sigh. "Do excuse me."

I hurry upstairs. "You have no sense of occasion, Madam," I say, looking down at Esme in her cot, her face screwed up, mouth open wide, tears glistening on her cheeks. I glance round and shut the door before unzipping my dress. Fortunately Esme settles after being fed and soon goes back to sleep.

"Sorry about that," I say as I return to the dining room. "Emergency order at the milk factory."

Winona looks up, crossing her legs and tugging at her skirt. She and Matt have finished their main course. "Are you sure you want another one?"

"Sometime maybe," I mutter. I've considered going back

on the Pill, but there's little need for it at the moment.

"Do you want to reheat that up in the microwave?" says Matt. I shake my head and eat my dinner.

"I was just showing Matt these," says Winona. She reaches across the table, holding out her phone. "Pictures from Greece." She went with her boyfriend, the one she's apparently just split up with. It looks very warm and sunny. In several shots, Winona is in a bikini. "I don't wear that in the office, I hasten to add."

"I can vouch for that," says Matt.

When Winona leaves, we walk her down to path to her car. We did offer to put her up in the spare room, but she preferred to travel home tonight, even with the long drive. Maybe she didn't want to risk being woken by Esme in the early hours. She kisses us both.

"Good luck on Monday," says Matt.

"Thank you." She turns to me. "Job interview. It'll be promotion if I get it."

"Very best of luck," I say.

"You'll smash it, Winona," says Matt.

She holds up her hand, thin fingers crossed. "Hope you get a good night's sleep, Matt."

I notice she didn't wish me that. As she drives off, she waves at us.

"Oh, she'll get it," says Matt, hands in his pockets. "All things being equal, they'll pick the one who puts *she/her* in the email sig. She's not going to go off and have kids any time soon. I know they can't ask that."

"It shouldn't be just that, surely. Isn't she the best at the job?"

"If she isn't, I don't know who is."

"That's all that should matter, then. It's not as if they'll give the job to the one they want to bang the most, is it?"

"Of course it isn't. I think one of the interviewers is a woman, anyway."

"That's not necessarily a contradiction in terms. Anyway, your boss's mum probably had to leave work when she got married, certainly when she got pregnant. It's not the Seventies anymore, Matt. Good luck to her. It's not a plot by the women to put the men down. Anyway, you didn't apply for the job, did you?"

"No I didn't. I'll stay where I am for the time being."

"Anyway, why did Winona wish you a good night's sleep?"

He sighs. "Naomi gave me a bollocking yesterday. I was dozing off at my desk. She said it was dangerous being so tired behind the wheel of a car."

"And you didn't tell me this?" I don't add, *And you confided in Winona before me?*

"Telling you now. I didn't want to worry you."

"You have now, Matt. Thanks a lot."

He slips his arm about my shoulders. "I do try to have a doze in the staff room in the lunch break. I set the phone alarm to wake me up after half an hour or so. Doesn't always work, though." He takes his arm from my shoulders and walks back to the front door. "I don't know about you, but I'm going to bed. I am so fucking shattered."

I stay outside for a little while, idly scrolling through my phone as I perch myself on the outside wall. When I stand up to go back into the house, Marilyn waves at me as she closes the curtains.

"Tea up," says Marilyn, bringing in a tray with three cups and a plate of biscuits. Opposite me in her front room is Norah, her walking stick resting against the arm of her chair. "Get that down you," Marilyn says to her.

Above the mantelpiece is a framed print I haven't seen

before, of Marilyn and her husband, taller than her and bearded, arm about her waist. Behind them in the distance is Uluru. Marilyn sees me looking at it.

"Oh, I found that the other day. I thought I'd better hang it up. Ayers Rock we called it then. You can't see all the flies in this picture. They were brutal."

"You look young and in love," says Norah.

"Oh we were. I think I was preggers then, didn't know it though. We took an excursion there, wanted to do it while we could. Five hours each way from Alice Springs. A very long day."

"Did you live in Australia, then?" I ask.

"We were there five years. My husband was working in Alice. It so hot in the summer. My son was born there." She takes a sip of her tea, dunks a biscuit. "They say if you see the Todd River flowing three times, you're a local. We only managed it once. Then we came home. My daughter was born here. Conceived here too, in this very house."

"The bull comes to the cow," says Norah.

"I'm sorry…?" I say.

"The bull comes inside the cow."

"Yes, thank you, Norah," says Marilyn. "We all know how it works."

"And then the bull…"

"Yes, okay. Let's let him have his moments of pleasure, though. He's done his job."

I frown. "How did your husband die, if you don't mind me asking, Marilyn? He looks about the same age as you."

"Two years older. He had an accident, fell over and hit his head and never recovered consciousness."

"I'm so sorry."

She shrugs. "That was it. All over in a second. It was a long time ago, now."

203

"My husband had an accident too," says Norah. "He was electrocuted, before my very eyes." And she begins to cry. I hurry over to her, hold her. Her tears stop and she dabs at her eyes with a handkerchief. Esme is asleep in her basket on the floor but I take her out and let Norah hold her. Esme stirs, gurgles a little, then settles again.

"You're another broody one, Norah," says Marilyn. "If you could have a baby at your age, you'd be first in the queue."

Norah looks up. "I'd need to meet a nice man first. Not that many at my age. Even the toy boys are retired."

I check Matt is asleep, which he should be—he took a sleeping pill earlier. I normally sleep nude, but I quickly put on a pair of pyjamas. It's warm enough outside for me to wear only that and sandals on my feet. I rock Esme gently in my arms, but she doesn't wake. I was worried she might start crying and wake Matt up, so he'd find out I'm not there.

It takes me five minutes to walk to the pond. There are no lights on, but as I go through the gate onto the dried-mud path, Marilyn says, "Phoebe, welcome."

She is standing on the grass, a foot away from the path, naked. Her hair is loose and halfway down her back.

"We've been waiting for you."

"Sorry I'm a bit late," I say.

"Not to worry. There's plenty of time."

Along both sides of the path are rows of women, They are all naked. Lizzie, the nearest on the left, smiles at me as I approach. I glance round. One woman, whom I see now and again in the village shop, is completely hairless. Her hair was a wig and her eyebrows false, I now know. Two other women have one breast each, a fold of skin and a scar where the other ones were.

"Lizzie, can you do the honours, please?" says Marilyn.

204

"She'll need to be naked too," says Lizzie. "She's only a few months old, but she's female too."

"Good point," says Marilyn.

I remove Esme's bedclothes and nappy—clean, fortunately—and rest them on the ground. I hand her to Lizzie. "I hope she behaves."

"Oh she will," says Lizzie. "Aren't you gorgeous, Esme. Look what your Mummy's going to do."

"That's your cue, Phoebe," says Marilyn. "We won't look if you don't want us to."

"Oh what the hell." I unbutton the top and place it next to Esme's clothes, then the bottoms follow it. I stand upright, kicking off my sandals, looking down the path to the edge of the pond. I hold my breath and start walking forward. One step at a time. As I pass each woman, she claps, stopping again as I'm on to the next. Some of them reach out and touch me, fingers glancing off my arms, my elbows, my sides, my hips, my breasts. And I reach the pond. The water is surprisingly cold on my feet.

"Go on," says Marilyn.

I hope I won't slip over. The Moon is high over the trees, trailing silver sparks across the water. There is quite a sudden slope and the water is up to my waist. Then to my neck. I hold my breath and I'm fully submerged. I open my eyes underwater but all is brown and black with faint light above me. A warmth inside me, a wholeness, as if I've dissolved in this water and will come out a different woman. I stay until I can hold my breath no longer, then turn and walk back to the shore and the women waiting.

They all applaud.

One of them hands me a towel and I dry myself.

"I wondered if you'd get as far as you did," says Marilyn. "One lady who did it years ago, she couldn't get underwater so she had to squat down and almost fell arse over tit. But she was just over six feet tall. You're one of us now, Phoebe." Lizzie hands Esme to me. "She slept through it all. Lovely."

"Glad to hear it. Hopefully she'll sleep through the night before too long." I dress Esme, managing not to wake her. "I'd better be getting back home, then. I hope my husband hasn't woken up."

He hasn't. I put Esme back in her cot, then take my pyjamas off.

"Fee…?"

Standing at the side of the bed, I gaze down at him. "Sorry, did I wake you?"

"I thought you weren't there."

"I'm here." I sit beside him. "I thought I heard Esme. But she's sleeping. Sleeping like a baby. Well, she is a baby, obviously."

"Come to bed."

I climb in next to him, facing him, pulling the duvet cover to my waist. He rests his hand on my side, the fingers of his other hand brushing my mouth, my nose, my eyelids, as if he's a blind man only able to perceive by touch.

"Your hair's wet."

"I had a shower."

"In the middle of the night?"

"I felt like one. It's supposed to relax you; make you sleep better."

"Hope it works." His hand moves up my side, over my hip and down into my waist, rests on my breast. "You're so…full."

I smile. "That's one way of putting it."

My hand travels down his front, toying with his navel with my forefinger. Further still, and I take hold of him, my fingers closing round him. He's aroused, and not just because he woke up that way.

"Mmm, that's nice."

"The bull comes to the cow," I whisper.

His eyes widen. "Does that make you a cow, then?"

I smirk. "I've been called worse."

"So I'm the bull?"

Slowly I stroke him. "Yes. There I was, in the field, chewing the cud, minding my own business. And then you trotted past, saw me and mounted me."

"The sexy way you waved your tail. Gets me every time."

"I bet it does."

He lets out a gasp, just preventing himself coming into my hand.

"Shhh," I say. I straddle him and guide him inside me.

I'm sitting on the toilet in Marilyn's house, the skirt of my summer dress hitched above my waist. *So undignified.* But I said goodbye to dignity when I gave birth to Esme. The plastic strip is between my thumb and forefinger. I gasp. *Oh well, here I go again.* I shouldn't surprise myself, but I do: I begin to cry.

Marilyn is waiting in the kitchen. She ordered the kit for me, so it wouldn't show up on Matt's and my credit card bill. Given her age, the algorithm must be thoroughly confused by now.

I hold out the strip. "Marilyn, it's pink!"

She grins broadly and hugs me. "Oh, how wonderful! The bull has come to the cow. The bull's done his job." She kisses me full on the mouth, her arm slipping about my waist. I rest my arms on her shoulders. "Two cows together. It's going to be so lovely." With her free hand, she lifts her phone and takes a selfie of the two of us.

Fens Sutton
Emma Coleman

"Nothing can be more depressing to the spirit than grey rain hammering into this pitiless sea. Sheets and sheets of grey rain, stretching all the way out to that flat, obscured horizon, over which there is probably blue sky and sun."

Edward stood alone at the window on the third floor. The room had grown darker behind him as he stared out to the late summer sea, watching the endless motion of doleful waves, creeping and rolling, disappearing, one after the other beneath the rainclouds.

He suddenly bristled with silent fury.

Great Aunt Ada. She had been the cause of all this gloom; the storms. She was responsible for this dead-end, lifeless little coastal town, for the boredom, and the people who didn't like him. And the fish, always fish for breakfast and dinner, fresh fish. Freshly caught, but still stinking fish, every day, as relentless as the bloody waves they had been dragged out of.

He once thought he wished to live on the coast—Dorset, perhaps, or even Devon—somewhere south, but not east. Especially not East Anglia. Especially not Norfolk.

Edward stood with hands held behind his back. He tightened them, hearing her incessant voice in his head, pecking at his brain with her high, quivering register.

"…as I was saying, Edward, Norfolk has a beauty all of its own…the light, you know, on the Broads in early summer is exquisite. We would take a few days touring the county…I don't think I ever told you, Edward, about my summers in Norfolk. As a little girl, Papa and Mama would indulge me and take me in a pony and trap to the nearest seaside town for freshly caught crab. There would be a puppet show on the beach, and a man selling sugared almonds. Oh, such fond memories of my childhood…are you paying attention, Edward? Edward? Edward, you are not listening to me…"

Edward narrowed his eyes and ground his teeth. Aunt Ada, how he despised her.

The unrelenting downpour began to darken but Edward remained in the gloom; his eyes never averted from that distant horizon, that hidden fine line between blocks of sea and sky, the edge of the world.

She'd insisted on moving here. The doctor had insisted. Fresh, invigorating salt air for the crippled lungs. A simple life, gentle rambles on the clifftops or on the beaches. Bracing! A clean life, with good people and plenty of fresh fish, so good for keeping the brain in good order. And the heart.

The Norfolk coast, then; the flatlands and the Broads, fenland and waterways, the sea for miles…and Aunt Ada had such happy memories of Norfolk, there would be no debate.

But, one night, only four weeks after moving into the large Georgian house on the seafront, Aunt Ada had died. The attack happened suddenly, without warning; Ada had been getting stronger by the day, her lung capacity gaining, and her coughing fits lessening. The roses in her cheeks were now genuine and not blush, and all because of the time she spent on the beach in her bathing chair, sitting, breathing, and looking out to sea and recalling her childhood.

Edward blamed his great aunt for dying in the manner she did; the locals would never trust him now. He knew they all thought he'd bumped her off.

Steel waves rolled in under the pebble-dash of bullet-rain; the panes of glass shivered at the increasing wind coming in from the sea, and Edward, eyes fixed on the morbid flat line of the edge of the world hidden behind sheets of grey, inwardly cursed.

He hated his aunt, perhaps even more so in death.

As her only living relative, Edward had to remain in the property throughout the entirety of its leasing. These instructions had been witnessed and made legal. Ada had her nephew on a leash as a constant companion and errand boy, a proffered ear in which to pour her tiresome reminiscences, and she would use her silent slave every hour of every day for the rest of her life.

"If you want to inherit anything from me, you must earn it, Edward. I didn't get where I am today through idly sitting by and waiting for others to give me a fortune."

Edward tried to laugh.

Four weeks at the seaside. The last four weeks of an indulged and indulgent life.

There came a knock at the door and Edward, without turning away from the sea view, muttered, "Come in, Harriet."

A young housemaid entered, dressed smartly but with locks of unruly black hair, carrying a basket of tapers and matches.

"Is it time to light the candles, sir?" she asked.

"I suppose so," said Edward.

Only Aunt Ada would choose to reside in such a backward place as this hovel, it doesn't even have any of the modern conveniences!

"Harriet," he asked, turning from the window. "How do you survive in a place like this?"

"Sir?" Harriet held a long glowing taper, her eyes upon Edward with a look of confusion.

Edward slumped into an armchair.

"How do you live. What do you *do* here?"

"Work, mostly," she replied, lighting a candle.

"Yes, of course, work," muttered Edward, looking into the black mouth of the fire grate. He paused for a moment before continuing, "What I mean is, do you never get tired of the sea? Do you not wish for another view, something green and wooded? Fine spires of churches on hill tops? This panoramic seascape makes one feel ill. I confess I feel as though I shall go mad with only the water to look at, and that wretched sky. I am at my wits' end, Harriet."

Harriet blew out the taper after lighting the last of the candles.

"It must be hard for you, sir, coming as you do from the Midlands, and not being able to leave here as you want, begging your pardon."

Edward waved away her apology, his face miserable.

She watched him for a moment and gave a sharp sigh.

"Come now, sir, whatever shall we do with you? It's a good job I haven't lit a fire, the way you're glooming at the grate ; you would have put the blessed thing out. I tell you what, I shall get one started now for you, make the room a bit more homely, and then I shall bring in Cook's tea. She's been baking a fruit cake and Lord knows what else, so you can't be miserable then, can you?"

Edward rubbed his forehead and nodded; he liked Harriet, she seemed to be the only person in Norfolk who didn't despise him, and he rather enjoyed the way she spoke to him. She had wisdom and a knack for putting him in his place, but it was a nice place, he often thought. Somewhere between a toddling child and a schoolboy, yet despite musing on this, Edward was hardly even aware of his deep-rooted need to be a little boy again, with all its freedoms and doting females.

Aunt Ada, of all the people why did it have to be her? Aunt Annie, Auntie Beryl, even Aunt Gladys, father's sister, out of all of them, why couldn't you have died first? Why must you have been the one to outlive them all?

"I'll get that fire going, sir, and bring in some tea," repeated Harriet.

Edward didn't hear her.

Later, Harriet came in with a tray of tea and cake and crab paste sandwiches; Edward hadn't even noticed she'd left the room, nor seen the bright flames lapping up the chimney breast after she had lit the fire. He was consumed with a depressive self-pity, and convinced he'd remain in that state for the rest of his life.

The maid stirred the tea in the pot, tapped the spoon twice on the edge of the rim and popped the lid back on. She turned to Edward.

"Shall I pour for you, sir, or do you wish to wait a while?"

Edward said nothing.

"I'll pour you a cup, sir. But mind you drink it while it's hot. And there's some nice fresh crab paste sandwiches that Cook's done for you, and she's cut the cucumber wafer thin as you like it."

Crab paste. Crab paste. Crabs live in the sea, the sea out there that goes on forever...

Harriet poured the tea and placed the cup and saucer on the round side table next to Edward's chair.

"There we are, sir, I'll pop the cosy on, so the pot stays nice and warm."

Pots. Lobster pots, with the seaweed tangled all about. And those great armoured creatures from that wretched deep sea, waving their claws and twirling their antennae, while the fishermen fling them out on the grey, miserable harbour...

Edward, disgusted by the image of crabs and lobsters fighting for their lives, swiftly turned to Harriet and said, "Would you mind taking those sandwiches away, please? And let Cook know that from now on I shall only want beef paste bought, no more of the crab, thank you."

Harriet, bemused, picked up the plate from the tray and said, "I was thinking about what you said, sir, about wanting a green view, trees and things, not the sea all the time. There's a little place called Fens Sutton, it's a beautiful village—just as you want, sir—with an old-fashioned inn and..."

"Fens Sutton?"

"Yes, sir, and it's not too far really. You could probably get there in an hour, sir, if you went in your motorcar."

Edward grimaced; he had bought the motorcar on his Aunt Ada's instruction, but he detested driving the contraption, much preferring to travel by bicycle, or else take the train.

"Aren't there any train stations near this place?"

"No, sir, it's very much out of the way, it's got an oldy-worldy sort of a feel about it, a bit like going back in time. We went there last summer, for a day out. I remember it being very romantic..."

Edward looked at Harriet in surprise and she stood up a

214

little straighter.

"Romantic, is it?" queried Edward.

"I mean it has charm, sir."

"Many villages do."

"Oh, but not like Fens Sutton, sir. You'll understand what I mean if you do pay a visit."

"This inn you mentioned…"

"It's the oldest in Fenland, sir, and has a very good reputation."

"And what does one do when one gets to Fens Sutton?"

Harriet's eyes sparkled.

"One can dream, sir, and forget that anything bad exists in the world."

Edward took a sip of his tea; he looked at the fire, and thought to himself, *Forget anything bad exists in the world…*

He glanced at his housemaid who remained in a semi-enraptured trance

"Thank you, Harriet, I'll think about it."

Edward took the motorcar in the end and as he sped along the lanes, away from the coast, his sense of liberation made him giddy; he whistled merrily, burst into snatches of song, and laughed out loud at nothing specific except for the feeling of breaking free of drudge, oppression…

"…and that bloody endless sea. God Almighty, if I never see that sea again, I shall die a happy man."

His world opened out to the wide, flat lands of the Fens; no longer the sea stretching as far as the horizon, but lengths of vivid green and rich brown earth meeting the lower sky, while the rest of that vast powder-blue purity went up and up and up, higher and beyond clouds, taking in Heaven on its way.

Even the weather had changed for the better. It was all

perfect.

Edward stopped the car. He got out and walked to the edge of a dyke where, further along, there were men working by the water.

He called out to them. "Hello there, I see you're hard at it."

The labourers turned, raising their hands to their eyes against the light and one of them called back. "Tha's right."

They returned to their work and Edward strolled over.

"What is it that you do here?" he asked, putting his hands in his pockets and nodding to the water.

The man who had spoken thumbed his cap back and looked up at Edward. The rest of the gang paid him no interest and carried on with their work.

"Water's bein' dragged," the man said.

"Oh, yes? Whatever for, lost treasure?"

The man shook his head slowly.

"Not less you considers a dead body treasure," he replied.

As he said this, a shout went up from the other workers, and the man turned from Edward. Edward peered into the water and there, caught in the mechanics, was a wet, white arm, blotched with silt and weeds.

"Get 'im out, then. Careful, with 'im, careful."

The old man crouched and took hold of the rope. Without looking at him, he called to Edward, "You best be on your way now, 'tis a bad sight for a gentleman like yourself to see."

"Before I go, may I ask if I'm heading in the right direction for Fens Sutton? Do I follow this lane, and is there a turn-off at some point?"

The old man and the workers began heaving the corpse towards land. Edward glanced at the arm as it slipped; the hand with its stiff fingers trailed the water, leaving lines of ripples on its bright surface.

"Fens Sutton? You carry on this lane, there's a turnin' abou'

216

three mile down, take it and keep on it for another foo miles along that dyke and then there'll be an old bridge as what takes you right into Fens Sutton."

"Thank you for your help. I'm so sorry to have interrupted your ghoulish work," and Edward, a little jocular, turned on his heels and sauntered back towards his car. He whistled and looked up at the sky, reaffirmed by the sight of a dead body. He was still alive and had much more life ahead of him.

Perhaps I can forget the bad things, after all.

He glanced behind and noticed the old man standing and looking after him, while the others sat crouched over the corpse.

Edward gave a gesture of farewell, but immediately the old man walked towards him.

Edward stopped.

The man stood within three feet of him, and he peered at Edward with a strange expression; there was contempt, and curiosity, his eyes narrowed.

"Yes, what is it?" asked Edward.

The old man took off his cap and turned it in his hands.

"You had a death in your family recently?"

His voice was quiet and, after speaking, he set his lower jaw forward and averted his eyes for a moment.

"That is rather an impertinent and unusual question for a stranger to ask," chuckled Edward, bemused, "but yes, I have. Why do you wish to know?"

The man looked at Edward and pulled his cap down on his head. He took a step back and put his hands deep into his corduroy pockets.

The old man, with a tone of simplicity, said, "Don't go to Fens Sutton."

Edward laughed.

"Why ever should I not go?"

"I've told you once, give you a chance. Go somewhere else."

And the man, turning his back on Edward, slowly made his way to his workmen, who all stood together in a tight group, watching.

Edward shrugged and stepped down from the ridge of the dyke.

He went to his car and reached through the open window for the crank handle on the passenger seat.

After locking it in place he quickly wound the engine but looked back to the men with their corpse as he worked.

The engine started, and he tossed the handle through the window; he glanced once more at the group, who all faced him, and shook his head, giving a baffled laugh.

He then sat himself in the driver's seat, gripped the steering wheel tightly and pulled away onto the dusty road.

As he approached the men, a couple of them twisted to get a better view of him while the others continued to peer down at the dead body by their feet.

Edward waved as he drove by, but nobody returned his farewell except for the old man, who gestured something, that Edward didn't understand.

He shook his head again and smiled, shifting in his seat and driving faster. The light on the land changed as large clouds shifted slowly across the impossibly wide sky, and Edward started singing at the top of his voice.

He arrived at Fens Sutton twenty minutes later. As he pulled close to the medieval bridge that crossed the dyke—the water sprouting with fresh green reeds and yellow iris—he knew what Harriet had meant about the romance.

Edward slowly drove over the narrow bridge, looking down at the water with its darting coots moving between the

218

green leaves, and felt an acute sense of relief. He had made it; he had got away from the coast, the ghost of his Aunt Ada, the misery, and here he was, in Fen's Sutton, a spot of magic in a flat landscape.

The bridge led onto a winding lane, and Edward saw the small, white cottages on either side; they hugged up to one another, propping each other up, while their single bulging bay windows twinkled with diamond-panes that caught the sunlight.

Fresh and unfussy, they had rich red roof tiles and a tiny diamond window in their pitches, like smiling eyes peeping out at their sweet world.

He followed the lane, reaching the open green with its border of beautiful, jumbled cottages and shops, the most handsome of all the buildings, the inn.

"And it even has a village pond," whispered Edward, as he drove into the heart of Fen's Sutton, watching the ducks spinning on the glinting water.

He pulled up in front of the inn, Wayfarers Wherry, and a young man immediately stepped out of the wisteria-clad latticed porchway, and walked down the steep, uneven steps.

"Hello, sir, welcome to Fens Sutton. Are you staying with us, sir?"

Edward jumped out of his automobile and greeted the man with a firm handshake.

"Hello there, and yes indeed, I plan on staying at the inn, if possible."

After shaking hands, the young man walked to the back of Edward's motorcar and began unstrapping the two suitcases, calling over at the same time, "I'm sure we're able to find you a room, sir, if you'd just like to step inside, sir, the lady at reception'll take your particulars."

Edward nodded and jogged up the steps.

He entered another world; the scent of wisteria heightened the sense of the past, and the hallway could have been conjured up by Scott, with its oak panelling that glowed like amber from centuries of rubbing, alongside exposed stone walls, William Morris furnishings and drapes, and small windows at differing levels beaming in shafts of warm light.

Even the guests had an air of historical wistfulness about them; everyone seemed to be dressed in their finest fashions, sitting amongst the brocaded cushions upon gilt-edged settees, or at small, elegant tables conversing quietly, intimately, either playing with a curl of hair, or stroking down a prim moustache.

And there were many guests, more than Edward had expected for such an out-of-the-way and slumbering village as Fens Sutton.

He clapped his hands briskly and stepped over to the young woman sitting behind a desk. He tapped the bell unnecessarily.

"Good morning, sir, do you 'ave a reservation?" she asked, giving a welcoming smile.

"Well, no, I'm afraid to say I don't have a reservation. I must admit that this trip of mine was rather a whim, a spur of the moment adventure. Someone recommended Fens Sutton and I came. And now I see how busy you are, I have a horrible feeling you're going to tell me you're full up to the rafters?"

The receptionist picked up a pen and shook her head.

"No' at all, sir. We do in fac' 'ave a number a rooms free, 'ow long were you thinking on staying with us at Wayfarers Wherry?"

"Well, I hadn't quite thought about that. Could I leave it open-ended, as it were?"

"Yes, a course. May I ask if you travelled by motorcar, sir?"

"Indeed, I did, it's parked outside the entrance."

"In tha' case, I shall ask someone to drive it round the back for you. Righty-ho then, I shall give you room number eighteen, sir, it's on the top floor and 'as a very pretty look-out onto the green. Now if I can just 'ave your name, sir, and address, and then I shall get Samuel to take your luggage upstairs for you."

Samuel came into the reception, holding onto the suitcases as Edward gave his name and home address. The lady then turned and reached for the key hanging on eighteen's hook and handed it to Edward.

"There we are then, sir. Dinner is served at seven-thir'y, luncheon at one o'clock and breakfas' from six till eight, all in the main 'all which is through there, sir," and she pointed to her left. "We 'ave a bathroom on the second and third floors, sir, and a maid will see to your comfort in that department. And if you find you require anything, there is a bell-pull in your room so don't be afraid to use it."

"Most kind, thank you," and Edward bowed a little, "but if I may trouble you for a moment longer, I wish to know about local sights of interest."

"Well now, mos' of our guests come for the beauty of the place—we 'ave very pretty walks, and then there's the fishing, and you can take a wherry trip up the waterways, sir, if tha' takes your fancy. And the old windmill past Turberry Hythe is worth seein', we can always make you up a picnic to take along with you, sir, tha's something we're keen on doin' for our guests. But the place mos' people want to see is the moated mansion. Elizabethan it is, sir. Quite takes your breath away when you first see it…only ruins in some parts, but it makes for a very romantic experience."

Harriet.

Edward smiled. The receptionist blushed and grinned.

"That's wha' our guests usually comment, sir, romantic."

"Well, I'm sure I won't be the only person to stay in Fens Sutton who *doesn't* feel the romance."

He smiled and turned on his heel, sauntering his way to the oak staircase, with Samuel following closely behind.

One morning, after four days at the Wherry, Edward debated whether to visit the mansion house or see the windmill past Turberry Hythe.

In the end, he decided he would take a trip on the water, but without company; so far, his days had been spent chatting with other guests and laughing at jokes over the dinner table, flirting shamelessly with a young lady—Evelyn Barratt— from Northampton, and existing on optimism and joy.

He had made new friends and swapped addresses for future correspondence, even inviting them to stay at his seaside home next summer.

But on this day, he wanted to dream about all that had happened since his arrival, requiring time to be alone, to reminisce, and smile with his eyes softly closed against sunlight.

He took off his dressing gown, flung it on the bed, and then went to his wardrobe, picking out a suitably lightweight outfit for a day out of doors in the summer sun.

...besides, the romance of the Elizabethan ruins and the moat requires the company of a lady, and the company of a full moon on a warm summer's night...

Edward's imagination set to work; it would be a full moon casting long shadows, and the white light would pick out a pale-faced but beautiful woman, in a lace gown, running for her life.

Edward had expectations of the lady shaking and stumbling with fear, sobbing loudly as she ran...

And she would cry out for me, calling "Edward! Rescue me, Edward! Help me, Edward!" And I would hear her cries, sharply turn my head and see her running up the exposed stone stairs, crawling perhaps, yes, crawling up them and sobbing her little heart out.

Ghosts and bats, the terror of the dark, all would chase the lady towards the ruined battlements and Edward would rush to save her from harm.

"Evelyn Barratt! Come back!"

Edward gave a smirk at his fantasy while pulling on a pair of linen trousers.

Evelyn would reach the very top and tremble in the moonlight, the ghosts still haunting her, but Edward would rush to her and snatch the fainting figure in his arms.

Edward gave another smirk, picturing the finer detail of his gothic dream; Evelyn swooning as her flowing lace gown billowed in the breeze, the sigh on her lips, with his face close to hers—so fearful and stricken with love—his own lips brushing against her lips. She'd wake, revived by his earnest passion, and tell him…

"…sweet and dearest Edward Harris, you have saved my life, you are my saviour, my love…"

She'd be in my debt, then, saving her life once would be the easiest way to keep her in her place…if I really did want to save her life, of course. What if I let her fall? Or should I give her push?

He all at once pictured himself shoving Evelyn from the moonlit battlements and, for some reason, he rather enjoyed what he saw.

"But not today, though, today I want to be alone with a picnic by the windmill."

Edward finished dressing and looked in the mirror as he thought of Miss Barratt, sitting with her mother and father at the breakfast table.

"Perhaps I shall ask her to come with me one evening, act

out my little fantasy. A secret assignation amongst the ruins."

Evelyn Barratt was a passing amusement; he had no real intentions towards the girl, but so what, he wanted gaiety, a toy to play with—*don't I deserve some fun for goodness' sake, after all I've done*—and the often-repeated promise of romance in the fens was tantalising.

He *had* to have romance. It was all part of the holiday.

Edward left his room and strolled down the oak staircase; it was seven-thirty, he would have his two cups of very sweet coffee, his slice of toast with marmalade and perhaps a peruse of a stray newspaper.

When he entered the sunlit dining room, he saw the Barratts rising from their table; Evelyn looked directly at him, giving a soft smile and a slight nod of the head, while Edward cried out, "Hello there," and gave an unromantic salute, something both parents found little amusement in, but gave the impression it amused them greatly.

They laughed as he approached, Mrs Barratt laying a hand across her neckline in a genteel manner, and Mr Barratt holding out his hand to shake Edward's.

"Good morning, good morning!" Edward enthused.

After shaking the father's hand, he took hold of the daughter's and gave a quick kiss.

"Shall we have the pleasure of your company today, Mr Harris?" asked Mrs Barratt.

"How kind of you to ask, Mrs Barratt, but my plans today require solitude and reflection and, alas, that means I shall be depriving myself of your excellent conversations and generous company."

"In that case, Mr Harris," said Mrs Barratt, beaming, "we shall press you no further on the subject and bid you good day."

The family went to move away when Mr Barratt stopped

and said, "Oh yes, Mr Harris, do you recall that first evening we dined together—your first day here, in fact— and you told us of your unfortunate encounter with a dead body on your way to Fens Sutton?"

"Yes, of course." Edward had related the episode with gusto, relishing his description of the stiff, waxen arm dragging its fingers through the surface of the water. "Why do you ask, Mr Barratt?"

"We heard news of the dead man late last evening from our neighbour in the adjacent room. By all accounts, the man—a Mr Jack Fincham—had been seen by a young local boy, days before his disappearance, running from the windmill past Turberry Hythe. Rumour has it, Mr Harris, that this Fincham character murdered his only brother barely a week before coming to Fens Sutton."

"Extraordinary…but on what authority do you have this piece of hearsay?"

"The gentleman next door overheard a conversation between a constable and the receptionist last evening; she was most upset. Do you know this fellow had set himself up for over a fortnight at the inn as the perfect gentleman, when all along he knew himself to be a cold-blooded killer wanted by the police. And to think we even spoke to the blackguard on friendly terms only two days before he disappeared."

Edward shrugged.

"Dear me, though I suppose it shows you can never really tell what someone is truly like."

"My opinion precisely, Mr Harris. But why choose Fens Sutton, for Heaven's sake? Of all the places to try and hide, it's hardly the spot for criminals."

"I expect that's precisely why he chose Fens Sutton, it's in the middle of nowhere. Whoever would think to come looking for a killer in a place such as this?"

"It all seems rather distasteful...though I did tell the ladies not to distress themselves, the villain certainly can't cause any harm now. I thought you'd be interested to hear the news, Mr Harris, seeing as it was you yourself who informed us of the grim encounter in the first place."

"Of course and thank you for the facts. Ladies, you would do very well to take heed of Mr Barratt's sound advice and not let it spoil your holiday."

He bowed slightly and smiled; the two ladies nodded at his gesture and then all three retreated from the dining area, but at the doorway Evelyn looked back and gave a small wave.

Edward chuckled.

"Quite a pretty girl...still, never mind," and he wandered over to his table by the window.

He sat for no more than a minute, vaguely pondering the news of the dead man, watching the comings-and-goings of people outside by the green, when he was served his hot coffee by a young waitress. He asked if it was possible to have a picnic made up for him.

"...I intend to visit the picturesque windmill beyond Turberry Hythe and wish to spend the whole day there, weather permitting. So far, it would seem a perfectly dry and bright day ahead."

The young girl under her white lace cap nodded several times and murmured something Edward didn't quite hear, yet took to mean, "Yes, sir, I shall ask Cook straight away, sir."

He dropped three lumps of sugar into his coffee with a pair of silver sugar-tongs, and then after stirring thoroughly with a tiny silver spoon, he took a sip. He stretched out his legs, hidden by the floor length primrose-coloured cloth, and gave a self-satisfied sigh.

"Today will be a very nice day."

Wherry Trips. Four times daily. Fair price. Speak to
Joseph N. East.

Edward and one other passenger sat aboard the wherry;
Joseph East, the boatman, sat and steered the vessel in serene
silence, cutting through the water as he had done for decades.

It had just gone ten o'clock and was to be the first trip of
the day, but Mr East, in his quietness, was already concluding
to himself that he would not take the wherry out again that
day; the first trip usually gave a good indicator of how he
would fare, monetary wise, for the day ahead, and today
looked to be one with little profit.

He reached down by his feet for a hunk of cheese and a
piece of cut-up apple laid on an open teacloth; he put the
slice of fruit in his mouth and then took a bite from the
cheese, squinting into the blue sky and chewing, wondering
what jobs he should start on when he returned.

"Excuse me," someone called from behind, interrupting
his wonderings. He dropped the lump of cheese and shifted
in his seat, peering over his shoulder.

"Wha's tha'?" he asked in a soft, low voice.

Edward raised a finger and then pointed to himself.

"Excuse me, but may one ask for a brief informative guide
to this wherry, please? My fellow traveller and I have both
paid a rather high fee for this trip, and some colour and
history would be most helpful."

Joseph appeared to ignore this request and returned his
gaze to the view ahead, still chewing his cheese and apple.

"I's fifty-four fee' and used to carry cargo, no cargo like
yourself, but hay and the like. This un sometimes carried
cabbages, dependin' on the season…"

"I beg your pardon, but I cannot hear you, would you mind

turning this way, or speaking up?"

Joseph raised his voice.

"…and mos' times manure from the town streets, loaded it were, with fresh manure collected from all them towns we passed. And we'd bring the stuff back for the farmers, nice and fresh. For'y tons this un can carry…not nowadays, though…" and after this Joseph became quiet.

Edward sighed; he could hardly hear what the old fool was saying, between his low tone and accent, and he folded his arms over his chest.

"Stupid old man," he muttered, and the other passenger seemed to take offence at his remark.

"Well I'm sorry, but he is," and he shifted, turning sideways on the narrow bench, looking out across the flat landscape.

He propped his elbow on the edge of the boat and rested his chin against his clenched fist.

Stupid passenger, too, I was asking for us both.

There were no sounds out there in the exposed landscape, except for the quiet constancy of the slicing of water, and the sharp cries of marsh harriers in the distance.

Edward glared angrily at the flat fields.

Don't allow these people to ruin your day.

"…and she got jus' the one sail, as you can see," suddenly went on the boatman, "and when the wind do blow, she fair flies along, but if the wind do die, well, we got a grea' big pole as push us through 'em reeds down there…", and then he became silent.

The wherry sailed calmly, cutting the green water. Edward looked down at the thickly packed reeds, wavering in the wake, and at the ripples writhing behind them.

The calling of a marsh harrier close by called Edward's attention and he just caught a glimpse of the bird as she flew straight along the length of the waterway, and then beyond

228

them.

He had a pang of awe, and then, in an instant, he became morose.

I only ever get to see those awful gulls, hundreds of white stains against the sky or perched on the railings, all of them screaming and gobbling and fighting amongst themselves. I don't want to spend another eighteen months in that damned place. Aunt Ada, you despicable and spiteful old cow. Great God, I hate you so much.

He felt the anger churning his belly…

What the hell is that down there?

Edward's rage vanished; he gripped the edge of the wherry with both hands and leaned right over, peering at the water.

"Hie, boatman! There's something stuck to the vessel!" Edward cried.

Mr East feigned deafness and stared ahead, chewing more of his apple and cheese.

Edward turned to the other passenger.

"You, come here, come and see."

But his fellow traveller said nothing, ignoring Edward entirely. Edward, exasperated, muttered insults under his breath and peered back down at the water.

A fish? Or an otter perhaps?

The wherry jolted unexpectedly and a little violently, turning into the reeds; Edward lost balance and nearly fell overboard, and in that moment, the thing in the water disappeared.

It had been a lot bigger than a fish, and of a strange hue; a strange shade of pink, fleshy and almost glittery.

Joseph got up and stepped over to the long pole lying against the portside, apologising to his two passengers for the jolt, and he couldn't understand how it had happened. He grabbed the pole and started to prod at the bank.

"It must've been a fish or something," Edward said out loud, but to nobody in particular.

His tone had changed, and he sat down primly, staring across the wherry and at the big sky, unaware of Joseph pushing them away from the reed bed and back into the slipstream.

I dare say it may've been a reflection of some kind, he thought, and with a feeling of disquiet he dared to take a tentative look over the edge of the boat.

But there were only the tall reeds and the dark agitated water, nothing else, nothing disturbing, and the boat, with Joseph back in his seat and chewing on another piece of apple, resumed its gentle way towards Turberry Hythe.

Edward stood on the ancient port, now grass-grown and lonely, watching Mr East steer his wherry back towards Fens Sutton.

The grasses bristled, rustling in the gentle wind, and Edward felt their sharp stems jab through to his skin. But he continued watching the blue and white vessel, standing still and holding the picnic hamper tightly as if for comfort, until the wherry and the two people aboard had gone.

'I'll be along to collec' you at six o'clock, get you back to the inn for dinner time. Tha' a'righ', Mr Harris?'

It had seemed a perfect idea ten minutes ago, when he'd agreed heartily to the plan as he got off the boat, but now Edward wondered if he should've stayed with Mr East and the other passenger, the other gentleman having decided to remain on board and make the trip another day as he had a peculiar dislike of Mr Harris.

"So, here I am," Edward said, quietly.

A lonely spot, the old Hythe.

Edward turned about, looking in all directions; there was nothing but sky, and fields of green and brown, except to the south where a painted windmill stood black and white, its four sails unmoving, despite the wind becoming a little stronger.

The strengthening breeze gave Edward the impression of it wanting to chase him away. It whipped at his loose clothes and whistled fiercely into his ears.

With his picnic basket and leather satchel, he headed for the old bridge connecting the Hythe to the mainland. He breathed deeply to assuage his anxieties, kicking his way through the tall stems.

Edward's nerves were unexpected, his trembling legs a concern.

"What's the matter with you, for Heaven's sake?" he admonished himself, as he trudged across the quiet landscape towards the windmill.

Why aren't you at the seaside?

Edward stopped and looked all around.

It must've been his own voice, in his head again.

Who said you could leave?

But he knew it was Aunt Ada.

Determined to carry on with his day and rise above whatever nagging there was in his mind, he pushed onwards.

You shouldn't have gone to Fens Sutton.

"Stop it, stop being silly."

He walked faster, lifting the picnic basket and tucking it underneath his armpit. He stared ahead to the windmill which grew ever bigger with each step.

He thought of the boatman on the wherry, and without realizing, Edward looked over his shoulder to the Hythe, hoping to see it steering towards land.

His heart sank when he saw that Mr East wasn't coming.

"Pull yourself together, for goodness' sake, what the hell's got into you?"

He raised his head. The wind blew, bitter and sharp, and

Edward shivered; his linen clothes flapped like flags, and his teeth started to chatter.

"Just get to the windmill, you'll be out of the wind and soon be warm again."

Yet when he made it to the black roundhouse, and to the steep ladder steps that led straight up into a black, empty rectangle, Edward found he couldn't make himself go up them.

His hand gripped the rail; his index finger tapped madly on the cold-iron while he tried to work out why he couldn't take that first step, or why he felt frightened of the black gaping doorway.

He lifted a foot, as if to take a step, but quickly changed his mind; he chewed on his lower lip, realizing he had nowhere to go.

"There's nowhere to hide," he whispered, unaware of saying it.

The isolation he'd craved had become desperate loneliness, and he had hours to be in the fens, alone.

He turned away from the windmill, telling himself to wait on the Hythe, read one of his books to distract himself from his increasing anxiety, and not look back at the black rectangle at the top of the steep ladder.

Edward reluctantly peered over his shoulder; he felt certain something waited for him, up there in the dark room of the windmill.

He could see nothing, and as Edward turned to look ahead, he saw his Aunt Ada.

"What are you doing here?" he asked, but he heard his voice coming from somewhere else.

His aunt stood on the Hythe, both hands clutching the top of a walking stick, which she leaned on heavily.

"How did you get here? What are you doing here?"

Edward heard his voice in the distance shouting angrily at Ada yet faint on the wind.

His aunt made no answer.

"Why aren't you at the seaside? How did you know where to find me?" he heard himself cry.

Edward watched the scene from the edge of the field; he saw himself on the Hythe, looming over his unmoving aunt, demanding answers, but she stared at her nephew watching from the bank.

Edward's heart tuned to ice. He tried to swallow, his mouth dry, pleading with himself to turn away, but he couldn't even blink.

"Answer me, damn you!"

Ada smiled at him, a sickly, fiendish smile, and as she did so, her whole face appeared to slip down, sideways.

Edward, frozen to the spot, heard his other self shout, "Was it Harriet who told you?"

Ada made no reply but leaned further forward over her walking stick, her shoulders hunched, her head sinking lower, yet her eyes remained fixed on Edward where he truly stood, on the edge of the bank.

"Did Harriet tell you I was here?"

The Edward on the Hythe was an angry man.

You've always been angry, Edward, even as a child you were angry, and you always got your own way because of it.

Edward let go of the picnic hamper; it rattled and clinked and a glass smashed, and his satchel dropped from his shoulder to the grass.

Edward gaped in horror.

"It can't be real," he managed to utter.

They all made such a fuss of you. Spoilt.

"What are you doing here, you're dead aren't you?" Edward yelled aggressively, yet Ada remained unmoved; she gradually withdrew her sickly smile with her eyes now fixed on a point beyond her nephew, towards the windmill.

Something creaked behind him and Edward started to shake; he dared not turn around, but he heard himself say as if whispering into his own ear, "You know I did it, don't you? That's why you're here."

And the murderous night played out in vivid detail.

The old lady in the bed, the pillow over her face, her struggles to tear at her nephew's arms as he pressed down harder. The faint groans and pleas for him to stop, his own name being begged for mercy, the twitching body underneath the blankets, all disordered, his reflection in the window with his contorted features, willing death for Ada, determined, "die, die, die."

Her weakening attempts to stop him, his grinning image in the window, her limp arms dropping onto the crumpled blankets as he continued to push down harder, her head pressed so far back he could feel it impressing on the mattress, and then nothing. He pulled away the pillow...

The sails of the windmill groaned.

"She made my life a misery," Edward muttered, "it wasn't my fault."

"You're a naughty boy, Edward, and naughty little boys must be punished."

The grass on the Hythe rustled, rolling like yellow-green waves in the breeze as both Ada and his other self stood watching him.

The sails of the windmill creaked again as they started to turn; Edward, compelled to see what was happening, looked behind as the sails spun smoothly in the ever-growing wind, with the sky so blue and bright.

The bitter wind whipped about him, stinging his face with

234

unexpected violence, like cat claws striking his cheek, and he gasped.

Edward tentatively touched his face and was shocked by the sight of blood on his fingertips.

The icy air blew harder, bringing tears to his eyes, and he shivered and shook, when there came another strike of cold claws.

Edward yelped like a terrified animal.

Without time to recover, a sudden gust of ice-cold air struck Edward hard in the chest, and he was flung backwards off his feet.

He wheezed, winded and in shock, his hands sinking into the cold earth.

Edward choked on the scent of the peat, spluttering out again and gasping for air, when he realized he wasn't sinking into the earth, he was being pulled.

The sensation was horrific; gritty and cold, it moulded about his hands up to his wrists and sucked onto his limbs, slowly bringing him closer to the ground.

Edward screamed and sat back as far as he could, leaning against nothing. He gritted his teeth, growling in pain, but soon he felt the release of his arms and he fell back onto the grass, heart racing and panting for breath.

There's nowhere to hide.

Edward scrambled to his feet, vaguely aware of the way his arms had turned red, the sleeves of his linen jacket now gone.

Nowhere to hide, Edward.

He spun around in panic; Ada and his other self stepped forward, closer to the edge of the Hythe, both grinning.

Nowhere to hide.

They each turned to water; fluid green, like the murky water of the fens, they crashed and folded into the waterway without making a sound.

Edward watched the shifting of something under the surface. It moved without effort and it moved for Edward.

"Someone! Help me!" he cried, but he knew there was no one. He stumbled backwards; eyes fixed on the thing in the water.

It got closer, nearing the bank where he stood when, slowly, the top of a thin, pale pink head broke the surface, and a pair of circular black eyes set deep in rings of wrinkled skin, glittered.

Edward fell back a few steps before turning and running as fast as he could along the edge of the dyke.

His chest burned with the effort to run as fast as he could, his breath agony in his lungs. He tried to glance quickly over his shoulder, but his unsteadiness prevented him and he nearly stumbled to the ground.

He pushed on, drawing in loud, wheezing breaths, but he had only open land to run towards; nowhere to hide, nowhere to get help, a lone figure in a vast space.

Without warning, he fell over when his foot got caught by something under the grass. He landed awkwardly, his ankle twisting as he crashed down onto his backside.

A sickening rush of panic overwhelmed his entire being; the peaty earth swelled and sucked onto his foot, like a gritty mouth of wet soil closing about his ankle.

Edward heaved himself backwards, scooting back on his hands, all the while staring in horror as the ground tried to swallow him up.

He pulled at his leg, begging God for help.

"Help me, God, please, God, help me!"

He groaned with the effort of dragging his foot out of the dark earth; he leaned back, his tears blurring the blue and white sky above him, and he roared with desperation when, at last, Edward freed himself from the grip of the peat.

Edward's shoe had gone, and the cuff of his trousers shredded, but he didn't notice. He didn't even notice that the lower part of his leg dripped with blood, or that the skin of his foot was now lacerated.

Dizzy and in shock, Edward stood half slumped, rocking from side to side. He slowly drew up his face, knowing that something stood watching him, and there, six feet away, was the creature.

It had pale pink skin that shimmered, partially reflecting its surroundings; there were dashes of green and brown, and a faint blue from the sky on its face and shoulders, but the black spherical eyes were as hard as jet.

"What are you?" Edward whispered, beginning to cry, but there came no response.

"What are you?" he whispered again, exhausted.

It had no mouth or nose, or ears, only the two black eyes set deep within ripples of wrinkled pink skin.

You murdered me in my bed.

Edward's face creased as he sobbed, "Yes, yes I did," and bubbles of saliva popped between his barely parted lips.

I was an old lady. Murderer, murderer, murderer.

"I know!" screamed Edward, bending over and crying harder.

When he had the strength to stand, he found himself staring into the eyes of the pink figure.

Edward couldn't breathe; he saw himself looking at his own face, his own image, but with the creature's hard, glinting eyes of jet black.

I saw you coming, Edward.

Edward stared at his reflection, hearing Ada's shrill voice in his head.

The face began to subtly alter; Edward had never had a moustache, but his reflection now showed a trim, blond moustache, twirled at each end.

I see you all coming here.

The lips beneath the facial hair were larger than Edward's and they stretched into a wide smile.

This one will be on his way soon.

The man Edward looked upon was younger than himself, perhaps twenty, and he suddenly remembered the old labourer working on the dyke, and the strange way he had looked at him after the corpse had been dragged from the water.

"Was...was that me? Did the dead man have...did he have my face?" he asked.

The image of the young man vanished as the pink figure grabbed Edward. It wrapped its damp, cold arms about him and held him tight.

Edward closed his eyes.

In one swift movement, they both plunged into the dyke.

As Edward slowly sank through the darkening water, the creature melted away, turning to the green and black of the waterway, weaving amongst the reeds.

Edward, his face bloated and grey, drifted to the bottom of the dyke, where his dead body settled in the silted weeds.

One damp, autumn day, when the body of Edward Harris had finally been dragged from the dykes at Fens Sutton, a young man skipped up the steps and sauntered into Wayfarers Wherry.

The receptionist looked up as he smacked his hand down hard upon the counter bell.

"A room for a week, darlin'."

He jangled the coins in his trouser pocket.

"I can afford to stay as long as I please, you know, I've come into a bit o' money, see."

He winked at the young woman, still jangling the coins,

but she ignored his comment and reached for a booking slip.

"I ain't got no money worries now, not a bit of it."

The receptionist gave a quick smile but barely looked at him.

The man gave a shrug, unaffected by her silence, and reached into his jacket pocket; he pulled out a packet of cigarettes and tapped one out, cocking it into the corner of his mouth before reaching out and striking a loose match against the stone wall.

He lit the cigarette, one eye closed tight against the glare of the flame, and then he shook the matchstick which he tossed over his shoulder, at the same time slipping the packet back into his jacket pocket.

He leaned on the counter, giving the young lady a suggestive grin and blowing smoke in her face.

"Do you know summat, girly, some interfering sod working by the river back down the road told me not to come here."

He nodded in a way that suggested she didn't believe a word he said.

"It's true," and he took another drag on his cigarette, "true as I stand here. Told me to stay clear of Fens Sutton if I knew what was best for meself."

He paused for a moment.

"There was some dead man they'd pulled out the water, know anything about it?"

"One of our guest's wen' missing a couple a months ago, it migh' be something to do with that. And it's a dyke, no' a river."

With the thumb and index finger of his left hand, the young man smoothed down his blond moustache.

"Fancy that, then," he said, ignoring her correction, and he had another drag on his cigarette, "poor old sod."

He flicked ash onto the carpet and then gave the receptionist a wink and a cocky smile.

"What time do you knock off today? I could take you for a nice romantic walk along the river if you fancy it. How about it?"

How Do You Like Your Feather Bed? How Do You Like Your Sheets?

Tom Johnstone

ere lies Lady Margaret, sprawled over the rolling hills of England. Well, one of them at least. One arm thrown over the side of her head, the other clutching her broken heart. Her long hair is splayed out as if on a duck-down pillow. All rendered in the white of the chalk under the green of the grass, the skull beneath the skin of the English countryside's face. She cuts a pitiful figure out there on the cold, cold downland, her eyes sad green hollows above a triangular nose-hole and a mouth whose skeletal grin belies her woe.

I smile. *Serves her right, the home-wrecking bitch.*

Someone went to a lot of trouble to carve such detail out of the chalk grassland four centuries ago, on the steep incline of this hill that's much older, though as an iron age fortress artificial too, whose contours seem to undulate alongside her female curves. Nothing but the best for Lady Muck, or rather Margaret, not an unsung heroine but a tragic figure of an often-sung ballad. It was a long climb to reach the point where the best view is to be had. I have to hurry because slate-coloured clouds loom overhead, bringing sullen misty rain to ruin the view, but I got in there in time to see her suffer, a proxy for another whose thoughtlessness made *me* suffer.

There's a bench at the bottom where someone left flowers, bedraggled in mizzle-soaked, see-through plastic. Sweet Williams of course. How appropriate! I threw them straight in the bin nearby, the one near the National Trust sign that retells the story, linking it to the Lady of the Hill ——

Of how Lady Margaret is sitting in her high bower room, combing at her long yellow hair, and who should she spy but Sweet William and his bride on their way to the church down there.

Then she throws down her comb, tears off in high dudgeon and is never more seen there. But later, after killing herself or pining away quietly, it's never clear which, her ghost turns up in the bridal chamber, saying archly to William:

> *How do you like your feather bed, how do you like your sheets?*
> *And how do you like your fair young bride, a-laying in your arms asleep?*

He answers in the same vein:

*Full well do I like my feather bed, much better do I like my
sheets,
But best of all is the fair young maid, a-standing at my bed
feet.*

I feel sick to my stomach when I read the plaque, wanting
to tear it down. I don't of course. Not for the first time, I
remind myself why I came here—it wasn't to commit criminal
damage against footpath signs relating to this geoglyph, but
to see it. My original reason for this field trip was to collect
versions of this folk song. I wanted the best one possible
to present to the band before we began recording the new
album. It brought me to the village of Wilbury, where I met
the old woman who told me about the Lady of the Hill, after
singing the version her mother taught her, handed down
from her mother before her, etc., etc,...

She didn't comment on my rumpled clothes or my
unwashed hair or the dark marks under my eyes after another
sleepless night, just recounted the changes human hands
have made to the image over the centuries. *She's a changeable
one, that one,* she said, making me ask if she meant weather
damage—the hill is rather exposed to the elements after all.
*Oh no, dear. There's some who like to add their own little touches from
time to time. Can't say I always approve, mind. Some of them are silly
or even downright rude...*

Of course, it was human hands that put her there in the
first place, unless we are to believe that godlike aliens carved
her out of the chalk with lasers. I'm being facetious of
course, recalling the Nazca Lines hoax I remember from my
childhood obsession with the discredited theories of Erich
Von Daniken and his ilk. I'm an adult now, and I know that
the local squire barked out instructions from the other side
of the valley through a large iron funnel, a kind of primitive

loudhailer, to his lackeys, who must have been hanging from ropes to do the job considering how steep the hillside is where she reclines. That's what it says on the plaque anyway. Nevertheless, it does sometimes feel with chalk figures of this kind, even relatively new ones like this one, that they have dropped out of the sky like stone tablets, while any additions or embellishments, prankish or otherwise, feel like the work of mortals, scuttling over the hillside with their trowels and spades and wheelbarrows to interfere with her. From what the old woman said, such adjustments to the Lady are of a juvenile or even lubricious nature, perhaps a representation of Sweet William a-lying down beside her to enfold her in a necromantic caress and plant a kiss on her clay-cold lips.

Not that this representation has any lips to cover its death's head grin.

In any case, there's no such alteration to the geoglyph today. I feel almost disappointed, having secretly wished for a sardonically obscene defacement to take the shine off Lady Margaret's martyrdom. Why should I prostrate myself in pity for a woman who coveted another man's husband and would have stolen him away given the chance? Indeed, arguably she did, as later verses show him a-pining away unto death over her, visiting her cadaver to plant a succession of kisses upon her clay-cold lips and various other parts of her body. How very unflattering to his young bride that he thus expresses his preference for the dead over the living.

In much the same way, in another traditional ballad that's almost the mirror image of this one, having just slain his rival Matty Groves in a duel, Lord Darnell hears his wife tell him she'd rather have a kiss from Matty's dead lips than all his finery. His answer? To run her through, pinning her to the wall with his broadsword. Sweet William's bride is permitted no such satisfying redress for her humiliation. In fact, she

244

gives him permission to seek out her rival. How very sweet of her. How very touching, the description of William's heart crushed within by the spectacle of his dead lady. How very heartless of me not to appreciate the tragedy of these star-crossed lovers in the way his meekly submissive little bride obviously does.

Quite a contrast to the bloody violence of 'The Ballad of Matty Groves', which is in many respects similar, even sometimes sung to an almost identical tune. When Lord Darnell surprises the lovers, he confronts Matty with the same mocking, but in this case more menacing, refrain, a mirror image of the bedroom verse in 'Lady Margaret and Sweet William':

> *How do you like my feather bed, how do you like my sheets?*
> *How do you like my lady fair, who lies in your arms asleep?*

To which, Matty replies with ill-advised brass neck:

> *Full well do I like your feather bed, much better do I like your sheets,*
> *But best of all is your lady fair, who lies in my arms asleep.*

This wasn't how the conversation went on my front doorstep between my husband and hers.

When the red mist has lifted from my eyes, I notice there is in fact a change to the chalk lady on the hillside before me, subtle but unmistakable. I must have been quite beside myself with rage and anguish not to have noticed some prankster lifting and delving and hewing the turf to move the thrown-back arm so that it is now down beside her, the other one still clutching her heart, though a little lower. How did I miss this? It could be the mist distorting it, I suppose, to give the impression of a slight alteration. Also, I was a little distracted for a moment there, remembering that contretemps of which I could hear but snatches.

It's not been a week, a week, a week, not even three…

I had to get away, using the pretext of a long-delayed song-gathering field trip. Of all the songs I could have chosen… Then again, there's usually a fair bit of anguish in all these narratives. Sexual betrayal's one of the milder traumas on offer in their verses. Maidenhead's never a town in Berkshire in these songs, which are set in wilder, grimmer locales, but it's a commodity whose loss in a woman is invariably catastrophic, leading to death so inexorably that they're almost synonymous.

But why chose that one? Maybe I wanted to torment myself. Then there's the fact it's the only chalk figure I knew of with a ballad connected to it.

But it does strike somewhat closer to home, this one.

I tried to kick Martin out after I dragged the full details of his indiscretion out of him, but he refused to leave, although calling it refusal suggests a more proactive man than he is. I couldn't stay under the same roof as him, so I had to leave, or I might physically do him harm more serious than the hefty slap I'd dealt him. It was this exchange, overheard through the open bedroom window that overlooks our front door, that got my spider sense tingling: my husband's voice whining, *But she said you'd given her your blessing;* her husband replying, *That what she told you, is it?*

Yes, that —and that you never gave her…

I couldn't hear the next bit, didn't want to, just sounds of a scuffle, grunts and laboured breathing, an angry parody of sex. All one-sided I assume. My husband, like the eponymous Matty Groves, is a lover not a fighter.

Oh, God, Martin, you've finally done it, haven't you? Please tell me you haven't.

The way he looked down to avoid my gaze was enough to open a sinkhole beneath my feet. Right then I wished one would actually swallow me up. He'd been too spineless to tell me the truth before. He was too spineless to keep up the lie now he sensed the game was up. Too passive and too lazy to fight back when I slammed him against the wall, but too passive and too lazy to leave either. He left that to me as well. I'd long vaguely planned a trip to collect folk songs linked to the chalk hill figure, as a way of kick-starting the new album. He never left the house except to go to work. Probably where he met this man's bored wife, and she spun him a yarn about her marriage being dead from the waist down and her having hubby's approval to seek solace elsewhere.

Well, I never gave you my blessing! I screamed at him as he stood there pathetically clutching his smarting cheek, his shiny adulterer's shirt rumpled and torn, whether from my slapping and grappling with him or the cuckolded husband roughing him up, I no longer knew or cared which.

Is it the fog playing tricks on my eyes and my imagination again, or is her other hand now covering her thigh, as if stroking it lasciviously? I'm not sure, but Lady Margaret's outright fondling her left breast rather than clutching her heart at this point. I wonder if the inner turbulence caused by my recollections about Martin's confession of infidelity, the details as painfully extracted as a mouthful of rotten teeth, have again allowed the Phantom Chalk Figure Adjuster to do his or her work undetected. Maybe it was an earth tremor like the one I remembered within me that day that moved her arms about. Or maybe it was the mist that obscured this activity by a kind of archaeological Banksy, one so elusive he or she manages to cross open country unseen by me. Indeed, I haven't seen a single other person out here, with or without a set of turf-cutting tools, ropes, crampons…

I consider the highly unlikely possibility that it was me that changed it. Since I found out about Martin's affair, I've had nightmares so vivid they make waking existence seem less real than dreams, panic attacks so severe they cause me to black out and end up in unexpected places, not knowing how I came to be there. It's just possible I went all the way up the hill during a lost half hour or so and changed it myself, but there's been no mist descending over my brain to mirror the one kissing the hills. I stare at my hands, looking for traces of mud and chalk, but they look clean. I wouldn't know how to anyway. I haven't got any tools. Besides, I'm in exactly the same place as I was before the figure changed.

I close my eyes, remembering that terrible, heartbreaking day that turned my world upside down, tore open that sinkhole in my life. He'd always had a roving eye. I had no illusions about that. But roving hands, a roving mouth and dick…? I didn't think him capable of going through with an actual affair. I thought he'd just content himself with unrequited infatuations, or the juvenile flirtations I sometimes discovered when I surreptitiously checked his phone. Physically cheating? I didn't think he had it in him quite honestly, especially after I'd told him if he ever did, it would finish us. Well, he certainly called my bluff, didn't he? Sounds like it was just a game when I put it like that. But it was worse than that. I also told him it would finish me.

Once or twice, I'd suggested to him he was only with me because no one else would have him, and I understand now that the affair was his way of proving me wrong. But the unforgivably cruel thing, the heartbreakingly heartless thing about it, was this: He was prepared to risk my utter breakdown in order to prove the point; not just to me, but to himself, because he'd started to believe it—the bit about

248

how no one else could want him, that is. Perhaps he didn't really believe I'd fall apart, thought I was just saying I'd crack up to blackmail him into staying faithful. Yes, maybe that's the most charitable explanation. That and maybe he thought I didn't really want him either.

But the truth is, I did want him. Still do.

And now I've sabotaged myself by leaving him home alone. Left to his own devices, he'll no doubt cheat again. I've given him the perfect excuse now. He may be lazy and passive, but he can be quite proactive when he wants to be. He was uncharacteristically hardworking when it came to betraying me. Maybe he'll go back to *her*, bring her back home this time, something he claimed he never did before. Maybe now it's out in the open, he'll have the brass neck to screw her in our bed this time. No more sneaking around to hers when her husband's out, the one he believed didn't mind her unfaithfulness to him apparently but balked at her doing it in the next room while he was there. Or maybe he'll find someone new. Now he knows someone else will have him after all, the world's his oyster.

I open my eyes again, in a sudden panic. What's she up to now? What new changes have there been in Lady Margaret? Is her hand squeezing her breast more tightly? Has her other hand crept between her legs to compensate her for what Sweet William is unable to provide? Is her head thrown back, her skeletal grin now a grimace of ecstasy? Was that an earth tremor I heard earlier, or just a rumble of thunder?

I don't know, but it looks like the earth is moving for Lady Margaret.

I squeeze my eyes tightly shut to try and make it go away, and when I open them again, red and blotchy, the mist has descended, heavy and opaque this time, as if some kind god, the soul of discretion, wants to spare me this chalk-carved obscenity. I realise I'm soaked to the skin by the mizzle, the sort you don't feel until it's seeped into your bones. My face is wet, both from the weather and my tears.

Finally, the fog lifts again and I see the hill, a blank green canvas. She's gone. It's as if she was never there.

There was something else the old woman said about the Lady of the Hill. I dismissed from my mind at the time. I thought she was talking nonsense ——that knowing look in her bird-black eyes, as if she knew what he'd done, the real reason I came here, irritating me, rattling me, so that I made my excuses and left her cottage, ill-concealing my fury.

I must hurry back home. If I'm quick, I'll get there in time. But the traffic is terrible. The slowly creeping cars and trucks and lorries backed up along the motorway taunt me. It's getting dark. I tap out a rhythm on the steering wheel in my impatience. It takes me a while to recognise what it is I'm compulsively beating out…

How do you like my feather bed, how do you like my sheets…?

I feel sick with anguish and fury, imagining chanting those lines to whoever is trespassing there when I catch them at it. Eventually, I switch on the radio to stop my relentless tapping. Late night experimental music drones and screeches on Radio Three. Impatient drivers change lanes to try to get ahead of the pack. I wonder if I should do this, but I can see it's pointless. There's an exit coming up soon for an alternative route.

I take it, drive back along winding roads to my destination. It's almost too dark to see without a full beam. I keep flicking between that when the road ahead is empty and the dimmer headlights when there's traffic coming the other way, but then I can barely see the edges as curved as a woman's thigh.

250

My wheels screech as I steer and brake too sharply, narrowly avoiding veering off the road or into the path of cars coming towards me in the opposite lane.

It seems to take forever, but finally, I'm home.

I creep into the house, opening and shutting the front door with extra care, as if to surprise him in tangled sheets with another. Yet, I also hope he'll be awake to surprise me with flowers or at least a kiss and contrite words. But there's only silence. I suppose he must be asleep, but it's deeper than that. As I approach the bedroom, his snoring doesn't greet me. I can't even hear breathing. Perhaps he is with another, only not here.

As I open the door, I let out a gasp of relief. He is both here and alone.

But all is still. So still.

The only sound is a whisper from the darkness, or more an indistinct hissing mutter, which might be:

> *Is she in her parlour?*
> *Is she in the hall?*

Martin lies sprawled naked, amid tangled sheets, his blue pyjamas nowhere to be seen. I can make out clothes strewn about the floor. My heart pounds in anguish at their suggestion of a passionate struggle to discard them. Yet he's quite alone. If there was anyone else here, she must have done a midnight flit. No smoking gun from his womanising.

He's also quite still.

He doesn't even stir when I open the door wider, letting the light in from the landing.

> *Is she in her chamber high*
> *Among the gay ladies all?*

These muttered words appear to come from the edge of the room where the darkness still lingers. I can just make out a bundled shape, which could be the curves of a woman lying with her back to me. No, it can't be, because I have a strong sense of a face staring at me, mocking eyes glimmering in the darkness, which would mean the head was turned right around at an impossible angle.

> *No, she's in her cold coffin*
> *Face turned to the wall*

Not this time. Her body's facing that way, but not her lambent eyes.

In furious terror, I turn on the light to banish the impression, which I now see comes from a bunched up, discarded duvet: The two of its shining buttons visible at the end account for the impression of sardonic scrutiny. He must have thrown them off in his restlessness.

But now he doesn't stir.

Martin, I say, and there's a catch in my voice, as I see his eyes are open but staring blindly, chalky finger marks all over his bruised throat. Then I remember what the old woman said about the Lady of the Hill, her words that I dismissed as old wives' nonsense—*she's the scourge of both jealous wives and unfaithful husbands*—and I wonder which deadly sin summoned her here: his lust or my wrath.

A Hunt One Morning
Thomas Wren

And what will you do there?
O, we may not tell you.
We'll hunt the Cutty Wren.
  "The Cutty Wren", a traditional folk song

There is something awful alive in this place
We are most relieved to leave behind
  "The Ghost of a Tree" by Richard Dawson

I

Instructions had been slid under the door, ready for the morning. The first to rise was Milder, from his cot in the corner. He stretched his back as he did every morning: by arching his chest forward to get rid of the aches of his middling years in a series of cracks and groans. The fire needed feeding, so he did that, reaching into the scuttle for two more pieces of coal. He stirred the embers and eyed the instructions flat on the boards at the foot of the door. He would wait for Festel.

Molder crashed down the stairs, sliding first on his backside, but then twisting around so that his face scraped on the wall on the way down. The heap of his body scrambled around in a circle of arms and legs trying to right itself, swearing and huffing. Milder stood, immobile, but jumped to him eventually to help.

When Molder finally stood up, he rubbed his body, pulled the neckline of his nightshirt into place and flopped into one of the chairs at the kitchen table. He scowled at the wall. Eventually, he said "Morning," to Milder and Milder responded with the same. Milder patted his arm.

"Shall we wait for Festel?" said Molder, having seen the instructions on the floor, but he knew what the response would be.

"Of course," replied Milder. He sat across from Molder and clasped his hands.

There were no birds singing.

Festel climbed up from the cellar, picked up the instructions and sat in a third chair at the table. Milder and Molder looked at Festel as he read the instructions. They waited for him.

Fose emerged from the back room, yawning and reaching her arms above her head. She touched the teapot to check if it had been boiled. It hadn't. She filled it from the tap and set it above the fire. She drew her dressing gown around her against the cold and sat in the fourth chair. "Did you sleep okay?" she said to the room.

"Fine," said Molder, rubbing his neck.

"Badly," said Milder.

Festel was still reading.

The side door banged open and John walked in covered in snow. He shook so hard his fingers could barely grasp at his freezing body. Sprinkling snow across the floorboards and rug, he stood next to the growing fire, warming first his front and then his back, switching every few seconds and enough to make him dizzy. The rags wrapped around his nose were brown, bloody and stuck to his face.

"Morning, John," said Milder. "Did you sleep out there?"

John's teeth chattered as he replied, quietly, "You know I did."

"No," Milder said, still looking at Festel, "I meant, did you *sleep*, as in, get some rest."

"No," said John.

"Shame."

"My nose really hurts."

"Serves you right for getting into it."

Molder said nothing.

Festel placed the instructions down onto the kitchen table. Everyone stopped.

"So," he said. "Instructions are. We're to go after the Wren."

II

Milder threw himself onto his cot and wailed into his pillow.

"Are you laughing with us right now? Are you having a laugh with us?" squealed Molder as he stamped his foot.

Festel didn't respond but walked to the cabinet and poured himself a tumbler of whisky. He sat down again, not touching his drink.

Fose paled and excused herself. Vomiting was heard from the bathroom.

John crouched by the fire and put his battered head into his hands.

When everyone had calmed down and returned to the table, Festel passed the instructions round so everyone could read what it said:

THE WREN

When they reached John, and Festel gave him a nod, he tossed the instructions into the fire.

"Is that all it says?"

"You read them the same as us, John. I'm not holding a secret second piece of paper," Festel said. He rolled a dry piece of bread between his fingers into a ball and flicked it at him.

The bread bounced off his forehead. He turned to face the fire.

"Why did they take so long to read?" asked Fose, scraping her chair back in response to the whistling kettle. She nudged John out of the way of the fire with her foot; he strained to stay close to the flames and looked around her legs like a puppy.

"Making my mind up about the plan."

Fose poured herself a cup of tea and added milk from the jug in the fridge. They would need to figure out where they would get more as their last provider had disappeared.

Festel rapped on the table and regarded everyone in turn. He looked out of the window at the pale rising sun.

"Let's get ready."

III

Milder shaved the last few hairs from under his nose, the cuttings littering his vest, and he tucked the straight razor into his belt. He brushed the hairs onto the floor and went to find something to stop the bleeding spots on his cheeks.

Having finished his preparations and sharpened his blade, Molder lay flat on his back next to the oven and stretched his spine.

Festel counted out each of his sharp-nosed bullets into three rows on the kitchen table and cut marks into them with the end of his knife. He shut his eyes to see the symbols and cut what he saw.

Fose span in a circle. Stopped. Aimed for a spot to punch and kick. Went again.

John re-dressed his nose. Fibers still stuck in the mess in the middle of his face and it still dripped a munge of blood and snot.

Once all of the bullets were etched and accounted for, Festel stood up. Everyone else shuffled to meet in a circle in the middle so that they surrounded Festel. He checked each in turn, turning in an arc and making adjustments to their clothes if necessary. When he was satisfied, he handed them all rags from his coat pocket. Hunting the Wren brought with it strategies they wished they'd never have to use, whispered about and shared from those they came across outside.

Milder started to cry again. He scrunched his eyes up and tears bulged out and down his cheeks. Festel squeezed him on the shoulder and led them all outside.

IV

Milder continued to snivel as they all walked through the field that surrounded the cottage. The grass sat in frozen fringes on the ground and hid the hard lumps of mud dug up from past, failed plantings. The fields rolled out until the trees in the distance.

Molder cut at the grass with his sword, a rusted, chipped rapier he'd found one day on another trip. He swung it in time with his strides and lopped the fringes off into raggedy patches. He smiled when they reminded him of Milder's shaving earlier in the day. He whispered this memory to Milder as they walked, which brought a smile to his face and stopped the tears for a short while.

The rifle was slung over Festel's shoulder and it bounced off his back with each step. He thumbed each bullet between his fingers and felt each mark he'd made earlier, deciding which should go first.

Fose pushed one hand deep into her coat pocket, while, with the other, she raised her piece of wood at different angles to see which blocked the sun the best. All failed. She swapped arms when she got tired.

Hanging back, still sore from the night before, all John could think about was Molder clapping him in the face with the table. Or had he clapped the table with his face? How everyone had laughed and how they'd thrown his things outside. His head hurt, either from the ripples of pain from his nose, or the drinking.

All at once it seemed they reached the forest.

V

The trees were patchy at best and those that still stood were twisted and turned, reaching out more than up. Milder blew into his hands and rubbed the tear tracks from his cheeks. He tested the sharpness of his razor on the bark of a tree, managing to chip off a shard. He put it in his pocket.

Molder kicked at an old bucket rotting halfway out of the ground. He kicked it again.

Festel loaded the first bullet, one etched with a five-lined box, into his rifle, ready.

Fose took her club into her right hand. She remembered playing rounders when she was little and hitting the ball so far over the school fence she was given a nickname. She couldn't remember what the nickname was now.

John gave his nose another rub and adjusted the bow strapped onto his back.

A car, as if trying to dig away, was buried nose-first into the ground. It had been painted and painted again, once. The back wheels were slashed. Festel climbed on top of it and sat on the roof, his rifle angled up over one shoulder.

"Okay," he said. "From what we all know, the Wren won't be a straightforward catch, not like the last one."

Fose chuckled. "He was easy."

"Today will be different." Festel looked down at the others and they looked up at him like scolded dogs. "We've heard the stories, the things we might have to do, so hopefully they'll help. The rest is up to us. And there's five of us, one of them."

"We hope," murmured Milder into Molder's ear.

Festel jumped down from the car. "If none of you have anything to say, we'd best begin while the sun's still up. Put the rags around your eyes."

The group did as they were told. Once each rag was wrapped tightly around each face so they couldn't see, Festel said, "And now turn."

Everyone began to turn in sloppy pirouettes; Milder and Molder bumped into each other as they staggered with their arms out; Festel turned slowly, his lowered rifle dragging a circle in the earth around him; Fose twisted quickly, careful to keep as much of the same patch of dirt beneath her feet as she could; John rotated, wanted to be a tree.

Before the world could spin any further, Festel called "Stop," and all did. They all faced different directions but didn't know which.

"You know what to do," Festel said. "When you think it's time, take your mask off." The group was silent.

"Ready?"

No one replied.

"And walk."

VI

Milder stumbled over a knobby root as he shouted, "Where are you going?" in the direction of Molder, not knowing that Molder had already fallen down a bank into the teeth of some nettles.

Molder, blacked out by his rag, lay as still as he could in the patch of nettles. He could hear his dad in his ear saying *Grab it quickly and you won't get stung*, but knew the dead advice was useless when he was covered, surrounded by the things already needling his palms.

"We may not tell you," shouted Festel, reminding them all of how it needed to go. The Wren should have no idea they were coming. He used his rifle like a dowsing rod to help nose his way through the forest, waiting for the right moment to take off his mask. He felt a hand caress his calf but carried on in spite.

Fose began walking, like she was told, but carried herself into a sprint when the panic of wearing the mask took over. She hurtled headlong into wherever she was going, blurring past trees, tripping, but not tripping enough, over parts, undergrowth, things.

"We're off to the woods," said John to himself. After walking, he stopped when he bumped into an obstruction. He felt along its surface and his fingers came back with splinters. He rocked it back and forth, and it creaked and complained, clearly a fence, rotten and ready to lay down and die. He didn't take his mask off yet and followed the fence to the right.

VII

Milder snivelled with his arms outstretched, banging into trunks, tripping over everything. His poorly angled razor dug into his hip; his trousers began to fall down despite the belt. After three attempts to keep his trousers up, he gave up and carried on shuffling through the woods, ankles hindered by the pooled denim. At once, when he felt a stillness surround his head, he paused. Everything was quieter. Milder pulled his rag off his face, trousers still down, and looked around. He couldn't see anyone else, but the forest went on the same. He pulled up and refastened his trousers and drew his razor.

Molder hauled and swore his way out of the nettle patch until he stood over it. Without taking his mask off (it wasn't time), he pulled his blade from its makeshift scabbard of garden hose and aimed vaguely around him. The nettles quivered and died with every rush of his sword. He stamped on them all and kicked them into the air. When he was satisfied and his breathing slowed down, he walked on, sword still drawn. After twelve more paces, he fell down another hill. When he reached the bottom, he removed his mask.

Festel's feet, used to the gnarled earth, hesitated when a harder ground took over, something like cobbles. He took his mask off to see squat buildings sit either side of a road. It was as though they were sulky and refused to look each other in the eye; their angles were haphazard and sharp. Festel couldn't tell if the road had come first or the buildings.
Fose came to a halt when the muscles in her hips threatened

to tear. She collapsed forward in the dark behind her mask and she fell shoulder first into a hard, hollow thing. Rolled onto her back, she untied her mask and looked up at a huge blue and grey sign. It was split into two arrows and read: THE SOUTH M1, and pointed to the left, and THE NORTH M1, and pointed to the right. Fose hadn't seen it for a long time. Didn't know what it meant anymore but tried to remember. She couldn't, so beat the leg of the sign with her wood. When she grew tired and felt no more anger towards the sign, she continued the hunt.

John took his mask off after hearing a robin call in his right ear. He looked up and saw the robin and saw the bark of the tree through its feathers. The faint little bird called again with its trilling voice and looked down at John. It took off over a field and blended into the sky. John looked over the field and saw the way back to where they lived. He didn't know what to think.

VIII

Milder wished he could see everyone again, wished Molder was there to talk to him about what he was feeling, and most of all wished he hadn't seen behind the wall he'd come across. He stood against it, not looking around the corner, his razor pressed flat over his heart. If Molder were here.

The hill Molder'd fallen down had swollen his ankle and led him to a steaming bog. The trees were sparser here but still poked up through the half-ground in surprised patches. Molder dragged his useless foot behind him and felt out a solid enough path. He looked down at the bog around him and saw the submerged grass, and the glowering fires sunk deeper below. More fires sprouted on land next to the trees and burnt the landscape away into smudges. A scream started behind him and he knew it to be Milder. He clutched the grip of the sword tighter as his palms began to sweat and pressed on into the bog.

When no one answered his knock at the first door, Festel kicked it open. The house was dusted with yellow lichen that started with a deep, mustard colouring close to the window and fanned out across the floor, table and chairs into whorls of mucus green. Festel stepped onto the thin, flaky scales. The boards didn't creak underfoot. He remembered seeing a documentary when he was little about the caretakers of moss in Japan. They wore *jika-tabi*, specially designed boots with a cloven toe, to minimise damage to the moss as they pruned and farmed in the quiet groves. Festel crunched his way over the lichen which travelled up the stairs. He could see an eaten carpet poking its way through the growth, the fibres looping in and out of the lichen. Upstairs, he heard someone say "Shh!".

Fose smacked the weeds along the verge with her stick, trying to remember what her nickname was. The sky opened up into harsh sunlight. She stopped and squinted upwards, enjoying the vague warmth on her cold face. She continued on, following the verge, only half thinking about the job to be done, instead thinking back to their last. The boy was easy to find and easier to kill. They found him playing in a hedgerow before they dragged him out and did it. They all got home to eat, get drunk and watch John fight Molder over the last portion of soup. She remembered John being thrown out into the back garden with his bust nose, silly man. Fose heard a gunshot and stopped.

John circled the yard around their house. Everything seemed to be in the right place. He pushed the front door open and scanned, trying to figure out the reason he'd ended up here again. He stepped over to the kitchen table and saw a spray of blood, his own, from the night before where Molder had banged his face downwards into the wood, making his nose split. He touched his nose then, numbed by the cold, but still sore if he thought about it too much. He'd fallen in with them all two years ago after he stumbled in one evening, his arm bleeding and twisted, and, after a brief alarm and drawn weapons, Festel attended to him. The others followed, making tea and giving him bread, and they were together from then on. He'd loved them. The door to the basement opened with a drawn-out whine. John turned. The door was wide open for him. He watched and waited, still, but nothing emerged. He stood, exhaled, pulled the murky bandage from his nose which caused the wound to open again, and drew the bow from his back. He notched an arrow and walked downstairs. The house was quiet and the basement door swung closed.

IX

Milder could still hear the chewing noises from behind the wall. He had to do something, he knew, but he couldn't bring himself to, until he then heard a sigh and a moan. *Was he still alive?* If he was, he had to help John, as much as he was an arse with Molder yesterday. He took three more breaths, opened up the razor and stepped around the wall to see fully what he didn't want to see: a boar scoffing its way through John's belly. Without thought, he launched himself at the boar, blade out, and hacked at its ridged back. It bucked and twisted against Milder's slicing; Milder clung on with his free hand and swung with the knife, cut into the boar again and again. It eventually turned its head and Milder came face to face with a tusked Molder, his eyebrows lifted in shock and his eyes drooping with tears. Milder kicked himself away, leaving his blade in the thing's scored back. Molder looked at Milder, swooned, tried to say something and collapsed next to John's body. When neither John or Molder had moved for some silent moments, Milder started to cry again and inserted himself between the bodies.

Amid the bog fumes, Molder thought of the first time he'd met Milder. He had been trapped in a hole and was banging two stones together after his voice had worn out. After the third night, Milder had appeared holding a razor. They didn't speak for a while, and Molder held his hands up after dropping both stones. Eventually, Milder said, "Need help?" and hauled Molder up with a rope. He took him back, grubby and starving, to the house, and they looked after each other. A calling bird broke him out of his memory too late. Before his mouth was sucked down into the bog, he saw a small bird. He could not tell what it was.

The barrel of Festel's rifle smoked. The kick-back had made his shoulder ache, but he was used to it. The man lay back on the bed as if half asleep, boots still planted on the floor. His two children cowered together around a bedpost. Festel leaned the rifle against a bedside cabinet and stepped quickly over to them both. He caught them both by the chin, looked into their eyes, saw nothing, and let them go. Both children scurried out of the bedroom over the carpet of lichen. Festel climbed onto the bed and sat next to the man. He was as nicely dressed as could be, considering. Festel unbuttoned the man's shirt and revealed his chest, punctured with the bullet and pooling blood. Festel rolled up his sleeve and dug his fingers like tweezers into the hole, up to the second knuckle. The age and power of both rifle and bullets worried him, but at least they did what was necessary, and kept, like he wanted, the bullet in the body. He felt the cooling metal and gripped it hard, pulling it out. When he saw that it wasn't the bullet with the five-lined box, but one with a curving zag instead, he swore and jammed the bullet back into the body. He fished the remaining bullets out of his pocket; he was missing two.

Fose ran, stick raised, in the direction of the shot, along the verge, burdock standing like sentinels along her path. She cascaded down a hill, rushed into a copse, and stopped short, nearly tripping on a knot in the frozen mud. She remembered her nickname. On that April afternoon at school, the sun hot on the rounders pitch, ready to hit the bowled ball from Isaac Westhill from class SW4, all she heard were the cheers of the other students around her. Isaac bowled, aimed right through her shoulder blades, and she swung her bat, elbow jarring with the force, and the ball flew high, up and over the school fence. She careened round the posts, the school cheering her on, and when she got back to home base, her team-mate gave her the nickname. Fose smiled at the memory. The copse around her lightened. She heard a whimpering in the ground ahead of her.

X

When Milder woke from his exhausted sleep, the bodies of John and Molder had started to turn to leaves. He clutched at Molder's body, falling to mulch, and held him as tight as

268

he could to his chest before the leaves all browned and fell through his arms. Molder sat between the piles of leaves and cried. He knew this is what the Wren did, what the Wren could do, but he missed Molder too much. As soon as he pulled Molder up from that hole, he knew he'd be okay with him. They spoke easily and made each other laugh; before, none of his friends were like that and he went coldly from job to job with no one to tie him anywhere. In all of this, with everything that kept happening, he was relieved to finally feel safe with someone in the world. Milder lay down again between the leaves, knew this is what the Wren could make him feel, and fished around in the leaves for his razor. The Wren, he thought, made him feel like this, like he'd never see Molder again, knew it, knew he wouldn't, so Milder drew his knife over his own neck. He didn't turn to leaves for a long time.

The rest of the village was empty, as far as Festel could tell, and he started to wonder why they all didn't live here. Plenty of space, a house each. He knew they wouldn't find this place again, but they could try another day. The building at the far end, a flat-roof pub he could see was called *The Shovel*, might still have some food left behind, he thought, so he headed there, rifle loaded with a bullet scratched with three v's. The pub had a raised stage at one end with a backdrop of old tinsel streamers. They smelled of his grandma's house at Christmas and would have glinted if the lights worked.

The moaning Fose heard was ahead in the middle of the copse. She approached, stick ready, the trees forming a circle around the sound. The noise came from an old man in a shallow hole. He was curled like a millipede around himself and his roving eye rolled around his head searching out who

269

had found him. He was naked except for a translucent grey down covering his shoulders and neck. Despite what the moans were supposed to make her feel, Fose knew what he was. She gave him no chance to do anything and brought her stick down on him, across his head and side, ensuring to catch the eye, until the stick was in splinters. His moaning had stopped. She couldn't make out the eye in the aftermath. Fose dragged the body from the hole, unfurled, and pulled it with her towards home.

XI

Festel, holding up the rifle with one arm, fished around under the bar for any crisps or pork scratchings; finding none, he cleared a shelf of glasses with one arm, smashing them all on the gummy floor. He saw a stringy blot, like a hulking wrack of kelp, move out of the corner of his eye and onto the stage. He tried to raise the rifle, but was blocked by the bar, and it went off and drove the bullet into the wood. Looking up at the figure on stage, standing there, Festel panicked and loaded another bullet into the chamber, not looking at which one it was. He lifted, breathed out, fired. The figure disappeared with a rustle behind the tinsel. Festel dropped the rifle, a coldness spreading from the centre of his body outwards into his limbs. He fumbled with his own shirt as his fingers numbed to find the hole in his chest. He looked down at the bib of blood pouring down his clothes and onto the floor as he dug the bullet out of himself. When it was out, he didn't recognise the marks.

The body was heavier than it looked and kept getting stuck in the roots of trees or divots in the earth, but Fose knew she needed to get it to the house to complete the work. After retracing as many of her steps as she could, and seeing things she hadn't seen before, she found the sunken car and the edge of the field. Fose couldn't, now that the act was cooling in her head, look back at the body she was pulling across the frozen ground. She was sure at first, sure with every strike of her bat, but now, was he just an old man cringing in a hole?

XII

Fose left the old man outside ready for whoever would collect him and, after staggering into the house, collapsed into a kitchen chair. She fell asleep, head lolling backwards, and dreamed of the dying man in reverse. With every swing of her stick, he became less broken, the eye unburst, the collapsed chest and skull shored up and fixed. Fose woke in the morning, the winter light pouring in through the window, but no one else was here. Another set of instructions lay flat at the foot of the door. She waited to see if Festel would rise to read them, but after an hour, she wasn't sure. Fose retrieved them herself and cried when she read what was there.

Shifting Sands

Liam Hogan

Winston, when he was in the quayside pub, when he'd had a few pints and was feeling garrulous, when he was asked the inevitable "*What do you do?*", would proudly answer: "I move beaches."

The locals, the ones in their tattered cable-knit jumpers, sitting with their favoured pints at their favoured perches, knew exactly what he meant and weren't impressed. The Winthorpe Harbour Reclamation Project had been running for over two years and was headed into overdue and over-budget territory long before Winston arrived. The dredger traversed slowly back and forth across the silted-up harbour, sucking and clawing tonnes of sand from the seabed, to be deposited in great mounds on the quay, where yet more claws and jawed scoops tipped it into murky-yellow tipper lorries. All so that Winston and the other drivers could truck

273

it around the headland to the tourist beach they were trying to establish.

Hubris, scoffed the weather-beaten men propping up the bar or half-hidden in dimly lit corners. Winston wasn't entirely sure what they meant but understood the tone well enough. "King-bloody-Canute. It's the *sea* that moves beaches, son, and a lot more besides."

"Like what?" Winston asked.

"You'll see," they muttered darkly, "if you dig long and deep enough."

Which was exactly the faux mysterious, utterly useless reply he'd expected. Besides, Winston *didn't* dig. Did his damnedest not to touch any of the stuff he shifted, the rotten stench of dredged estuary sludge, left to drain for a couple of days before being loaded onto his truck. The smell others said he'd get used to. He didn't *want* to get used to it; he was just a lorry driver, his HGV licence newly printed. Paid to drive his truck to the quay, queue until it was loaded, then drive the five miles to the shingle shore they were burying. Queue again until someone told him where to dump it, then drive back and repeat.

He made up to five circuits a day, depending on the queues. There were *always* queues. Workmen waving trucks through the bottleneck at the harbour, or down to the fake beach, while Winston and everyone else looked on from their cabs, awaiting their turn. If he was lucky or canny and timed it just right, he'd arrive too late for that fifth run and get to knock off early. Not that he *minded* his mindless job, mostly, but an extra half an hour in the pub, especially on paydays, never went amiss.

The distance from the neglected harbour they hoped to transform into a glittering marina, to the pebble beach they wanted to turn golden, was a lot less than five miles as a seagull flew. But the road was forced to take the scenic route, unable to cope with jagged, crumbling cliffs, arching along the headland almost as far as the automated lighthouse at its tip, before swooping back down the southern side to the sheltered cove and future tourist trap. There was a more direct route, but his on-the-job training, which had amounted to a single circuit with the foreman sharing the cab and sharing his hard-earned wisdom, ruled that out.

"Don't," the foreman said, as they came to a turning not far from the quay they had loaded at, "ever take *that* road."

"Why not?" Winston had asked. Reasonably enough, he thought, not that the 'road' was much more than a dirt track.

"Oh? You want *reasons*, do you? For starters, it's too steep when you're fully loaded, and too bloody narrow even when you're not. Up at the top there's a village, where the road gets narrower still, kinks around the ruins of a church and a walled graveyard, and I don't want my trucks scraped to buggery, or worse, *stuck*. Besides which, the few villagers up there don't much like traffic and are liable to complain, and that complaint comes through to *me*."

He eyed Winston bleakly. "So the main reason not to cut the loop is because I *say* so, and because it's an instant dismissal if you do. Copy?"

"Copy," Winston agreed, agreeably, swinging out onto the coastal road. Not that he needed anyone to tell him which way to go. You just followed the trickle of sand that each truck left behind, twin tramlines that the sparse traffic slowly cleared. Last thing he wanted was a short cut. There was too much hanging around in this job, too much sitting in the cab going nowhere. The five miles there, five miles back (when, unloaded, he could *almost* get up to forty miles an hour!) were the highlight of the circuit, when he was his own man, giving a casual nod to the other drivers of the other trucks he passed going the other way. Anonymous ants scurrying back and forth. Look upon thy works, etc., etc.

Sometimes, when Winston turned up at the harbour in the morning, there was already a truck waiting for him, ready to go. More usually, he joined the 'rush hour' queue, the half dozen dumper lorries not yet strung out by the tedious process of loading and unloading. Time enough to grab a coffee from the Portakabin canteen, from the stolid woman whose legs he'd never seen and whose name he didn't know and who had never said a single word to him in all his three months on the job.

Every so often he'd have a passenger, someone wanting a lift between the sites, a brief exchange of gossip his scant reward. Mostly, he was on his own. Which suited him just fine. Not that it stopped him complaining about the tedium, as he did to one of the equally idle engineers, who was waiting for a tender to carry him out to the dredger.

"Least your job is nice and safe," the engineer said, squinting to the steel horizon.

"Safe?" Winston followed the man's gaze, to the dumpy ship, its crane swinging another scooped load to the attendant barge. "Because I'm not at sea?" A sea as flat as a pancake, at least until you cleared the sheltering headland.

"Because of the bombs."

"*Bombs?*"

"Big ones, from world war two. They dredge them up sometimes. Back then, Winthorpe, harbour already clogged by the shifting sands, was a decoy port."

"A decoy?" Winston a parrot, echoing each startled word.

"Yeah." The engineer, whose name might have been O'Connor, or O'Connell, Winston wasn't sure, laughed. "A load of ancient hulks, with empty crates stacked high on the quay, pretending it was far more important than it was. To

276

protect ports and docks further along the coast. Mostly, the bombers didn't take the bait. A few did. Enough to make a pretty mess of parts of Winthorpe, which is why it's such a ghastly mix of old and new. But some of those Nazi bombs didn't explode, and were swallowed by the sands, turning up seventy years later. Keeps the navy bomb disposal unit on their toes, when the dredger unearths a thousand-pounder."

"Christ." Winston glanced over his shoulder to where Winthorpe clustered, an amphitheatre of concrete, studded by the occasional wooden-framed building, the pub foremost. "What about the locals...?"

"Oh, they were evacuated. Even the military aren't stupid enough to paint a bullseye on an *inhabited* town. A few brave souls—invalided soldiers, mostly—set the lights each evening, lit fires to create enough smoke to make it look busy, but that's about it." The engineer squinted towards the rocky cliff. "Other than those up on the loop."

"The town on the hill, the one the lorries avoid?"

"Town? *Shit.* Ain't more than a dozen buildings, most of them empty. Maybe twice that many, back in the day. *Before.* The residents refused to leave, just as they still do, the crazy coots. They claim to have been there since this headland was an island." The engineer shook his head, giving Winston a sly glance. Winston realised this was a camp-fire ghost story, even if there was no camp-fire to sit around, and even if it was daylight.

"The MOD figured they were insignificant enough and *probably* far enough away from the harbour. And they were mostly right. But one night, 'round about this time of year, in the teeth of an unseasonal storm, a Junker—or was it a Heinkel?—heading back across the Channel, dropped its last bomb up there, for want of a better target. Took out the church tower, the priest, *and* the congregation; around half the town's inhabitants, gathered for evening service."

"Christ," Winston repeated. "Terrible luck."

"Some say that," the engineer nodded. "Others say they were warned, and not just by the MOD. Seems one of the villagers, a blind, old crone, foresaw the tragedy. Told them not to go to church that night. Those that survived were the ones that listened. Otherwise it would have been even worse."

Winston latched onto the nugget of information even the engineer had sounded doubtful about. "So this used to be an island?"

"So they say. Until the river, dumping its silt into the estuary, bridged the gap. Mind you, they say it might become an island again, what with rising sea levels. I suspect that'll suit any folks who remain up there just fine."

So the bombs were what the locals had warned might be dredged up with the sand. Winston blamed a gust of wind that tugged at his hi-vis jacket for the shiver as the engineer clambered aboard the tender, ignoring the foreman's glowering scowl for not waiting out of sight in his cab, taking all of an extra fifteen seconds when he was finally waved forward.

After that dark little bedtime story, every time Winston hit a bump in the road or took a corner too sharply and felt the tug of the lorry as it tried to continue in a straight line, he couldn't help but picture some rusted WWII bomb shifting in its disturbed bed of sand, the ancient mechanism implausibly restarted and ticking like something out of a James Bond film. Or maybe there would be no warning at all, maybe the unstable ancient explosives would just decide that today was the day, that *this* was the long-delayed moment, no possibility of escape. One tiny jolt of energy triggering a much, much bigger one, and all that would be left of him and his tipper lorry would be an ugly crater in the road, a

278

few twisted fragments of metal for the investigators to piece together, a layer of sand, and silt, and Winston, spread for a hundred meters all around.

Neurotic nonsense. But what else did his mind have to occupy itself as he drove the lonely stretch of coastal road, nothing but seagulls for company? The haulage recruitment company had warned him that it was a tedious job, not suited for anyone with an imagination. Winston had been quite happy to assert he didn't have one. Now he wasn't so sure.

The locals laughed even more when he tried to tell them why he was so out of sorts.

"Ain't *just* the bombs," they said, grinning with yellowed tombstone teeth. "Out there, a mile out, there used to be whole 'nother Winthorpe. Back oh... god alone knows which century. Before the loop was an island, and before it wasn't, again. A storm surge wiped the prosperous fishing town out, overnight, separated the mainland from what remained, and drowned every man, woman and child who lived there. The only survivors were those who had retreated to the top of the loop, to Cranfar. Someone had warned them disaster was looming, so the tale goes, not that many listened.

"Afterwards, the surrounding towns came up with reasons for their neighbour's destruction: their pride and wealth, or devil worship, or that traditional scapegoat, *witches*. Or maybe it was a witch that warned them, that they ignored. All that is certain is that, on quiet nights, 'round this time of year, you can still hear the solemn bell from the Old Winthorpe church, the one the dark waters swallowed."

In a pig's ear. Winston heard echoes of that other tale, the one about the bomb. Storytellers recycling key components. Warnings, and churches, and storms, and almost everyone lost. Maybe they didn't have much imagination. Maybe there was a sliver of truth, sandwiched between the tall tales. Most likely, both stories were a crock of shit.

"And that should have been that, consigned to the history books, nothing but a mile of tidal marsh to mark what had been there before," the teller went on, plodding to the end, not that his audience was listening. "But tides are fickle, and for a while, the sandbars the old town had sat on left a protected channel out to sea. So they rebuilt Winthorpe around a brand-new stone harbour, the one here now, and the town prospered once more. Until the tides changed again."

The locals shook their heads in wry amusement. Winston kept his sniggers to himself. But he swapped the tale with O' whatever his name was, as they circled the loop back to the harbour. The engineer had heard it before.

"Planning for *any* sort of future is a fool's game, if you ask me, which no one does," he said in judgement, after a decent pause. "Like, I'm guessing the town planners aren't looking beyond twenty years. Probably no more than five; the developers will sell their swanky new holiday homes and bugger off somewhere less bomb and flood prone. They certainly won't be the only leeches to profit—curious how there are so many real-estate owning councillors!"

This was one of the engineer's more frequent refrains. Winston knew all the conspiracy stories, wads of brown-envelope cash and expenses-paid holidays to luxury resorts. His passenger lent back and put his sandy boots up on the dash. "If it *does* take off, though, that might be even worse. The Winthorpe bottleneck, and this coastal route, will be a nightmare come summer. Chock full of caravans and screaming kids." He shook his head. Winston peered down the lonely road. Even with the eternal convoy of dumpers it always felt empty. He tried to imagine it bumper to bumper, his truck in danger of overheating as it crawled along, stuck between exasperated holiday makers. But his job would be long over by then.

Sometimes, as he was sat in his cab waiting for another load, he wondered how much sand he'd shifted so far. How many tonnes. Wasn't there something about there being more grains of sand than stars in the sky? How many galaxies had he shifted?

Sometimes he was told to dump the sand onto an existing pile, sometimes to inch forward as it poured in damp clumps from the tail gate. The trucks couldn't dump it direct onto the beach, any more than they could reload by going for a swim in the harbour. The workmen at the beach shifted tonnes of the stinking stuff with caterpillar tracked diggers, busy building sandcastles.

At the shoreline, the sea sorted through the pebbles, something it had been doing for centuries and still hadn't finished, hadn't yet rearranged them to its satisfaction. The dumped sand didn't stretch quite that far—it would only get washed away again if it did. He could almost hear the locals' smirks of derision.

Driving slowly back to the quay, watching the clock tick towards his first pint, Winston wondered what else lay hidden beneath the sand. Would those ancient corpses of Old Winthorpe be nothing but dust by now, distinguishable only under a microscope? What about the coffins, and gravestones, from the flooded churchyard?

The evening echoed his thoughts. Clouds were gathering, heavy rain was forecast. He might get tomorrow off. Sometimes, it rained so much the trucks couldn't go anywhere, the sand too heavy or wet or something. He didn't care about the reason, grateful for the day off, even if it was unpaid and even if the weather that caused it meant there wouldn't be much to do but drink. There had been fewer such days as spring edged onwards and the weather began to warm, his cab windows wound down as often as up. Not this evening, though. The changing weather had brought a chill to the air. He was glad the forecasted drenching had stayed off until after his last run. Happy that in less than half an hour he'd be cosy in the pub, where the storm could lash and howl as much as it liked.

"Hold up," the foreman called as Winston was leaving his cab, spinning the keys in his fingers while diggers optimistically loaded it for tomorrow morning. "Where are you off to?"

Winston looked pointedly at his watch. "Won't be time for—"

"Ah *sure* there will!" the foreman grinned. "An hour to sunset, at least."

"Sunset?"

"Did you think this was a nine to five?" He scoffed. "Days are getting longer, so *you* work longer. Pretty soon they'll be shifting the start time earlier as well."

Winston blinked. He should have paid more attention to his contract. How many hours a day did they expect him to work? How many hours could you drive for, under the HGV rules? Except, of course, most of the time he *wasn't* driving, just sat in the cab. No chance of exceeding the regs.

The foreman nodded, as though he could hear Winston's thoughts. Or maybe he was just responding to his stifled groan. Either way, he seemed to relish this.

"More hours of light means more hours to dredge. So don't you worry, Winston my son, there'll always be plenty to shift. Right, you're re-loaded. Best get a move on, this *will* be the last run of the day."

The trucks that had come in after his were lined up and empty, a fading babble of laughter as the drivers drifted away. Winston cursed his luck. In trying to give himself an extra fifteen minutes in the pub, he'd arrived just in time to get an extra hour of work instead. Fat raindrops splattered across the windscreen as he pulled out.

The sun hadn't set yet, but it was a lot darker when he arrived at the dumping ground. Black clouds roiled in from across the sea, upper edges fringed with the gold of late evening. As soon as those clouds hit land and were forced to rise, they'd be merrily shedding their load. Which was, it appeared, something *he* couldn't do.

"Tailgate's jammed," the workman at the beach informed him.

"Sorry?"

"Tailgate. Jammed."

Winston emerged from the cab and headed to the back of the lorry. Not that there was anything he could do. The mechanics of the hydraulic system that tilted the flat bed of the truck until the contents reluctantly submitted to gravity were beyond his pay grade. He'd only gone round to see the impossible for himself.

"Tailgate's jammed," he agreed. "So... what now?"

"Truck will stay here—no point in driving it back full— until an engineer can take a look, but that won't be until morning. I guess you're done for the day."

Winston took a look around. No other lorries parked up, his being the last to arrive, and the only one not to depart again. Just a couple of cars and a pickup. "Can someone give me a lift?"

The workman laughed. "Sure, if you don't mind waiting a couple more hours. We don't knock off early like you lot do. Or you can stretch those long legs of yours?"

Winston frowned. "It'll take me that long to walk."

"Not if you cut the loop," the workman said. "Then it's only forty minutes. So, your choice. Wait, or walk. But best decide soon, before it gets any darker, or wetter."

At that the workman seemed to lose interest, in both Winston and his truck. Winston bristled. So many people he'd given a lift to, (including, he suspected, this bloody workman) and now there was no one willing to give him one in return? Not for a couple of hours, anyway. Valuable drinking time.

He peered up to the craggy bluff that terminated the pebble beach with its spreading carpet of sand, watching a seabird navigate the blustery conditions. If that obdurate rock wasn't there, hugging the sea, the Winthorpe road could pass either side of the headland, instead of going around the houses. He raised his collar and trudged reluctantly away.

He almost missed the turning in the gloom. Nothing more than a rubble-strewn track. Maybe smugglers had used it once, or wreckers, on dark, stormy nights like this. Maybe there was a smuggler's pub up there. No one from—what had the locals called it? Cranfar?—ever descended to the harbour pubs in Winthorpe. He would have met them, by now. He stomped up the hill, the hi-vis jacket doing little to keep him dry or warm, buoyed by the thought of some smoky local, perhaps no more than a single room, once someone's parlour, with a name to match. *Molly's*, or *Keefe's*, or something—

A shape loomed out of the darkness. He squinted from beneath his baseball cap, rain dripping from its curved visor. Took a moment to recognise it as an oddly squat church. Then he remembered *why* there was no soaring tower and wondered where exactly the bomb had landed. Winston was still gazing upwards when he realised he was being watched. But it wasn't until he was a yard in front of her that he saw the old woman with the stout walking stick must be blind, eyes like moonlit clouds.

She knew he was there, though.

"Ain't no way through," she spat, and if he'd thought the old sailors in the pub had bad teeth, this was a real horror show. Was it because she couldn't see to clean properly? Or because she hadn't been to a dentist since they started working for the NHS, and had probably now missed that particular boat?

"I'm on foot..." he began to point out, as though she'd have this conversation with a fifteen-ton truck.

"Ain't no way through, lad," she repeated. "You been warned. Not *tonight.*"

If the weather had been fine, he might have headed back. Or struck out off-road, skirting the truncated church and narrow walled streets and its crazy inhabitants—or inhabitant, since he'd seen no signs of anyone else. "Look..." he false-started before biting off the sentence and beginning again. "I only want to get home."

She waved her stick dangerously as though in search of a pinata, as he edged along the far side of the narrow street, the walls of the church on one side, the walls of the graveyard on the other. He went as quietly as he could, but she still turned her sightless eyes to track him, her ruined mouth gaping ajar, her dark cloak flapping in the wind like raven's wings.

Winston turned back when he got to the end of the cemetery wall, and almost stumbled. From this angle, the church looked like it still had its tower, a dark spire, topped by a weathervane, cockerel spinning in the gusts, the faint squeak coming from on high. He heard something else, the drone of an air-plane, the thrum of propellers, passing almost directly overhead, an unseen carrion bird. There was a weird, shrill whistle, undercutting it, getting louder, getting closer, and his every nerve screamed at him.

He turned and flung himself into the darkness as lightning rent the sky and a single cataclysmic bark of thunder announced the end of the world.

Ears ringing, eyes blinking with jagged after images,

palms scuffed and bloodied by grit and knees bruised, he cast around for the old woman, unwilling to go back the way he came, over the rubble-strewn road. If she hadn't got in his way, if he hadn't given her such a wide berth, how close would he have been when lightning struck? There was no sign of her. No sign of anyone, despite the noisy heralds of the storm's arrival. Rain fell in earnest, quickly drenching and chilling him, as he staggered down the hill towards distant Winthorpe.

An hour later, and until the last bell of closing time, he sat huddled by the late-in-the-season pub fire, listening to old sailors tell their tales of storms and bombs and witches, nursing a pint he didn't want, and saying nothing.

The Clootie Tree
Selina Lock

Tie a ribbon 'pon the hawthorn tree
Say a prayer, let your wish fly free
Clootie Tree, Clootie Tree, We worship thee
[Anon. Trad.]

Maureen trudged up the little path between the fields. Even though it was overgrown, she liked to walk this way to the woods. It felt like her very own secret passage, as she never saw anyone else. Even the local dog walkers weren't aware of it. She'd made this trip every week since she was a girl. Back then it was with her grandma and great aunts. It hadn't seemed weird at the time that they'd make this pilgrimage straight after church on a Sunday. Going from one form of worship to another, like water flowing downstream. Grandma always said God and nature were two sides of the same coin. They were both about body and soul. One wanted obedience and penance, while the other wanted nurturing and offerings

In those days she skipped along the well-worn path holding ribbons and homemade charms. Now, she gripped her Bag for Life and tried to ignore the ache in her calves. She didn't bother with church, coming straight after her Sunday shift at the local supermarket instead, and her ribbons were rice paper, much more eco-friendly.

The path petered out as she got to the edge of the woods. It had shrunk, as the industrial farmlands encroached. She walked around the treeline until she found the small gap in the undergrowth she'd always used. She squeezed through and felt the world recede as trees deadened the sound of the nearby A road. She made her way to the Clootie Tree at the centre of the woods, the sacred well little more than a collapsed wall and hole in the ground. Moss and weeds grew over and around the stones.

The hawthorn tree itself still stood tall, though some of its branches had grown straggly. Traces of cloth and ribbon remained in the highest branches, among the blossom buds, frayed and weather-worn. A few wooden charms still dangled here and there. Maureen checked the lower branches and saw that several of her paper ribbons from her last few visits still survived. They hadn't seen much rain for this time of year. She rummaged in her bag and withdrew several new rice paper ribbons. She smiled, pleased with this week's effort. An online purchase of paper with real flowers embedded in it. She stroked the ribbons, savouring the feel of the petals. She liked to work her way around the tree during the year, so she carefully tied the strips to the next branch clockwise.

She pulled a small picnic blanket from her bag and placed

it beside the tree. Lowered herself to the ground with a groan and leant against the trunk. She retrieved her travel mug and sipped lukewarm tea with own-brand Rich Tea biscuits. She mused on her weekly wishes. Keeping her job was the main one. They'd all been in a tizz at work since redundancy rumours started their rounds again. She didn't fancy applying for a new job at her age, the mortgage on her flat with years still to run. As a girl she'd wished for adventure, as a young woman for romance, but her pleas to the Clootie Tree had grown mundane over time.

She started to get chilly and struggled to her feet. She tipped the last of the tea over the roots of the tree, thanking it for remaining her constant companion. She crushed the last biscuit, sprinkling crumbs in the same area. The tea and biscuits hadn't been part of her grandma's ritual, but it just seemed the right way to do things nowadays to Maureen. Plus, the birds might like the biscuits.

She packed everything neatly away and retraced her route out of the woods. As she neared the edge, she heard voices and paused to listen.

"We thought we might get some pushback from the locals," a smug-sounding male voice said. "You usually do with this kind of rural land development, but nada. Council were on our side and pushed it through. Know which side their bread is buttered."

"Good to hear there's no issues." Another man, but his accent gave him away as a local. "Always a pain if you get protestors. My lads will be finishing up that Surrey job in a few weeks, then we can get all the trees cleared ready for your contractor's start time."

"Excellent. Now you've seen the lay of the land, let's get back to the car..."

Maureen remained rooted to the spot as the voices drifted

away. They couldn't mean what she thought they meant. A part of her wanted to run after them and demand to know their business, but she'd just look like a local busybody if she did that. She marched home, out of breath by the time she got back to her flat. She flung her coat and bag down and reached for her phone.

The next week she spent researching. Combing through planning permissions and the council website. As she'd feared, they were building a new housing estate on several acres around the wood. She vaguely remembered some work colleagues talking about it. They were a little surprised when she started asking around at work about the plans. It was less surprising that her colleagues were mostly in favour of the plan, citing affordable housing, new people bringing new business and all that. They didn't seem to know it was all going to be luxury detached houses for commuters who shopped at Waitrose, not from local businesses like theirs.

She tried to get people interested in petitions or protests or appeals, but they ignored her, as usual. A sympathetic council worker intimated that money in the right place had made environmental pressure groups pipe down. She talked to a local historian about the importance of the Clootie Tree, but they were more interested in recording an interview with her to preserve the stories for the local archives. As the deadline for the tree clearing loomed, Maureen sat in her flat and cried. It was such a magical place to her, the only special thing she had left. She had to do something.

One night, she lay in bed, on the edge of sleep, and a memory surfaced of her grandma, her great aunts, of blood, of chanting and red, red ribbons. The next morning, she had her answer.

The butcher didn't have much call for blood anymore but cheered to see someone carrying on the British traditions.

Maureen had Googled a recipe for black pudding in case he tested her. Why anyone would want to make it from scratch she couldn't fathom but she blathered on about locally sourced ingredients and he seemed happy enough. The other things she needed were much easier to get hold of.

She'd convinced the development project manager to meet at the woods on a Tuesday afternoon. It had taken multiple emails to their PR department, threats to go to the press, some judiciously edited quotes from the local historian and a fake petition to get him there. She'd taken the day off work and went up to the woods at sunrise. Every branch she could reach was weighted down with red ribbons. Rich velvet, shiny polyester and even some with Christmas patterns on. The beribboned old hawthorn tree looked like an Easter bonnet from a classic film. Ready to parade its glory. She poured the pigs blood in an anti-clockwise circle around the trunk of the tree, tipping the residue down the ruins of the sacred well. It felt sacrilegious, but Maureen also felt like the earth was waking, the heat rising through her feet.

The working done, Maureen went home, changing into her most respectable outfit. She made tea to fortify herself, using the good China, and McVitie's Rich Tea. She felt the occasion required more than own-brand biscuits. Then she headed back to the woods.

Typically, the developer was nearly half an hour late for their meeting. He reeled off a half-hearted excuse when he arrived at the treeline, gesturing for her to lead the way.

"If we could get on, please, I have several more important meetings to get to today." His face was sweaty and scrunched with annoyance. He couldn't wait to leave the natural world and return to his concrete one.

Maureen just nodded, "This way."

They made their way along the path Maureen always

followed. She hoped it wasn't the last time. The man swore as he caught his feet on tufted weeds, scuffing his expensive shoes. So out of place in his slim-fit, check suit. His pale hands contrasted with his bottle-bronzed face. Glancing back, she saw him waving his phone about, forlornly hoping for a signal bar. No phone masts to be found here.

When they got to the Clootie clearing, he shoved his useless phone back in his pocket.

"You have been busy," he commented. "But you'll need more than a few ribbons to turn this into a site of religious importance. This is a ridiculous waste of my time."

Maureen was only half listening, as she stepped behind him. She took off her long red chiffon scarf and looped it around his neck. He stumbled as she pulled it towards her. Luckily, he wasn't big man, while she was a sturdy woman. He let out a surprised wheeze, grabbing at his throat as the chiffon drew tighter.

Maureen began to chant. "Save the Clootie. Accept my offering. Save the Clootie. Accept my offering…"

Not the most original words. Certainly not the ancient words her grandma had used in that ritual over fifty years ago, but Gran always said the intention was more important than the words.

The developer thrashed around, catching her in the stomach with an elbow, winding her. Her grip started to loosen and he almost broke free. Almost. Roots erupted from beneath them. They grew, twisting around the developer's legs. He yelled for help. Maureen let the chiffon go as he was dragged away. The gauzy red fabric became entangled with the rhizomes, building a tuberous cage around him, pinning him to the ground.

The roots emitted creaking groans alongside their unnatural progression. Then she heard flapping from above as a murmuration of starlings swirled in midair before diving down towards them. She threw herself under the dripping red ribboned branches of the Clootie, sheltering as the voice of the wood grew louder and louder.

The starlings were joined by finches, tits, blackbirds, even a woodpecker. The man's screams were almost drowned out by the rattling of their beaks and whistling of their wings. A pulsating mass of feathers in a riot of colours above his body. The mud turned rusty as his blood mixed with the soil. Cries became gurgles and then he was silent.

Maureen continued whispering "Save the Clootie. Accept my offering..." Still, the birds didn't stop, their beaks scarlet, their black eyes beady. The remains of his clothes were gore-sodden scraps, prizes that the birds tore away and carried up to serve as fresh ribbons for the branches.

As quickly as they had arrived the birds took flight, whooshing into the sky and Maureen was alone with the Clootie Tree. She crawled through the blood-soaked dirt towards what little remained of the businessman. With trembling hands, she picked up a humerus and flung it into the sacred well.

She just needed to tidy up. When she had finished, she found her travel mug. A cuppa was just what she needed. She followed her tradition. As she poured the dregs around the hawthorn, she thanked it for granting her wish and accepting her offering. They had won this battle together, but this would not be an end to it. She would redouble her efforts to convince others. Or it might require stronger offerings than tea.

Red, Red Wine

KB Willson

The creature regarded her quietly from the foot of the bed, its large, oval eyes focused unblinkingly upon her own. Neither she nor the creature moved. It was waiting for an answer; an answer to a question she had pushed firmly to the back of her mind, but which had suddenly reappeared like a ghost at the feast, consuming her waking hours and devouring her dreams. Players across a poker table, they held each other's gaze, hardly daring to breathe. Truth was, she had run out of options. By the time she realised the significance of the question, it was already too late. The thing at the end of her bed held all the cards.

Exactly a year had passed since their last encounter, soon after they had bid a final farewell to her mother, the matriarch of the family and powerhouse behind the success of their business. They had given her a good send-off. Her brother, in whose shadow she had spent her entire life, had spoken well and from the heart, and she was thankful he had taken that responsibility from her shoulders. They clutched each other, as though neither could stand on their own, tears flowing freely as the curtains closed around the coffin—and then she was gone. Their guiding light, irrevocably extinguished. Back at the house, surrounded by the awards and trophies picked up by the vineyard over the last few years, they cracked open several bottles of the 2016 and celebrated a life well lived. The next day, dosed with paracetamol to combat a furious hangover, she had joined the rest of the family at the solicitors to hear the reading of the will.

To this day, the shock of the announcement still resonated, as Mr. Dunwoody pronounced her the sole heir. At the time, nauseous as she was, it passed over her in a cloud of unreality, but to her brother it was a dagger through the heart.

"… and to my firstborn, my daughter Meredith, I leave the house, the vineyard, the winery, and all associated goods and chattels. The business known as Littlebrook Wines shall pass to her in its entirety, along with all extant contracts and goodwill, and I have every faith she will do all that is necessary to ensure its continued success under her stewardship…" A chair scraped across the wooden floor and the solicitor paused, lifting his eyes in time to see Meredith's brother rise and leave the room. It was to be the last time they would see him. For her own part, Meredith heard the words but not the meaning, swimming as she was in a thick fog of befuddled incomprehension. Only later, back at home and nursing a balloon glass containing the remains of a 'hair of the dog', did the full significance sink in.

Her mother had been ill for some time, a progressive and pernicious anaemia that seemed unwilling to respond to treatment. In the beginning it simply manifested as tiredness,

296

which the family had put down to the heavy workload she'd taken on. Growing grapes on England's Jurassic coast was a challenge, to put it mildly. It took nerve, and she'd been on the verge of throwing in the towel many times, before the 2014 vintage put them on the map, garnering an armful of prizes and setting the business on the road to success. But as the vineyard prospered, so her mother's health declined.

The fatigue was soon accompanied by shortness of breath, and she complained of feeling cold all the time. Meredith tried to get her to see a doctor, but she dismissed the idea with a curt 'there's nothing wrong with me that a good night's sleep won't cure,' so it continued, until the afternoon her son had found her unconscious on the floor of the winery. Despite her protestations that she'd skipped lunch and just needed a good meal, she was taken off to the medical centre where anaemia was diagnosed, iron tablets prescribed, and a new diet regime put in place, none of which improved her situation.

Meanwhile, the 2015 vintage hit the market to great acclaim, and suddenly everyone wanted to drink Littlebrook wine. Meredith became the face of the vineyard, talking to the press and managing their online presence, while her brother assisted their ailing mother with the everyday running of the business. Her eyesight had begun to fail, dizziness and nausea were common occurrences, and the fainting was getting worse. After more tests showed her red blood cell count continuing to decline, she was sent to see a consultant haematologist, who diagnosed hypovolemic shock, and ordered a transfusion.

"It's as though she's lost a lot of blood," the consultant told the siblings, "but there is no sign of a wound, and your mother seems unable to account for what's happened to her. I've run some basic tests, and it doesn't seem like she's bleeding internally, but at this stage I can't know for sure. Ideally, I'd like to admit her, but she is absolutely against the idea. Maybe you can persuade her that it would be in her best interest. The blood we're giving her will help her get back on her feet, but unless we can get to the bottom of how her blood supply is depleting, I fear you'll be back here again within six months."

Back home, the argument that ensued shook the walls, and resulted in their mother literally barricading herself in her room. The following morning, she was back at work as though nothing had happened, and it was never spoken of again.

Soon after their trip to the hospital, Meredith had googled 'loss of blood volume' and in the absence of any other explanation, had reassured herself that it was most probably a natural decrease due to her mother's age, and left it at that. Nonetheless, it niggled at her for a couple of months, until sheer volume of work forced the matter to the back of her mind.

There was indeed a great deal to do, and that year's grape harvest turned out to be a bumper crop, exceeding all expectations. Meredith also had the upcoming launch of the 2016 vintage to occupy her thoughts, with little time for anything else. In truth, the siblings had grown used to their mother's ill-health, took her admonishments 'not to fuss' to heart, and so became blind to the warning signs. Until, on the eve of the launch event, their mother collapsed. By the time the ambulance arrived, she was dead.

And so it was, just ten days after the funeral, that the creature first appeared at the end of her bed.

The shock of the sudden appearance sent Meredith into a spiral of panic. A hot sweat soaked her nightclothes as her mind struggled to comprehend what she had just seen. She tried to edge away, but her back was hard against the bedhead and there was nowhere to go. She was pinned like a butterfly on a board, while the wet, bulbous eyes of the little creature watched her, quizzically. Finally, it spoke, a sound like grinding glass, through which recognisable words rose and fell.

"Where is the other woman?" it asked, through a lipless mouth that barely moved.

"The other..." Meredith paused, unable to process the question; then understanding dawned. "Oh..." Her tongue seemed twice its normal size and stuck to the roof of her mouth; she could hardly control her voice. "She died. A couple of weeks ago."

The strange little thing took a moment to digest this information, during which Meredith's mind worked overtime, desperately trying to categorise the creature, to attach some identifiable label to the thing, to convince herself she wasn't going mad. Roughly humanoid in shape, though less than a third the size of a normal man, it had spindly arms and legs emerging from a truncated torso, which in turn was covered by a beribboned smock. Its skin was cream-coloured and glistened like wax. In the absence of a nose, two slit-like nostrils entered directly into the face, and dark-brown hair hung lankly to its shoulders. Most striking, though, were the eyes, which were too large for its face, somehow lending the whole abnormal visage an incongruous 'puppy dog' appeal.

Fairy? Pixie? Sprite? Goblin? Gnome? In an effort to give a name to the curious creature she ran through the stories from her childhood, finally fixing upon the poem 'Goblin Market', which seemed the closest fit. Probably.

Just as the refrain from the poem began to echo through her mind, the creature spoke again.

"Then it falls to you to honour our contract."

In that moment, Mr Dunwoody's voice came back to her,

the words she had scarcely heard through her post-alcoholic stupor: '…along with all extant contracts and goodwill'. Surely the business had no contract with this weird little goblin fellow—how could it? Up until this moment she hadn't known he existed. "I'll have to check the paperwork," she stammered, unable to think of anything else, "then I'll get back to you. If a contract exists, of course I will do my best to honour it."

"Paperwork…" mused the creature, as though struggling to comprehend the term. "Your mother and I had… an agreement."

"But if there's no paperwork, I'm afraid there is nothing I can do." Heart pounding, but determined to signal an end to the interview, Meredith swung her legs over the side of the bed and stood up. Though she towered over the goblin, she couldn't shake the feeling that she remained at a disadvantage. "We're under new management, you see. I'm very sorry." The huge, oval eyes still held her gaze, and she braced herself for whatever might be about to happen. In the event, nothing did.

"It is your prerogative. It saddens me that you will not continue our arrangement, but your mother resisted too, in the beginning. I will give you a year to consider, then return for your final answer."

"But I don't know how to…" Meredith got no further. The little creature had disappeared.

Both unnerved by the encounter and at a loss to know what kind of agreement her mother might have had with this strange freak of nature, she found herself replaying 'Goblin Market' in her head despite the fact there were whole sections that she simply couldn't remember. There were definite parallels. Might her mother have entered into some unearthly contract with the goblin resulting in her wasting away, like the sister in Rossetti's poem? The long night stretched before her and, aware that sleep would prove impossible, she pulled on her dressing gown and went downstairs into the office, pouring herself a large measure of single malt on the way. Fortified by the warmth of the glistening liquor, she pulled open the filing cabinet and began her search. By 5 a.m., having drawn a blank with the hard copies, she was searching through the files on the computer. By 7.30, as a watery sunlight crept into the room through the cracks in the curtains, Meredith was slumped over the keyboard, fast asleep.

Winter came and went, one of the wettest she could remember, but as spring took hold and the sun began to lighten her spirits, the first of the complaints started to filter through. There was a problem with the 2016 vintage. Customers were sending it back in their droves. Meredith was at a loss; this was the wine with which they had toasted their mother less than six months earlier, and it had been superb. Well balanced, medium bodied, oaky, with hints of cherry and chocolate. As far as anyone knew, Littlebrook Wines were on to another award winner. So what had happened? Could the problem have occurred within the bottle itself? She doubted it. They were meticulous at every stage of the process, and those first bottles they had opened were all fine. Yet consumers were reporting a taste akin to rotten cardboard. Meredith had no option but to recall the entire vintage.

Then, in early July, the current crop began to wither on the vine. Meredith and her estate workers spent frantic weeks investigating possible causes, from pest and fungal infestations through to viral attack, but nothing proved conclusive. Eventually, they were forced to admit defeat and incinerate every plant in the vineyard. As thousands of pounds worth of vines went up in smoke, Meredith returned to her office and wept.

The weeks flowed past in a flurry of desperate activity, as she launched her rescue bid for the business. The house was remortgaged, support loans secured, the vineyard stripped out and prepared for replanting, all achieved with much grovelling, soul-searching, and ruthless application of a pared-down business model. Half the staff were dismissed, which above all else caused Meredith the worst pain; most of them had been with the enterprise since the beginning and had always been fiercely loyal to the business and the family. The severance pay almost crippled her, but not as much as the knowledge that she had stabbed them in the back, betraying her mother's trust in the process.

Throughout these last interminable months, she had been trying to contact her brother. Since he'd walked out of Mr Dunwoody's office, Meredith had been weighed down by the irrational belief that she was somehow to blame for his exclusion from the will. Guilt had gnawed at her soul until finally she accepted that she would have no peace until she had made things right with him. And as the catalogue of disasters unfolded, she concluded that perhaps, just *perhaps*, everything that assailed her was in some way retribution, karma for the way he had been treated. But every avenue she tried had drawn a blank. He appeared to have vanished from the face of the earth.

In one last ditch attempt to track him down, she had engaged the services of a private investigator. It wasn't cheap, and she baulked at the cost, especially when she'd just laid off so many of the workforce, but within three weeks they'd succeeded where her own efforts had signally failed. The email, when it came, made difficult reading. It seemed her brother had moved to France, where he'd attempted, unsuccessfully, to get a job with a series of notable vineyards. Too proud to accept any other kind of employment, he became a recluse, eking out an existence in a one-roomed apartment in Paris until his money ran out, finally ending his life with a packet of pills and a bottle of the Littlebrook 2016.

For Meredith, coming on top of everything she had endured throughout the year, the news struck a hammer blow. She screamed at the screen, sweeping it over the side of the desk, where it dangled on straining cables between desktop and floor. Shrieking invocations to the uncaring gods, she threw herself back in her chair, which in turn toppled and tipped, depositing the hapless woman onto the floor and landing heavily on top of her, castors spinning. Battered, bruised and sobbing, Meredith crawled out from beneath the wreckage of her life. She was done. It was over. She had done everything to live up to the faith her mother had placed in her and had been found wanting. She flipped herself onto her back and stared up at the underside of the desk, the computer screen swinging gently above her.

And that was when she saw it.

From her current viewpoint, looking directly at the underside of the desk, a section of the detailing on the front of the apron appeared to be standing proud of the rest, revealing a small gap, invisible from any other angle. Raising herself to her knees, she inserted her fingers into the space and pulled. With a surprising lack of resistance, a small drawer slid out of hiding; a drawer containing a slim cardboard-covered notepad. It wasn't old, could have been bought anytime over the last few years, but the simple fact that it had been secreted away piqued her interest. Lifting the pad from its mahogany nest, she opened the cover. At first, she thought it must be a diary but dismissed the idea almost immediately. It read more like a ledger; each entry painstakingly crafted by her mother's hand. Heart pounding, Meredith righted the chair, slumped down onto the accommodating leather, and began to read.

The book, though not going into specific details, explained a great deal. Reading between the lines, Meredith now understood how her mother had managed to build the business against the odds, how she achieved such extraordinary success in such a comparatively short time, and the heavy price that she paid. And although not itself a contract, it left her in no doubt as to the nature of the agreement between her mother and the strange little creature that had visited her so soon after the funeral. By the time Meredith turned the final page, she knew she had a stark choice to make.

And here they were, just one week later, staring in silence across the expanse of her dark blue duvet cover. She felt the coin clenched hard in her fist, just one of several discovered in a velvet bag beside her mother's bed. A tiny thing, yet of enormous significance.

"You have made your decision?" asked the goblin, more statement than question.

"I don't see that I have much choice."

"Of course you have choice. You could go somewhere else, leave this land to us. We will tend it, nurture it, *husband* it, as we have always done. Your mother was merely the latest in a long line of tenants. The land has always been ours."

"But then my mother's sacrifice will have been for nothing… and I will have failed."

"Yes. You go forward on your own and fail, or you continue our agreement, and succeed. That is your choice."

Its bluntness took her aback. The negotiations with the bank were as nothing compared to this. She had often referred to the banks as leeches but had never meant it literally.

"But if I agree to your terms, I will almost certainly go the way of my mother."

"Everything has its price. This is ours. It is rent for the land,

304

and our goodwill. A bargain sealed with blood and silver, as old as time itself." The large eyes were expressionless, but as she watched, a milky fluid began to seep gently from their corners. *Crocodile tears*, she thought. *To him, it is just business; there can be no place for sentiment. Just business.*

"…all extant contracts and goodwill," mumbled Meredith. Since finding the notebook, the terrible significance of those words had rung through her head like a death-knell. She felt lost, adrift, out of her depth. Her mother had been wrong to entrust the vineyard to her. Why hadn't she just handed it over to her brother and been done with it? Meredith was no hard-headed businesswoman. For her, it was *all* about sentiment.

And there it was, the key to the whole sorry business. If ever there was a time to repay the debt she owed to her mother, her brother, her family, it was now. She was *proud* to be her mother's daughter. Any normal, sane person would just pull out, she knew that; leave the land to this impossible creature and whoever might come after. But there was nothing normal or sane about this situation. They had come too far, suffered too much. Making this sacrifice would guarantee the success of the vineyard and secure her mother's legacy. It really was that simple. The mantle had been passed, and she wasn't about to walk away. Wiping the tears from her own eyes, Meredith cleared her throat. "As I say, there is no choice."

"Then our contract stands," said the goblin. "I will take the first payment now. You will feel nothing and will recover quickly. Payment will be due every complete cycle of the moon."

"Yes, I know," she whispered, closing her eyes as the creature crawled across the bed toward her. A silver sixpence and a pint of blood. A small price to pay.

In the Forest There are Doors

Pete W Sutton

My friend Jo went missing. The police found her VW Polo, all banged up, on a track an hour or so drive from Bristol, where we both lived. I saw it on the news—looked as though people had thrown stones at it. The windscreen had impact fractures of stars of white glass, the side windows were smashed, large dents in the bodywork. She loved that car, seeing it so degraded made me angry. I wanted to find the people responsible and make them pay. I wanted to find Jo or find out what happened to her.

On her YouTube channel she said she'd downloaded an app called RandoNautica and was checking it out. Her car had been found in the Forest of Dean. Of course we weren't supposed to go into Wales during the lockdown.

RandoNautica is an app that encourages you to explore your local area. Basically, you give it an 'intention' and it gives you a randomised set of co-ordinates. There's supposedly some quantum gubbins on there with the randomiser and people on YouTube and TikTok make much of the spooky coincidences they get when using the app.

I watched Jo's YouTube videos for hours, rewatching the last one over and over. Looking for a clue. All she says is that her intent was 'blood.' That's pretty morbid right? But lots of Randonauts put in stupid things like 'something creepy,' or even 'death.' Nutters! She got co-ordinates from the app—but didn't put them on screen, which was pretty infuriating. Why someone with a known love of unicorns and a sparkly purple phone with bunny ears would have the intent 'blood,' I'll never know.

I also watched a lot of YouTube of Randonauts and videos like 'The Top Ten Scary RandoNautica Trips.' You could tell a lot of them were faked. But there were a small number with genuinely weird coincidences.

I tried to get the police interested but they were thinking in strictly 20th century terms. Young woman lured into the woodlands type of deal. They didn't seem that interested in the app. Not even when I told them about the famous case where teenagers had found a body in a suitcase in Seattle when playing with it.

Despite lockdown I got my mate Mark, and his girlfriend Sue, to help me. I needed wheels and they were willing. They were also upset at Jo's disappearance and the seemingly lackadaisical response from the police. Mark drove, Sue in the passenger seat, me in the back. We assumed that Jo had gone via Gloucester—due to the lockdown—so went the same way. M5 north out of Bristol, through Gloucester and onto the A40 through Ross-on-Wye. When we got to the turn off for the Forest we stopped at the petrol station. Mark and Sue waited for me in the car. Part of the deal was for me to pay for the petrol.

"Have you seen this girl, or this car?" I asked the spotty local behind the counter showing him the photographs I had. He grunted and pointed to a badly photocopied and grainy picture of Jo, filling up her car at the station, stapled to the notice board. There was a 'have you seen this woman' title and a number to call the police if you had. "Were you working that day?" I asked.

He shrugged, sniffed, wiped the back of his hand across his nose and said, "no."

I was glad he was behind Perspex. The door opened and a businessman in an expensive-looking suit, who'd been filling up a gleaming black BMW, came in. His blue facemask looked fancy, one of those luxury N95 ones. He kept his distance. I decided that a retreat was required. I wasn't going to get anything from the spotty teenager but it was worth knowing that Jo had stopped here. I clicked a phone pic of the notice and then scuttled out of the shop.

"Anything?" Sue asked as I climbed back in.

"She filled up here on the day she disappeared. But the boy behind the counter didn't know anything about anything." I clicked the seatbelt in.

"Where to now, bud?" Mark asked.

"I guess we should go straight to where her Polo was found?"

Mark started the car and we rolled out of the petrol station. I glanced back and, in the window, I could see the attendant watching us. His spotty face expressionless. The businessman also stared at the car. Bit creepy.

Of course, because we were now almost in Wales it started raining. Big black clouds had gathered overhead and the few spots of rain turned into a downpour. I had a rain jacket with me but this was some serious weather. The paths around the river Wye would be muddy, wish I'd brought wellies.

Immediately the B road leading to the Forest of Dean narrowed to a single track with large hedges on either side. Mark took it slow and I hoped we wouldn't come across too many folks travelling the other way. I took note of passing places, just in case we came across a tractor or Land Rover full of locals. Luckily the road remained deserted as we penetrated further into the forest. The occasional houses got fewer and further apart the deeper into the woods we travelled. I couldn't tell one tree from another usually but spotted that many of the same type of tree in the woods seemed to be dying. The radio cut out to static just before we lost satellite signal and our Satnav gave up. We'd been travelling through white space for a bit.

"That's weird," Mark said.

"We're in a dip. Radio black spot. Happens a lot in these rural places," I replied thinking he was being a bit of a townie.

"No. Listen," Mark turned up the radio—just within hearing, almost lost in the static it sounded like a man crying, sobbing in fear or pain.

"Turn it off!"

"Okay. Okay. There. Calm down, Sue. It's just a stray radio signal," Mark said, trying to calm Sue down. She looked at me in the rearview mirror. Looking for reassurance?

"It was pretty weird. But probably just picked up a radio play or something," I said. I didn't convince myself and by the look Sue gave me, I hadn't convinced her either.

We reached a fork in the road. No signpost. Mark slowed and stopped. The car idled in the silence of the country lane.

"Fuck. Anyone see which way we were supposed to go?" Mark said pulling out his phone.

The Satnav was stuck on 'updating route' without a signal.

"I think when there was a bit of a map there it was just one straight road wasn't it?" I tried to remember if there'd been any forks. I vaguely remembered there were some roads off the main route, if you could call this single track a main route.

"When in doubt go left," Sue said. "Like in a labyrinth?"

"If we go wrong, we can always come back," I said.

"If we can turn around," Mark muttered. He put the car in gear and we started down the left-hand path. I spotted a curious magpie watching us from a tree. One for sorrow.

The road deteriorated a few hundred yards further on and became a gritted path with large potholes. The hedges loomed either side of the car, too tall to see anything but the green tunnel we drove down. "This doesn't feel right," I said.

"I'm not reversing all the way back. There are ditches either side of the road, if we go down one, we'll be stuck." Mark took a deep breath and snorted out through his nose after delivering that opinion.

"Onwards then."

Mark slowed the car to a crawl and we bumped our way down the track. After ten minutes or so we came to a wider area where the track did a loop. The stand of birch? trees, in the centre of the grassed area the track circumnavigated, looked stunted and misshapen. A wooden gate with a sign on barred the entrance to a path through the woods. Mark rolled the car to a stop opposite the gate. "What's the sign say?"

Both Sue and I peered out at it.

"Can't read it," I said.

"You'll have to get out," Mark said and pulled the handbrake on.

"What?"

"Get out and read it."

I looked at Sue and she shrugged.

I unbuckled and got out of the car. The rain poured, I could hear rushing water, no birdsong, no insects, the wind blew through the trees making a sound like the sea on the shore. Under the trees, the air was so gloomy it may as well have been night-time. I dashed over to the gate. The sign said, 'White Rocks Nature Reserve' and underneath, in red pen, someone had written 'Doward' and below that 'beware of the inbreds.'

I turned back to the car and caught the sound of a motor or generator somewhere in the distance, beyond the trees.

I hurried back into the car.

"Does Doward mean anything?" I asked as I got in.

"I think that was on the map," Sue said.

"I should never have got rid of the paper map," Mark mumbled.

"Does it help though? Where's Doward in relation to where they found Jo's car?" I clipped myself back in and Mark started the car.

"I don't know," Mark replied.

"Okay, let's go back to where we turned left," I suggested.

We hadn't gone far before a large van came round the bend, headlights on full beam stark in the gloom of the downpour. It skidded to a halt a little after Mark did.

"Shit." Mark put his arm on the back of the passenger seat and peered over his shoulder out of the back window.

"Let him reverse?" I suggested. I tried to remember where the nearest passing place was, we hadn't long passed one, a turning loop while the main track went straight on. Actually Mark was probably right and letting the van get to the turning loop was a good call. He shifted into reverse and eased the car backwards. The people in the van—I could see two silhouettes—didn't give us much room, they came forward at the same pace. "Turn, turn!" I shouted as we started to edge into the ditch. Mark over-compensated and we almost went in on the other side. "Left a bit… right a bit… straighten up…" I gave directions as we proceeded backwards. I breathed a sigh of relief as we approached the loop. We went down the left-hand part, the van went straight and I turned to watch the van assuming Mark would stop and as the van passed us, we clunked into the ditch with a bang.

"Fuck. Fuck. Fuckity fuck." Mark bashed the steering wheel. Face red.

"Shit. Sorry, man!" I should have carried on directing.

Mark carried on swearing as he put the car into first and tried to go forwards. The tyre spun in the ditch throwing back mud and smoke. He clanked into reverse and tried again, and the car stayed where it was, wheel spinning. The smell of burning clutch and scorched rubber permeated the inside. "Stop. Stop!" While we'd been spinning our wheels the van had pulled up behind us. "Look, we'll have to get out and push," I said to Sue.

Her eyes were round in the mirror. "Nuh, uh. There could be serial killers in that van."

"Well we can't just sit here."

"They're getting out!"

I spun in my seat to watch the van passenger door spring open and a tall figure drop to the track. It stalked up to us and I took in the wet-weather poncho the figure, a man, was wearing. More prepared than us. He carried a long flashlight, substantial-looking, like a club. He tapped on the window.

"Oh my God, oh my God, tell him we're fine, tell him we're okay, tell him to just go round us," Sue babbled.

"Shush now," Mark said and wound down the window.

I could smell unwashed body even over the burnt rubber smell. A face that could kindly be called weathered, with straggly beard, long thin, pointed nose the rain dripped off, and a mouth full of wood-coloured broken teeth loomed in. "You folks need some help?" The accent was as thick as tar. Real Forester, born and bred.

"We could do with a push," Mark said.

The guy sucked his teeth. "We could do that, big van like ours should be able to oik he out."

"No. I meant, a few people to—"

"Going to take more'n manpower." The face disappeared, hawked, spat. Re-appeared. "Stick he in neutral and we'll give a push, like."

The man turned and marched back to the van. Mark wound up the window. "Beware of the inbreds," I said.

"What?"

"That's what the sign said."

"You've got to be fucking kidding me," Sue said.

"Listen, let's all just keep our shit together and let the nice locals push us out of this ditch." Mark had put the car in neutral and the van behind flicked his headlights on and off. Mark wound the window back down and put his arm out and signalled forward. The van edged up to our rear and pushed us forward, slowly. Above the sound of the rain, we could hear the man behind us shouting something.

"What's he saying?"

"Pop it in gear," Mark said, doing so and putting his foot down. We juddered forward and with a bang leapt free of the ditch but there was a horrible grinding thumping. Mark pulled away from the van and then stopped. "Fuck."

"What was that sound?" Sue asked.

"Sounded like we've broken something," Mark replied.

The guy in the poncho came back.

"He's out now," he said.

"Yes. Thank you. But, well. Sounds like something broke."

The guy wiped rain off his face. "Let I have a look." He

314

disappeared around the back of the car. Gone a few moments then popped up at the passenger window. Sue gave a little squeal of surprise. Mark controlled the electric window opener and wound down her window.

"Summat's knacked back passenger wheel—it ain't sat right." He gave a sniff. "You got a tow rope?"

Mark shook his head.

The guy sucked his teeth again. Stood up and waved to the van. Its diesel engine the only sound apart from the rain and wind I could hear. The woods definitely edged into darkness now. He leaned back down. "We dunt have one neither. There ain't no phone round here. We can give one of 'ee a lift to the main road? We'll have to push him back so we can get past. Hold on, I just let me mate know what's up."

He walked back to the van giving us a chance to debate.

"I'll have to go," Mark said. "I'm the one with the roadside coverage, it's my car."

"Should we all ask to go? Better if we stick together, right?" I said.

Sue nodded.

"He said one," Mark pointed out.

"Look, it's probably best if you stay with the car. I got us into this, I'll go. Give me your membership card."

"It's my car," Mark started.

"Just let him do it, Mark. I'd prefer it if you stayed." Sue looked at me, "No offence."

"None taken."

"I'll phone the breakdown people and then get these guys to bring me straight back here."

I could see that Mark wanted to argue but our friend with the long nose was back.

"Well?" he said.

Mark glanced at Sue who gave him a pleading look.

"Okay. Here's the card, the number's on it." He opened the glovebox and took out a scrap of paper and a pen. "Here's the registration."

I took everything and put them where they'd stay safe and dry. The rain looked to be easing up somewhat so at least there was that. We all climbed out and the two guys from the van helped us push the car backwards—something clunked as the back wheel went round. Definitely wrong.

When it was out of the way I followed the guy back to the van, giving Mark and Sue a cheery wave I didn't feel. "Aff you," Long-nose said and pointed into the van. I climbed aboard, noting the rust on the bottom of the door and the threadbare seat, some of the inner foam showing. The stench inside the van reminded me of onions, because it made my eyes water. The fug of cigarette smoke didn't mask the human odour. The driver was smoking a ratty rollup that stank like rat's piss. I shuffled in and the guy who'd done all the talking climbed in after me. Right cosy. It was a transit without a window to the back and my mind started supplying all sorts of things the rear space may be full of.

"It's really kind of you to go out of your way like this," I said. The driver just gave me a stare and Long-nose gave a sniff, hawked and spat out the window.

"You smoke?" he asked digging out a pouch of rolling tobacco and some papers as the van pulled away.

I shook my head.

"Good for you. Filthy habit," he grinned. His tobacco-stained remnants of teeth confirmed what he said.

"I'm Eamon, the silent one there is Tony." I introduced myself and said that Mark and Sue were the ones in the car. "What you doing out in the woods?" Eamon asked.

"Er... my friend, Jo, went missing and her car was found out in the woods and, we, well. We thought we'd take a look...

316

and see if we could work out what happened," I babbled. Should have lied. Sue saying that the van may be full of serial killers popped into my mind.

"That the banged-up VW on the news?" Tony, the driver, said without turning my way. I examined him, stubble like blue felt, nose broken many times, tatty dreadlocked hair under a filthy baseball cap that may once have been green.

"Yes. That's the one." I wished I'd stayed back at the car now. Regretted saying anything about Jo. But these guys sounded local. They could know something. Equally, they could be responsible for her murder.

"Shame what happened to her," Eamon said.

"Erm. Do you know what happened?"

Eamon sparked up the cigarette he'd rolled and blew out a long stream of grey-blue smoke. "Car was found down near Biblins. Load of reform boys there on a camp-out. Good for city lads on wrong side of law to be given outdoor recreation. Assume they pelted her car."

"Why?"

"They's wrong 'uns innit."

We travelled on down the lane, the occasional branch scraping down the side with a banshee wailing of wood on metal.

"But that doesn't explain what happened to Jo."

"No. I guess not." Eamon had evidently done his talking. He took another drag on his cigarette. Tony concentrated on the road. We jounced and bounced on poor suspension.

"She's still missing." I pointed out.

"Rasty."

"Does anyone around here know anything about it?" I asked.

"All sorts of folks came here during lockdown to do God knows what. Outsiders. Meddling. But more likely she fell in a hole. Land's riddled with mines and caves."

We pulled up at the petrol station on the A road. I pulled my phone out and I had a signal. Not a great signal but enough to make a call.

"You waiting here for the breakdown man?" Eamon asked as we pulled up to park.

"I was rather hoping you'd take me back to my friends once I've called the breakdown service," I said. I mean I could wait here, but I'd have to wait in the shop probably. The rain was still persistent. Even though the car had broken down only a couple of miles away it felt like a different world.

"Can't," Tony said.

"'Fraid we has a date," Eamon said.

Well. They had gone out of their way to bring me here I suppose. I thanked them and stood in the forecourt to make the call. Perhaps whoever had written 'beware of the inbreds' had it all wrong, the locals were good guys, even if they needed to invest in plumbing and shower gel. I waved them off after giving them profuse thanks for the help they'd given us.

If Jo's car had been stoned by young offenders then perhaps she had just fallen down a mine shaft. Maybe she hadn't even been in the car and they thought it had been abandoned. Like kids would throw stones at derelict buildings to try and break the windows. I decided that we should abandon the search. Leave it to the professionals. It was only a couple of miles down the road to where Mark and Sue were. I could walk back in less than an hour. I'd get a bit wet, but that'd be better than hanging around a shop during a pandemic with lots of random strangers wandering through; most without masks if the last few customers I'd seen were anything to go by.

I phoned the breakdown service and explained the problem and where the car was. They said it'd be a few hours. Skeleton service because of the pandemic and also, we were in the middle of nowhere.

I started to walk back to where Mark and Sue and the car were. What a wash out. I phoned Jo's phone, just to hear her voice, hear her say: 'this is Jo's phone, you know what to do, beep,' the old reassuring message. It rang and rang and was answered.

"Hello?" Was it Jo? "Jo? Can you hear me? Hello?" Could she have a signal somewhere in the forest? The police hadn't said anything about finding her phone. I listened carefully to the receiver and above a slight crackle I could hear a man crying distantly. Sobbing like he was in pain or fear. Then the phone cut out. I stared at the screen and the lack of bars. I turned around and walked back to the main road until I had a signal and phoned again. This time it went straight to answerphone. And the next time too. Cursing I hesitated near the petrol station. I had to get back and tell Mark and Sue that the breakdown services were coming but also if I kept trying Jo's phone maybe she'd be able to answer again. Or someone would. I tried another few times, but it'd obviously been a fluke that it had been answered the first time.

Right, I needed to go back to Mark and Sue. I hoped that because Jo's phone had been answered she was still alive. I phoned the number of the policeman who'd asked me to call if I'd thought of anything about Jo that could help. That rang and then went to answerphone. I explained that I'd got through to Jo's phone, it had been answered and that she might be lying somewhere in the forest, injured. Maybe Mark could help me look in the woods while Sue sat with the car.

New plan in hand I walked back up the hedge-lined lane so I could get back to the broken-down car. My trousers were soon soaked through and I discovered that my shoes weren't waterproof. I trudged down the lane until I heard a car approaching. No passing places in sight I squashed myself against the side hoping they'd see me in time. I spotted the car as it flicked its lights to full beam—I must have been lit up, I waved—and it sped up towards me. I tried to squirm into the tree my feet slipping on the mud and grass and the car roared. It deliberately drove at me. I had time to see it was a black, new BMW that somehow looked familiar, before it hit and I was tossed upon the bonnet and flipped over, smashing my head and blacking out.

A ding, ding, ding—a door open alarm.

The road hard against my cheek.

Grit in my eye.

Sharp pain.

Blackness.

Movement.

More pain.

Soft leather against face.

I realised I'm in the moving car.

I tried to sit up and my body was a fist of pain beating me. The car jounced over a rutted path. In the footwell I spotted a purple sparkly phone.

"Stop. Please… "

"Sit tight, my friend, you'll soon be at your final destination."

"Wait… you can't do this… my friends are waiting, the police—"

"The police are useless. We've been defunding them for years. You were seen going off in a sketchy van with some hillbilly Foresters. No one is going to save you." The voice was assured, rich, cultured. The car was obviously very expensive.

"Why are you doing this?" As I came more awake, I became aware that among the pain points my leg was screaming. I looked down and saw it lying at an odd angle. Something the size and shape of a thumb pushed at my trousers around knee height. I felt nauseous. Something stabbed at my chest as I breathed in. My head felt lumpy, I couldn't see out of one eye.

"Why? Because we can."

We? "My friend Jo?"

"You'll soon be with her. The wonders of modern technology. RandoNautica brings us victims. Your phone call alerted me to the inconvenient fact you came looking. The drone I flew over the forest saw you break down, the hillbillies, you going off alone." The man driving the car chuckled. I finally sat up enough to look out of the window and watched as the turning, down which Mark and Sue were waiting, disappeared behind the car. We rumbled over tarmac. The car turned off the road to Biblins signposted Great Doward. I saw the man in the rearview mirror, he wore a full-face bone-white animal mask, a badger skull made large enough to fit a human head, triangular, dangerous-looking fangs. Not the N95 mask from earlier. What the fuck?

I grew dizzy and had to lie down again. If I could reach my phone, or Jo's I could phone the police. If there were a signal.

The car turned into a driveway. Pulled up outside an innocuous-looking cottage. Several cars in the driveway, Porsches, Mercedes, BMWs. Mark's car, no sign of Mark and Sue. The front door opened and several men and women emerged wearing long black gowns, like barrister's robes or graduation robes, and masks, bone-white, animal-skull masks.

The door lock popped as a gaggle of men approached.

"Welcome to the retreat. A home away from home. You won't be happy here, but we'll have fun," the man said. I reached into the footwell and snagged Jo's phone. I thumbed the screen, it was locked of course but I knew the code, had seen Jo enter it so many times. No signal. On the call list 999.

Jo had desperately phoned 999 without getting through. The car door opened and a meaty pair of hands roughly grabbed my leg and pulled. I screamed as I was moved and my broken leg was jostled. I dropped the phone, I hoped that before doing so I'd managed to phone the emergency services.

As I fought to remain conscious eager hands dragged me from the car and lofted me, passing me across a forest of arms and towards the house. Upside down I saw the women part and within the gloom of the house a tall antlered figure waiting.

Carried within I spied a swirling maelstrom of images as I was passed from hand to hand and spun around. Through the French doors I spotted a tableau of horrific proportion—a small hill set with randomly-spaced wooden doors with figures displayed upon them, like stations of the cross, but carved from life.

The walls span past and the bizarre artwork adorning them flipped in a frenzied kaleidoscope—woven from human hair, animal pelts, feathers and bone, plaited and elaborately curled into alien arabesques. Somewhere a flute started a discordant and jarring tune, and many hands took up a drumming beat.

As I was brought to the garden the life-size tableaus were revealed to be people tied, nailed, bound to wooden doors. A dozen doors in many colours stood upright, planted in a pattern hard to discern through the dancing procession that led me in a spiral uphill toward the centre. A wicker barrier snaked throughout, linking the doors together.

I passed a woman splayed upon her door, naked bar the thorn-laced brambles wrapped around her pricked and bloody limbs. A man crucified and nailed to his gate, his arms threaded with black and white feathers, quills embedded in his flesh.

Mark, his eyes dull and confused, his hands flayed, shocking white bone exposed, antlers nailed through his shoulders binding him to the door.

Sue, ripped open from crotch to throat and the flaps of skin pulled back and nailed to the door in a grotesque pattern. In the void where her internal organs once were a bird struggled, a crow? Bound with her tendons, wings beating bloodily.

And just before they brought me to the centre, I saw Jo with great jagged shards of mirror, silvered glass greasy with blood, shoved in occult patterns everywhere in her body, slivers glinting in her hair cutting her again and again as they blew in the breeze, her crying anguished eyes turned in my direction. My wish to find out what had happened to her had brought me here. Now I knew.

They brought me to my own gate, awaiting its symbol, its token. The final piece of whatever puzzle this was creating. The base of the door jammed into bare earth, worms and beetles danced among the many, oh so many, bird skulls of all sizes. The drumming intensified, the flute swirled to a crescendo and then silence crashed in, like an uninvited guest.

Slammed against the door rude hands starfished me and incongruously a corpulent man, with dog skull mask, wielded a nail gun. Four swift percussions and I was spread-eagled and hanging—my broken leg a wildfire, sharp pain at my wrists a counterpoint. The handle cruelly jabbed into my back, stabbing pain into a kidney.

I could sense the palpable excitement run through the gathering like a hot wind. While the door behind me chilled where it touched, apart from four hot points of pain.

Here, at the centre, at the highest point, I could see the spiral of doors. And behind them I sensed there was a multitude of beings, and yet one power, waiting to breach our world from some unknown place.

The stag-headed man strode to within a foot of me then

turned and howled. The congregants howled back and turned to watch the doors. The first, the bramble tied woman, slammed open, fast and violent, the woman squashed into the wicker fence which trembled all the way to rattle to either side of me. "He comes!" cried one of the celebrants. I did not see what force opened the door, a celebrant was presented to the void within and fell thrashing to ground, back arching in agony, or ecstasy?

One by one the doors jerked open and there were ecstatic cries from the throng, some fell to their knees, one woman ululated, a man tore his robe and beat his chest, others followed suit, several had knives with which they carved runes upon their freshly exposed flesh. Each void received a celebrant.

As each door opened, the token, the manifestation—the representation—hung upon it screamed their last scream. I fancied that the air darkened and, quickened in the doorways, indiscernibly at first but soon moving from door to door a shade at the very limit of perception.

"He comes!"

Mark's hands beat against the door, a rattle of bones as his wrists flipped backwards ripping a scream from him, unearthly in its terror. And then he was gone and I could sense the presence upon the threshold pause a moment before joining with the existing manifestations.

Sue's door rattled prior to opening and the bird, with a harsh guttural rattling call, a magpie's call, burst free and leapt then flew above the door and away in a spray of blood. There was no pause this time, the manifestations merged and moved onwards. More writhing figures on the ground.

Jo's mirrors exploded as her door flew open and the darkness within was joined by the blur of air I had tracked from Sue's door. There were no more doors but mine.

The great summoning was almost complete. Most of the celebrants now knelt, many raised their arms to the sky, the stain upon the air swirled among them, a couple slashed their wrists as it passed, the air drinking the spray of blood, one man slashed his throat and his body lifted clear off the ground as the darkness upon the air reddened. And, as the stag-headed man bowed I sensed that the presence had turned its hungry awareness onto me.

The door rattled.

They brought forward a female celebrant.

A vast presence gathered behind me.

The handle suddenly jerked and fresh stabbing pain ran down my back.

The stag-antlered man was the last sight I took with me before the door burst open.

Nature Morte

Marisca Pichette

Porter was still settling into his alcove when Ynes crossed under the beam from her bedroom. His dark brown fur was damp from whatever drizzle he'd encountered during the night, claws scratching the wood as he found a suitable perch for sleeping. Porter was not a bad tenant; he kept the mosquitos down and Ynes hadn't encountered a single moth since he moved in. After the first few mornings, however, she'd placed a dish under his perch to catch (most of) the droppings.

"Good morning, or night, or whatever," Ynes muttered to the bat, placing a clean willowware plate under the beam.

She made the rest of her rounds—watering the plants scattered across the windowsills, leaves hugging doorframes and creeping across the floor, reaching for toes and chair legs. Ynes had been the one to fill the house with flowers;

Luca had preferred animals. As she bent over the litter box, scooping out the ferret deposits, Ynes wished they were still here. Hansel still slept on Luca's side of the bed. He'd always liked them more, liked the warm impression their body left in the morning.

Ynes sometimes wondered if she left any heat behind her, any impression at all. She slid the lid back onto the tin of Hansel's litter and stood, rubbing her lower back. Her fingers pressed in, feeling for lumps. She remembered how they felt on Luca's back, her hands caressing as they lay in bed, finding something that didn't belong.

She walked into the kitchen, the light flashing on in response to her motion. She winced, squinting in the brightness. Installing the automatic lights had been Luca's idea. They believed it would discourage thieves. Too often, one of the pets set them off instead. *At least my plants don't move*, Ynes thought. The pots lined up along the walls were still. Looking at them reminded Ynes what she had to do today.

She took her time with the rest of her routine—all the jobs she used to share with Luca.

In the kitchen she emptied a squirming scoop of bloodworms into the long black tank that covered most of the wall. Stheno slithered from the tank's depths, one grey eye fixing on Ynes before the eel gathered up her breakfast in a few darting bites. Bloodworms were Stheno's preferred snack, but Ynes was in the habit of tossing other morsels into the tank while she was cooking. Hearts were especially popular.

With Stheno fed and Hansel's bowl filled, Ynes had only one thing left to do. Wiping her hands against her thighs, she opened a kitchen drawer and removed two candles. Her fingers were cold as she pocketed a lighter and left Stheno swimming laps, black ripples creasing the top of the tank.

The grass felt cold and wet under her feet. Ynes inhaled the dense humidity outside. She and Luca had made their home on the edge of town, close enough for Luca to ride their bike each day and visit their patients. Ynes stayed in most of the time, putting together charms and potions using the plants in her garden. She liked the silence of growing things.

She didn't like the *other* silence—the kind none of her potions or charms could stop.

Standing outside the door, she faced that silence. Her destination was a small outbuilding on the other side of the garden. Some people set up the Quietus in the house for ease of checking. They found it comforting.

Ynes preferred to put distance between her life and what remained of Luca.

She stood in the moist air for as long as she could before crossing the grass to the Quietus. A simple latch held the door closed. Ynes lifted it and took a long breath as she pushed the door in, the candles and lighter clenched in her fist.

After weeks, the smell seemed to be improving. She could breathe without choking. And for the first time she didn't feel like retreating back to the house without practicing the ritual.

For Luca. She wasn't sure she believed it, but she took the candelabrum from the shelf by the door. Melting the bases of the new candles with the lighter, she wedged them down on top of the old stubs.

It was traditional to check weekly, but after the first week, Ynes pushed her checking to every ten days. She wanted the first phase to pass quickly, pull Luca apart without her having to see each step. It would be easier, she thought, to come back in a year and see fragmented remains. But she knew that Luca would have checked on her weekly—maybe even daily—so Ynes kept coming.

She lit the candles and walked deeper into the Quietus. It was little more than an old tool shed, though quite spacious now that she'd finally sold the VW Camper. That was a month before Luca. They'd dreamed about travelling, but Luca's position here became so valuable…that dream slipped away. Witches were rare these days, and two of them together? Ynes and Luca had to stay. The house, Ynes' garden; it was all so permanent. Until it wasn't.

She walked forward, stepping into the space where the camper used to rest. *Twisted luck*, Ynes thought. If they hadn't sold the camper, she wouldn't have had anywhere to put Luca.

The centre of the Quietus was enshrouded in plastic curtain, sheets hanging heavy and still around a table which was really two sawhorses and a sheet of plywood. Unable to access Luca's life insurance until a month after their death, Ynes couldn't afford anything better. She'd carved sigils into the wood, but she wasn't sure she believed in them. Their shapes were wrinkled, slanted from the shaking of her hands as she'd carved them.

She moved towards the curtain, drops of moisture clinging to the other side. The smell grew stronger. She approached from Luca's feet; she always came from this end. It was less shocking that way.

Skin and fat had slid from Luca's bones and gathered against the rim of the container. Ynes looked for Luca's nails, which had fallen from their hands and feet last time she checked on them, but it was hard to pick out anything specific in the liquid remains.

Holding her breath as much as she could, Ynes walked around the container, clutching the candelabrum. Luca's ribs hovered over the rest like dead branches half-submerged in a swamp. Luca had been naked when they were placed in the container. Ynes now wished she'd put them into a dress to cover their ribs. She had the strange notion that they might be cold. *I should have made a sigil for warmth, she thought, her gaze sliding up to Luca's head.*

Luca's face was gone. Ynes focused on the sunken sockets, pools of multi-coloured ooze where their eyes used to be. Used to be brown. Used to reflect so many things.

Wax dripped from the candles onto Luca's skull, sliding across the not-yet-bare bone before hardening into something like tears.

At the beginning of the checking, she'd cried every time she visited the Quietus. She'd cried when Luca's eyes sank away and their teeth fell out. She'd cried when the mould covered their chest, replacing the dress she should have brought to cover them.

When the smell got to be too much, Ynes backed away from the container. Its sides were translucent, tinted pink. She imagined Stheno swimming underneath, feasting on skin and muscle and fat.

She thought that she would have preferred that, somehow.

Ynes' mother had refused a Quietus for her wife. When Ynes' stepmother died, she'd helped her mother build a scaffold of bamboo. They'd placed Steph on top and checked her daily, letting the birds claim her eyes and ears, the bats descending at night to catch the flies as they laid their eggs in her chest. Ynes had liked seeing Steph reclaimed, not confined to a container in a Quietus.

She set the candelabrum on the shelf by the door. The candles had burned down half their length. She always stayed until they extinguished themselves, just to be safe. Luca never wanted a pyre. That, at least, they'd discussed.

But Ynes wasn't sure anymore whether a Quietus was right, either. She stood in the doorway and watched the plastic curtains, condensation sliding down to join in puddles on the cement floor.

If only Luca had told her what they wanted. If only they'd seen what it was like, checking every week (or ten days), living alongside the Quietus, trying to garden when the breeze blew the wrong way and brought the odour of the one you loved into your face, mixed with the scent of potting soil.

She stared at the curtains, the blurred image of Luca resting on the other side. Silent. Silent, but not growing. Ynes wished she could reverse what she was seeing, come to find Luca more each week, not less. How long until they were bones? The mortuary was due to come in a few days to remove what liquid remained. *They'll be cold then, won't they?* Luca used to produce so much heat; they kept barely any for themselves. Ynes pictured them lying in bed, the blankets swirled around them, adding to their curves, turning them even softer. Elegant.

In bed. *That's where Luca should be.*

The candles were still burning when Ynes left the Quietus. She walked across the grass, dew slicking her feet.

Time for something new.

In the kitchen, she unhooked the ladle from over the stove and pulled a stack of pans from the cabinet. Stheno watched her leave, one grey eye pressed to the glass.

Ynes pushed back through the plastic curtain, Luca's scent filling her nose. She placed the pots in a circle around the sawhorses with their slanted sigils. Then she straightened, staring into Luca's no-longer-brown-eyes.

"I'm sorry. I can't wait any longer," Ynes whispered. She didn't know if this is what they wanted. Maybe they would have preferred Steph's scaffold. It burned Ynes, not knowing this final detail about her partner. All the years, and she couldn't figure out how to keep them, how to let them fall apart.

Without knowing, Ynes had to guess. Holding her breath, she raised the ladle and dipped it into the liquid surrounding Luca's bones.

She filled one pot, then another. She moved around the container, ladling all of Luca's softness into pans she normally used for making potions and dying cloth. She filled all six pots, but there was still more of the stuff. Ynes hauled the pots outside, past the sputtering candles, now almost burned all the way down.

Liquid spilled over the edge of the first pot, splashing onto her feet as she hauled it to the edge of the garden. It was shockingly cold. Ynes grunted, pouring it out alongside the hostas. *For warmth.*

She managed not to spill the second pot, carrying it from the Quietus to her herb patch. The soil accepted the viscous liquid better than she had expected. *For health.*

The third pot she emptied under the nectarine tree. *For sweetness.* The fourth she brought to the other side of the garden and poured at the base of the hydrangea. *For brightness.*

Ynes' legs were slick by the time she tipped the fifth pot out over the pumpkin leaves, their trichomes clinging to solid bits while the rest slid down the vine. *For solidity.*

She carried the empty pot back to the Quietus and set it with the others. She bent to pick up the sixth, wincing at the ache in her shoulders. She only carried this one as far as the roses, emptying it just as a thin drizzle began to fall.

For us.

Back in the Quietus, the candles drowned in their own wax. Curls of smoke twisted out of Ynes' way as she returned with the sixth pot. She picked up the ladle and spooned the last of the liquid into it. The pot filled three quarters of the way, leaving the base of Luca's container clear, save for a layer of viscosity.

"There." Ynes wiped at damp on her face, not sure if it was sweat or rain or tears or Luca.

Lying in the container were Luca's bones, remnants of tendons and cartilage still clinging to them in places. She thought her partner looked more like themself than they had since decomposition set in. She touched the hardened wax on Luca's face.

"Now, I'm going to make you handsome again," Ynes whispered. Her throat ached. She turned away before she lost control, pulling bags of soil from the shed's shelves.

It took much less time to refill the container, the rich black soil filling the spaces between Luca's bones, replacing their flesh with something new.

Two bags were all it took to turn the container into a planter. Ynes' hands turned black as she pressed the earth under and around Luca, paying special attention to the area by their head. She made the soil deeper here, like a pillow.

It was dark when Ynes walked back across the grass to the house. She set the last pot in the sink and fell into bed, exhausted.

Ynes' shoulders screamed. She dragged herself from bed, cursing as she trod on Porter's dish, fresh guano sticking to her foot. After washing and replacing the dish, Ynes fed Stheno and Hansel. She stopped in the bathroom and felt along her back. Her muscles were stiff and aching, but the area around her spine was smooth. She exhaled, staring into the mirror. Every day it was the same. She was the same.

When she entered the kitchen, she wretched. The last pot sat in the sink where she'd left it, too exhausted to finish what she started.

She hauled the pot from the sink and carried it past Stheno and outside, setting it firmly on the ground next to the door.

She took two full breaths of morning air, her gaze falling on the Quietus. It was almost better. *Almost.*

She went back into the house and gathered up as many potted plants as she could carry. Back across the wet grass, she paused only to open the door.

One fell as she struggled with the latch, but the rest passed safely into the repurposed shed. Ynes set the pots on the shelves and rescued the unlucky aloe from its broken vessel. She nestled it beside the other succulents in the space over Luca's shoulder. She cleared away the pottery shards and returned to the house for more plants.

She made three more trips back and forth, repotting her chenille, African violets, setcreasea, myrtle, and fuchsia. Colours spread over the fresh soil, green and purple, red and orange. Ynes smoothed the earth, patting the base of the aloe before stepping back to look at her newest garden.

Luca lay like they had since the mortuary installed them over a month ago, their arms at their sides, naked except for the tattoos of vines curling down their arms and over their hips. The tattoos were gone with every other part of Luca Ynes touched in life. Looking at them now, there was little of Luca's remains that was anything like the person Ynes had loved. Only bones. Bones and flowers.

She stood in the Quietus, breathing in and out, the air clearer than it had been in a month. She wiped her hands on her thighs, letting the soil stain her clothes. She didn't mind. That was something she could deal with.

This—she could deal with this.

Before she left, Ynes uncovered the shed's windows. When had they been covered? Had she done it, or the mortuary? She couldn't remember. The fresh light reflected off the flowers and bones and wax. She pulled down the curtains and piled them in the corner before walking back out onto the grass.

She had one last task to tend to.

She lifted up the final pot and carried it back into the Quietus, which was no longer exactly a Quietus, but wasn't a shed either. It was something else, something new. Something silent and growing.

Ynes leaned over the container and poured the last of Luca over her plants, holding the pot up until the very last had dripped from the rim and sunk into the darkened earth.

For you.

She lowered the pot, tension leaking from her shoulders.

"I'll check on you tomorrow," she said.

She left the door unlatched.

The Trembling of Dog, the Fierceness of Sheep

Laura Jane Round

I need to find the perfect gift. Something to smooth things over.

It was all Dina could think as she looked out onto the garden of the bed and breakfast. The cold summer scene was quiet, the trees rustling in the breeze, as if trying to shake off the chill. Her cup of soup was long since drank, but she didn't feel like closing the glass door of her room just yet. The smell of rain soothed her somewhat.

Inside, there was a pink towel, a blue towel, a large bed with dolphins leaping out of stitched waves on a duvet. This was a room *made* for couples. Dina smiled wryly, feeling a slight but persistent ache in her sternum. *Jon,* she thought, *you're really quite mean, making me look at these atrocious dolphins alone.* She checked her phone, but no signs of life—not even a weak signal. He was mad at her. What else was new? Dina knew she could be stubborn, but when he'd started making jabs at her article—

—*What?*

Suddenly there was movement, more movement than the rustling of trees. Dina's long eyelashes swept across her face as her gaze fell upon… something. Was that a deer? Was it a moose? Here, in the English countryside?

Lanky, dark and dappled fur. Elongated ears. Horns, curved in a way that somehow struck Dina as bizarre. And when those dark eyes looked at her, she felt such a chill down her spine that she sprang into action.

She went to reach for her phone, fiddling with the touchscreen. Her frantic freckled face looked back at her. She'd dropped the phone on the coach, the hard, lumpy carpet a poor cushion for such precious cargo, and the screen had been fickle ever since. She needed to get a picture; she needed proof it was real.

When she'd looked up, the creature was gone.

Fuck! She pinched the bridge of her nose, sitting back in her wicker chair.

Her mind might be playing tricks.

It was over a full English, sat with the couple who owned the bed and breakfast, that Dina finally got some answers.

"It's probably Dave's," one half of the couple, Larry, happily relayed. "He lives next door. Breeds rare sheep. They 'ave all different coats, big feet, small feet, massive 'orns… Must've given you a little fright!"

Dina tucked into the blood pudding, before remembering her manners and answering—albeit with her mouth slightly full. "No, no," she said, swallowing quickly. "It was fine. My eyes were tired; I just couldn't make out what it was."

Erica, Larry's other half, smiled in a rather patronising way (if Dina did say so herself). "Well, if you need anything, just knock on. Larry can shoo away any demon sheep!"

Dina forced a returning smile, looking back down at her plate and swirling a finger through the blood pudding residue.

"So, are you planning to go into town?" Larry asked, setting down his teacup. "I can drive you up if you're ready to go now."

Dina shook her head. "I'm here to write."

"Ooh, a writer! How exciting!"

Down, boy. Dina's smile was becoming more strained as she suppressed a sigh. "Ah, um, it's not all that glamorous." She'd come out here for the quiet, the greenery. A place to clear her head and get some words down on the page—whether Jon wanted to come with or not. That fight before they'd left had really jangled her nerves-

"-What do you write?"

"Articles, short stories... whatever sells," Dina said, taking a swig of her lukewarm tea. She was categorically *not* a people person. She just wanted to get up and leave, but they had been so nice, so accommodating, that she wanted to extricate herself with minimum rudeness.

"I can't imagine that makes much money," Erica said. "Still, if you're doing what you love..." she trailed off, head tilted to the side, like she was trying to make up her mind about something.

"I need to go, um, freshen up," Dina said, pushing her chair back as she stood. "Might go for a walk to clear my head before I sit down to write. I'll see you later?"

"Sure, sweetie. Don't get lost!"

I can read a map better than you can read the room, Dina thought as she made a swift exit.

...Okay, so maybe she was a little bit lost.

The rain had picked up with gusto. Dina's newsboy cap

was a lost cause, and her anorak was being tested to its very limits. She needed to get back to her room with the atrocious dolphins, maybe take a hot shower and wrap herself in one of those unnecessarily gendered towels. Why did she do this to herself? Why was she out here in the sticks when she could be somewhere with recognisable roads and working Wi-Fi?

Everything smelled so wet and green, something that had charmed her the previous evening, but now just reminded her of how far she was from civilisation.

Even if he wanted to give me a sign, she thought, *he wouldn't be able to get a hold of me*. Ugh. Self-pity. So unattractive, and even more unattractive from within.

"Hello!"

Dina's head whipped up, droplets of water flying.

"Are you okay?" called a woman, her bright yellow jacket a shaft of light in the grim English skies. She stood on a small hill, seeming to tower above Dina in that moment. All thoughts of self-sufficiency vanished, and Dina breathed a shaky sigh of relief.

"I'm lost!" Dina admitted, and the woman started making her way over.

"You sound like you're not from 'round here," the woman said with a smile, and Dina felt an irrational stab of self-consciousness aimed at her—carefully cultivated—classless accent. "No wonder you got lost, these roads are difficult to navigate if you haven't grown up with them."

"If they can be called roads," Dina shouted over the rain, and the woman snorted in amusement.

"Lauren," the woman said, extending a hand. She was the plain kind of pretty. A country girl through and through, Dina supposed.

"Dina," Dina replied, clasping it in a soggy handshake.

"Pub?"

Dina smiled. "Pub."

"So this is summer?" Dina said, hoping the hot chocolate in her hands would stop her shivering soon. It was a rather cosy pub, built for comfort rather than maximising space.

Lauren shrugged from where she was curled up in her armchair. "Pretty regular summer down here," she said with that lilting accent. "We're not exactly a tourist trap. Walking holidays are probably the most popular scenarios." She paused; hesitated. "Kids move away when they grow up and realise there's nothing for 'em. Farming is our thing." She looked up from the rim of her cup—an Irish coffee. "But surely you knew that?"

Dina gulped down a mouthful of her drink. "Not really. I picked on a whim." She stared over at a tapestry on the wall, paying attention to each fraying stitch. "I needed to get away. Someone was coming with me, but it turned out he couldn't." Jon. *Jon.* Why couldn't she stop thinking about Jon? She guessed she shouldn't have left things that way.

Lauren's brow wrinkled in what looked to be concern. "Are you alright?"

Dina looked down at the black screen of her phone. Freckles. Crow's feet. Tired brown eyes. "No," she said, "I'm not sure I am."

There was a lot of giggling by the time they reached the bottom of the gin bottle.

"And then he said," Dina said, pausing to laugh, "he said I couldn't make it as a writer! Me! The one who paid for his fucking rent!" It wasn't funny—it'd stung like a bitch, the first time she'd heard it. But still she laughed, Lauren laughing with her, and everything back home felt distant and fuzzy, a figure of fun. So what if she should be writing right now?

She was on holiday!

"He sounds like a bitch," Lauren cut in, accent stronger than ever.

"Hah! You might have a point." Dina paused, considering. "Still…he's *my* bitch."

"Cheers to that!" A clink.

"No, no," Dina said after knocking back the contents of her glass, "He's not that bad. I'd…pushed him pretty far. Was away a lot. And then," she said, holding up a finger to punctuate her point, "when I *was* around, I was really cold to him. Stressed with work, And his little face…" She sighed, pinching the bridge of her nose. "I would not recommend going freelance."

She held up her glass. Another clink.

"Amen to that," came a low voice. Dina looked up from her fifth impulsive toast of the evening and found a bespectacled man sat on a chair next to her.

When had he sat down? Dina didn't remember him approaching. Surely, she would have heard him? Her instincts must be dulled from all the gin.

"Oh, hi Duncan," Lauren said, her entire body language shifting from open to closed-off.

The hair on the back of Dina's arms stood up.

"And who's this lovely lady?" Duncan asked. He looked like a subpar specimen—thick-rimmed glasses, a receding hairline and premature jowls to boot. But his arms were well-formed, his posture self-assured, a classic warning sign in any man.

Dina preferred them insecure.

"Eve," Dina lied. It was good to lie. It was good to know *how* to lie.

"You want a drink, Eve?" Soft voice. So soft. Still waters, they run deep—Dina knew that better than anyone.

"We've had enough," Lauren said, with a tone that had a touch of finality about it.

"Well, I can give you both a ride home?"

"No thanks," Dina said, not thankful in the slightest.

A glass shattered somewhere in the back, a chorus of quintessentially English "*wheys*" ringing out in its wake. The clock chimed. Short, sharp, jarring.

Duncan held her gaze for what felt like hours, before sliding out of his seat and to his feet.

Thank fuck for that. After he'd made a swift retreat, Lauren whispered to Dina in a more sober voice: "Let's get out of here."

They were walking home from the pub when Lauren tried to kiss her.

Dina was unphased; this sort of thing happened a lot. Being out in the sticks like this couldn't be good for a lesbian love life.

"I'm sorry," Dina said, voice neutral. "You're not really my type."

Lauren's pupils were dilated. "…What is your type?" She smelled like apples. Probably her shampoo.

Dina looked in Lauren's general direction, not quite meeting her eyes despite their continued proximity. "Trust me. It's not something you want to be."

The unholy sheep from that first night watched her from the window as she ate breakfast.

"I think he likes you!" Larry said.

Dina, hungover and not in the mood to get into a staring contest with a sheep, nodded along just to avoid talking further. She was too busy to discuss livestock with Larry when she was already writing a new short story in her head. Creepy

English locals and drizzly weather. Something unsettling for sure. Perhaps with a lesbian twist?

Maybe Jon would find it funny if she told him about last night—the Lauren incident. Then again, he didn't find much funny these days. She should probably take up Larry's offer of a lift before she went home; she still needed to find that perfect gift.

Larry laughed as the sheep gave a loud bleat, interrupting any train of thought to be had. Dina, suddenly wishing for mutton on her plate, furiously stabbed at a sausage.

The clacking keys of Dina's laptop permeated the silence of her room. She felt a layer of sebum settling on her skin. Her clothes were rumpled and forming creases on her back. She sighed in discomfort—she always got like this, writing. Poor posture, forgetting to eat, getting the kind of hunger pangs where you sweat and shake.

She sighed, wriggling a little on the firm mattress. A hangup from living at home with her parents for so long. Her bedroom had been her sanctum, perhaps too much. She remembered when she'd moved out for the first time, looking down at her bare mattress, seeing the dip of where she had lay, laptop balanced on her knees, furiously typing.

She sighed again, checking the time. Her phone lay blank next to her bed. She didn't exactly have to wonder what Jon was up to right now—his routine was pretty regular—but she wondered whether he was thinking about her. She hoped he knew she wasn't being unnecessarily cruel. Signal was a bitch out in the country. God help her, but she actually missed his little face...

"Oh, Jon," she murmured, maybe just because she could.

An owl hooted outside. It was a dark, damp and cold evening. What else was new here? Romantic propositions from locals notwithstanding, she supposed she should make the most of going outside and seeing her surroundings. Her English folk horror effort had run out of steam without the damp moss beneath her feet. It wasn't her style at all, and who knows when she would write it again?

Decision made, she reached for her hat and coat, fully prepared to fend off some demon sheep if need be. She grabbed a breakfast bar on the way out before she forgot, hands still trembling a little as she tore it open.

The sky was clear—not even a drizzle, giving the pitiful mush of grass some reprieve. Dina had to admit that the clear air had dissipated her hangover swiftly. Jon didn't like it when she drank.

Well, he'd just have to make his peace with that wouldn't he?

She hadn't strayed too far this time. She was busy mapping everything out despite herself, eyes quickly adjusting to the dark of the clearing. Her brain could never switch off; she knew it was her fatal flaw. Different places to crouch, hide, reassess. Every writer she knew did this. Maybe not to this extent, but...

She heard rustling behind her. She stiffened, hands clenching into loose fists.

There was an inhale, then a soft voice. "Eve?"

Ah. Duncan.

"Hello," she replied, because what else was there to say?

Two people in a tiny excuse for a forest, conspicuously alone. *My goodness, what will the neighbours think?*

"I thought it was you," came that soft, almost hypnotic voice. The perfect predatory tool lay in the way he took care with his vowels, Dina was sure of it.

"What brings you out here?" she said.

"I lost my dog."

Dina suddenly had an absurd image pop into her head—Duncan, eyes as clear and dead as they always seemed to be, leash in hand as he led that bizarre sheep around a paddock. She suppressed a snort. "I'm sorry to hear that," is what she said instead, voice neutral. "How long has it been gone?"

"A while."

"Well, what does he look like?"

"Black. Shaggy."

Dina sighed under her breath. Why the pretence? "Duncan," she said, turning to face him.

Something flickered behind his eyes, but his expression didn't change. "Yes?"

"This is a bad place for it."

A flicker again; confusion. Downturned mouth, if only for a moment. "What do you mean?"

"This clearing. People would find out."

She could see the wheels turning in his head. No emotion, of course—calculations. Risk assessments. And suddenly, those big arms didn't seem all that much of a threat after all. "What do you mean?" he said.

Dina smiled. She couldn't stop herself. *Poor puppy*, so naïve. "If you take me to the backroads closer into town, there'll be more people, but there's a larger area to cover. A person could get lost so easily."

Silence. That downturned mouth. She put a hand in her coat pocket, feeling the metallic crackle of the breakfast bar wrapper. "Did you see the mud on my shoes?" she asked, changing tack.

"What?"

"The mud," she repeated. "It was drying out, but it was caked on there pretty thick. I got lost, you see."

"Lost?" That hypnotic voice. Those surely violent hands,

346

held at his sides. Someone softer could have been so easily pulled under. Well, someone weaker.

"Like your dog. Those backroads, I was helpless." She took a step closer to Duncan. "I didn't know where I was half the time. My map was drenched with the rain, it was *ruined*. If Lauren hadn't showed up… who knows?"

Duncan's pupils were dilated; she could see it now. Just from the dark? She wasn't so sure. "Just something to think about," she whispered.

She took the wrapper out from her bag, tossing it into the mud. It floated, twirling on the breeze like a feather before it reached the ground.

Duncan seemed to shift on impulse, mindlessly reaching down to pick it up.

Good boy.

"You know," Dina said, turning her back on him, intentionally, suggestively, undauntedly. "A few years earlier, you might've been my type." As she made her way to the edge of the clearing, it almost felt like the trees were opening up to let her through.

"Goodnight Eve," Duncan said.

"Have a pleasant evening, Duncan."

Two people in a clearing, one conspicuously leaving.

"I want to go into town," Dina said, setting down her glass of orange juice.

Last night had invigorated her. Call it the clean country air, the bracing walk, the look in Duncan's eyes as he picked up her mess—she felt like she could take on the world. Writing would not be a problem when she returned home, she was sure of it. She would make up with Jon, soothe his nerves, and she would also show him that she could "make it" as a writer. Step one: a gift. If only she could see him right now!

Her thoughts raced—she wished she could bottle this feeling.

"Perfect," Larry said, getting up with some difficulty. "I'll drive you in."

She flashed her teeth. "Thank-you."

The sheep gazed at her as the Larry's car engine sputtered into life. Curious, that that particular sheep was the only one to stray this far. Perhaps he was the bravest. Perhaps he was the most stupid.

She no longer felt the need to reach for her phone as they pulled out of the drive. She knew she would remember the slotting curve of its horns, the elongated slope of its neck, for years to come.

"Thanks for your custom," a white, dreadlocked girl who smelled terribly of patchouli said as Dina exited the shop. Dina refrained from telling the poor woman that her nose piercing looked infected.

Away from the shadowy alcove of the hippy shop, Dina smirked as she looked down at her purchase. A Jig Doll? She'd never heard of one, but apparently this little town was famous for making them. Jon would see the humour in it, she hoped. Satisfied, she amused herself with it for a while, making it dance to the faint tune in her head before something caught her eye.

An elderly woman was waving her over, trying to get her attention. Dina frowned but ultimately put her new friend back in the mandala-covered bag before approaching.

"I'm sorry, do I know you?" Dina asked.

"You should watch yourself," the woman answered with the same lilting accent as Lauren. Her hair was pulled up into a tight bun, her wrinkles thrown into heavy relief.

The patient smile froze on Dina's face. "Excuse me?"

"Those dolls… They can be a heavy burden."

"I'm sorry, um, I don't understand."

"That girl in there. She's not a good person."

Dina was confused. What exactly was this old lady trying to get at? "What do you mean?"

"She doesn't make them the right way, the authentic way."

"Um, okay?" Dina resisted the urge to pinch the bridge of her nose. "So *you* make them, is that it? You make them in a traditional way?"

"No, no," the woman said, trying—and failing due to Dina's step back—to take hold of Dina's hands. "Please, just be careful—some say they are cursed. All, all these new people, coming into this town, forgetting the old ways, setting up ungodly shops—"

"—Okay," Dina said, showing her teeth. "I have to go now, I'm leaving soon."

"Promise me, please, be careful," the woman tried again in that frail, cracking refrain.

Dina backed away before the strange woman could try to touch her again, heading in the general direction of the bus station, mind already on the road.

Safely on the coach home, Dina sat back on the cool leather seat, watching fat raindrops blot at the window. The winding hills were giving away to flatter terrain, and the coach was almost empty. Dina guessed she should be soothed, soothed enough to rest her eyes for a while at least, but, as usual, she couldn't switch off.

That crazy woman… Duncan in the moonlight… The gaze of the sheep.

It had to mean something, right?

The countryside was a creepy place, no doubt. *Nowt so queer as folk*, as some of her Northern friends said. She was glad nothing too harrowing had happened to her, and that she was still in one piece. Jon would surely be glad for that fact, too. And the story ideas… being around creeps had its benefits.

As if she had summoned him, her phone gave a soft but unmistakeable 'beep'. Signal.

It felt like the smile on her face would split it in two. Frantically swiping at her dodgy screen, she finally accessed the app she had been thinking, no, dreaming of since she had first left her house that awful morning. She felt flushed, overbright, like a schoolgirl again.

A crackle, static, buffering. Whatever the interference was, it finally dissipated and as it fell away, Dina finally got a glimpse of that sweet little face.

"Jon," she said to herself. A little prayer.

Jon looked up at her—naked, chained, shivering. He couldn't see her, hear her. But she liked to think he was aware of her presence. He was a good boy, after all.

"I'm coming home, Jon," she said to herself. "I'm coming home."

All things considered, the trip to the countryside had been a success. Fresh air, exercise, some fairly good gin and plenty of time to write. Switching off from social media had Dina feeling more like herself than she'd felt in years. Ideas flowed easily from her like lightning from her fingertips. She had the perfect gift for Jon, something to occupy him while she was away (poor boy always asked for his phone, but how could she possibly allow that?). And she had met some interesting, unexpected, unsettling people, which didn't happen every day.

Still, she thought, sitting further back in her seat with her too-wide grin, Jon's despairing eyes peering out of her screen, *there is something to be said for the wonders of civilisation.*

350

About the Authors

Emma Coleman is a writer from Northampton. She has had short fiction published in the anthologies *Noir* and *Shadows on the Hillside*, and a novella *May Day* published by NewCon Press, which was recommended by Ellen Datlow in *Year's Best Horror*. Her debut collection of short stories, *The Glasshouse*, was also published by NewCon press in 2024 as part of their highly praised Polestars series.

Gary Couzens has had stories published in *F & SF*, *Interzone*, *Black Static*, *Midnight Street* and other magazines and anthologies, with the collections *Second Contact and Other Stories* (Elastic Press, 2003) and *Out Stack and Other Places* (Midnight Street Press, 2015). "The End of All Our Exploring" was reprinted in *Best of British Science Fiction 2021* (NewCon Press, 2022). Film and book reviews have been published in *Black Static*, *ParSec*, *Interzone Digital* and *Cine Outsider*.

Paul Crosby is a writer based in the UK with an interest in the fantastical, the uncanny and the absurd. He has previously been published in collections by Supernatural Tales, Pulp Cult and Air and Nothingness.

Epiphany Ferrell's stories appear in more than 90 journals and anthologies, including *Wigleaf*, *Ghost Parachute*, *Best Microfiction*, *Best Small Fictions*, *Pulp Literature*, *Unnerving Magazine*, and the Stoker-nominated anthology *Shakespeare Unleashed*. Her work was selected for dramatic performance at SIU Carbondale as *Epiphanies: Performances of Flash Fiction*. She is a two-time Pushcart nominee, and a Prime Number

Magazine Flash Fiction Prize recipient. She lives on the edge of the Shawnee National Forest in Southern Illinois. epiphanyferrell.com

Ren Graham is an illustrator, designer and writer living in the rainy Pacific Northwest. Ren is fascinated by history, biology, and folklore, and especially how these elements can combine to make a spooky story. They are fond of isometric RPGs, their three cats, and a warm cup of tea.

Rachel Henderson lives in New Orleans, where she spends her free time writing horror fiction and playing bagpipes. Her stories have appeared in *Take a Breath: A Collection of Claustrophobic Horror, After Happy Hour Review, Neither Fish Nor Foul,* and elsewhere. In 2021, she won first place in the NYC Midnight Short Screenplay Competition.
Find her at www.rlhendie.com.

Sam Hicks lives in south east London. Her fiction has appeared in various anthologies including the *Fiends in the Furrows, Vastarien, Dark Lane, Nightscript,* and the *Best Horror of the Year.* Instagram@ahorrorof hicks

Ivor K. Hill originally wrote "The Crow Who Burned" to practise writing in a fantastical setting with a voice inspired by his hometown of Belfast. He had so much fun that he decided to write an unrelated novel but with a similar voice (just finishing it now, June 2025). When it comes time to brave the rigours of pitching that novel, he'll be able to look back on his inclusion in *Hiding Under The Leaves*—alongside so many talented writers—for wee jots of confidence. His debut novel, *The First Scars,* was longlisted for the 2025 Self-Publishing Fantasy Blog Off (SPFBO).

Liam Hogan is an award-winning speculative short story writer, with stories in *Best of British Science Fiction* and in *Best of British Fantasy* (NewCon Press). He volunteers at the creative writing charities Ministry of Stories, and Spark Young Writers. Sci-Fi collection: *A Short History of the Future* (Northodox Press). Fantasy: *Happy Ending Not Guaranteed* (Arachne Press). More details at http://happyendingnotguaranteed.blogspot. co.uk

Tom Johnstone is a Council gardener, so he knows certain lawn mowers are demonically possessed. His fiction has appeared in various venues, including, in 2024 alone, *Chthonic Matter Quarterly, Supernatural Tales, Creepypod, Shadowplays* (PS Publishing, co-writing with Colleen Anderson), *Body Shots* (Subtle Body Press), *Medusa* (Flame Tree Press), *Ethereal Nightmares: The Second Sleep* (Dark Holme Publishing) and I*nfernal Mysteries, or a Compendium of Gothic Reveries and Dolorous Tales* (Egaeus Press). His story "Body Worlds", which first appeared in *Body Shots*, was selected for reprint in *Best Horror of the Year, Vol. 17* (Night Shade Books). More information at tomjohnstone.wordpress.com.

Dr. Frazer Lee is a Bram Stoker Award-nominated author and Edgar Allan Poe Gothic Filmmaker Award-winning screenwriter/director. He is Reader in Creative Writing at Brunel University of London and resides with his family in Buckinghamshire, just across the cemetery from the real-life Hammer House of Horror. Crisps are his downfall, talk him down from the ledge at: www.frazerlee.com

Emma Levin is a writer of comedy, sci-fi, and horror. Her short stories have appeared in anthologies (e.g. *The Best of*

British Science Fiction 2019 & 2021), in magazines (e.g. *Shoreline of Infinity*), online (e.g. *Daily Science Fiction*), and in many recycling bins. She received training in writing for broadcast through the BBC's 'Comedy Room' Writers' Scheme, and some of her jokes have turned up on the radio and in video games. You can find her online at: emmalevinwrites.com

Selina Lock is a mild-mannered librarian from Leicester. She was the editor of *The Girly Comic* and has written strips for various comic strip anthologies, including for the double-Eisner nominated *To End All Wars*. She has had several short stories published, including one in the British Fantasy Society shortlisted anthology *Dreamland: Other Stories*. Her novella *The Periodic Adventure of Seňor 105: Green Eyed and Grim* is available from Obverse Books. She has M.E./CFS, is a member of The Speculators writing group and one half of Factor Fiction alongside her partner. More info: www.factorfictionpress. co.uk

Tim Major's books include *Jekyll & Hyde: Consulting Detectives* and a sequel, *Jekyll & Hyde: Winter Retreat*, plus *Snakeskins, Hope Island*, three Sherlock Holmes novels and short story collection Great Robots of History. Tim's short stories have been selected for *Best of British Science Fiction, Best of British Fantasy* and *The Best Horror of the Year*, and his story "The Brazen Head of Westinghouse" won the British Fantasy Award for Best Short Fiction in 2024.

LJ McMenemy wears many hats: Editor-in-Chief at Horror Tree's Trembling With Fear; marketing for the British Fantasy Society; event curator for Writing the Occult. With almost three decades as a professional writer across media and marketing, Lauren also works as a coach and mentor.

Her own fiction revolves around occult and folk horror with a gothic lean. You'll find her at events stepping up as a host, interviewer, moderator, and general cheerleader, or haunting South London, where she lives with her Doctor Who-obsessed husband, the ghost of their aged black house rabbit, and the entity that lives in the walls.

Marisca Pichette is a queer author based in Massachusetts. Her short fiction and poetry appear in *Strange Horizons, Clarkesworld, Vastarien, Fantasy Magazine, Asimov's, Nightmare Magazine*, and others. Her poetry collection, *Rivers in Your Skin, Sirens in Your Hair*, was a finalist for the Bram Stoker and Elgin Awards. Her eco-horror novella, *Every Dark Cloud*, is out now from Ghost Orchid Press.

Kev Rooney is an author, illustrator, graphic novelist and game designer from the UK. He's aware of the phrase 'pick a lane' but couldn't tell you what it means. The curious can seek him out at cultofnyx.com.

Laura Jane Round is a writer, editor, and performance poet from the West Midlands. Round has a BA (Hons) in Creative Writing from Liverpool John Moores University.
Round has been published many times, in places such as the Trickster Anthology, Lumpen Journal (of which they later went on to guest edit), the Beyond Queer Words Poetry Anthology and Sad Girl Review. *The Coveted*, Round's debut pamphlet, was released in 2021 by Cerasus Poetry. 'TEATH' was published by Alien Buddha Press in 2022. More about their work can be found at www.laurajaneround.co.uk.

Pete W Sutton is a writer and editor. His two short story collections—*A Tiding of Magpies* and *The Museum for*

Forgetting—were shortlisted for Best Collection in the British Fantasy Awards in 2017 & 2022 respectively. His novel—*Seven Deadly Swords*—is available in all good bookstores. He has edited a dozen short story anthologies and is the editor for the British Fantasy Society's *Horizons* fiction magazine.

Matt Thompson is an experimental musician and writer of strange fictions. His work has been published at *Black Static, PseudoPod, Vastarien, Cosmic Horror Monthly, Tales to Terrify* and many more worthy venues. You can find him online at http://matt-thompson.com.

KB Willson is a British author currently living beside the sea in Dorset with his miniature dachshund dog, who likes to sit on his lap while he is writing. He has had work published by NewCon Press, Little Red Writers, Timber Ghost Press, Quill & Crow Publishing House, The Slab Press, Other Worlds Ink, Gypsum Sound Tales, Underland Press, Wildside Press (*Black Cat Weekly*), and PS Publishing (*ParSec Magazine*). He also has a story accepted for publication by Red Cape, date yet to be announced. For more information, please visit www.kbwillson.com

Thomas Wren is a writer, poet and teacher based in Leeds.

Acknowledgements

I'd like to thank everyone who has ever bought a book from me: you've convinced me there might be legs in this publishing malarkey as a way of life. Let's all continue to be readers, dreamers, and doers! Many thanks to Kev Rooney for his brilliant artwork. Above all, thank you to my husband, Neil K. Bond, who has supported me through what has turned out to properly be a mid-life career change. We weren't expecting anything like this, were we?

Donna Scott

LAUGHS IN SPACE

An anthology of humorous science fiction stories, hand-picked by editor Donna Scott, who is not only a BSFA-Award-winning editor, but an Old Comedian of the Year and Some Antics Comedy Competition finalist, and a cast member of the multi-award-winning children's comedy group, The Extraordinary Time Travelling adventures of Baron Munchausen. Featuring stories by Lavie Tidhar, Ian Watson, Ida Keogh, Fiona Moore, David Gullen, Gary Couzens, Andrew Wallace, and many more...

VIVID WORLDS

Vivid Worlds brings together twenty exciting, new science-fiction stories by writers from all over the world. The emerging genre of solarpunk weaves imaginative storytelling with optimism and innovation to address some of the challenges humanity is facing today and is likely to face in the future due to climate change. These short stories not only offer fantastic examples of cutting-edge science fiction, they also explore the concept of humanity's survival from both a technological and philosophical angle. These stories offer hope, just when we need it the most.